The Magic of Love . . .

Falling in love is simple . . . except when vampires, Faerie Princes, ghosts and other apparitions are involved. . . .

"The Man of Her Dreams"—Oddly, Kristen wasn't surprised when Barry, the perfect man she had been literally dreaming of all her life, walked into her dull office party. What was surprising was how boring perfection could be.

"Mushroom Tea"—Kromcek is an average guy. All he wants is a house big enough for his collectibles and a date with his favorite waitress. What he gets is a talking coffee cup with opinions on his romance problems. . . .

"The Enchanted Garden"—Glendon was a Faerie Prince about to be married to twenty virgin brides. Penny was desperate to win the local flower show to impress her father. When she tried a New Age growing spell on her plants, the last things she expected to pop up were a ladybug the size of a turtle and a gorgeous man with wings. . . .

**More Imagination-Expanding Anthologies
Brought to You by DAW:**

ALIEN PETS *Edited by Denise Little.* What if all our furred, feathered, or scaled companions aren't quite what they seem to be? What if some of them are really aliens in disguise? Or what if space travel requires us to genetically alter any animals we wish to bring along? Could we even find ourselves becoming the "pets" of some "superior" race of extraterrestrials? These are just a few of the ideas explored in original tales from some of science fiction's most inventive pet lovers, including Jack Williamson, Peter Crowther, Michelle West, Jane Lindskold, David Bischoff, and John DeChancie.

LEGENDS: Tales from the Eternal Archives #1 *Edited by Margaret Weis.* The Eternal Archives are the repository for all that has or will happen on every Earth—the history, myths, and legends that have molded our destiny Let such talented Archivists as Margaret Weis and Don Perrin, Dennis L. McKiernan, Josepha Sherman, Mickey Zucker Reichert, Janet Pack, and Ed Gorman led you through the ancient passageways, the dimly lit rooms which few mortals have been privileged to see. Open for yourself the dusty tomes from which legends will once more spring to life in never-before-revealed tales of both mortals and immortals.

CAMELOT FANTASTIC *Edited by Lawrence Schimel and Martin H. Greenberg.* Arthur and his Knights of the Round Table live again in original tales set in that place of true enchantment—Camelot! Let such heirs to the bard Taliesin as Brian Stableford, Mike Ashley, Nancy Springer, Rosemary Edghill, Gregory Maguire, Ian McDowell, and Fiona Patton carry you away to this magical realm. You'll find yourself spellbound by stories ranging from the tale of a young man caught up in the power struggle between Merlin and Morgan le Fay, to that of the knight appointed to defend Lancelot when he's accused of adultery with the queen.

A
Dangerous
Magic

Edited by Denise Little

DAW BOOKS, INC.
DONALD A. WOLLHEIM, FOUNDER
375 Hudson Street, New York, NY 10014

ELIZABETH R. WOLLHEIM
SHEILA E. GILBERT
PUBLISHERS

Copyright © 1999 by Tekno Books and Denise Little.

All Rights Reserved.

Cover art by Luis Royo.

DAW Book Collectors No. 1113.

DAW Books are distributed by Penguin Putnam Inc.

All characters and events in this book are fictitious.
Any resemblance to persons living or dead is strictly coincidental.

If you purchase this book without a cover you should be
aware that this book may have been stolen property and reported as "unsold and destroyed" to the publisher. In such
case neither the author nor the publisher has received any
payment for this "stripped book."

First Printing, February 1999
1 2 3 4 5 6 7 8 9

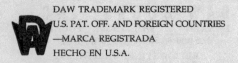

DAW TRADEMARK REGISTERED
U.S. PAT. OFF. AND FOREIGN COUNTRIES
—MARCA REGISTRADA
HECHO EN U.S.A.

PRINTED IN THE U.S.A.

ACKNOWLEDGMENTS

Introduction © 1999 by Denise Little.

A Little Death © 1999 by Susan Sizemore.

Old Delicious Burdens © 1999 by Peter Crowther.

Woman of Character © 1999 by Yvonne A. Jocks.

Slow Dance for a Dead Princess © 1999 by John DeChancie.

Nine-Tenths © 1999 by Laura Hayden.

The Man of Her Dreams © 1999 by Tim Waggoner.

Legacy © 1999 by Roberta Gellis.

Teel Rules © 1999 by Mark Kreighbaum.

Churchyard Yew © 1999 by Andre Norton.

Mushroom Tea © 1999 by David Bischoff.

The Enchanted Garden © 1999 by Deb Stover.

At Eternity's Gate © 1999 by Gary A. Braunbeck.

DreamStitching © 1999 by Kristin Schwengel.

The Face in the Leaves © 1999 by Diane A. S. Stuckart.

Sunrise © 1999 by Michelle West.

CONTENTS

A DANGEROUS MAGIC

MAGIC and fantasy have always been a part of our world. In the dim and distant past, they touched the lives of all people—kings and priests, Druids and vestal virgins, knights and serfs. When tales were told of King Arthur plucking Excaliber from the hands of the Lady of the Lake, or of Theseus fighting the Minotaur, listeners believed what they heard was fact, not fiction.

Even today, in this age of relentless rationalism, magic and fantasy influence us. Most of us spice up our lives with a bit of fantasy—whether it is thoughts of Miss June or Antonio Banderas or even the fleeting image of a despised acquaintance turning slowly on a spit in a cannibals' camp. As for magic, face it—every time you use a microwave oven, aren't you convinced somewhere deep in your heart that it works by magic rather than science? Magic and fantasy are still a vital part of our day-to-day lives. They are often the only comfort we have when the real world surprises or disappoints us. Sometimes they are the only explanation we can find—for better or worse—for the bizarre twists that our lives can take.

This is especially true in matters of the heart. For the majority of us, the most fantastic rite of passage that we are likely to personally endure is that incredible, amazing, frustrating, intense, unbelievable experience called love— the most dangerous magic of all.

1

Love can rip our hearts out, make us smile like idiots for no apparent reason, turn the world rosy, or drag a sunny day down into the depths of despair. It can inspire us to new heights of greatness, shred the sanity of the most balanced human being, drive a pacifist to kill, or turn an ordered mind into a quivering mass of chaos. Anyone who has ever been through the mill knows exactly how wonderful a good case of love can be, and will appreciate the extremes to which a really bad case can drive you. On a more practical level, sharing a bathroom with a member of the opposite sex is enough to make anybody believe in monsters and aliens. . . .

Given the power of the emotions involved, is it any wonder that many of the best pieces of fantastic fiction, classic and modern, involve the adventures of the human heart in one way or another? From *The Left Hand of Darkness* to the realms of Valdemar, from *Restoree* to *Dracula,* the ties that bind us have formed the underpinnings for remarkable works of prose.

Here in this all-new collection of fantastic fiction, some of today's finest writers explore the dangerous magic we call love. The tales they've come up with range from the cutting edge of modern life, through Victorian fancies, right back to stories pulled from ancient mythology. The protagonists are not always (or even often) entirely human, and the tone varies from heart-wrenching to hysterically funny, from bravura to bittersweet. As in real life, no two stories are alike . . . and happy endings are occasionally optional.

Given the subject matter, this is entirely appropriate. After all, as everybody knows, love is a *most* dangerous magic indeed. . . .

A LITTLE DEATH

by Susan Sizemore

*Susan Sizemore read her first vampire novel (Stoker)
when she was thirteen, her first fantasy (Tolkien) at
fourteen, her first science fiction (Heinlein) book at six-
teen, and her first romance (Woodiwiss) at nineteen. She
is still happiest when reading or writing in any one of
those genres. Actually, she's happiest when mixing those
genres. She backed into professional romance publishing
by writing a time travel novel, and into writing vampire
novels by being the fan of a television show. When not
writing, she's either at a movie, or walking her dog.*

"ALL I want is my life back, and I end up as the Angel of
Death. This is called what, irony?"

"Seniority. You don't have any."

"I don't want seniority. I want—"

"We've heard it before."

Carmen sighed. The fact that she didn't have any lungs
or any need for air didn't make the experience any less
real. Being dead didn't make anything less real, it just com-
pounded the frustration. "Any news?" she asked, though
she supposed she wasn't, technically, a *she* anymore.

No, no, SHE couldn't think like that. If she let down her
guard even a little, God was going to get His way, and that
would lead to harps and wings and eternal joy in Heaven.
No way she was going that route.

"The Mills of God grind slowly," she was reminded.

"Ain't that the truth. So?"

3

"Your appeal is still under consideration. In the meantime, you have your assigned duties to perform."

Garbage detail again. She could tell by the Heavenly Spirit's tone, though tone was too small a word to encompass the aura that accompanied the words. Angels. Real Angels—been around since the Beginning ones like her boss here—were scarier than hell. Carmen had never been one to let herself be intimidated. But since The Will of God had spoken, she supposed it was time to hit the streets and get to reaping.

"Going to be a long one," she muttered as she willed herself out into a cold, rainy night in the urban hell she used to call home. There she went again. "This *is* my home," she said, though none of the mortals around her could hear, see, speak, touch, smell, taste, or in any way sense her presence. Not that there were that many mortals out anyway. "I should hope not. No one should be out on a night like this. Not in this weather, in this neighborhood, at this time of night."

She, on the other hand, had an appointment to keep. She stood at the mouth of a narrow alley for a moment, getting herself used to what she was about to do one more time. She'd had thousands of hours of practice by now, but she always felt as though she were starting over at the beginning of every shift. Carmen told herself it had something to do with being out of the linear time-loop these days, but she knew it was really a respect for the gravity of the job she was about to do. Okay, so she said a little prayer. Nothing wrong with that. Didn't mean she was an angel, or had any plans to be in the near future. The people she came for could use a little praying over. Lots, in most cases.

"Speaking of future," she said to the junkie who came wandering out of the alley. "You don't have one."

The junkie didn't hear her, not yet. Currently, his attention was centered on the sensations of his body shutting down from a massive overdose. He stood weaving in the watered light from a streetlamp over the alley mouth for a few moments. Then he fell to the cracked and oily pavement with an awful groan. He began to twitch.

She checked her watch. "Five . . . four . . . three . . . two . . . one . . . Hi, there. Welcome to the afterlife." She held out her hand and helped the dead man's soul to rise.

Once he was on his feet, she formally shook his hand, then surreptitiously wiped her palm on her jacket.

The hand didn't exist, neither did the jacket, or the filth she wiped away, but it sure seemed that way at the moment. The recently dead had a way of bringing a bit of the mortal world across the divide with them. It dissipated within moments, but was quite a rush while it lasted. Carmen lived for these brief moments—except that they tended to be accompanied by junkies, hookers, winos, gangbangers, dealers, pimps and other low-life scum. Her existence had boiled down to one big Quentin Tarantino movie.

"I don't suppose you can dance?" she asked the late junkie.

"Am I dead?" the junkie asked her.

She nodded gravely, and prepared to put a consoling hand on his arm. It was something she'd been taught in an AOD orientation class, but found she rarely had to use.

The junkie gazed sadly down at his cooling body. "Dead. It's not fair."

"Tell me about it."

"What?"

She didn't reply. Better to keep quiet. It was a chance comment from her AOD that led her to discover that there was some question about whether or not she was scheduled to actually die the day it happened. She'd inadvertently found out that the incident was scheduled as a Life Altering Event but that her life hadn't necessarily been the one that was supposed to get altered—as in ended. She'd used the information to lodge her protest with the celestial bureaucrats.

The fact that one person's wrong decision robbed her of her own choices pissed her off to the point where she simply wouldn't accept the fate that had been dealt her. Pissed her off then, pissed her off now. Her undying anger was the main reason she refused to back off on her protest no matter how hard the office angels made it on her.

One protest a millennium was quite enough for the feather pushers. All AODs were under strict orders not to allow any other souls to slip through the cracks in the gray area between life and death. Carmen figured it was better for her case to keep her nose clean and just do her job.

Besides, so far she hadn't reaped anybody who wasn't destined to go.

"Your time is up," she said to the soul, respectful but firm.

He looked at her worriedly. "Am I going to go to Hell?"

Here was the tricky part. She answered carefully. "Do you think you should?"

He nudged his body with his foot. "I've been there already."

Good answer. She took his arm and turned him away from the corpse. The darkness began to fade, so did the filth-littered street. From the distance a golden glow grew toward them. She pointed. "See that Light?"

The soul beside her radiated awe and sudden peace. "Yes. It's beautiful."

"Just walk toward the Light." Her words weren't necessary. He was already on his way. Good. One down. She checked her watch again. She had a burglary to get to. Not that anything interesting was going to happen until she arrived.

Richie D'Augusto entered through the same broken window the burglars had used, with his Glock in his hand and his partner's warning in his ears. Three different guns fired at him as he dropped to the floor. They all missed. He fired back and people ran. Richie went after them.

His partner, he assumed, was calling for backup before she followed him in. Tracy always went by the book. The same book Richie had thrown out four years ago. It was a wonder he was still on the force. A wonder he was still alive, as Tracy among others frequently pointed out. He'd glimpsed three, maybe four, perps before they'd scattered like cockroaches. Three against one. He liked the odds.

He smiled. People who lived by the rules just didn't know how to have fun.

The warehouse was dark but for the infrequent overhead lights that shed only tiny intermittent pools of illumination. The place was a cold, mysterious maze. He heard running footsteps ahead and to his right, but saw nothing but narrow rows of stacked crates. It was dangerous, risky—an adrenaline rush. Most fun he could have with his clothes on.

Someone swore. There was an answering furious shout. There was more gunfire. Sounded like they were arguing among themselves, a trio of panicked kids with automatic weapons and no respect for human life. They were angry with each other for being spotted by the cops. Two of them were old enough to do hard time and were really pissed off at the teenager who'd talked them into the break-in. They wanted to kill the cop, but it looked like they might kill each other first. More shots were fired.

Grinning, Richie headed toward the deadly noise. Maybe he could get a little action going.

What was that saying? *It's a good day to die, my brother?* "Day, night, doesn't matter to me."

It was going to be messy, but at least she was in out of the rain. There was a lot of blood on the floor where she appeared. Blood. Two bodies, both still breathing. She ignored them for the moment. They weren't going anywhere without her. She followed the staggering footsteps of the one who was closer to dying, but still going after the cop. Since he figured he didn't have anything to lose, he planned to take everyone he could with him.

When he fell onto the already bloody concrete floor, she tapped the soul that remained standing on the shoulder. "Just what the hell did you think that was going to get you?" She pointed at the gun, so real to the recently deceased that he'd brought it out of the world with him. Behind him, the friends he'd killed in a fit of temper were now standing over their bodies, blinking stupidly in the Light that grew toward them out of the darkness.

She focused her angry attention on the soul in front of her. She didn't have much time to try to get through to him. "You're going straight to Hell."

"So what? Who cares?" He pointed the gun at her. "You wanna come with?"

She grabbed him by the front of his jacket. "Listen to me, you stupid bastard!"

What was that?
Where?
The voice had been low, but the angry snarl of words were impossible not to notice.

"Do you know the difference between justice and revenge? Have you ever heard the word *consequences*? You will be learning the meaning of it shortly."

Richie tilted his head sideways, eyes closed even though he was surrounded by darkness already.

He didn't need his eyes, not with what he had going for him at the moment. He was full of the energy buzz that was part fear, part anticipation, controlled excitement, and fierce concentration. The air around him glowed and hummed. His senses stretched, strained toward the danger, for what he knew waited for him in the darkness. He was so alert that he was half out of his body. Richie was well into that hunter's high when he heard the girl's voice.

"Let me explain to you just how and why you are in so much trouble. Let me give you something to think about."

Even though she whispered, or at least sounded like she was speaking from a million miles away, he heard the girl on the other side of the wall of crates quite clearly.

But he didn't stop to listen to any more because getting to her and the other perps, making the collar, that's what he was here for. He opened his eyes and considered his options. He glanced down the long row of stacked crates to either side of him, then he looked up. Up and over was the faster route. Richie slipped his gun back into his shoulder holster and began to climb.

There were three bodies on the floor on the other side of the wall. He saw them clearly from a perch maybe eight feet off the ground. Besides the three corpses, he saw two columns of human-shaped smoke floating toward a tunnel of brilliant white Light that stretched down out of the sky, a wall of flames licking up from a hole in the floor, another smoky human shape a bit more substantial than the others, and one very ticked-off Angel of Death.

She was darker than the night around her and a creature of light all at once. Terrible. Implacable. Beautiful. The girl of his dreams.

He'd seen her before, caught just the faintest glimpse sometimes out of the corner of his eye. They worked the same streets, knew the same people—it made sense that they'd run into each other occasionally. He'd been waiting for an introduction for a long time, but nobody had yet been good enough to do him that honor. He wanted desperately to feel the brush of her hand, to take a long, deep breath of her intoxicating perfume.

It made Richie jealous to see her talking to somebody else.

"Hey, sweetheart!" Richie called as he jumped down off the crates.

He landed between her and the other guy with a bone-jolting thud, barely missing the body sprawled on the blood-soaked concrete. Richie was somewhere between the light of Heaven and the flames of Hell, maybe a foot or two closer to Hell.

"Hi," he said, and noticed that Death was a lot shorter in person. There was something delicate and vulnerable about her that made him want to embrace her more than ever. "I love you," he told her.

And Death finally looked his way.

She had dark eyes, of course. Black eyes, soft as velvet, sharp as obsidian. Discerning, Devastating. There was nothing cold or forbidding in her glance. But there was a hell of a lot of astonishment.

Somebody shot at him out of the darkness a heartbeat after their gazes met.

Richie blinked. The warehouse came back in focus, and his reflexes took over.

What the hell? What had he—?

He ducked and drew his gun, vaguely aware that he'd been experiencing some kind of hallucination. He couldn't quite remember it. Something with a girl? It didn't matter. He had a situation to deal with.

Police sirens sounded outside, and running feet pounded toward him. The cavalry had arrived. He'd been right in thinking that there'd been more than three burglars in the warehouse. Instead of continuing to hide, this last kid had decided to try to shoot his way out.

"Bad choice," Richie murmured. "Police!" he added for form's sake. "Put down your weapon."

He dived to the floor and rolled, rising and firing as a second bullet plowed into a crate behind where his head had been. One shot took his assailant down. The boy stumbled forward and fell as Richie rose to his feet. No need to check for a pulse. Not on any of the four bodies. Richie looked around, straining in the darkness for—what? The sight of a pretty girl who wasn't really there? He could almost . . . feel her . . . moving among the corpses, behind his back, just out of the range of his vision, as though she were being careful not to walk on his grave. A cold chill went up his spine.

He didn't want to think about it. It was all his imagination anyway. Right?

Richie was still looking down at the bodies when Tracy and a bunch of uniformed officers reached the scene.

"Cheated death again, I see," his partner said to him.

"No," he murmured, too low for mortal ears to hear. "She cheated me."

He'd seen her. He'd talked to her. To her! Impossible. He said, "Hi" and— No. People simply did not talk to AODs that way. Even suicides didn't greet death as more than a professional acquaintance, an official they needed to do personal business with. The cop's greeting had gone far beyond professional courtesy. He'd been smiling when he spoke to her.

Smiling. At her.

The memory sent a shiver through Carmen. Not a cold shiver either, but a pleasant, tingling warmth. His smile did that to her then, and the memory of it did it to her now. Which was another impossibility. She wasn't standing next to any just-departed souls, not getting any reflections of emotions. She was actually feeling something about somebody other than herself. Impossible, but true.

One of the things she felt was annoyed. What did he mean she'd cheated him? Sounded almost like he meant she'd cheated on him. Like he was possessive, jealous. Like he had a right to be. Something definitely needed to be done about a man with an attitude like that.

But what? It wasn't as though she'd had much in the way of dates before she was gunned down in a drive-by shooting. She had lots of brothers that she had bossed around all her short life. It had been good preparation for her current line of work. But this guy's attitude toward her had been anything but brotherly. Her reaction to him was anything but angelic. Just the sight of him had almost distracted her from her work. Thinking about him sent sparks through her, even though there was no her. She had to see him again.

Just to straighten out his attitude, of course.

Truth was, she needed to see him just to see him. And in the hope that he could really see her. Which he probably couldn't, so the whole affair was moot before it even got started. Affair? Now there was an odd way of thinking about it.

Carmen checked her watch. She had some time before Mr. Petty was due to be loaded in the ambulance where they were scheduled to meet. Maybe she'd just drift on over to the street behind the warehouse where all the police cars and emergency vehicles were currently parked.

The young woman standing at the edge of the small crowd beyond the yellow police tape looked familiar. She looked so familiar, and so forlorn, that he was drawn to her. Richie didn't know why anyone who didn't have to be at the cleanup of a violent crime scene was there anyway. Crowds always gathered, though, especially when somebody had died. Body bags just seemed to get people's attention. Even well after midnight on rainy nights like this.

Only this girl's attention was concentrated on him, not on the black plastic bags the medics loaded into the Coroner's van. Her focus was so intense it was scalding. He liked the heat that flared through him, though. It warmed his senses as nothing had in years. He couldn't quite define it, because his reaction to her went instantly beyond wanting to ask her to jump in the sack. He wanted to ask her to not only jump in the sack with him, but to have his babies.

No way did he believe in love, let alone love at first sight. But . . .

He knew her from somewhere, and he'd loved her for a long time.

"Hey, sweetheart," he said as he came up to her. "You okay? You look cold." He reached out to put his hands on her shoulders, as if touching her would somehow make it all better for both of them. Surprisingly, her denim jacket was quite dry despite the rain.

She gasped as his hands came to rest on her, but didn't try to shake him off. "I'm—here," she said, sounding like she didn't quite believe it.

He slid his hands slowly down her arms until he grasped

her small hands in his. She seemed fragile, but he could feel her strength. Not so much physical strength, but he could feel her energy, was aware that she had a spirit that was as tough and uncompromising as steel.

She took her gaze from his for just a moment to glance at one of the long black bags two medics brought out of the warehouse. She shook her head sadly. "Those kids—" she began.

"DOA," he told her.

"Like AOD, only—" she said, still distracted by the body. "I never noticed that before."

"Yeah, right." Maybe she was dyslexic. Maybe he didn't care. She was cute. Besides, if she had some kind of learning disability, maybe he could help somehow.

Since when did he ever try to help anybody? Richie D'Augusto cared for nobody but himself. He asked her, "You want to get a cup of coffee or something?"

"Aren't you on duty or something?"

He shrugged. "Got paperwork waiting. No big deal."

She took her hands out of his and put them on her hips. She gave him a stern look. "Which means you make your partner do all the boring stuff, right?"

"She likes it."

"Really?"

She was skeptical, but also sounded as though she really cared. He started to shrug nonchalantly again, but there was something about her attitude that sent a ripple of guilt through him. It was as if she expected the best of him, that she was disappointed in him for shirking his duties and all that. She reminded him of his third grade teacher.

"You're not, like, a nun or anything, are you?"

"Like a nun?" Her eyes laughed at him even though her expression remained perfectly serious. Her lips lifted in the tiniest of sardonic smiles. "Not a thing."

"Good. 'Cause I've never wanted to kiss a nun before."

"You want to kiss me?"

Her eyes went all soft at his words. Full of surprise, too. As if it had never occurred to her that somebody would ever want to kiss her. She had really gorgeous eyes. Dark brown and incredibly expressive. And that mouth. Totally kissable, with that easy, articulate smile. She could say anything with those eyes and that smile.

"Of course I want to kiss you. But how about that coffee first?"

"How about you do your share of the paperwork?"

He didn't know why she thought it was important for him to be responsible, but for some reason he couldn't just blow her off like he did other people. "After the coffee?"

What was the matter with her? Here was a man who could actually *see* her. A man who said he wanted to kiss her. Kiss her. Imagine that. And they'd just met. She wondered which one of them would be more astonished if he tried. It could be heavenly—but for whom?

What was she doing? Lecturing him. What was he doing? He was standing there oozing charm, which was certainly more attractive than what most people who saw her oozed. He was attractive, in a lean, nervy, intense way. There was something preying on his mind, though, something eating at him under all the charisma he turned on her. The darkness was as attractive to her as the seductiveness.

What was the matter with this scene? He'd killed somebody a few minutes ago. She'd sent that soul on its way. They'd met on the job. Lots of people did that. But. But.

"Let's go get that coffee."

He slipped into the booth beside her. She could actually feel him sitting next to her, all warm and hard-muscled and alive. She could smell him, the wet leather of his jacket, the faint hint of male sweat on his skin. He was so much a part of the world, and for this moment so was she. She didn't understand this, but it was great and terrifying.

The only logical explanation was that she'd gotten summarily transferred to the GA Division. Only, she knew there was a long waiting list and a rigorous training period for guardian angels. Heaven's management was heavily into Tests and Learning Experiences. She hadn't applied for a transfer. Didn't want a transfer. She wanted to go home. Had Somebody decided to make her a GA without telling her?

No, whatever was going on here had nothing to do with Heaven and everything to do with the cop. Who was rather heavenly to look at, come to think of it. He was full of energy, the raw, sexual kind. She felt as if she were feeding off that energy, existing simply because of it.

She didn't know whether to be grateful or pissed off about that. Depending on somebody else, shining in his reflected light, wasn't her thing. But—he believed in her. She had always believed in herself, living and dead, but it was so very hard. It was—nice—to have someone else share that belief.

"You're confusing me."

"It's my sex appeal," he answered without missing a beat. "Drives women crazy."

"You drive me crazy."

His grin was pure boyish mischief, but with a dangerous edge to it, and pain behind it. "Good."

He moved subtly, so that his thigh pressed against hers. She felt age-softened denim and hard muscle. His body heat poured into her, fueling the knowledge of just how cold being a disconnected soul was. But she wasn't disconnected. When their gazes met—

He'd looked into those eyes before. He had held her in his arms once, long ago.

She knew him. Even with all the distance of life and death between them, they were together. As they'd always been and always would be. They'd formed that connection when—

She couldn't remember when, and didn't want to either.

"Richie."

"Carmen."

He didn't remember when he'd told her his name, or when he'd learned hers. It didn't matter, not when they could see into each other's souls—

Richie looked quickly away, dropped his gaze to the table. What she must have seen wasn't worth looking at. What was he thinking? That he'd found a woman he could relate to? Keep? That he deserved? He deserved nothing and no one. That he couldn't make himself get up and leave her frightened him. He'd never had any trouble abandoning women before.

"If you're smart, you'll walk away," he said, not able to look at her. "Just go." He hoped she would, and prayed she wouldn't. "You don't know what I am."

She snorted, not the most feminine of sounds, but he found the sarcasm endearing. "I think I can safely say that that goes for both of us." His hands were twisted together on the tabletop. She pried one hand from the other, and twined her fingers with his. "And I thought I was cold," she said when she held his hand in hers.

"It must be the rain." As he said the words Richie noticed again that her clothes were perfectly dry. He leaned his head closer to hers, brushing his cheek across the long fall of her black hair. It had a smoky sweet scent to it. "You smell like church. Like that incense they use at High Mass." She chuckled as he flagged down a waitress and ordered.

Carmen wasn't surprised when the waitress only brought one cup of coffee. When Richie looked up to complain, Carmen squeezed his hand. "That's okay. I'm not thirsty."

She could smell it, though, as he brought the cup to his lips. Divine. She wondered if she'd be able to taste it as long as he was touching her, but decided not to risk it. Better abstinence than disappointment. Besides, it was pleasure enough just to be with Richie. Why push it?

When was the last time she'd known pleasure? She'd deliberately forgone all the benefits of the afterlife for the sake of proving a point, of winning her case. She'd chosen to do something useful in the limbo between the flesh and the spirit rather than give in and go on to whatever waited. Being with Richie confused her, made her doubt what she wanted, what she should do. Did she want to give in and go on? Or did being with him just make her hungrier to regain what she'd lost?

"You piss me off, D'Augusto."

He brought her hand up to his lips. The gentle kiss sent a stream of warmth through her. "I piss everybody off sooner or later. What's wrong, sweetheart? Why'd you look so sad? What are you thinking?"

He sounded like he really wanted to know. He also looked surprised that he really wanted to know. It made her smile. "Thinking about free will," she answered. "Exercising it's a real bitch, you know?"

He dropped her hand. His expression went cold, his eyes hard and flat. "I know all about it," he said. "I never made the right choice about anything in my life." He shrugged. "You've got to do like me, and learn not to care."

"You care. You just have to get past whatever it is that's eating at you."

He gave her a blistering look, but before he could manage an equally blistering retort, the raucous blare of a passing ambulance caught Carmen's attention. She jumped up.

"Mr. Perry! I forgot all about him. Gotta go!"

"No. Wait! I'm sorry. Don't—"

"It's not you. It's my job. I have to leave."

Carmen was gone even as Richie grabbed for her hand. He sat back hard on the booth's worn padding. He wondered where she'd gone, and how. Mostly he wondered why he missed her already. And why *her* overblown sense of responsibility made him feel like a jerk. Just because she had this need to do the right thing didn't mean that he—

"Damn it, why I am suddenly thinking so hard about everything?" He hated thinking, especially about himself and the things he did. What was it about the familiar-looking girl that made him want to not only take stock of his life, but take control of it as well? He liked being out of control, for God's sake! Better if he never saw her again. Lots of reasons. He didn't want to think about them. He didn't want to think. Couldn't stop.

Maybe it was the coffee.

Fortunately, before his brain could actually get up and running to the point where he'd be spending another sleepless, pacing night, he got a call about an assault in progress. He left the diner with a happy smile.

The truth was, Carmen wanted to be back at the diner. The fact was, she was making her last call of the evening, at the top step of a tenement stoop. Mr. Perry had been sent on his way, though he'd complained about her keeping him waiting. She apologized, and vowed not to let herself get distracted anymore. Instead of yielding to temptation she went on to her next assignment. Now, despite the solemnity of the moment, she thought about Richie as she looked down at the body of a woman who'd been on the losing side of a domestic dispute for the last time. Carmen prepared to calmly reassure the dead woman that she was going to something better. She held out a hand and helped the soul to rise.

"Somebody ought to kill that bastard husband of mine," the woman's soul said as she got up from the corpse. She shook off Carmen's touch and put her hands on her wide hips. "Maybe the cop who took off after him will get lucky."

A jolt of worry broke Carmen's concentration. "Cop?"

The woman pointed down the dark street. "Got here about a minute too late to help me. He was really mad about it when he took off after Chuck."

"Cop?" Carmen repeated worriedly. "Tall? Lean? Dark hair? Big gun?"

The woman laughed. "Honey, I didn't see his gun. But it was D'Augusto all right."

"You know him?"

"Everybody in the 'hood knows that wild child. You ought to get somebody to look after him before he gets himself killed. He could use an angel on his shoulder." The soul scratched the back of her neck and looked around curiously. "Isn't there something I should be doing here?"

Carmen chafed to be away, to find and protect Richie, but she carried out her duty. Asked the proper questions. Gave directions. Once the woman was on her way to the next world, Carmen ignored the fact that she should go to wherever it was she existed between shifts. She thought about being with Richie. In the next instant, that's where she was.

Just as a large fist connected with Richie's jaw, not for the first time. She saw that his gun had been dropped in what looked like a nasty hand-to-hand fight. The man he struggled with was more than twice his size, and mean with it. There was blood on Richie's face, but he was grinning. When the man dived for the fallen weapon and came up with it, Carmen screamed. Richie just laughed, and put himself in the way of the gun. The man shot. Richie jumped, spun, and kicked at the same instant. The bullet missed, but the big man went down.

Richie was cuffing him and reciting the Miranda mantra a second later. When he was done, he added, "Damn it, Chuck, you missed. Why'd you have to miss?"

Carmen couldn't take it anymore. Heart racing with anger and terror, she planted herself squarely in front of Richie D'Augusto. "You idiot! You could have been killed! What did you think you were doing?"

He gave that characteristic shrug. "Thought maybe I could get a little action going. Didn't get lucky tonight."

He sounded like he was talking to himself. Maybe he didn't quite know she was there. She grabbed the front of his leather jacket and shook. The glazed look didn't leave his eyes, but they did focus on her. As the excitement of the fight cleared out of them, they slowly filled with something far more frightening to her. Love. Pure, intense, hungry love. And longing for something he thought she could give him.

"You came for me." His voice was a husky whisper. He reached for her.

Carmen jumped back. She finally understood why he could see her. If she weren't already dead, she would have wanted to die. It hurt that much. Oh, yes, he wanted her all right. The reality of her, the truth of her, what she really was. Bitterness poured through her, as fiery as that other thing he'd made her feel, that thing she wasn't going to call love. Richie here knew what love was, and it was ugly. Right now, her perpetual, seething anger at the cop who'd gotten her killed was a small, insignificant flame compared to the fury at Richie D'Augusto that lit her soul.

She backed away from him, shaking her head.

He took a step after. "Please, I need you."

"No." She held up a hand to fend him off. "No. I'm not easy." He smiled his charming, seductive smile. He held his arms out to her. God, but he was attractive. Carmen kept her distance. "No," she said again. "You can court Death all you want, but Death isn't interested. Not me. Not tonight."

I've got a headache, she added to herself, and went into that limbo where she belonged.

"What do you want?"

"Not what you're hoping for, that's for sure."

He put his hand on the doorframe, blocking the entrance. He wished he hadn't answered the knock. He wished he weren't glad to see her. He didn't know what he wished. He looked down into those beautiful, belligerent dark eyes and asked, "Why are you here?"

"Taking a holiday." She smiled. "Can I come in?"

That smile did him in. He didn't know why he was angry at her anyway. He didn't know how she knew where he lived. He wondered where she'd gone when she'd rushed out of the coffee shop a week ago. He'd had an odd dream or hallucination or two about her since then, but that wasn't her fault. She was here now, and he was glad. He stopped blocking the doorway and let her inside.

Carmen looked around. His studio apartment was in the sort of broken-down building where even the cockroaches needed to carry Uzis. It could be called "home" only by virtue of containing a couch, a television, an unmade bed, a bathroom, and an area that might, technically, be a kitchen.

"Nice toxic waste dump you have here." She shook her head at the squalor. It had a far too deliberate look to it, stage dressing for the role he chose to play. "You can do better than this, D'Augusto."

"What? You want me to get slip covers?"

"No. A little more self-respect."

"I'm working on it," he admitted, much to his own surprise. He moved a pile of magazines from the couch to the floor. He was absurdly pleased to see her, even if she was a nosy, nagging little thing. Also embarrassed to have her see his apartment. He cared what she thought of him. This was a new, scary thing. "Your standards are too high," he muttered.

"Always have been," she agreed. "I tend to expect the best of people."

"I don't have a best."

"Let's work on disproving that, shall we?"

Richie didn't want to argue. He wanted to tell her to get out before it was too late. For him. He said, "Have a seat. Want coffee? Want me to do the dishes first?"

"Yeah," she said. "I do. Want me to help? You don't have to do it all on your own."

He knew she wasn't talking about the dishes, but that's what they did anyway. He washed, she dried, he basked in her extraordinary smile and managed to touch her whenever he could. It was a tiny kitchen; there were plenty of opportunities to brush against her while they did the work. They all felt good. And he talked. Normally he was the strong, silent type. Not with Carmen.

"I missed you. I mean, really missed you. I had the feeling you were angry with me and I didn't know why. I knew I wanted to make it better, though. To fix whatever I did wrong. I just wanted the chance, you know? Then I got to thinking that maybe it was because I'm a cop. Lots of people are nervous and scared around cops. If that's it—"

"No. I work around cops all the time. Most of them are okay. There was one once, but—never mind." She went all sad and distant for a moment. It made him ache to take her in his arms and make whatever hurt her all better. Then the moment passed, and she brushed the back of her hand across a healing bruise on his jaw. "Hurt?"

He shrugged. "No. But it gave me the excuse to take a few days off. I needed to think," he admitted. "Don't you just hate having to do that?"

"No."

"I thought you'd say that." He snagged an arm around her waist as she put the last dish away. He pulled her close. "I'd rather do this."

Carmen had never been kissed before. It blew her away. It caused a delicious, tingling ache to run all through her. The hot, wonderful sensation only intensified when his hands moved over her. She molded herself to him, touched him in turn, and drew far more than reality from the contact. This couldn't be happening, of course, but she didn't care. She wasn't going to think about it. She slid her hands down his back, cupped his ass, and pulled him closer.

She'd come back because she couldn't bear to leave a soul in pain. She'd had this *need* to help him. It turned out her anguish and need was as great as his. As the kiss deepened and intensified, regret and sorrow shifted and changed as a new type of craving grew in her, between them, was shared. They were in this together, all their senses entwined, feeding off each other. Passion was terrifying and intense; it burned away everything in its path. It felt great.

When he picked her up and carried her to the bed, she was shaking with desire and with joyous laughter.

Richie laughed with her. He hadn't laughed, really laughed, in years. Suddenly, he didn't just need to have sex, he needed to have fun. It turned out Carmen was not only incredibly responsive, but she liked it when he tickled and teased and took his time. He was happy to oblige. And she was happy to take her time with him in turn. He wasn't quite sure where their clothes went, but it didn't matter. What mattered was that when they finally came, it was together, and it was pure heaven.

Carmen knew it hadn't really been sex they'd shared, that simply wasn't possible, no matter how much reality his belief loaned her shade. But they had made love.

"Works for me," she muttered, and ran her fingers through his sweat-damp hair. His head was resting on her shoulder, a great deal of the rest of him was planted on top of her. "You're heavy, D'Augusto."

"Want me to move?"

"No."

"Good. I don't plan to." They rested like that together for a long time, sated, content, happy. Gradually, though, she felt tension tighten his muscles as the anguish that was so much a part of him reasserted its hold. Maybe not as tight as usual, she hoped.

"I need to talk."

She stroked his hair again. Their gazes met. "I know."

"I killed a girl."

He both expected her to be repulsed and hoped for forgiveness. A tiny stab of dread began inside her. Something else stirred as well. She didn't want to know. She already did. "Go on."

His heart tried to tear itself out of his body rather than let him give up his secrets. Her steady, neutral gaze helped him go on. "I was a rookie, working the east side. You know what it's like down there?"

"Intimately."

"My partner stopped our patrol car to talk to some gang bangers he'd been working with. There was a girl with them that night. She was yelling at her brothers, trying to get them to go home. She looked at me and smiled. Boom. We connected, just like that. Her eyes were—"

"Mine."

"Then she went back to yelling. Didn't miss a beat. I was laughing at that when I looked around and saw the car coming up the street. I saw the guns aimed out the windows, knew what was going to happen. Somebody shouted. People started to scatter."

"The world slowed down."

"I turned. I was so close to her. All I had to do was push her out of the line of fire."

"You froze."

"I could have saved her. I know I was supposed to save

her." He looked at her with the same wild expression he
wore when he saw an Angel of Death. Only this time she
knew he saw her—the girl she had been. "You died in
my arms."

"You kept telling me how sorry you were."

"You told me you didn't care. That you weren't going
to die. But you did."

"I've been trying to get back."

"I want your forgiveness."

"You should."

"I can't forgive myself."

"No, you shouldn't."

"I don't want to go on. I want death, but— Ow!" She'd
hit him hard on the side of the head. Just like he'd seen
her do to one of her brothers before—

Carmen pushed him off her. She was on her feet.

Richie rolled up off the bed to stand facing the furious
woman. He didn't question that they were both fully
clothed when they'd been naked an instant before. "Forgive me, Carmen. That's all I want from you."

"You want to die. That's why you want me. That's what
you find so attractive about me. I can't give you death."

"I want you to give me peace."

Carmen shook her head, and damned the compassion
that was so much a part of her, living, dead, and in between. She didn't want to feel it for this man, but it was
there, permeating her soul, trying to guide her actions. Why
did she have to be so damned *nice*? To keep the compassion at bay she reminded herself that *it's all his fault*!

"I was going to college," she told him. "I was going to
help people. Get married, have babies. It *hurts* not to have
those things."

"I'm sorry."

"Good. Stay sorry. Don't ever stop being sorry." She
grabbed his shirt and pulled him close. "Just stop trying to
get killed!"

"I deserve it."

"Everybody *deserves* it. Eventually. Even I don't argue
with that."

"You'd argue with God himself."

"If I could ever take a meeting with Him, yeah. I don't
know why I didn't remember you sooner," she went on.

"You were so cute, so cocky back then. I wanted to eat you up then and there, but I needed to get my brothers home more. Why'd you have to turn out to be such a loser just because I died?"

"It was my fault."

"I know. Spare me." She pushed against his chest, and he ended up sitting on the bed. She felt the need to loom a little, which was hard even for an Angel of Death when she was only five feet tall. He looked up at her with those big, brown, soulful eyes of his, and she couldn't help but smile. What was the matter with her? "You're like a puppy," she complained. "You make me want to swat you on the nose, then cuddle you."

Richie didn't know what to make of her reactions. "I thought you hated me."

She waved a hand. "Yeah, well. . ." She wasn't good at hate. Righteous anger, yes, but not hate. Carmen drew herself up and tried to look like an Avenger Class Angel. She pointed a finger sternly at Richie. "If you expect me to say you have to forgive yourself, forget it. Guilt and self-loathing can be very useful incentives to leading a responsible life. I don't want you to forgive yourself. I do want you to get on with living, D'Augusto. And stop thinking about me all the time," she added, though she knew it was condemning herself to sensory-deprived limbo once more.

Richie clutched hard at the edge of the mattress as the pain he'd lived with for so long began to let up a little. "You forgive me?"

She looked disgusted. "Yeah. I guess. Sure." Carmen bent forward and kissed him, sweet and life-giving. "And I love you."

Then she was gone.

"That was one weird dream."

Richie reached out, half expecting someone to be in the bed beside him. Then he sat up and rubbed his hands over his face. He needed a shave, but the bruises didn't ache anymore. He felt more rested than he had in a very long time. He glanced around his small apartment, wondered when he'd done the dishes, and remembered the long, vivid dream. In it, he met the girl he'd let die. They'd gone out for coffee, then come back to his place to make love. It should have been macabre. It should have been a nightmare, but it was bittersweet and beautiful. Some kind of catharsis.

Like she'd given him a blessing to go on with his life, or something.

Maybe he should take her up on it.

Carmen went back to her assigned duties, back to waiting to hear about her case. She tried not to mark the passage of time, especially the time without Richie in it. She never thought about the cop who had gotten her killed anymore, but she thought about Richie a lot. He never sought her out anymore, and she was glad of that. Really.

They worked the same violent streets; they were bound to run into each other again.

The emergency room was already packed with people and equipment when she arrived, but Carmen had no trouble squeezing into the crowd around the table. Her clients didn't normally make it as far as a hospital before they met. Carmen felt out of place in the brightly lit room.

"I'm used to walking the streets in the 'hood," she told the dying man as she took his hand.

"I could bust you for streetwalking, you know," he answered, and held on tight.

"You could try." AODs didn't cry, but she wiped tears away just the same. "How you doing, D'Augusto?"

He would have shrugged if he had the strength, or been conscious. "Been better."

The people around them were frantically busy. Their gloved hands were covered in blood. Carmen shook her head at the mess. This was such a waste.

"How'd you get shot?"

He looked embarrassed. "I—uh—took a bullet meant for my partner. I'm a hero. It's a redemption thing, I guess. Didn't hesitate this time," he added with pride. "Thanks for teaching me that, sweetheart."

She was impressed. "Congratulations." Various alarms began to beep and buzz. One of the doctors swore angrily at death. She didn't take any offense. The line on the heartbeat monitor wavered and began to flatten. "Looks like you're about to get what you wanted from me, Richie."

He scowled. "Yeah, but I don't want it anymore."

"Bummer."

"I still love you, Carmen. Always have. Always will. You. Not what you are." He sighed. Or maybe it was his last breath. "It's nice to know you weren't a dream."

His words didn't help her grief any. She was about to lose him forever. He'd go on to whatever waited for him, she'd keep on doing what she did while the God damned Mills of God kept grinding her up, inside and out.

When she started to help his soul rise, a large, very large, glowing hand, pulled her back. Fear and awe raced through her. Carmen whirled to face a real Angel—her title was just a courtesy one—a being of light and love and terrible splendor. She had no idea how he fitted the wings into the already crowded emergency room. This Angel wasn't her boss, but a complete stranger. Instead of obeying the urge to fall to her knees in veneration, she turned back to the dying man.

"It's okay," she told the intruder Angel. She dashed away tears again. "This is my job. I can do it. He needs me."

The Angel touched her again. He spoke with the Voice of Authority—sort of like James Earl Jones and Sean Connery rolled into one. "I came for you."

Carmen spun back to face him. Everything around them disappeared. She was engulfed in The Light of Heaven. "What?" She looked around frantically for Richie, but nothing existed but the empty shining whiteness.

"Come."

"What are you talking about? What's going on?" she demanded, frantic and afraid. "Where's Richie? He needs me. Don't you know how much I need him?"

"Your case has been decided."

"What?" she shouted angrily at the Messenger of God. "You're kidding. I'm not going to Heaven," she protested. But . . . That must be where Richie was going. She could deal with Heaven if he was in it. At least it would give her somebody to argue with. She took a deep breath to try to calm down. "Okay. Fine. I can do this." She closed her eyes. "I'm ready."

"You're not going to Heaven."

"Huh? What do you—"

She was grabbed around the waist and thrown to the

ground before she could finish. A body covered hers. The concrete under her was hot and hard. So was the muscled body on top of her. She heard the staccato blast of nearby gunfire. Then an engine roared, tires squealed away. There was shouting, and lots of swearing.

"Get off my sister, man!" her brother Hank demanded.

Her protector shifted. He rose to his feet, and helped her to stand. It felt odd to have somebody help her rise for once, but Carmen brushed the strange feeling away. The handsome young cop who'd saved her looked deep into her eyes for a moment. Her heart lurched, and not because of any fear or panic reaction in the aftermath of the drive-by shooting. They smiled at each other.

He was still holding her hand. She didn't want him to ever let go. Words between them were completely unnecessary. She managed to say, "Thanks."

"You're welcome."

"D'Augusto, get over here!" the other cop called.

When Richie looked away, Carmen remembered everything that hadn't happened. Her brothers rushed up to her, but she wasn't able to do anything but nod to their worried questions. She'd deal with her brothers later, use their fear for her to get them away from the gang life. She had to concentrate on capturing the memories right now. She didn't think she was supposed to remember, and that made her even more stubborn than usual about keeping them.

In her memory Richie made the wrong choice, froze instead of pushing her to the ground. She remembered dying but refusing to give up on life. She'd been able to make a case for returning to the world because somebody told her Richie had made the wrong choice. She'd had to wait for a Decision. While she'd waited, Richie went nuts. When they met again, he was in love with death. They'd had a fight about that. And then—something awful happened. And an Angel came and told her she wasn't going to Heaven.

"Who wants to go to Heaven?" she asked. She looked around, at the hot summer concrete, the sagging buildings, the worried faces of her brothers—at the cocky, confident cop who was coming back toward her. "I've got heaven right here," she said as he took her hands again. Her brothers glared, but she didn't care.

"My name's Richie D'Augusto," he told her. "Who are you?"

"Carmen."

He put his arms around her. "Carmen what?"

Something that might have been memories of things that weren't going to happen now filled his eyes. She put her arms around him. "We won," she whispered. "It's going to be fine."

His smile was all the Light she needed. "But I still don't know your last name."

"How about D'Augusto?"

He didn't hesitate for an instant. "Fine with me, sweetheart."

OLD DELICIOUS BURDENS

by Peter Crowther

*Peter Crowther is the editor or coeditor of nine antholog-
ies and the coauthor (with James Lovegrove) of the novel*
Escardy Gap. *Since the early 1990s, he has sold some
seventy short stories and poems to a wide variety of
magazines and chapbooks on both sides of the Atlantic.
He has also recently added two anthologies,* Forest
Plains *and* Fugue on a G-String, *to his credits. His
review columns and critical essays on the fields of fantasy, horror, and science fiction appear regularly in In-
terzone* and the Hellnotes *internet magazine. He lives
in Harrogate, England, with his wife and two sons,
where he is currently working on two novels—one genre
and one mainstream.*

*Still here I carry my old delicious burdens,
I carry them, men and women, I carry them with me
   wherever I go,
I swear it is impossible for me to get rid of them,
I am fill'd with them; and I will fill them in return.*

   Walt Whitman, from 'Song of the Open Road' (1881)

"GEOFF . . ."
   At first, the word sounds alien, intrinsically strange and
nonsensical, a mere utterance and nothing more, the sound

of exhaled breath through throat and lips and teeth, caught in a certain, never-to-be-repeated coalition of form and relationship. All around him is dark and warm, still and silent, the whispered single word an intrusion.

He waits, unaware that he *is* waiting, his eyes closed and his mind turned off, no lights flashing on any cerebral panel, only the faintest digital LED glow somewhere, down deep inside himself, to confirm that the power is still connected.

He is asleep. Of that much at least he is aware. Or rather he *was* asleep. He was talking with . . . who? He was talking with his solicitor. And his accountant was there, too, dressed in the simple clothes of a sheep-herder. He remembers trying to count sheep to get to sleep.

Without opening his eyes, he feels himself drifting to the surface of consciousness, reluctantly, like a thwarted suicide hauled back from the welcoming and undemanding darkness of the depths of the East River, with the river's myriad currents and undertows gently pulling and pushing him, kneading him into some semblance of wholeness. Hauled back to the light.

The sound comes again. "Geoff!" it says, this time more urgently.

The voices of the water through which he passes mutter, making little sense at first but then, as though benefited by some wondrous translation device, they cajole him and tug at his brain. And amidst the whispered mutterings of *divorce*—the end of its final syllable dragged out into a sibilant chant—and *alimony*, they speak directly to him. *Your name,* they say to him, *that is your name.*

His eyes open and, at first, he drinks in only the bedroom door, momentarily frowning at the disappearance of his solicitor and then trying to recall what Simon was wearing . . . it was something strange, but already the recollection of it is puzzlingly and annoyingly fading . . . fading, fading . . . *gone,* like ice in the sunlight. He allows his eyes to move side to side in rapid succession, looking to freeze-frame familiar objects, each pause lasting the merest hint of a nanosecond. He is unable to find any.

He is in bed but this is not the bedroom he shares with Louise. This is the guest bedroom, where they have never

slept before. He frowns. Then why is he here? Then he
remembers.

He remembers the harsh words delivered like swords,
parried and thrusted; he remembers the feints and the
blocks, each one carefully and systematically devised on
the spur of the moment by two people who have become
professional in their ability to hurt and to inflict wounds.
Amidst these word-memories he recalls tears, some from
Louise and even some from him, though none of them had
been tears of regret. They had been tears of frustration.

Then, with Louise's vitriol pouring up the staircase after
him, he had gone up to their bedroom, the one they had
shared for—how many years? Almost thirty-four. Thirty-
four years.

And he had started removing clothes from the closet—
pants and shirts and jackets—throwing them onto the bed
in a semblance of order. Then the socks and the underpants
from the shelves, the ties and the shoes from the bottom
of the closet . . . all thrown haphazardly into a pile on
the floor.

And Louise had come in then, striding to her own closet
at her side of the communal room, thrusting the doors
wide, pulling out blouse and skirt, sweater and hose, tossing
them in a flutter and a whump of crinoline and cotton, a
blaze of discarded color and design, tossing them even onto
Geoffrey's own clothes already there on the bed, creating
a Rorschach amalgam of shape and texture and color—
primary and pastel—which suggested many things but not
togetherness. Despite their proximity to each other, never
togetherness.

They had continued in this way for several minutes—not
a long time in real terms but more than long enough to
render the room uninhabitable. Then Geoffrey and Louise
had paused for breath, their respective closets virtually
empty save for one or two items reluctant to respond to
their fevered grasps and pulls and tosses, instead hanging
listlessly on rails or forlornly over the edge of shelving, all
folds carefully administered at the moment of their incarceration now gone and replaced by careless creases and
brutal bulges.

They had paused for breath and seen the extent of their
anger: the bed was buried.

At which point Louise had declared her intention to sleep in the guest room, advising Geoffrey that he could sleep downstairs on the sofa.

Incorrect, Geoffrey had boomed dramatically, finger aloft, almost laughing. *It is* you *who will sleep on the sofa. I* will *sleep in the guestroom.*

And so, almost farcically, the two of them had rushed for the door of the guest bedroom, a room in which they had not only not slept before but also had never even entered together . . . and for the briefest of moments there they were, the two of them, jammed between the two uprights of the door frame trying to establish sole sleeping privileges in their own house.

Neither would relinquish those rights and so, in silence, they had removed their clothes, pulled on nightdress and pajamas rescued from the debris of their own room, and got into the bed in the room which, in many ways, represented a kind of no-man's land.

Geoffrey blinks away the memories. "Uh?" he groans. Then, almost barks out, "What?"

"I heard something," his soon-to-be ex-wife says, her words a disembodied voice from behind him in the bed. The bedroom door swims back into focus and he blinks, blinks again. And listens.

"I don't hear anyth—"

A hand clasps his shoulder but still he does not move. "Listen," she says.

He listens.

Did he hear anything? He tries to ignore the feel of Louise's hand, fights off the urge to reach up and lift it away and push it back to her. He doesn't want it. He doesn't want her hand and he doesn't want her . . . though he wonders, deep down in a hidden part of himself, if that is only because she doesn't want him. He concentrates, keeping as still as he is able, and hears only the dull, rhythmic thud of his heartbeat, not the imagined sound of a foot stealthily mounting a stair somewhere close by.

He closes his eyes and concentrates.

Somewhere beyond his heart he can hear the sounds of the house, floorboards settling, radiators clicking, a myriad insects padding almost—but not quite—noiselessly about their business beneath the floors and behind the walls. Outside, it is raining. He can sense rather than hear the rain—rain falling does not have a sound, he thinks absently; not unless it's actually lashing down, beating against the windows and the paintwork and the stone. But yet one can tell when it is raining, possibly because it removes sounds rather than adds to them. Is silence then a sound itself?

"Go to sleep," he says. The irritation is clear in his voice, along with the sound of thick saliva and a throat rasped by too many cigarettes, too much coffee, maybe one too many glasses of bourbon and a whole lot too much conversation. Far too much conversation.

It was a long evening—the evening they have just finished.

And it was a long life—the life spent together they have just finished during that long evening.

His eyes still hurt from staring, alternately at her and at the clear honey-gold liquid he kept swilling around his glass, looking for answers. His jaw still feels stiff from being clamped tight, the muscles being forced to work, grinding teeth together.

Talking to her had been like talking to a mirror. He had been able to see the same shallow, tired stare looking at him, see the same movements at the corners of the jaw, see the same straightness of leg and awkwardness of arms tightly linked. No emotion. The discussion had come and gone almost entirely without emotion—at least until the histrionics of the emptying of the closets and the subsequent disagreement over sleeping arrangements—and yet, even at the end of it all, with everything decided and agreements already made, he had felt a sense of loss.

Looking at her, as they had silently prepared for bed, he had seen that same feeling tugging at his wife's eye corners. *We blew it,* the eye corners had said silently, and he had had to look away, away from their knowing sadness.

"Louise," he says, keeping his voice soft and steady, "I do not want to talk about any of this anymore. If this is your idea of—"

He stops.

"See," his wife whispers. She kneels up behind him and peers over into his face. "You heard it then, didn't you?"

He frowns and lifts his head from the pillow.

Yes, he wants to say to her, *but what did I hear?*

You heard the sound of nothingness, a voice says in his inner ear. *That is what you are most familiar with, it is a sound you know well.*

"No," he says, "I didn't hear anything."

"Liar!"

He turns around and glares at her. He can see the anger in her eyes now, but there is something else there, too. He recognizes it immediately: fear.

She pulls back from him and frowns, glancing up at the partly closed door and then back at his face.

"What?" he asks. *"What?"*

"Is this something to do with you?"

He pulls himself up now onto his left elbow, twisting around to answer. "Is *what* something to do with me? Louise, there's nothing *there.* You're imagining it. You're just—" He closes his mouth and traps the words.

"What? What is it, Geoffrey? What little homespun philosophy have you worked out to deal with this one?" She sweeps a strand of hair back from her eyes and shakes her head. "There are people . . ." she waves her arm, ". . . wandering around our home and you're blaming it on my imagination because I'm . . . because I'm *upset*? Is that it?"

He moves his head side to side and glances away, stifling a yawn.

"My God, that's rich," she says, the words as soft and piercing as gossamer-covered razor blades. "Coming from you," she adds.

For a second, an oppressive stillness descends on the room and across the bed, calling into crystal sharpness Louise's features and her mouth, partly open. Her eyes look moist. She shakes her head and reaches out, slams her hand against the headboard, once, twice, and shouts, "We're up here!"

He lurches across and pulls her away from the headboard, gripping her hand tightly, forcing it down onto the bedclothes, feeling a mixture of accomplishment and regret when he sees her eyes narrow in pain. "What the hell do you think you're *doing*?" His voice is hoarse and low, the words coming out singly, separated by brief pauses, and as he speaks he glances over his shoulder at the door. Did it move just then, then . . . when his eyes first saw it? Was it in

the process of opening even as he turned, with someone—
some*thing*—standing on the landing?

"Did you see that?" Louise asks.

"I saw it."

"The door moved."

"I said, I saw it." He lets go of her hand and quietly
pulls back the sheets. "Probably just the wind," he says,
trying to keep the blind hope out of his voice as he searches
with his feet for his slippers.

"Why would there be any wind out there on the
landing?"

Geoff decides not to answer that. He stands up from the
bed and, suddenly feeling very exposed and vulnerable,
he adjusts the cord on his pajama trousers, pulling the fly
closed.

"What are you going to do?"

He waves her quiet without turning around and steps
forward against the wall, keeping the open door on his left:
this way, at least, he won't get flattened if whoever's out
there pushes the door open.

He crouches down, making his frame more compact—
less of an easy target, eh? the small voice in his head says
with what sounds to be a trace of amusement—and holds
his hands in front of him. He tries to ignore the fact that
they seem to be shaking.

"Should I call nine-eleven?" When she speaks, Louise's
voice is so low that Geoff can hardly hear what she says.

He shakes his head, not daring to take his eyes from the
doorway as he shuffles his back along the wall.

From somewhere in the darkness beyond the door, a
faint sound echoes, a rustle of clothing, a creak, and
then . . . a soft chuckle.

"Jesus Christ," Geoff says to himself.

There really *is* someone out there. And they're laughing.
Are they laughing at him? Have they seen him, sliding
along the wall, his hair looking like a bird's nest, and just
been unable to contain their amusement? Are they laughing as they flick off the safety catch before they storm in
and shoot them?

Maybe they're going to do other things first, the voice
says.

"I'm calling nine-eleven," Louise says.

Geoff stops where he is and waits, breathing in deeply, but does not take his eyes away from the open door. He hears her punching the buttons, grateful that they had had the foresight, all those years ago, to include an extension in the guest bedroom.

"Geoff," Louise whispers.

Now he turns and looks at her.

"There's someone on the phone."

He frowns at her. Someone on the phone? What the hell does that mean? Is it the police? A wrong number? "Well, tell th—"

Louise points down with her hand. "*They're* on the phone, downstairs."

Geoff looks across at the curtained windows and thinks about walking calmly across the room and stepping out into the rainy night. As if on cue, a car goes by, momentarily bathing the windows in its headlights, the sound of its engine Dopplering away, from wherever to wherever, its driver's future shining brightly in those same headlights.

Geoff suddenly doesn't hold out much hope for his own future. He looks at Louise's face and sees the terror in her eyes. Nor hers. Particularly not hers.

"What are they saying? They calling someone?"

Louise shakes her head. "I don't know," she says, putting the handset against her ear and carefully covering the mouthpiece. "I can't make it out. It's like whispering . . . distant whispering."

He glances back at the door and then moves quickly to the bed, holding out at hand. "Let me hear."

She hands him the handset and he listens.

It's like wind on the wires, the sound of breath-words flitting half-formed and indistinct, the auditory equivalent of a moth trapped in a jar, its wing brushing the sides in an effort to escape. Then, his eyes widen and he looks at Louise.

She leans her head close, trying to hear. "What is it?" she says.

Geoff gives her the handset. "It sounded like . . ." He frowns. "It sounded like you."

"Me?" Louise places her hand flat on her chest, then clenches the fingers and scrunches up the pale blue nightdress. "What was I saying?"

"I couldn't make it out," Geoff says, "not entirely."

"The bits you *could* make out."

"It sounded like . . . like you were asking me to pick up Nick."

"Oh, Geoff, why are they doing this? *How* are they—"

"You were saying something about my picking Nick up at his dance class on the way home."

Nick was Nicholas, one of their two sons, now almost thirty years old, long since moved away from home and living in Baltimore where he spends time working in a men's outfitters while he waits for auditions. He *is* a dancer. He no longer goes to dance *lessons*. Hasn't since he was fourteen.

"You said I was asking you?"

He nods.

"Did you hear . . . did you hear *yourself*?"

Geoff thinks, replaying the trapped voice-winds in his head. "I . . . I think so. Christ, I don't know. It sounds ridic—"

"Let me," she says, holding her hand out.

Geoff shakes his head and places the handset carefully on the cradle on the table next to his side of the bed.

They both stare at it, imagining what the trapped voice is saying . . . what *all* the trapped voices are saying, for both of them had heard many voices and tones and rhythms.

"That means," Louise ventures, "they've recorded us?"

Geoff shrugs then shakes his head. "That would mean they've been watching us for almost twenty years."

"Then they're *imitating* us?"

Geoff looks at her and frowns. "Can't see that either. It would mean the same thing . . . that they had somehow been listening to our conversations for all that time."

She looks at the bedroom door and winces as one of the downstairs doors opens and closes softly. "What do they want, Geoff?"

He stands up and, for a second, feels completely in control. It's the first time he's felt this way in a long time. "Only one way to find out," he says, realizing he sounds like a character out of a movie.

Geoff strides to the door and stands for a few seconds, wondering what he's waiting for.

Louise says, "I'll come with you," and he understands

that that was what he was waiting for. Maybe he should tell her, *no, you stay here,* but he doesn't want to. He's frightened, and he wants her with him. And anyway, if they do something to him down there, it'll sound even worse to Louise waiting here upstairs . . . listening to them dealing with him . . . waiting for their footsteps to begin up the stairs to where they know she sits, cowering.

He waits until she is standing next to him, pulling her robe around her shoulders, and then he places a hand firmly on the edge of the door and pulls it toward him.

The landing is dark. But more than that, it seems a little foggy out here . . . as though a bunch of guys have been having a poker game, the smoke hanging over the table like a mushroom cap.

Geoff takes a step forward, so that his toes are touching the change of carpets between bedroom and landing, and waits for a few seconds, his head tilted upward and over to one side, straining to hear.

Behind him, Louise whispers, "What *is* all that *noise*?"

Geoff doesn't have any idea. He just listens.

There's a lot to hear and yet there's nothing.

The noise is a mosaic of sounds and whispered voices, moving around the two of them as they stand there.

Then, their eyes accustomed to the darkness of the landing, they start to see things.

In a diaphanous flurry of whiteness, a figure passes them in the weak light cast onto the landing by the bedside lights in the guest bedroom. But it is not so much a figure but rather the *suggestion* of a figure. It appears, suddenly, at the head of the stairs, pirouettes, and then, amidst a distant, throaty chuckle, whirls past Geoffrey and Louise before it stops, its arms thrust outward as another figure appears from the storage room beside the bathroom along the hall.

The second figure is that of a man. His features are similarly indistinct to those of the woman, but Geoffrey and Louise have no problem identifying either of them.

In a daze, his eyes so wide he feels they might just tumble out of his head and roll across the floor between the gossamer feet of the woman, Geoffrey hears himself say, "Hide 'n' seek. We were playing hide 'n' seek."

Behind him, Louise says, "It was the day the decorators left."

She looks around at the high ceilings and the paintwork, the papered walls and the silent doorframes, picking out the familiar curves and corners even in the gloom. "What's happening, Geoff?"

The two figures fall together in a muddle of outstretched arms and muted laughter, spinning themselves around as though to an unheard rumba or fast waltz, and then, slowly, they disappear.

From their own darkened bedroom they hear a cacophony of moans and sighs, of silent voices uttering pledges and promises. Geoffrey turns around and, with one arm, pulls Louise back so that she is behind him. He pushes open the door and flicks the light switch.

"Oh . . ."

"They can't hurt us, Geoff," she says. "They're us."

And so they are.

Through the partly open bedroom door, on the ghost of the bed that even now lays buried beneath a welter of thrown clothing, they see a hundred—no, a *thousand*!— images of themselves. The phantom pairs are locked in embraces, their bodies—some naked, some fully clothed and others still in various stages of dress or undress—intertwined and moving: here they are moving fast, here slow, and here they are not moving at all, only lying together, one arm resting on the other's shoulder, their eyes closed and their faces peaceful. And each one, though the features are blurred like television stations with poor reception, is either Geoffrey or Louise.

"My God, what is happening to us?" Geoffrey asks. He turns around and looks into Louise's face. "Are we dreaming?"

Louise shrugs and casts her gaze down to the floor, averting it out of respect of the privacy of the myriad shades of themselves in the bedroom. "Perhaps we are," she says at last. "Or perhaps we're haunting ourselves."

Geoffrey runs his hands through his hair and moves to the head of the staircase.

In front of him, at various places on the stairs, he can see himself holding onto the wispy figure of his wife, sometimes going down and sometimes coming up. And there are sounds to accompany the images, some of the sounds laugh-

ter, most of them some form of conversation and in one or
two the Louise figure appears sad, even crying.

"There," she points. "That one. Nick had just gone to
college, remember? We couldn't come to terms with how
empty his room was." She walks to Geoff's side and leans
on the balcony. "You had said that we would put back all
of his posters. 'Let him buy new ones,' you said," Louise
says, mimicking Geoffrey's voice. " 'I want his room back
the way it was.' "

"I remember," he says. "God, but we were lonely that
night."

"Mm hmm. We didn't think we were going to make it."
She is silent for a few seconds and then she says, "You
cried yourself to sleep."

Geoffrey doesn't say anything. He watches the couple
reach the foot of the stairs and disappear through the
closed door into the living room.

Already the downstairs hallway seems alive with whirling
whiteness, a blur of shape and movement. But most of the
sound is coming from the living room, with figures occasionally materializing out of the wooden door and moving
this way or that way, bringing with them the sounds of talk
and laughter and all the things that hover around two people enjoying their life together.

Louise moves past him onto the stairs, carefully placing
one foot in front of the other as though creeping up on a
feeding squirrel, out in the park, to watch more closely.
"Let's go down."

"Go *down*. I don't know—"

"I want to see," she says.

They move down slowly, passing through memories of
themselves with every step, holding out their hands to feel
the apparitions but without success. In the soft glow of
the nightlight on the hall table, the figures move and talk,
whispering to each other secrets that they once knew, the
real-life Geoffrey and Louise, but which the passage of time
has eroded as surely as the wind and the rain erodes even
the strongest rock.

"We're still asleep," Geoff says, his tone almost reveren-
tial. "We must be. Maybe . . . maybe we could wake ourselves up?"

"No," Louise says, watching a shimmering memory of

herself, its hair longer than it is now and filled with the shine and vitality that only youth can give. "I don't want to."

She reaches the bottom of the stairs and pulls her robe tight around herself. Looking down at her, Geoff sees his wife seemingly standing in a crowded hallway, figures appearing and disappearing around her and through her, half of them himself and half of them her, but these are Geoffs and Louises that once were and have since metamorphosed into a new Geoff and Louise.

With a glance at Geoff, who has stopped a few steps up, she strides to the door of the living room and pushes it open.

The whispering tumbles out of the room like gas.

It is an aural miasma of sound and confidences, of promises and commitments, of information and conversation, affection and concern.

She steps inside and out of sight.

"Oh, my goodness," she says, her voice drifting back into the hall.

Geoff trots down the final few steps and enters the room to stand beside her. The room is filled to bursting, with figures overlaying other figures like transparent images through which multitudinous variations can be seen, each one formed of the same opacity which permits still more versions to be observed.

"These are ghosts," Louise says softly, looking up at her husband. "They're the ghosts of what we once were. The ghosts of happiness."

Geoff watches a younger Geoff locked in embrace with a younger Louise, their bodies linked as one, writhing on the sofa amidst others, some sitting, some lying, some even asleep with the attendant other gazing affectionately at their partner, smoothing hair or stroking cheek.

"We weren't always happy," Geoff says.

"Maybe not," comes the response, "but we were always happier than we are now."

They continue to watch.

"Geoff," she says. "Is it my imagination or are there fewer of them now? Fewer than there were when we first came in."

He looks and the room certainly seems less crowded.

It seems that, as one pair completes its performance—its memory-play—it simply fades away. Now there are but forty or fifty of them, half Geoff and half Louise. He nods as an image of a youthful version of himself—doesn't look any older than thirty or so—wraps his arms around a long-haired Louise, rests his head on her shoulder and then fades from sight.

"Know what I think?" she says. "I think we've killed them."

"How can we kill them? They're just shades of things that were. Of the *people* we were. Nobody stays the same forever." Right now, Geoff is desperately wanting to wake himself up. He feels a gnawing sensation in his stomach, as though he hasn't eaten for days.

"Maybe memories live on only so long as they mean something. Maybe, when people grow tired of each other, there comes a time when they no longer have a place." She turns to him. "Maybe it's the house's way of letting us know what we had . . . and what we've lost."

"But we still have it. We still have all these memories."

Louise shakes her head. "That's what I meant when I asked if it looked like there were fewer of them than when we first came in here. That's what I meant when I said we were killing them."

She takes hold of his arms and says, "Now, try think of all the times we were in here . . . maybe making out, maybe sitting watching a movie or maybe just sitting talking, together."

He looks at her and frowns, allowing his gaze to drift across the room to a younger version of his wife's naked backside, with a partially obscured younger version of himself sitting in front of her on the sofa, its eyes looking up at her face and then working their way down. Moments later, when she has taken his youthful self's hand and led him across the ghosts of strewn clothing to the door, they stop and look horrified at each other. Then, giggling madly, they scurry to the discarded clothing and pick it up, frantically stepping into underclothes and pulling on pants and sweaters.

"It was Simon," Louise says. "He just called on the off-chance that we'd be in. The doorbell rang just in time; a minute later and Simon would have been looking through the front door at our bare asses walking up the stairs."

Geoff sniggers. "I remember," he says, imbuing the statement with a tone of amazement. "Would've served him right."

In front of them the younger figures, now clothed, fade from sight.

They look at each other and Geoff sees a tear on Louise's cheek.

"Now do you remember?" she asks. "Now that they've gone."

He looks back at the spot where the images were and down at the floor where the clothes had been discarded, and he frowns. It's there, the memory, but now it too has faded leaving only the faintest hint of itself.

All around them the images are disappearing.

They watch until only a few remain, recalling each instance, and then, eventually, there are only one Geoff and one Louise, sitting on the sofa staring into the corner where the television used to be in a previous version of the living room. The Geoff of this memory is asleep, his legs laid across Louise's knee. As they watch, the young Louise turns to her sleeping husband and, smiling, looks at his face and his chest, watching its gentle movements. Then she shuffles herself, clearly careful not to wake him, rests her head on a cushion beside him and closes her eyes.

Seconds later the image fades and Geoff and Louise are alone.

There are no more bygone Geoffs and Louises.

The house is still and silent. No whispered laughter, no conversation.

"That's it," she says. "Show's over."

Geoff moves out into the hall and looks around.

"They've all gone," Louise shouts to him. "*We've* gone. It's all finished."

He sits down on the bottom stair and shakes his head. "I can still . . . you know," he says to Louise as she comes to stand beside him. "I can still remember a lot of those things happening but I can't for the life of me recall the exact detail."

Louise nods, sees the desperation growing on his face

and, suddenly, she feels sorry for him. Sorry for both of them.

"We shouldn't have let it go so wrong," he says.

She is silent for a while. Then she says, "Maybe . . ."

He looks up. "What? Maybe what?"

"Maybe it's not too late to do something about it."

"About all those memories?"

She shakes her head. "Uh-uh. I think they're gone for good. But maybe other memories are gone, too."

He frowns at her, the question unspoken.

"Well," she says, "I mean, you know, can you recall exactly what we were fighting about last night?"

He looks at her, moving his eyes around her face, drinking in the familiarity of that face, seeing the tiny lines that have developed over the years to turn the girl he fell in love with into the woman he loved more than anything in the world, and, as he looks, he tries to think.

What *had* it all been about, that fight to end all fights?

Something to do with work and the reduced attention they gave each other . . . was it something like that? When he thought of it, thought of it in such a general way, it seemed so ridiculous. So inconsequential. It had to be more than that, didn't it? Didn't it have to be something big for it to end their marriage . . . to bring to an end their lives together?

"I can't remember," he says, "not exactly."

"Me neither," she says. "So we've not only lost the good memories, we've lost the ones that weren't so good, too. And that's . . . that's good, I guess," she adds with a smile.

He nods. "The bedroom is a mess. I remember that much."

She giggles and wipes the tears from her eyes. "It'll tidy. There's nothing that can't be fixed."

"Yes," he says and, with a deep breath, he holds out a hand.

Louise looks at him, sees the thickened chin and the thinning hair, sees the tiny wrinkles around the eyes, wrinkles made with time and love and laughter, and she takes his hand in her own and squeezes it. "Love you."

"Love you, too," he says.

Louise pulls her hand free and walks past him up the

stairs. Seconds later, after one final look around the empty hall, Geoff follows.

There is a click of the bedside light and then the house is quiet again.

Down on the stairs a pair of gossamer figures materialize: one seated on the stairs and one standing alongside, their hands clasped in rediscovered affection.

When they have completed their brief performance, the figures grow even more translucent and shrink down into carpet, cornice and floorboard, becoming one with door frame, wall and wood-stained balustrade, until they gradually fade from sight. Gone to await new companions.

WOMAN OF CHARACTER

by Yvonne A. Jocks

Yvonne A. Jocks has written since she was five, publishing her first short story at the age of twelve. Under the name Evelyn Vaughn she sold her first novel, Waiting for the Wolf Moon, *to Silhouette Shadows in 1992. Three more books completed her "Circle Series" before the Shadows line closed. The last,* Forest of the Night, *was named Favorite Science Fiction Romance in Affaire de Coeur Magazine's '96 Reader's Poll. Yvonne resides in Texas with her animals and her imaginary friends and teaches junior-college English to support her writing habit . . . or vice versa. All sentence fragments in her story are for effect. Really.*

"I can't do this," I said, stopping in the middle of the airport terminal. Announcements and conversations and a muffled rush of jet engines roared in my ears. My peripheral vision faded until I could barely see the flow of passengers detouring around me, like a river around a boulder.

A paralyzed, thirty-something boulder wearing too nice a dress to panic in.

"So stay on the ground," said my best friend, current chauffeur, and fellow boulder, Moira. "You won't miss tonight's episode of *Sky Marshal* that way."

"I promised! It's important to Dad." Because of the tunnel vision, I had to turn my head to see her; only then did I realize she was bluffing. As if either my fiery death or missing the season finale of my favorite television show were joking matters. "I've got to do this."

"Then commit to it and breathe deep. In through the nose, Erika. Out through the mouth."

Moira was a therapist.

I breathed. The shadows receded slightly. The loud-speaker, paging someone to the white courtesy phone, sounded relatively intelligible.

Outside the floor-to-ceiling windows overlooking the tarmac, distant lightning flickered. The better to show off the low-hanging, black clouds, my dear.

I whimpered.

"Remember the affirmation I gave you?" Moira prompted. She worked at a holistic wellness clinic. They did a lot of yoga and tai chi, massage and meditation—and affirmations. The idea was to repeat a goal over and over, worded as if already true, to create a mental shift that *makes* it true.

I know. It sounded suspiciously hocus-pocus to me, too. But I was desperate.

" 'My flight to London is safe and enjoyable,' " I repeated obediently. " 'My flight to London is safe and enjoyable. My flight—' "

Thunder boomed through the terminal.

I glared at Moira. "I'm going to die. I'm going to die. I'm going to—"

She covered my mouth and strong-armed me through the river of rushing passengers to a row of plasti-chairs near my gate. "*SIT*," she commanded.

I sat. Belatedly, I made my white-knuckled fist uncurl from its cramped hold on my carry-on bag. Was this a panic attack? It made no sense; I'd flown before. But something felt funny about this trip to London. Funny weird, not funny ha-ha.

Moira inhaled dramatically through her nose, like the "after" shot in an antihistamine commercial, then exhaled through her mouth. Her gaze held me so steadily, I found myself mimicking her. And it did help. A little.

"They won't take off if the weather's bad, will they?" I asked.

"Right; they only hire crews with death wishes," Moira said. "Erika, you have to get on that plane, or you'll miss your dad's wedding. You know flying is safer than driving. You know I did a tarot reading, and it indicated you'll be fine. Wonderful, even! Convincing yourself logically won't help." Okay, so *logic* might've been stretching the point there. "You've got to convince yourself emotionally. So say the damned affirmation."

I'm going to die. I'm going to die. What a disappointment, to be such a coward. "I can't."

"Okay, then," she sighed. "I didn't want to have to do this, but here goes."

I blinked at her, almost relieved to have something other than my own death to worry about. "Do what?"

"You'll have to make believe."

I stared at her. Then I looked quickly around us, in case someone heard—like anyone other than Clark Kent could hear *anything* in this madhouse. *Make believe?* Why not just offer Scotch to an alcoholic?

Only Moira knew my guilty secret: that the world of books and movies and television was more important, more real to me than my so-called "real life."

"Excuse me?" I asked, as sarcastically as possible considering my position of weakness.

"Look, it's not as weird as you think it is. A *lot* of well-balanced people have perfectly healthy fantasy lives. In fact, the integration of fantasy can improve their interactions with the world around them."

This from the woman who did tarot readings. "I don't think I'm one of them."

The truth? The truth is that I had more imaginary playmates as a child than I did real ones; to their credit, they could sleep over whenever I wanted, but on the debit side they never did learn to play a good game of catch. By the time I hit puberty, I was well-versed in the standard plot device of soul mates and love-at-first-sight, to the point that I rarely wasted my time dating. *He,* whoever he was, was fated to find me either way, right? I graduated high school, then college, turned twenty-five, then thirty, and we still hadn't found each other. Yeah, I'd started to harbor doubts about my romantic fate, but it was pretty late by then to take up a social life.

To watch TV—and oh, I did—you'd think any single woman who didn't have a date every Saturday night must be either a real loser or a major Fido or both. My friends assured me I wasn't unattractive. That left loser.

And how did I cope with that little snippet of reality? I scheduled my evenings around the TV. My bedroom was decorated with movie posters and stacks of paperback books—it wasn't like anyone ever went in there but me. And despite holding down a steady job, paying my bills, I was so unused to going out in the world that here I sat, afraid to get on an airplane that I knew was safer than a car.

"Role-playing is a standard therapeutic exercise," Moira reminded me.

I'd heard it before, and I wasn't buying it. "Uh-huh."

"Did you know that hundreds of people have visited a cemetery in Nova Scotia to visit a Titanic grave marked 'J. Dawson?' "

That got my attention. "Jack Dawson from *Titanic* is really buried there?"

"Actually, it's a guy who worked in the engine room or something, James Dawson. But that doesn't matter to the tourists. They're paying their respects to the guy in the movie, same as people in Glastonbury visit King Arthur's supposed grave."

"Then they're dysfunctional, too."

"You're not dysfunctional, Erika."

"I don't want to get on that plane, Moira." My dad had paid for the ticket already. He'd used frequent flyer miles to upgrade me to first class. I couldn't not get on that plane, but every cell in my body screamed that something different, something wrong, something life-changing—or life-ending—was going to happen aboard that aircraft. Probably *because* I had such a vivid fantasy life, and could so easily imagine everything that could go wrong. How functional was that?

A gate agent announced that my flight would board in five minutes. Outside, rain sluiced against the windows for that extra dollop of comfort I needed.

"Do you trust me?" asked Moira.

I nodded, and tried to breathe. In through the nose. Out through the mouth.

"Then imagine someone traveling with you," she insisted.

"Someone who can handle anything that goes wrong. Someone—"

"Sky Marshal," I said.

Moira sighed the sigh of someone who knew me too damned well. "That's who I figured you'd go with," she said, shrugging off the responsibility for what she'd started.

It was too late to call back the image now. " 'We need Sky Marshal on this one,' " I quoted from the show. Then I checked around us again, to make sure nobody had heard me.

Sure, the syndicated *Sky Marshal* series was pretty cheesy, a blatant takeoff on airplane adventures like *Airforce One, Passenger 57, Executive Decision*—you get the idea. Its plots were one-note: each week a crime took place aboard an aircraft and the ironically named Sky, a Federal Air Marshal working under cover for the FAA, put things to right. But it wasn't for the terrorism/hijacking/narcotics-smuggling suspense that I taped every episode, any more than people watch *Baywatch* for water safety tips—although I have been known, in the privacy of my living room, to whisper "Come on, Sky, you can do it!" at appropriate moments. No, week after week, Damien Ryder's portrayal of Sky Marshal himself, a lanky, blond, blue-eyed hero with a roguish smile that melted the heart, drew me back.

With Sky Marshal on this flight, I wouldn't worry. Yes, we'd be doomed to an adventure, as sure as any get-together with *Murder She Wrote*'s Jessica Fletcher will yield at least one corpse. But with the troubleshooting Sky on board, everything would turn out okay. He was that competent. And he was just the sort of hero to take pity on a really nervous passenger. He didn't just romance the younger ladies; he teased the older ones, buddied up with the male passengers, and defended children and animals.

I could imagine the meeting with surprising clarity. He would notice me from, oh, a bank of payphones. Scared as I was, I probably wouldn't see him until he folded himself into the plastic seat beside me, then drawled something painfully corny in that soft, deep voice of his.

Come here often?

I'd respond with a hint of sarcasm; what's a roguish hero without banter? *What gave me away, the hyperventilating?*

Nah. More like the wild eyes, trembling hands . . .

I looked at my lap. My hands *were* trembling. If Sky were here, he might lay one of his bigger hands over mine, warm and protective. Startled, yet strangely comforted by his familiarity, I would stare up into his blue eyes and see myself as he did, someone momentarily fragile but worthy of protection, maybe even . . . precious?

I felt warm certainty, a sense of homecoming. I knew those eyes. They'd widen, as if he knew me from somewhere, too. Or was he just that good at caring about people?

Sky. . . .

He would bluff away the earnestness of the moment with a joke. *Now if it were just the hyperventilation, I'd sit back and enjoy the scenery.*

Only once I'd huffed at his arrogance would I spot telling dimples, realize he'd said something chauvinistic just to goad me out of my fears.

God, he was gorgeous. . . .

"My stars, it's working," marveled Moira, drawing my attention from broad shoulders, searching eyes, dimples. I blinked, readjusting to the emptiness of the chair beside me. Wow. Maybe it was the fear, but that had felt like more than a daydream. More like an altered state!

"How do *you* know it's working?" I demanded, afraid that I'd embarrassed myself—spoken out loud, or drooled.

"Your aura." Before I could tell if she was serious, her head came up at a loudspeaker announcement that included the words, *And first-class passengers.* "That's you. Will you be okay, sweetie?"

An imaginary whisper tickled the hair on my neck. *Okay doesn't* begin *to cover it.*

I had no idea how to respond to either the blatant flattery or the niggling thought that I was the one creating it. Kind of egomaniacal, that. But I needed the security blanket too much to question it. Once I reached London would be soon enough for even badly needed psychoanalysis.

Okay? "I think so," I said to Moira. "Is it still lightning?"

Nah; just rain. Lightning isn't a big danger, anyway. They worry more about wind.

"Wind?" I echoed, glancing out the big windows.

"Neither one," Moira assured me, cocking her head.

The tower tracks wind shear, too. Leave everything to the professionals, Angel. Just sit back and, um, enjoy the flight.

There was definite double-entendre in that last piece. Were he really there, I would slant my eyes up at him to challenge his aviation knowledge. *Come here often, do you?*

And since air marshals travel incognito, he would widen his eyes with feigned innocence. *Me? Nah. I just read a lot.*

Yeah. Right. He *looked* like a scholar.

"Don't forget your bag," reminded Moira, handing me the carry-on case that, in my fantasy, Sky Marshal was already carrying for me. She and I hugged. I thanked her for the ride and promised to call. She swore she'd tape my show, Sky's show. But I must admit, I was distracted.

Considering my earlier panic, distraction was a *good* thing. Especially if nobody guessed *how* I was distracting myself.

Now, at least, as I showed my boarding pass to the gate agent and walked down the jetway to the DC–10, I had something on my mind besides my fiery death. Sky Marshal had that kind of charisma. For first class, he would choose his businessman persona; for some reason I imagined him without a suitcoat, sleeves rolled up to show corded forearms, but of course he'd have to wear the coat to hide his pistol. He would help me stow my bag in the overhead compartment while I settled into the luxuriously oversized leather seat.

What a coincidence, Sky grinned, dropping into the seat between me and the aisle. As an air marshal, he could probably sit wherever he wanted. But it felt right to have him there, nonetheless. *Looks like you'll have to put up with me all the way to England.*

Oh, no, not that, I teased right back. *Guess I'd better hit the booze.*

The flight attendant, an Oriental lady with an air of competence, stopped beside our seats. "Would you like a pre-flight cocktail?"

We laughed at her exceptional timing.

"Miss?" she repeated, and for a horrified moment I thought maybe I *had* laughed—out loud, right there in the plane, with nobody really sitting beside me to share the joke.

Don't mind me; I'm just a grown woman playing with my imaginary friend.

Silence assured me it *had* all been make believe. Sky didn't exist, and I was about to take off on a trans-Atlantic flight all by myself. Rain blew against the Plexiglas window beside me, and I jumped—wind? He'd said something about wind shear.

"Miss?" prompted the flight attendant.

"White wine?" I squeaked.

She nodded. "Absolutely."

Way to get airsick, Angel. Order water.

Wow, I *did* have some imagination, didn't I? *Water?*

Don't dehydrate yourself. Go with water or juice. Trust me. Another patented grin. *At least, trust me on this.*

"Excuse me," I said to the flight attendant, even as she turned away. She did an admirable job of not looking annoyed. "I'd rather have orange juice, please."

"Certainly," she smiled.

You'd better be right, Mister, I warned my imaginary seatmate. *I am NOT handling this flight very well.*

Tell you what. When we land in London, there's a great pub off the Thames where I'll be happy to buy you all the wine you can drink. If you want, I could even get you drunk and take advantage.

Moving a little fast, aren't you?

His voice dropped to a sexy purr. *Give it a try, Angel; you might like moving fast. Hyperventilation looks good on you.*

I barely noticed either the other passengers toting luggage by us or the engines vibrating into action; I was too busy seeing a truly remarkable me reflected in his rapt, imaginary gaze. Me as a woman worthy of romantic pursuit. I'd gotten my hair done for the wedding, and it did look cosmopolitan. I'd fallen in love with this blue, forties-cut dress the moment I saw it in a vintage clothing shop. The black pumps did nice things for my ankles.

I imagined myself smiling mysteriously. *Mmhm. I thought that after hijackers killed your partner, you swore off relationships until you quit C.A.S.* That would be Civil Aviation Security to folks who didn't watch the show.

The flight attendant brought my orange juice with a cocktail napkin. I thanked her and, as soon as I could, went back to picturing my handsome seatmate.

Then we DO know each other.

Not exactly. The air pressure changed; the flight attendants had closed the door. On the show, that made the aircraft Sky's jurisdiction. With an increased whine of engines, we began to trundle backward, safe in his hands now. Psychological crutch or not, this was working like a charm—I'd forgotten my fears.

Then the plane stopped with the slightest lurch, not twenty feet back from the gate, and I remembered them with a gasp. "What's wrong?"

Relax, Angel. Probably just some VIP wasting everyone's time. Despite his light words, he would be scanning the cabin, making sure he spoke the truth. Sky Marshal took very little seriously—except, of course, for truth, justice, and keeping the skies friendly.

We taxied forward again, back toward the terminal. I breathed deeply. There'd be plenty of time once we landed in London to wonder how my imagination knew so much about flying, right?

Maybe over wine, in a pub by the Thames—

Moira's tarot reading had indicated my trip would go wonderfully. For the first time, I thought past the flight long enough to wonder if my soul mate, the one I'd loved forever but had almost stopped looking for, awaited me in London. Problem is, when I tried to picture him, he looked like Sky Marshal. And Sky wasn't real.

If only affirmations *really* worked. I whispered a new one under my breath as I watched two flight attendants opening the door to the re-extended jetway. "Be real. Be real. Be real."

Over the noise, someone seemed to be complaining. "—*believe* you people almost left without me!"

When he stepped into the first-class compartment, I nearly choked on my juice. For a split second I was Cinderella and my fairy godmother had granted all my wishes. Either that, or my dementia was complete.

Sky?

Except, it wasn't Sky. Same height and shoulders, yes. Same strong facial features. But that full mouth of his pulled down at the corners in a way Sky Marshal's never did, even facing the worst perpetrators of aviation crime.

Uncharacteristic boredom dulled his usually crystalline eyes. He'd greased his hair back, darkening the already dark-blond so that he looked more brunet. And he wore jeans and a T-shirt that I somehow sensed cost as much as my entire wardrobe.

Be careful what you wish for. This wasn't Sky Marshal, it was—

"Damien Ryder," I whispered. Surely I said it quietly enough, especially under the whining engines, but maybe he could read lips; his gaze cut across the cabin to me, and his lip curled.

"I don't do autographs," he warned, and when the flight attendant pointed out his seat he sauntered to a place across the aisle from where Sky had been . . . I mean, across from the empty place beside me. His walk, almost effeminate, wasn't Sky's walk.

He must be one hell of an actor, I thought. Moira would say there's no such thing as coincidence, but . . . geez! I snuck a peek at the surreally familiar profile, one I'd never thought to see in the flesh. It was Sky, yet it wasn't Sky at all.

The actor shot another disgusted look at me, and I saw myself as he must: a mousy woman in a used dress, nothing special, maybe even pathetic. "Do you *mind*?"

I quickly looked out the window at the wet, bustling tarmac, and realized we were moving again. This was the problem with make believe. I'd liked the me I'd seen in Sky Marshal's eyes, but Sky Marshal wasn't real and neither was that woman.

Only the sense of loss was real.

Up front, the head flight attendant pointed out Clearly Marked Exits and strapped an orange cup to her nose to demonstrate how to use the oxygen, trying not to keep looking at Damien Ryder herself. A second attendant, male, collected my juice glass.

"Hey, steward! I could use a drink!" called Damien Ryder, over the safety spiel.

"I'm sorry, sir," said the attendant with a strained smile. "We're about to take off."

Ryder flipped him off. Welcome to reality.

The airplane made a wide, ungainly turn onto the runway and the crew moved to their jump seats. Then, with an even greater roar of engines, we challenged the laws of nature by picking up speed. G-force pushed me back into my seat, but I continued to stare out the window, watching the wind streak raindrops across Plexiglas. The point of no return. *I'm going to die. I'm going to die. I'm going to die.*

A hand covered mine, warm and protective. Everything in me went still.

The awkward bumping of tons of metal at high speed abruptly stopped, became miraculous weightlessness, and the plane started to climb. It banked to the left, tipping with the angle, revealing the airport and blue-lit runways beneath us, and only once we leveled out did I look at the seat beside me.

Empty. The closest person to me was the slack-jawed Damien Ryder, looking supremely bored with the triumph of aerodynamics. There was nobody—

That's the worst of it till landing. His voice, *Sky's voice*, was only in my head, not my ears. But it startled the hell out of me. *You okay?*

Uh . . . yeah. Sure.

Now THAT'S *convincing.*

Only when my focus readjusted from the empty space beside me to across the aisle, and the annoyance of Damien Ryder, did I realize I'd been looking at Sky. A Sky who wasn't there. It must've looked like I was staring at the actor. . . .

I turned my head. *This is* WAY *too weird. You aren't real. I can't imagine you with him here.*

The prima donna?

I would've smiled at his scorn, if the whole thing weren't so pathetic.

Why can't you be real, and him be a figment of my imagination?

You'd trade him for me?

In half a heartbeat.

Even if he's not yours to trade.

I was being lectured by my own out-of-control fantasy.

He prompted, *You don't really mean that, do you?*

Why are you—why am I even thinking this conversation? You aren't real.

Yeah. I'm sticking on that one, too.

I actually turned to stare at him—imaginary friends weren't supposed to question their reality!—and found myself staring through him to Damien Ryder again. Great.

So you're okay? asked the voice in my head—that clear, husky baritone of an imaginary voice. *No more of that cute hyperventilating?*

I'll be fine. As if he needed my assurance.

Catch you later then, Angel, he promised, but I knew that the only time I'd catch him would be watching reruns and videotapes until the fall season started. And he wouldn't be catching me at all.

Alone again—as if I hadn't been all along?—I readjusted to the chilled isolation of sitting in first class however-many-thousand feet in the air and climbing. At least I'd survived takeoff. That must be why my imaginary Sky had seemed so real—adrenaline. Now that we were airborne, it didn't do any good to be scared because I had no choice but to deal with whatever happened.

Breathe in through the nose, out through the mouth. Nothing would happen.

The fasten-seat-belts light went off with a chime, but the pilot made an announcement requesting that we stay strapped in as we might be hitting turbulence. The flight attendant offered another cocktail before dinner, and I shook my head.

She stepped to Damien Ryder's seat, apparently to ask the same question, but over the rush of engine and air I heard her add something about, "Big fan . . . looking forward . . . season."

She was a fan of *Sky Marshal,* too? But she seemed like such a competent, together woman to be a fan of cheesy syndicated television! Damien said something that froze her pleasant, I'm-here-to-serve-you smile. She shook her head as if she hadn't quite understood.

Oh, no.

Like one possessed I leaned closer, so when Damien raised his voice—that rich, baritone voice—I heard him clearly.

"No next season," he repeated, and glanced my way; he knew I was listening and didn't want to repeat himself. "We killed Marshal off in the season-ender."

The plane shuddered. Ding! The fasten seat belts light came on.

Damien Ryder laughed. "God, look at you two. Sky Marshal—it's just a character!"

It, not even he.

The flight attendant dredged up her mask of a smile and asked him again what he wanted to drink, then left to get it.

The chill I felt now had nothing to do with either the canned air or the turbulence, neither the rain blurring my window nor the strangely tactile, dark clouds barely visible past that. Sure, a storm put my life in danger. But as I've already explained, it seemed my real life was mainly a vehicle for my world of fantasy anyway.

Not Sky!

Damien Ryder got his drink, but we hit an air pocket and he spilled half of it down his expensive T-shirt. He mouthed some kind of curse, downed the rest of the liquor, then dug into his carry-on bag. The plane bucked and tipped. We were going to die. Sky Marshal already had . . . and maybe Damien Ryder wanted to, because he unfastened his seat belt and stood.

"Sir!" called the flight attendant from her jump seat. "You need to stay—"

"I've gotta take a leak. Sue me!" He made his unsteady way forward and vanished into the bathroom.

Sky wouldn't pull himself along the seatbacks like that.

The airplane pitched forward, then up; I tensed physically against the cries of several passengers. How pitiful, that my last living thoughts might be mourning a fictitious piece of beefcake.

In through the nose, out through the mouth.

The cabin lights flickered. I closed my eyes and tried affirmations. "I'm safe. I'm safe. We can handle this. Sky can handle this—"

No, it didn't make sense, but this wasn't about sense; I was clinging to whatever I could. Through my eyelids I saw a flash so bright, it had to be lightning.

"Sky has everything under control. I'm safe." I don't know how long I sat there, swallowing back nausea, empowering an image that I already knew couldn't be.

Only when a voice—a familiar, deep voice—said "Of

course you're safe. I wouldn't let anything happen to you," did I open my eyes.

Damien Ryder swung into the seat beside me, winked, covered my fisted hand with his. Except, he didn't look like Damien Ryder. His hair was lighter. His eyes were too kind. His mouth quirked comfortingly up at one corner. He wasn't even wearing Ryder's clothes; he had on dress pants and a once-white button-up shirt, both of which looked to have been tested in ways dress clothes shouldn't.

No, I recognized this man on a deeper level than I would ever recognize Ryder. This was Sky.

But . . . he was real?

The plane pitched again, throwing me sideways into his shoulder, and he grinned and widened his eyes as if to say: what fun! For that moment before I righted myself, his shoulder felt warm and solid. I could smell him—fresh air and clean sweat and hints of remaining aftershave. I wasn't imagining the hand steadying mine. Not this time. Which must mean . . .

"Very funny, Ryder."

The hunk beside me snorted. "Yeah, like that prima donna could *buy* a sense of humor. I bagged him in the john, snuck him down to cargo. It's accessible from the downstairs galley on DC–10s, you know. Timing couldn't be better, what with the chaos. I've got him stowed behind a doggie carrier with a St. Bernard in it."

Could Ryder be *this* talented? The closer I examined him, the more I marveled at the differences. Sky's jaw appeared stronger than the actor's; his nose looked to have been broken once. His shoulders—broader, were that possible. But even if it weren't Ryder, surely it was Ryder's *body*.

"I don't . . . how . . . ?"

"Yeah, I know." He ducked his head in feigned contrition. "Questionable ethics—although he made it a helluva lot easier by doing drugs in there. I just needed a chance to figure out why I'm here. Something's gotta be wrong, if I'm here. Something's *always* going wrong around me."

I just stared at him.

He frowned. "Angel?"

"I don't know whether to believe in you or not." I admitted, as unsteadily as the plane was flying. If this was Ryder's idea of a lark, it was downright sadistic.

But if it was real . . .

I caught my breath. The possibility felt so enormous, it frightened me. *If this was real. . . ?*

Sky held my gaze with his own, despite the turbulence. "You have to believe in me, Angel."

Were I a practical person, I'd tell him to get back to his own damned seat and leave me alone. It would be safer for my heart and my pride both. Hadn't I had enough illusions shattered for one trans-Atlantic trip? And, yet . . .

The truth? I wasn't a practical enough person to miss this.

I nodded, warily, and covered the hand he'd used to cover mine. Flesh and blood, all right. His roguish grin sent a rush of joy through me, lingering suspicions or no. "I knew I could count on you," he said.

"How could you know that?"

"Because I know you, Angel."

Uh-huh. "You don't even know my name."

"True." He reached across the space between us, pushed hair back from my cheek. "But I think I know your heart."

I'd been waiting for this man. Real or not, I'd been waiting for him forever.

"So . . ." I cleared my throat. "So what do you think is wrong?"

Surely it wasn't with reluctance that he glanced back to the cabin? "That's what I can't figure. I checked out the cockpit while I was still . . . me lite. Everything's fine. Lavs, galleys, cargo—the only unusual thing around here is me."

"About you," I tried. But our flight attendant appeared beside us, not quite hiding her surprise at seeing Damien—a man who she must think was Damien—beside me. "The captain assures me we're through the worst of the turbulence. Would you like to consider your dinner entree? Today we have a choice of beef tenderloin, pheasant, or shrimp."

"Thanks, Kim," said Sky, accepting the cardstock-and-tissue menus. *Her* name, he knew—probably from her nametag. "Look . . . I want to apologize for, uh, my behavior. Earlier, I mean. I was out of line."

She blinked at him, then at me as if to verify that she wasn't imagining him, then at him again. She was a fan of the show, too. Did *she* see the difference?

"Thank you, Mr. Ryder."

"Thank *you*," he insisted, sincere. Then, handing me a menu and looking at his own, he said, "*Man,* I'm hungry."

"*Hungry?*" My voice almost sounded normal.

"I'm physical now," he pointed out.

Over dinner, he recounted his last mission. In first class they did dinner right, white linen, china dishes, crystal glasses. We even had bud vases with a single rose in each.

Sky put the rose from his vase into mine. Part of me could melt from the romanticism of it, flying into the night with this handsome man . . . but part of me strained to decipher this before I risked basking in any of it. Any more of it, that is. I was already in trouble.

"So that's the last thing you remember?" I asked, after his narration. "Disarming the bomb and then losing your grip on the wing?"

"Yup. Free fall without the parachute. There was lightning . . . and then suddenly gravity was a moot point, 'cause my body seemed to fade out. I kept waiting for the tunnel, the light, the whole near-death package, but it didn't happen."

"Were you scared?"

He grinned his sexy, half-grin of bravado. "Nah; I knew the risks. I was more curious than anything. Then I heard my name, and pow, I was in an airline terminal—except I wasn't, not exactly, like in a dream. And you were there with your friend, all cute and hyperventilating—"

"I wasn't hyperventilating," I insisted, fighting a smile.

"—and I thought, someone should calm that pretty woman down, so I went over and we started talking." He frowned. "Sort of."

Damien Ryder couldn't know all this. I could hardly stretch my mind around the implications.

"You thought you were dead, and you still took time to talk me through my fear of flying?"

Sky shrugged. "Old habits die hard?" Not the whole story . . . but I could wait for that.

"So what happens now?"

"For now? Dessert." Well, that was a troubleshooter for you—apparently he didn't ruffle very easily.

That's why I'd brought him along. Weird thought, that.

"Tell me about this television show of mine—Erika."

I liked hearing my name from him . . . yet it unnerved me. How *could* this be real? Had I gone over the edge?

Did I mind?

After dinner Sky walked the length of the plane, even got Kim to wrangle him an invitation into the cockpit, but nothing struck him amiss. "Except that, for a jerk, the prima donna's pretty popular. I musta signed fifteen autographs for him."

"He's not popular," I insisted. "Nobody knows him from Adam. *You're* popular."

The cabin lights lowered, but we didn't put on earphones for the in-flight film. Instead, bathed in a pool of illumination from the panel above us, we whiled away what must be pre-crisis time in conversation. He seemed awfully well adjusted, considering. "I'm still me, no matter what plane I'm on. So to speak." He'd always resisted close relationships, what with constantly jetting off on dangerous missions, so he hadn't left anyone truly special behind.

"I've always felt like I was in a holding pattern," he admitted, "Waiting for the right person to show up. I'll admit . . . I was starting to wonder if she ever would."

The way he slanted his blue eyes at me as he put my own romantic philosophy into words stole my breath. If only he were real!

He is *real.* But I took his hand again, as if to prove it.

The movie ended; an engine-muffled silence stole over the cabin as passengers fell asleep. We turned easily to more personal issues than our disparate backgrounds. We talked about my parents' divorce and my dad's forthcoming marriage, and what he remembered of his own folks before their deaths in a major air disaster. We both loved dogs, Carpenters' music, and the Colorado mountains . . . where he wanted to start a commuter business after he retired. It felt . . . right. Sitting together, isolated by noise and shadows and tens of thousands of miles of open space—it felt fated. By the time we'd debated our favorite hockey teams, we were finishing each other's sentences.

Sky excused himself to check on Damien, down in the cargo hold. I stared out the window at the ocean far below, silver moonlight reflecting on its surface. Maybe I should have gone with him, seen for myself if Damien Ryder was down there. Maybe I didn't want to know yet. I tried not to think too hard about being 37,000 feet over the Atlantic, either—as if to question the physics of a DC-10 would steal its magic. As if to wonder about Sky . . .

I felt relief when he reappeared, looking even more like Sky and less like Damien. "Sleeping like a baby," he assured me, voice rumbling in his chest with the effort to speak quietly. "I made sure his circulation wasn't compromised. He should be coming to about an hour or so before we land at Heathrow; hopefully, he won't remember a thing."

Land?

For someone who hadn't wanted to get on this plane, I suddenly hated the idea of getting off it. "What happens then? If no crimes take place, I mean?"

"We change places." The *of course* was implied. Whether he'd be changing places to the cargo hold or something more ethereal, though, was up in the air.

"What happens to *you*?"

He spread his hands. "One way to find out."

I scowled, not wanting to accept it but knowing I had to. For now, anyway. Sky still had a few hours to come up with a plan . . . and so did I.

Kim the flight attendant brought us pillows and blankets, and we leaned our seats back, got more comfortable, and tried to stay alert with more conversation. We discussed our fears, our dreams . . . our perfect date.

"A pub by the Thames," insisted Sky in a deep whisper, trying to keep his eyes open. "Making you hyperventilate."

I love this man, I thought—and it was either the best or the most tragic thing that had ever happened to me.

When I woke, my head was pillowed on his chest, his chin on my head, and sun was streaming into the cabin. Although only an hour or two had passed, we'd flown into morning.

And nary a hijacker to be seen.

I'd often awakened clutching my pillow, curled up with dreams of him, but to know the reality. . .! I tested the idea, settled into it as I would a familiar quilt—warm and comfortable and safe. Tentatively, like feeling out uncertain footing, I opened myself to his presence. I let myself savor the steadiness of his heartbeat beneath my ear, his breath on my hair. I inhaled him. I cuddled slightly into his warmth. For the first time, I didn't feel cold on an airplane.

I lay there in the sunshine with a man I could very well love, and let myself feel joy.

"Erika," Sky whispered, not moving. The beginning of the end.

I didn't move either. "Mmhm?"

"I, uh, didn't tell you something."

I felt myself tense, even as I fought it. *No.* I didn't want this to vanish so soon! "What?"

"You know how many close calls I've had, working for C.A.S.? The things I've survived?"

"Yes."

His voice stayed low, thick with sleep. "It's because I had a guardian angel."

Intrigued, I sat slowly up, readjusted my pillow so that we were almost touching noses. "An angel?"

He held my gaze as steadily as he'd held my hand. "Every time I got into some fix no human should survive, I heard—no, that's not right. I didn't hear it, I *felt* it, inside. Someone, a woman, willing me on, saying, 'Come on, Sky, you can do it!' She kept me going."

Was he saying what I thought he was?

He leaned closer, brushed my lips with his, a tender, grateful kiss that needed no background music. "Thanks, Angel."

Where *did* the line between fantasy and reality stop? Not surprisingly, I no longer had any idea.

Kim came by with breakfast menus and "disembarkation cards" to fill out for customs. "My cue to go," Sky admitted.

I shook my head. Neither of us had come up with a plan. "Nothing's gone wrong yet."

He brushed my hair with the backs of his fingers, even though it probably looked awful. "The prima donna should eat something. And if I don't get down there before breakfast starts for real, I'll never make it into the cargo hold before we start our descent. If there's trouble, it'll find me."

"Do you have to switch with him?"

He brought his seat back to its upright position before eyeing me. "You'd choose my safety over his?"

In a heartbeat. Except . . . "It's not my choice to make."

"Exactly. It's mine." Damn heroes anyway.

He did his best to straighten himself up, but his already-stressed clothes stayed wrinkled and running a hand through his hair could only do so much. He still looked gorgeous. My blond-haired, blue-eyed rogue—and he was about to vanish into thin air.

"Meet me at the pub," I said suddenly. "The one by the Thames. What's its name?"

"The Lucky Albatross."

"Be there tomorrow night at sunset." Reading the conflict in his eyes, I added, "If you can."

"If I can," he agreed. Eye contact held his promise. If he *was* real . . .

I said, "It was hard enough being alone before this happened. Before . . ."

Before either a miracle or my nervous breakdown.

He nodded, put a hand on my shoulder. "I know. The thing is . . ."

I waited.

"*Were* we alone?" Huh. Maybe we weren't, not in our hearts. At least, I hadn't been. It was just a, shall we say, long-distance relationship.

Still, given my druthers . . .

This time, I kissed him. *"Go,"* I said. "Get to the lav, and I'll create a diversion."

He looked at me one long, last time—a serious, almost unfocused look that, were this the movies, would preface the words *I love you.*

Then he winked, saluted, and headed up the aisle. Cute butt. Good reason to keep all those videotapes. As soon as he'd vanished into the bathroom, I let out a shriek. "Oh, no—my *contact*! I cannot believe . . ."

Kim came to help. The male flight attendant came to help. Another first-class passenger joined in; what nice people there were in the world! We searched over the blanket that Sky and I had shared, the pillows, the seats. Only when I saw Damien Ryder stagger out of the galley, complete with stained T-shirt, did I end the game with the words, "Found it!" Then I took my imaginary eyewear to the lav, and spent a few minutes standing there in that roaring, stainless-steel closet of a bathroom, staring at myself in the mirror. My hair *was* frizzy, my first-class dress rumpled, my makeup just about gone.

And I looked damn good, too. If I crossed my fingers and made believe just a little, I could even look like a heroine. Even without him. Not that I was without him, exactly.

I crossed my fingers and touched them to my lips.

If it hurt to see Damien Ryder sprawled in his original seat when I came back out, I refused to think about it. Unless I'd fantasized the last eight hours, Sky and I had stretched the limits of reality together. Not many couch potatoes can say *that.*

He wasn't there to hold my hand during the landing, not even to make jokes in my mind. I even tested it. *Sky?*

With a bump, landing gear met solid ground. The entire plane rumbled as it reaccustomed itself to its role as ground transportation. No Sky.

But I wasn't scared any more.

I got my own carry-on bag from the overhead compartment. And when I found myself behind Damien Ryder in the line to go through Immigration and Naturalization, I stepped forward and touched his arm.

His arms were nowhere near as sexy as Sky's.

"What, already?" he demanded, rolling his eyes as if I'd pestered him every mile of the way. If he remembered anything about his incarceration, he wasn't talking. But he sure had looked confused at how friendly everyone seemed.

Yesterday I would have backed off, swallowed my own concerns. This was today, and either I'd had a true fantasy date, or he was one *hell* of an actor.

"Why did the writers kill off Sky Marshal?"

He looked away in disgust, like an aside to a nonexistent audience, but I waited long enough that he looked back. "I asked them to, okay? I've got a future in films to think about, and that stupid character was just a weight around my neck."

"In one season, that stupid character made you famous."

"So?"

"Don't you think you owe *anything* to him?"

"Geez, Lady, it's *just a character.*"

"No, he *isn't* just a character. Maybe some shows work so well because they plug into something real. Maybe another plane of existence . . . or maybe just something we all share in our hearts. But thousands, millions of people *cared* about that man. We cared enough to tune in every week, and that upped the ratings, and that brought in the commercials, and that paid your salary. You can't have it both ways. Either we care, and you're employed, or else he's just a character and not worth wasting our time—and you starve."

"My heart bleeds." He turned away, unrepentant.

But what mattered was that I'd said it. Whether Sky had been real—and I *had* to believe he'd been, was still—the result of my brief time with him was.

And that was a reality, too, of sorts.

"Sir," said the INS agent ahead of us, "I'd like to take a look in your bag, please."

Ryder said, "What?"

Someone touched my arm—Sky? No, a female agent, guiding me away from possible trouble. "Your passport and disembarkation card, please?" she asked calmly, but I recognized in her the same kind of alert competence I'd seen in Sky. Maybe there were some heroes on my plane, too.

Behind me, the agent with Ryder was saying something about "anonymous phone tip about drugs."

Had there been a bad guy to catch on this flight after all? Heroines try not to take joy in other people's misfortunes, so I didn't say it—not out loud. *My heart bleeds.*

An anonymous tip, huh? Breathe in through the nose. I still didn't *know* anything.

I had to do this without knowing.

My affirmation the next afternoon was short and sweet: Be there.

"Be there, be there, be there," I whispered to myself as I checked my outfit one last time in the hotel mirror, then headed out.

"Be there, Sky, be there," I continued to murmur, navigating the London streets to my subway stop. I didn't even say, "Be real." I didn't want to question that possibility, even once. "Be there."

When an old lady on the tube looked at me strangely, I smiled an apology, and she smiled pleasantly back. I said it in my mind after that. *Be there. Be there. Be there.*

Even the well-balanced people who lead perfectly healthy fantasy lives probably practice discretion.

I kept it up all the way to the pub. Only once I'd reached the Lucky Albatross—a narrow, Tudor-style building—and scanned its occupants twice, did my litany falter.

What if he'd gotten caught trying to get off the plane, or out of the airport?

Worse, what if he'd vanished, back to whatever realm he'd come from?

Worst, what if I'd made him up, after all?

Despite careful breathing, my shoulders began to sink. Then:

"Come here often?"

I spun. He looked even more like Sky, even less like Damien Ryder than yesterday, and not just because he'd cut his hair really short. Someone looking for Damien might not recognize this man—but I did.

"What gave me away?" After all, what's a roguish hero without banter?

"That sexy hyperventilating," he purred—then grinned.

And then we were in each other's arms, kissing as if we'd had years of practice, then just holding each other tight, marveling in the reality of our existence. Together. Only when people began to whistle did we sit. This was, after all, England; it took a while for them to whistle.

Sky ordered us wine. "My credit cards are good here; I'm not questioning it." We held hands across the table.

"Someone reported Damien for carrying drugs," I announced, memorizing him with my eyes.

"You, uh, don't say?" He ducked his head in feigned repentance, but his blue eyes sparkled. "I know—questionable jurisdiction. I didn't have a warrant, and he wasn't in plain view. But since I'm unexpectedly retired . . ." He shrugged. "Feels like a loophole to me. If you pretend hard enough."

I laughed. He had the right woman for that. "So you *were* there because something was wrong?"

"No. I think I was there because something was right." And he wove his fingers together with mine and held my gaze. And what I felt between us was most definitely real.

"More than right," I agreed, breathless.

And he grinned his charming, roguish grin. "Right doesn't even *begin* to cover it."

SLOW DANCE FOR A DEAD PRINCESS

by John DeChancie

*John DeChancie has written more than nineteen novels
in the science fiction, fantasy and horror fields, including
the acclaimed Castle series, the most recent of which,
Bride of the Castle, was published in 1994. He has also
written dozens of short stories and nonfiction articles,
appearing in such magazines as The Magazine of Fantasy and Science Fiction, Penthouse, and many anthologies, including First Contact, and Wizard
Fantastic. In addition to his writing, John enjoys traveling and composing and playing classical music.*

THE dream comes every night, the same dream as always;
the identical dark drear dream, the dream of flight and fear
through the million points of light bright as the sun, like a
thousand stars—and I run, I flee, daring no look over my
shoulder, and then to a coach, a strange coach that flies as
fast as the wind; I can hear wind whistling through the
mullions in the peculiar crystal windows, and the horses
whinny and snort and roar, and I have never heard horses
like these, more like dragons, these horses, monsters in the
night, and the wind shrieks through the mullions of the
crystalline windows and I feel the breath of the chill night
air, the lights outside fly by like stars as viewed from a
comet; and there is a city of lights out in the night, an
entire city built of light, and of course I think this is a fairy
city; fairies built it, towers of luminescence, towers so tall
they take your breath away, towers like willows that must

68

sway in the wind, they are so high, and the wind howls
through the crystal making a sound that hurts my ears, so
I shut the window and pull down the blind—is there a
blind?—I cannot remember—this dream plays tricks on my
memory—and the coach races ever faster and the lights are
streaks now, and ahead . . . and the dream always ends at
this point, and I wake up with a start and Griselda is there
with a cool cloth to my forehead and she says my lady, my
lady, wake up, you dream again, and then she and the room
resolve and I am back where I belong, in the Prince's castle
with its high parapets swept by winds from the sea and its
busy courtyards and warrens and its bustling life, but I have
had no life in this castle since the Prince betrayed me with
the Horse Mistress, this be my name for her, and though
it is not my nature to be uncharitable I will not call her by
anything proper and befitting, and I shut myself up in this
high room with my children—my children, I scream, my
sons, where are they? I shout to Griselda, and she laughs
and says, they are well, my lady, they are at the tanner's
watching him cure hides, and I take her by her collar and
say, are you sure? are you very sure, Griselda, for I had a
dream that I lost them forever, Griselda, lost them for all
time, and she takes great pains to reassure me that they
live and that I live, for I think I had a dream that I had
died, and Griselda says, that's nonsense, she says, for I let
her take liberties with me and answer impertinently and
though my peers say I should not indulge her in this wise,
I say the gulf that separates her class from ours is a an
artifice and should be treated as artifice; there are times
when we pretend and there are times when we are just
people to one another and no one has a right to impose
fabrication on what is real, but I rarely argue the point,
there is so much to separate me from my peers, from my
husband's family now, the royal family, huge barriers of
understanding such that I fear I shall never breach them,
nor do I think they are inclined to break through from the
other side; no, they subvert in other ways, they dig at the
very foundations . . . but I am not one to argue, I hate
discord, I fear strife, I don't want harsh words spoken in
the house as I hear in the hovels and hamlets outside the
castle, the raised voices and the shouts and imprecations,
the ugly words, for they hurt me so; I remember when as

a child I first heard such domestic discord my mother gathered me to her bosom and dried my tears with the hem of her shawl as we rode in the carriage through the streets of the rude hamlet, horses clopping through the muck and filth; but my mother is not nearby now to comfort me over the disharmony that sweeps through my own house, my castle, for it is mine, given me by the Prince, and I remember what he said, this castle which is mine I give to you, dear lady, dear wife, but it is not mine, for his minions have the run of it, his peer friends and their servants and pages and falconers and huntsmen and horsemen and ever so many more, they are the true masters of this castle, not I, for I hear their loud voices raised in drunken song even up in this high room, the refrains of those endless drinking songs and hunting songs and wenching songs that go on and on into the night, so late into the night, even unto wee hours that I sometimes fall asleep to their strains and then have the terrible dream, that dream again that comes and goes and brings terror in the night, the running, the desperate flight, and different parts of the dream are limned unto me on different nights, and one evening I will see those who pursue and they are swarthy and dark of complexion but brandish brilliant torches that flash in the darkness; torches that flame and pop like damp logs in the fire; and they chase us . . . who is us?—I know not, but I am not alone, for someone is with me, someone of whom I am fond but it is not the Prince, it is someone else that I . . . that I love?—saying it to myself somehow I am not convinced but does it matter, I don't think so, whether I love this person or not, for I am sure that I am inordinately fond of him . . . yes, a him . . . for the Prince's infidelity has driven me to the arms of another . . . a stranger, a strange man, a foreign merchant man, a wonderful man who shelters me and assuages the hurt, the betrayal, yet I do not think that I betray my husband, for I have had the lord solicitor draw up the papers of estrangement, and though the matter is not settled I shall not seek my husband's bed again, nor his company, nor his board, if I can manage it, so in my mind I am quite shut of him, though it be not as neatly legal as one would like with primly drawn up documents and seals and signs and signatures; he and I are as dead to each other, and though we still occupy

the same house we are as ghost and haunted, and I do not
know who the ghost or who the haunted; perhaps we are
both to each other; and in the same wise I know not what
the dream and who the dreamer, for the dream comes each
night and each night with increasing ferocity, like a great
black beast, like a demented giant, to romp and stamp
through the corridors of my soul, and sometimes I feel that
I am that beast and am in a rage, for though they say I am
gentle and mild of heart, there is anger in me as well, for
am I not only human? and have I not been wronged? and
should I not feel embittered? but I do not answer myself
and I remain in this high room in my bed as if in a fever,
thrashing and convolving in the sweaty sheets and it is if a
pox is on me and I hear the rats scurry with tiny pinprick
feet scratching scratching scratching across the stone in the
night; and I hear other things, I hear wailing, a strange
wailing like the behemoth come out of the deep at the end
of the world, a wailing like no other in the night, through
the mist and fog, as the sea sounds and crashes, or is it the
sea? or something else, perhaps the blood rushing in my
head, the humors sloshing inside me, disrupted and discom-
moded, and again the physician may have to come and
apply poultices and mayhap even bleed me again, for they
have done everything, all the physicians in the realm have
come every other day for a fortnight, each with their nos-
trums and specifics, their Greek potions and their Saracen
philters, but they do me no good, they do me no earthly
good, for my trouble is not on earth, not on this earth, but
in that dark dream world, the city of lights and the racing
carriage and the dark hordes that pursue me with lit torches
and slavering lips, the burning pitch smelling in the night,
and what it is that happens . . . something fearful happens
then but I do not remember it . . . and then I wake yet
again and it is daylight once more and Griselda my woman
is there and urges me to get out of bed, but I cannot,
though I try, and she tugs at me and pulls me up to sitting
and my head hangs low and I can only say, where are my
children, I want my children, my two sons, my beautiful
sons, and Griselda says, fear not, Princess, your sons are
with their father hunting, they fare well and you should not
fear for them, but I do, I fear I shall lose them for all time
if the dream overtakes me and I tell the woman this and

she says pshaw, what stuff and nonsense, phantasms cannot harm you and I say, this one can, this one threatens to become the waking and this, we here and now, will be the dreaming, and Griselda says, that is sheerest fancy, no such thing can occur, and I retort, no, the dream is that powerful, no dream was ever like this, and she says tell me about it and I say, it is the same every night and I tell her the dream and she sits on the bed and listens and grows frightened though she tries to conceal her fear, and I go on and tell her about the carriage that flies like the wind, at a speed that is almost unimaginable, and she interjects, you see, my lady, this is naught but musing, the stuff of daydreams, and I say, not daydreams, but dreams of the somberest sort of night, a nightmare from which there is no waking, and she pales and turns down her head and says in a low voice, perhaps, lady, there is a remedy, and I say, what could it be, no more physicians, I beg of you, and she says no physician of the body but one of the soul, she says, I know a woman, a woman of the fairy folk, it is rumored, and I say, a witch, she is a witch? and she says, no, a fairy folk, a fairy woman with the sight, the far sight, and I say nothing but Griselda takes my silence for assent and when the moon rises that night there is a stranger in the room, and Griselda is behind her at first, but then scurries round and bows to me properly as she almost never does for I do not insist on such amenities, and this other woman is there, tall and beautiful with eyes the color of amethyst and hair the color of lemons, but there is white in the hair and there are lines in the face and it comes to me that this woman is very old but it is so strange that she is yet beautiful, and it occurs to me that there is a spell on this witching woman herself that makes her something she is not, and I fear for what she is in truth, but she smiles and asks me to tell her of my dream and I do and she asks who is pursuing you, my lady, and I tell her that I think they have some Latin name and they are swarthy; ah, Italians, says the woman; Italians, I say questioningly, and what would Italians be wanting of me, and she says that she knows not the answer yet but she does know that these dark Southern people are lechers and worse and that I am fair and it is no wonder that they would pursue a fair woman, and it is true that my hair is golden though much darker than the woman's,

and I say what about the carriage, and she says, this is a
magic coach that rides on the wind, and I say, no it rides
faster than the wind, and she says it matters little the exact
velocity of the unearthly thing, the task is to winnow the
meaning of the dream, that is her chore, this strange fairy
woman says, and I tell her that I fear the meaning of this
eidolon, for that must be its nature, it being far too monstrous for a mere dream, and she says fear not, fair lady of
the high room, for though the appearance may be horrific,
the purport may be mild, for this is the way of dreams and
visions and the far sight, which you, lady, must have as well
as me, for the phantasms you see are the equal in wonder-
ment to those I see myself, and I am of fairy blood—and
I laugh, possibly for the first time in months and say, me
of fairy stock, what a silly notion, and the woman nods
solemnly like a priest and says it is not so foolish a notion
as you think, lady, for there is something fay in you, if only
for the immensity of the love shown by the realm for you
and the sympathy for your plight as regards your husband's
waywardness, and I say with another bitter laugh ah this is
my magic, is it, this is my fairy circle, that I am not disliked
and that my husband's dalliances are not well thought of,
and the drear fairy woman says, yes, remarkable this
shower of affection for one not born to royal station, for
one born to the lowest rank of nobility, because the subjects of this realm hold most of the nobles in contempt,
and I say after such magic what forgiveness, and the woman
lowers her head in silence and at length says, my lady, I
must study on this dream of yours, on this city of light and
the carriage that moves like a shooting star and the dark
hordes which pursue you, and I say forget not their popping
torches and their leering faces, though what they leer at I
have not the foggiest notion, and she says they leer at you
and at your beauty and I retort my beauty is much exagger-
ated though I grant I am no toad, my nose is overlarge and
I am horse faced a mite, and she insists that despite such
defects and blemishes—of which I am possessed—never-
theless the populace holds me the fairest in the realm which
speaks again only of the magic that holds sway over them,
the magic of the fay, and I say enough, fatigue overcomes
me and then the woman is not there any more and I realize
that I have fallen into a swoon and have waked yet again

and the memory of the dream lingers, though this time
there is more than usual, more of the dream, embellish-
ments that heretofore have not vouchsafed themselves, and
it is of a blood-red eye that convolves inside a crystal, a
brilliant eye of light as though from the fabled lighthouse
on the sea of the ancient city of Miletus that I have read
of in books, yet this lighthouse casts not a warm light out
to sea; it casts round and round an evil light, a dull red
light that turns and turns, and though I do not see the eye
directly its fiery light flashes in my eyes and sears them and
the fright of it is that it never stops, its turning and turning
goes on and on until I shriek or try to shriek in pain but I
can only groan, and I find that I cannot move, for unseen
chains bind me, and then voices—voices . . . the Italians
are here and there is the flash of their torches in this place,
which I think is a cavern . . . yes, a huge cavern of light,
for there is light everywhere in this city, the biggest city I
have ever seen, bigger than even the royal city of my husband's family, but now the dream is only a memory and I
cry out for Griselda, and she comes soon enough and answers my plea about my children, my two boys, and she
tells me they are still with their father hawking, she says,
and fare as well as ever, and I miss them dreadfully, for it
has been more than a fortnight since they have come to
visit me; and the dream comes yet again that night, and
more is revealed; the horses shriek as we enter a vast
lighted cavern with the Italians in hot pursuit and suddenly
there is a bump and a shifting of things and the world
careens around us and the horses rear and the carriage is
upset and all is still in the cavern and I am alone and a
prisoner, for I cannot move and my limbs are numb and
excruciating pain lies across my brow, and around me the
carriage is in ruins, crushed like an eggshell, its faceted
windows now crushed ice that lies everywhere, in my hair,
in my face, in my mouth; I spit blood and my chest is
wracked with coughing, and here the dream dissolves and
faces hover above me and there is a bright light that gives
pain to my eyes, and voices always voices in the bright
rooms, room after room they take me through borne on a
moving table and then eyes peer at me and there comes
the click of metal against metal and the prick of needles in
my skin and again the sound of voices conversing talking

about me as if I were dead, and a great lifting overtakes me and I am borne aloft into the clouds and I see greater lights and the city is below me and I float as a cloud above the moving white ways and the lights sparkling on the great river that runs through the city of light, and I wake again in a sweat with Griselda nursing me bringing me back to the land of the living and I say to her one more repetition of the vision and I shall be a part of it, I shall be dead for this dream is not a dream but a vision of the way I will die and Griselda says that is impossible for carriages do not fly and there are no great cities such as the one in the dream but I say this is a dream not of what is but of what will be after many years have passed and she says then how can you be in the dream of many years from now for it must be hundreds or even thousands of years for those miracles to come to pass and I say that is true but in another sense they are of the present but I do not know what sense that is exactly and Griselda says stuff and nonsense again and I cannot answer her; and this day is different for my husband comes to visit me, but he does not bring our sons the two princelings with him for he says that they are off to be tutored and they are hard at their studies and cannot be distracted and I tell him that they should come to their sick mother for I have not long to live and he says do not be foolish, your illness is but a woman's foolishness and it is only jealousy that eats at your vitals, and I tell him that it is not so much jealousy as the hurt that the betrayed feel, and he says how have I betrayed you, my Princess, for it is generations of my forebears that have sought solace from the monkish constraints of marriage in the arms of a mistress, and I say mayhap it be so, my Prince, but a life that is a lie is not a life to me but a living death, and he answers that he has given me the life of a princess of the realm, and is this death, he asks, and I say it is a fairy tale that is true but it is one that ends in death and he says how so, and I reply by telling him of the dream of my death and he says this is a strange dream you have been having, this dream of another life, another world, and I say yes that is exactly what it is, it is another life, and he asks what I am in this other life and I say I am a princess like in this one but the world is utterly strange and new and wonderful and terrible all at the same time, containing wonders that we

could not in this mundane world even dream about, and
he says tell me of your life as a princess and I answer that
it is as if viewed through a dark glass; it is a life of pain
and sorrow and hurting and it ends in death at a young
age in this strange manner of the coach that flies and upsets
in the cavern . . . no, for at that moment I see that it is a
great underground passageway for the conveyance of
horses and carriages, and this sets my Prince to marvel and
to wonder and such a thing, and he marvels over every
aspect of my dream that I tell him, and allows that my
vision fills him with awe, and I tell him that I love him,
and this he marvels at, for our marriage was set before we
even met, and I know that he does not love me, but my
telling him causes him to cast his eyes down and I thought
that there was shame in that casting down, and he turned
and went from my high chamber in the castle and visited
me no more there, and I felt for him, for he does truly love
the Horse Mistress, or so I think, God knoweth why he
does, but he does, and then it was evening and Griselda
brings the fairy woman in again and the fairy woman says
to me, my lady, I have divined the purport of your dream,
and I say tell me, and she says you have the sight and what
you see is the world as it is, for it is not one thing, the
world, though we think it so, it is many things, and I say
tell me what mean you by that, and she says there is not
merely one world but many and we lead many lives in all
these worlds and we live them at the same time, and all
the twists and turns of one life are not necessarily reflected
in another, for they are all like dark mirrors in a great hall,
and I say I still do not understand, and she says it is difficult
to understand, but that these many worlds are separated
by the thinnest of veils and sometimes they disturb one
another when a great mishap occurs in a single one, and
your dream is that one of your eidolons has met her end
in this nether world, in this dark mirror world, and I ask
do these mirror places really exist, and she says only in
possibility, the merest vapor of a possibility, and I say does
this other princess really exist, and she answers that this
other princess in the dark mirror world is but a reflection
of the eternal soul of only one princess, and that I am but
a reflection as well of this archetype or progenitor who
exists in eternity, for there is only one of me in the greater

universe which God did create but there are endless reflections of this progenitor, and what should I do about the dream I ask, and she says you must accept what happens in the dream, the life of that reflection ended and that reflection will now have no mirror in which to reside, and that I could guide her to reside in this world, for a reflection imposed upon a reflection is no contradiction, for the two only reinforce the other; and she says the next time you dream accept what happens and do not try to fight it for it is as real as what happens here in your world and you cannot change it, but you can guide your other self to rest and reside in a better world, and I said I will try, and I asked how she came by this strange cosmology and she said the fairy folk have known of this for aeons and that it is the basis of magic, and I say well I cannot do magic and the fairy woman says yes you can do magic if you wish, for this kind of magic is merely a reaching out to one's own soul, and the fairy woman was right, for night fell and with it comes the dream again, and the bloodshot eye turns round and round in its glass vessel and the Italian hordes flash their torches and the carriage races and the city of lights sparkle in the crisp summer night and the horses make a sound like thunder and we speed I and my paramour through the night and enter the vast carriageway underground, and suddenly the night is rent asunder and the carriage crashes against the pillars holding up the vault and the carriage flies to a million pieces around me and I know that my paramour does not survive nor does the coachman but the castle guardsman who was in the carriage will not die and how I know this I cannot not fathom, but it was true, yet I am dying as I lie in the crushed carriage, and the sea of voices inundates me and I cannot see anyone speaking, for the bruising pain is on me as if I am put to the rack and the boot and the screws all at once, as if a hundred torturers were on me at once and I try to scream but my voice gurgles with blood and my tongue lies thick and motionless in my mouth and I cannot breathe as if a thousand bricks lie on my chest and when they bear me away on a pallet I am in a swoon and I know nothing until I was wheeled through endless corridors with lights in the ceiling until I reached a great lighted chamber that was cold with shining steel and many strange things in it that I

could not comprehend and then I was in a great fright for
looking down then at me were many men in masks and I
thought the torturers are having at me again and in truth
they proceeded to prick me with their needles but in time
and in some way I came to understand that these men and
women in the great shining steel room with the hundred
lights did not mean to cause me hurt but to help me and
I smiled at them and fell again into a swoon for now I
understood this dream for in a moment I was not the princess I am in this world but the princess I was in that strange
world of the city of light and again there came upon me a
great updraft like a wind lifting me up and I floated to the
rafters of that great room and below I could see myself on
that pallet swathed in strange green cloth and all the people
were wearing either green or white and I thought myself
this mayhap is in Ireland or some such far land but then I
thought no not Ireland but France though I know not why
I guess that and these are French physicians who seek to
aid me and I love them for their kindness and compassion
but I can see that their battle is already lost and I am borne
ever upward and leave that great room until I soar over
the city of a million lights the tops of even its great towers
now below me and I fly ever higher and begin to attain a
great speed an even greater speed than that magic chariot
that crashed and the stars come within my reach and I
reach out but cannot touch them and below me the world
spins like a child's top and here the height is so dizzying
and the speed so much that I think that I am become the
wind itself for I am insubstantial I am a soul without a
body now and speed between the veils of all the worlds
racing across the vast reaches of space that is more than
space and time that is more than time and the universe
begins itself to dissolve into flakes of starstuff and glittering
dust and swirling whirlwinds of cold flame and ethereal air,
and I think I am lost but something guides me, and I know
it is love of home my real home not the one I left but the
one I know in this life for that is where my heart is and I
began a gentle descent down through pillars of smoke and
blankets of mists and fogs and then puffs of clouds and
then the sun comes into view and the castle heaves beneath
me and I settle settle gently gently downward until I come
to rest not surprisingly in my own bed, my very own bed

in the high room in the highest turret above the parapets and I awake and come back to life and throw back the covers and call for my chambermaid and Griselda comes and says my lady you are better and I say yes and get up from my bed and allow as after breakfast I would go out again from the castle for a walk in the meadows for it is spring and the grass is greening and the wildflowers spring to bloom in the wood and after I take some food I walk in the meadow with no guardsman to look after us for I send them away telling them that I now fear nothing and I do not tremble when men on horseback appear on the ridge but I do not even look at them for I am renewing my acquaintance with this world, this world of greenswards and woods and soft green hills and high tors and wooded dales and dappled glades and bowers a world so beautiful that it takes my breath away and I look up at the sky at clouds like dollops of whey and I know that this life is good and that dreams cannot assail it as long as I know what is real and what is not, and I hear a voice calling me Mother and I turn and it is my younger son off his horse and running to me and I take him in my arms and nearly crush the life out of him and he hugs me as if he has been away for years instead of months and he says that he will never leave me again and that he will come to live with me and my older child comes to me and I can see that he is a strong young man already and that he will be king one day they both shall be kings here in this land that has not turned away from kings and the tears pour out of my eyes and I give thanks that I am alive again for I did die but now am living again and I look up the hill and see the Prince smiling and I know that he has forsworn the Horse Mistress for all time and that is the way it should be and this is the life that could have been and should be for all time and all space and all the dreams of all the fairy mirrors forever and forever.

NINE-TENTHS

by Laura Hayden

*Laura Hayden hasn't found a medium she didn't like—
books, television, movies. This short story joins her list of
writing achievements—which include novel-length time
travel and paranormal fiction under her own name and
romantic suspense written under the name "Laura Ken-
ner." In addition, she has written for an Emmy-award-
winning television series and has completed her first
screenplay adaptation for an independent production
company in Florida. A winner of the coveted Golden
Heart award, she can be reached at suspense@suspense.net
or visit her website at http://www.suspense.net.*

THIS time, it started in the produce aisle. A blonde in a
leather miniskirt and clinging turtleneck held up two mel-
ons at chest level. "Do you think they're ripe?" she purred.

Greg Watson drew in a sharp breath, pointed the grocery
cart in the opposite direction and took off. Taking refuge
in the bakery, he tried to rivet his attention on a loaf of
pumpernickel, but someone approached. Fearing another
encounter, he pivoted, feigning interest in the baked goods
in the glass case next to him. Big mistake.

Focusing past the crullers and eclairs, he spotted a
woman arranging cookies on a tray. She stopped, caught
his eye, then rose slowly into view. Her smile deepened
from friendly to damned near lascivious. After licking her
lips, she spoke, managing to infuse a single, innocent word
with enough overt sensuality to make a sailor blush.

"Cupcake?" she asked breathlessly.

"N-no, thanks," he stuttered.

Enough was enough. He abandoned the cart in the middle of the aisle and battled his way out of the store, muttering a terse, but polite, "No," to each woman who tried to stop him. Once he reached the safety of his car, he shouted, "Angel!"

A feminine figure draped in diaphanous white and gold wavered into existence in his back seat. "Now before you start complain—"

He cut her off. "I can't take any more of this, Angel. I can't even go shopping these days without getting propositioned by every single woman in the place. You've got to stop it. Now!"

Angel crossed her delicate arms. "But you need a woman, Gregikins. Someone to love you and take care of you and—"

"Not like this, Angel." He pointed to the grocery store. "Not with strangers at a grocery store. And especially not with the strangers you keep bringing to the house."

Delicate wrinkles formed across her brow. "Why? Aren't they pretty enough?"

He sighed. "We've talked about this before, Angel. Remember? The 'looks aren't important' speech?" He decided to try a different approach. "Listen . . . I realize you think this so-called mission of yours is the way you'll win your wings, but you can't do it like this. If I'm going to fall for somebody, I want it to happen naturally. Okay?"

She faded a bit from sight, a sure sign she was unhappy. "Are you sure? All I want to do is make you hap—"

"Promise," he prompted. "Promise me you'll stop."

"I promise, Gregikins. . . ." Her whispered words echoed through the car as she disappeared completely.

An hour later, Greg finished his shopping at another grocery store without incident. He raced storm clouds home, praying he might get the groceries stowed before the bottom fell out of the sky. He finished just as gale force winds hit, making raindrops sound like bullets as they slammed against the kitchen windows. He allowed himself a sigh of relief. Angel would probably stay out of his hair for a while. She didn't like thunderstorms, television, beer, or his taste in reading material. So a storm meant he'd get some peace and quiet.

He stretched out on the couch, balancing his beer in one hand and groping under the cushions for a magazine he'd hidden from her. Opening it, he sighed in pleasure at the centerfold, a 1955 Ford T-Bird in all its shining splendor. If Angel were only interested in finding him the perfect car instead of the perfect woman . . .

As he was reading about the car's restoration, he was interrupted by the sound of someone knocking on his front door. *Not one of Angel's minions . . . please,* he thought. Maybe if he simply didn't answer the—

The knocking grew more persistent. Whoever it was, she simply wasn't going away. Greg abandoned the couch and headed for the door, hoping, praying that this wasn't another of Angel's little . . . gifts—another beautiful woman, ready to throw herself at him.

He opened the door.

The woman who stood on the porch looked . . . terrible. Her rain-soaked dress hung at an awkward angle. The wind and rain had turned her hair into a mess that covered half her face. Mascara streaked down the part of her face he *could* see. She held a broken shoe in one hand and was clutching the porch column for dear life with her other.

In other words, she was a damsel in distress and he was the Designated Prince Charming.

He started into his "You don't really want me" spiel, but the woman cut him off.

"Jeez, it took you long enough. I almost busted a knuckle beating on your door. Don't you farm folk believe in doorbells?"

Greg's mouth fell open.

She continued. "Or paved streets? I almost killed myself out on your pitiful excuse of road." She glanced at her high heel. "I definitely killed these shoes." She turned her critical gaze from her shoe to his rustic cabin. "Please tell me you have a phone." At his blank look, she released a heavy sigh. "Please tell me you know what a phone *is.*"

Greg now knew why hurricanes had once had exclusively female names. "Uh . . . a phone."

She nodded. "You know . . . you pick it up and say 'hello?' It has numbers on it, like 9-1-1."

Greg noticed the blood trickling down her leg then, and his conscience kicked in. "My God, you're hurt." He reached for her, but she shied away. A roar of thunder made the windows rattle.

"Sorry, but I've been manhandled already tonight. I'll do this under my own power, if you don't mind."

Greg stepped back and let her hobble unescorted into his living room where she managed to keep a wary eye on both him and the phone. She picked up the receiver. As soon as she put it to her ear, her bravado crumbled. She sank to the couch, tears mixing with the rivulets of rainwater that dripped from her. Gingerly, he took the receiver from her hand and listened to the silence.

No dial tone. The phone was dead.

He sat down beside her on the couch and listened to her woeful story—Zara Ryan and the blind date that had gone terribly wrong. When she'd been faced with the choice to "put out" or "get out," she'd taken her chances on the sunny country lane. Who knew a storm would spring up so suddenly? Or that she'd get lost? Or that no one would be home at the other houses she'd tried?

She drew a long breath and made an attempt to repair the storm damage—to her clothes, her hair, and her sense of resolve. "I can't stay here," she said. "I have to get home."

Greg peered outside, unable to make out much. "I'd gladly take you back to town, but the dirt roads around here are usually impassable in weather like this."

Her gaze narrowed. "So . . . "

"I'm afraid you're stuck here for a whi—"

She jumped to her feet. "No way. I've just been through the world's worst blind date." She glared at him. "I'm not stupid. Or vulnerable, for that matter."

Greg scooted away from her. "I never said . . . or thought . . . you were. I'm sorry you've had a bad night. But I'm not some serial killer laying in wait for a hapless victim. Keep in mind, I didn't even want to let you in. You're safe here."

"Prove it," she said.

How? Lightning and inspiration struck simultaneously. "Just a minute . . ." He fished around in his coat closet. A moment later, he turned around with his favorite wooden baseball bat in his hand. "Here. Her name is Betsy. Consider her a loan for the night."

Zara's color returned slightly when he held the bat out, grip first.

"Thanks." She hefted the bat, admiring its lines. "I used to have one just like this." She tapped the bat against her shoe. Water squelched from it and soaked the rug. She glanced down and made a face. "I'm a mess. Sorry about the floor."

Greg grinned. He'd seen drowned rats that looked drier. "Would you like to clean up? You're welcome to use the bathroom. You and Betsy, that is."

She contemplated the door he indicated, then him, then the bat. A tentative smile replaced Zara's earlier look of doubt.

"Thanks."

A half hour later, she emerged from the bathroom dressed in borrowed sweats, socks and a robe. She joined Greg on the couch where they listened to the storm and told each other dating war stories. From there they moved to tales of college hijinks, to sports, philosophy, and a dozen other subjects.

Sharing hot chocolate and popcorn made in the fireplace, they talked for hours. Finally Zara asked a question that had clearly been bothering her. "You know, I'd have you figured for a city dweller—this bucolic life doesn't seem like your thing. Why do you live out here in the middle of nowhere?"

Greg knew the explanation was unbelievably simple . . . or was that simply unbelievable? Angel. But there was no way he could tell Zara that his self-imposed isolation was due to an overly enthusiastic guardian angel. He stumbled through a half-assed explanation about escaping the rat-race world and attempted to change the subject.

Zara didn't buy it. "You're hedging. You know it and so do I. But—" she raised her hand in a dismissive gesture "—that's okay. God knows there are things I don't like to talk about. . . ." She stifled a yawn.

"Like the fact that you're too sleepy to keep your eyes open?" he supplied.

She yawned again and nodded. "It's been a long day and an even longer night."

He glanced at his watch. It was almost three a.m. They'd been talking for hours. He grabbed their mugs and took them to the sink. By the time he'd washed them out and turned around, Zara had already curled up on the couch and gone to sleep. So much for offering her his bed while he took the couch. He covered her with his grandmother's quilt, banked the fireplace to a crackling glow, and retired to his bedroom. Before he knew it, it was morning.

He sat up, trying to sort out last night's realities from last night's dreams.

Zara . . .

Real or fantasy?

He thought for a moment. Zara appearing at his doorstep—that was reality, right? And their talk until the wee hours of the morning—that did happen, didn't it? But the bit about them skinny-dipping in a Hawaiian waterfall—that was fantasy. He was sure of that. Angel made sure he experienced that dream every night with some woman she'd thrust into his path during the day. But this time he'd enjoyed the dream. For once, he wished his dream *had* been reality.

Leaving behind bedroom fantasies, Greg shuffled into the living room and glanced at the couch. It showed no signs of ever hosting a guest. Especially a pretty guest wrapped up in *his* robe. He sighed. Great. Now Angel was planting fantasy women in his daydreams as well as his nighttime ones.

Then he noticed the delicious aromas drifting from the kitchen, along with the sounds of someone humming.

Zara?

Or Angel?

He stepped into the kitchen, and felt relief when he recognized his robe and the curly-haired woman wearing it.

Zara.

He spoke softly, not wanting to startle her. "Uh . . . good morning."

She gave him a beautiful smile. "Good morning!"

Encouraged by her evident sense of security, he joined her at the stove, amazed to see that she was preparing enough food to serve a platoon. "You must be hungry."

She nodded as she expertly flipped an egg. "I couldn't

decide what I wanted. So I cooked a little of everything. I hope you don't mind."

He tried to smile. Another expedition to the grocery store meant running Angel's gauntlet again. But somehow, he didn't mind the effort if it meant receiving another smile from Zara.

He cleared his throat. "No, that's fine. I'm . . . hungry, too." He glanced out the kitchen window. "Looks like it stopped raining for the moment."

"I'm glad," she said. "I hate thunderstorms." She slid the eggs onto a plate next to a pound of cooked bacon. "Time for breakfast."

What followed was an eerily domestic scene; Zara insisted on serving him as if he were her lord and master, ladling heaps of food on his plate and jumping up every few minutes to bring him condiments that he hadn't even realized he had. Finally, he persuaded Zara to sit and eat with him rather than play kitchen wench. Zara looked uncomfortable, but she reluctantly allowed him to play host. As she ate, he scanned the living room, noticing subtle changes she'd made to the room. Fresh wild flowers sat on the mantle. The rug in the middle of the room had been shifted and he had to admit it looked better in its new position. As he glanced around, he realized his bat was nowhere to be seen.

"So you decided you didn't need Betsy?"

She looked up from her plate. "Who?"

"Betsy. The bat. You know—your stalwart protector?"

Then Zara did something completely out of character. She giggled.

"You call your bat 'Betsy'? That's the silliest thing I've ever heard, Gregikins."

He froze. Gregikins? Only one person ever called him that. He swallowed the sudden bad taste in his mouth. "Angel?" he whispered.

Her grin broadened. "In the flesh, literally." She stood and held out her arms as if modeling the robe for his approval, rather than a purloined body. "I saw her sleeping on the couch and I just couldn't resist." She ran her hand through Zara's hair. "I like the curls, don't you?"

He stared at Zara . . . at Angel within Zara. This was

wrong. Terribly wrong. "Angel," he said, "get out of her. Now!"

She began to pout. "But why? Don't you find her attractive?"

"Sure, but that's not the point. That's her body, not yours."

"Why in heavens did you think I was trying to find some-one for you? So we could be together."

He sagged to a chair. "T-together?"

She dropped into his lap. "Don't you understand? I love you. I've loved you from the first time I saw you. I figured if I could find a woman you'd find attractive, I could take her over."

He stared at her, speechless.

She ran her forefinger around the ridge of his ear. "Funny thing is—this one is smart. She really is. I can feel the facts and figures rolling around her brain." Angel/Zara wrapped her arms around his neck. "Who would have thought it would be so easy? But now this is my body." She leaned forward, her hot breath scorching his ear. "Mine and now yours."

Greg stood up, and Angel/Zara slid to the floor. "This is wrong, Angel. Really, really, wrong. Get out of her. Now!"

Her lips began to tremble. "But, Gregikins . . ."

"And stop calling me 'Gregikins!' " he thundered. "I hate that."

Angel/Zara stared at him in shock. "You don't have to yell." She buried her face in her hands. "I was only . . ." The rest of her statement was lost to wracking sobs.

Greg felt lost. The circumstances here were weird enough without this. Emotional women tended to unsettle him. Crying women? They unnerved him. And hysterical women? Unhinged him completely. But he couldn't afford to let Angel's tears distract him. Zara's life might depend on what he did next.

He knelt beside her and patted her shoulder in the most platonic manner possible.

"Angel, it's not right to steal . . . er . . . take Zara's body. I'm sure she has plans for it."

Angel looked up through Zara's green eyes; the effect was disturbing.

She threw herself at his feet, practically knocking him

over. Her sobs increased in intensity as she practically clawed her way up his legs. "But . . . I . . . did . . . it . . . because . . . I . . . love . . . you . . ."

He froze. "Get out of her, Angel."

She dropped the ineffective crying routine and went straight to Seduction 101. "But don't you find her attractive? Sexy? Don't you want her?" Her smile would, under any other circumstances, have brought him to his knees. "I saw into your mind," she said. "I know you dreamed about her."

"But I always dream about them—all the women you throw at me. You make sure I have that same stupid dream about them all."

"But this time was different. This time . . . you responded to her—" she drew her fingers down his chest, "—like a man is supposed to respond to a beautiful woman."

Greg grabbed her hand before it moved below his waistband. "You can't shanghai Zara, Angel. I won't let you." He pushed her away. "Get out of her. Now!"

Facing unyielding opposition, Angel's alligator tears turned into real waterworks, but Greg stood firm, refusing to let her touch him. She begged, pleaded, offered herself, swore, cried, and begged some more, but Greg remained resolute.

She finally made her last offer. "One kiss," she said. "Just one kiss before I leave."

It sounded relatively harmless, a small price to pay for Zara's release. And in Greg's heart, he knew one kiss from Angel wouldn't sway him.

"All right. One kiss."

Angel forced him backward until he felt the chair behind his knees. Another push and she'd forced him to sit down.

Angel straddled his lap, shifting her weight so that the pressure of her against him created a warm invitation that no red-blooded American male could resist.

"Just one kiss," he managed to say.

"I remember," she whispered. She splayed her hands across his chest and he fought his instinct to return the gesture.

This isn't Zara. It's Angel.

"I can do ten times more with this body than she ever could."

This isn't Zara.

"You know you want me."

This isn't Zara. His mind knew the difference, but his body began to weaken.

"And I want you . . . so bad, Gregikins . . ."

That name! It acted like a bucket of ice-cold water.

He was able to face her most seductive kiss with no response. His heart didn't even betray him with an extra beat. Try as she could, Angel couldn't get a rise out of him.

She stumbled back, panting as if the kiss had drained everything out of her. "How?" she gasped. "How can you withstand me?"

Greg straightened his shoulders. "Because you aren't Zara."

Pain joined exhaustion in her eyes. Her lip trembled as she spoke. "Damn it."

Greg watched Angel disentangle herself from Zara's body. The moment the glowing apparition separated completely, Zara sagged to the ground. Although fascinated by the process, Greg managed to catch Zara before she hit the floor.

He called her name softly, hoping it would help her surface from whatever place she'd been relegated to during the unlawful possession and reclaim her body. A few seconds later, she opened her eyes.

She struggled out of his protective grip and pushed to her feet, using the chair rather than him as a support.

"What . . . *who* in the hell was that?" she demanded.

What could he say? "A thorn in my side. An unwelcome thorn named Angel."

"An angel?" she scoffed. "Not in any theology I've ever studied. She's no angel. Maybe a devil. Or maybe a ghost. Either way—" Zara rubbed a place on her hip that looked like it might bruise "—she's a real pain in the ass." She picked up the robe Angel had discarded during the kiss and tugged it on.

"I'm awfully sorry . . ." Greg stopped. What was the etiquette for apologizing for an unlawful bodily possession?

She shook her head. "No need to apologize. I could hear and see what she was doing, as well as your response. You had nothing to do with it." A blush covered her cheeks.

"In fact, you're the one who kept her from . . . taking me. Thanks." She stood on her tiptoes and kissed him.

The kiss was clearly only meant to be a small token of thanks, but it rocked him to his toes. Zara jerked back, too, as if she'd been electrocuted. They stared at each other for a moment, then could resist no longer.

The second kiss was complicated, powerful. They broke away, both gasping for breath.

"Did you feel . . . ?" Zara stopped, unable to finish her question.

He gulped, then nodded. "You?"

She nodded as well, braced herself against the chair. "I didn't expect this. Not now." She ran her hand through her curls. "Not here."

"And not us. We barely know each other."

She glanced around the room, peering into the corners. "Is she here? Is she doing this to us?"

"I don't think so." He followed her gaze, scanning the room for any signs of the intrusive Angel, but seeing . . . feeling nothing but an incredible sense of connection with Zara. "I think . . . it's us." He turned to Zara. "Just you and me."

She shivered, then a smile crept across her face. "Shall we test that theory?" She flung her arms around him.

Too passionate, he thought. *Too fiery.* And containing none of the electricity of the previous kiss.

"Angel!" He pushed her away, wiped his mouth with the back of his hand to remove the unpleasant sensation of possessed lips against his.

She threw herself at him. "But Gregi . . . er . . . Greg, I'm the perfect woman for you. The sooner you accept that, the sooner we can build a perfect life together."

He extricated himself from the embrace. "We can't have a life together, Angel." Her name left a bitter taste in his mouth. "Angel," he said. "Zara was right. You're no angel. What in the hell are you?"

"Don't you know?"

"What?" he asked. "A ghost? A lost soul? What?"

Thunder ricocheted through the air and a flash of light sliced the room. For a moment, Greg was afraid this was her answer. Then he realized the storm had returned with renewed fury.

Angel flinched. But rather than flee the building storm as usual, she stood her ground. "A lost soul? Hardly. I'm your soul mate. But she's in the way. This Zara." She spat the name like a curse. "It's all her fault, and she ought to pay for it."

A terrible thunderclap followed her proclamation, forcing Greg to cover his ears and shield his eyes. When he opened his eyes, Angel was gone. Zara, too.

Greg sprinted to the door, but by the time he got to the porch, Angel had reached the dirt road, running like an Olympic sprinter.

He called her name, both of her names, but she refused to stop. She didn't slow down until she reached the small bridge over a fast-moving stream that bisected his property and emptied into the nearby river.

"Angel, stop. We need to talk about this." To his relief, she whirled around to face him.

"Talk? Why? You made it perfectly clear. You don't love me. Not now, not then."

He held out both hands. "You're mixed up. I never met you when you were alive."

She lunged toward the path that led to the river bluff. "It doesn't matter now. Nothing matters. I know what I have to do."

Greg charged after her, fear gnawing at his stomach. What circumstances robbed Angel of her life and condemned her to a ghostly existence? Had she died by violence, by accident? Or—his throat closed—by her own hand?

He ran parallel to the river path where the trees weren't as thick. He was gaining on her. "Angel, I don't understand," he called out. "Explain it to me."

But she said nothing as she headed straight for the outcropping of rock on his property that overlooked the river. It was a great place for a picnic. Or a handy place to drown herself in the rain-swollen waters below.

Angel skidded to a stop on the flat rock and faced him. "Don't come any closer. I'll jump. I've done it before. It only hurts for a little."

"Don't jump," he pleaded. "Don't do this to yourself again. This is your chance to do what most people can't, to learn from your mistakes. Maybe even correct them."

"My mistakes?" Her brows knitted. Evidently, he'd brought up a point she'd never considered.

"Sure." His mind raced, trying to find a rational thread in this irrational moment. "When you took your life, you lost your future. But if you save your life—Zara's life, then maybe you'll get back that future."

"With you?" she asked, taking a tentative step toward him.

He swallowed. If he told her the truth, he risked triggering a lethal reaction. Wearing his best smile, he held out his arms. "C'mere . . ."

To his relief, she responded to the openness of his offer and accepted his hug. He fought the instinct to lock his arms around her. Instead, he softly stroked her hair, keeping his voice low and reassuring. "It's not easy to make the right decision," he said.

She stiffened in his arms. He'd chosen the wrong tactic. She began to struggle, and despite his strength, she broke loose, clipping him under the chin with her head as she escaped.

Then everything happened at once; stars exploded in his head, the world tilted to the left and Angel's shrill screams echoed in his ears. A moment later, he found himself clinging for his life to the exposed roots of a tree at the edge of the bluff.

He stayed calm, due mainly to the fact Angel was a basket case. When she threw herself down to the ground in an effort to reach him, she caused a shower of rocks and dirt that hit him in his face, nearly making him lose his grip.

"Oh, God . . . . don't let go," she pleaded.

"I don't intend to."

"What can I do? What can I do?" she pleaded. She stretched toward him, her hand just grazing his. Another spray of dirt peppered his face. "I can't reach you. What should I do?" She repeated the words until her voice escalated to a scream.

"Get a rope," he gritted between his teeth.

"Rope," she repeated. "A rope." She scanned the trees as if expecting a handy rope to appear by magic. When it didn't, she began to wail. "I don't have a rope."

"Then find a tree branch. A long one."

"Tree branch. Right." She sped away. This time he had

the presence of mind to turn his face to avoid being pelted with dirt. While she rooted through the trees looking for a suitable branch, he fought for better purchase against the cliff face. He discovered a small crack where he could wedge one foot. As he pushed himself up to safety, a small tree limb landed inches from his face, startling him.

"Here!" Angel said breathlessly.

"Too fragile," he croaked. "It'll break. Get a bigger one."

Tears made muddy tracks down her dirtied cheeks. "But I could barely lift that one. You're going to fall, and die, and it'll be all my fault." She dropped to her hands and knees. "I never meant for this to happen to you, Greg. You have to believe me."

Angel buried her face in hands and began to wail as if she were already mourning the dead. As his grip began to slip, Greg realized that she might very well be on the right track. He changed his grip and averted disaster.

Then she raised her head. Although tears still cascaded down her cheeks, she spoke in a calm voice.

"I can save him."

Greg recognized the timbre of this voice. "Zara?"

Angel . . . no . . . Zara nodded. "Angel, you've got two choices. If you keep my body, then Greg will die. Give me my body back and I'll save him."

Angel's panic flooded back into her eyes. "Give it back?" she repeated.

When the tree root began to loosen, Greg was forced to turn his attention away from the argument going on at the cliff's edge. He had his own survival to worry about. He slipped from his precarious perch, and for a moment, he thought things were over. But then a piece of fabric snaked its way down the rock face toward him—the rope belt of his robe.

"Grab it!"

Zara or Angel? At the moment, it didn't matter. He wound the fabric around his arm and inched his way up the cliff. He made it over the edge and sprawled into the woman who'd rescued him, gasping for breath.

"Thanks . . ." He stopped. *Thanks who?* There was only one way to be sure. Sure enough, when his lips met hers, an unmistakable tingle of electricity danced between them.

After they broke apart, she smiled at him. "You're very welcome."

Greg rolled over on his back and closed his eyes. "I'm so sorry you got dragged into this."

Zara stretched out beside him. "Whoever said possession is nine-tenths of the law was wrong."

He leaned up on one elbow. "How did you get her . . . out of there?"

Zara cocked her head. "That's the funny part. I didn't do it. She did. She left voluntarily once she realized that I was better able to handle the situation than she was."

"Then what's to keep her from . . . repossessing you again?"

A voice filtered down from the trees. "Me."

They both looked up, then scrambled to their feet when they saw who spoke. Greg stepped defensively in front of Zara. "Now, Angel—"

"Don't worry, Gregikins. I learned my lesson."

He stared at her. She'd changed. Something new filled her face. An air of . . . serenity?

"You were right about having a second chance. This was the second time I'd tried to jump from this rock. And both times, it was over a man who I thought I loved but discovered didn't love me."

Zara stepped around Greg, unwilling to hide behind him. "You mean you killed yourself here? In the past?"

Angel shrugged. "Not quite. Before I could jump, I fell and died. According to the Powers That Be, there was a good chance I'd've changed my mind and simply walked away, sadder but wiser. So they gave me a second chance to face the situation and make the right decision." Her face darkened. "But I almost made the same stupid mistake over again."

"But you didn't." Greg felt a burden lift from his shoulders. "You made the right choice."

Angel graced Zara with a tranquil smile. "It helps to listen to the little voice inside of you. Especially if that little voice is the rightful owner of the body you're possessing. I'm sorry, Zara. What I did was wrong. Thank you for helping me . . . see the light."

"No. I should be the one to thank you." Zara slipped her hand in Greg's.

Angel turned to Greg. "She's the one, you know."

He glanced at Zara and grinned. "I noticed."

"Then it's time to say good-bye, Gregikins." Angel began to glow, became almost painfully bright before their eyes. A split second before Greg was forced to shield his face from the unbearable glare, he thought he saw two white-and-gold wings unfurl behind her. Then, with a clap of thunder, she disappeared, leaving behind a fading shower of gold dust in the air where she'd hovered moments before.

Zara squeezed his hand. "Did you see . . ." Her voice trailed off.

He nodded. "I think so."

They started walking back to the house, still hand-in-hand. A few steps down the path, Zara stopped suddenly.

Conditioned for disaster, Greg's pulse quickened. "What? What's wrong?"

She grinned at him. "Are there any waterfalls around here? I have this sudden desire to go skinny-dipping."

THE MAN OF HER DREAMS

by Tim Waggoner

Tim Waggoner wrote his first story at the age of five when he drew a version of King Kong vs. Godzilla on a stenographer's pad. Since then he's published over forty stories of fantasy and horror. His most recent work appears in the anthologies Alien Pets, Twice Upon a Time, Prom Night, *and* Between the Darkness and the Fire. *He lives in Columbus, Ohio, where he teaches college writing classes.*

KRISTEN was sipping a Singapore sling and trying to come up with an excuse that would enable her to leave as gracefully as possible when Barry walked into the bar. Oddly, she wasn't surprised, though she supposed she should have been. After all, until that moment Barry had existed solely in her dreams. But it seemed the most natural thing in the world for him to be here, weaving through the crowd, pushing past the drunken revelers from her office who had turned out to celebrate Lauren Foresca's promotion to regional sales manager, his gaze trained unwaveringly on her the entire way.

He stopped when he reached her table, nodded to the empty seat next to her. "May I?" His voice was the same mellow tenor that had spoken countless devotions to her while she slept.

She knew there was no possible way this could be happening, that seven years as a sales rep for a textbook publishing company had finally taken their toll and her mind

96

had snapped. Still, she smiled, gestured with her drink toward the chair. "Please."

He sat, moving with the fluid grace of a jungle cat. His eyes were the same deep blue as those of the Barry who inhabited her dreams, his hair the same blond, so bright it nearly sparkled even in the bar's dim lighting. Mustache neatly trimmed, no sign of beard stubble even though it was 6:45. His facial features were at once both rugged and sensitive, so much so that he could have been a cover model for the romance novels Kristen devoured so eagerly. He wore a light gray shirt, dark gray khaki pants, and freshly shined shoes.

"I bet you didn't expect to see me tonight." He smiled, displaying straight, even teeth so white they nearly gleamed. "Before you went to sleep, that is."

Before Kristen could reply, Lauren came walking unsteadily toward them, rum and Coke sloshing over the side of her glass. "You've been awfully antisocial tonight, Kristen. One might get the impression that you aren't exactly thrilled by my promotion."

Kristen hated Lauren. Hated her grating, brittle personality, her love of office politics—the dirtier, the better—the way she looked like she was in her mid-twenties even though she was pushing forty, hated the low-cut mini-dresses she favored. Right then she especially hated the way Lauren didn't take her eyes off Barry as she spoke, the way she leaned forward to display her cleavage.

"Sorry," Kristen said, doing her best to keep the venom out of her voice. "I'm not much of a party person, I guess." *Especially when the party's for you,* she thought.

"That's all right. You can make up for it by introducing me to your handsome friend here." Lauren flashed Barry a smile which said *I'm extremely available.*

"I'm Barry." He reached across the table and enfolded Kristen's hand in a grip of velvet-wrapped steel. "Kristen's fiancé."

Lauren looked as if she had just swallowed a very large and juicy bug. "Really?" She turned to Kristen, her voice suddenly cooler by several degrees. "This is the first I've heard about it."

"I proposed to her last night," Barry said, smiling. "In bed."

Lauren looked as if she might bring the bug back up. "How very nice for you both." She gave Kristen an appraising look, and Kristen knew what she was thinking: *How did a loser like you end up with a hunk like him?* "I suppose congratulations are in order."

"Thank you," Barry said. "Now why don't you go away and leave us alone?"

Lauren gaped. She was not used to being spoken to like that, especially by men. They usually fell all over themselves trying to please her in hopes of getting a close-up view of that cleavage. Kristen bit her lip to suppress a giggle.

Lauren scowled. "Now, listen here, Mr. *Fiancé,* I don't care who you are or what sort of brain damage you've incurred that's so obviously impaired your romantic judgment. But if you think for one minute—"

Barry stood and grabbed Lauren by the shoulders. He squeezed and she grimaced. She dropped her drink. It fell to the floor and shattered in a shower of glass and caramel-colored liquid.

The bar grew quiet; everyone turned to watch.

"Perhaps you didn't understand. I asked you to leave us alone." Barry's voice rumbled with barely restrained anger. "And I don't appreciate anyone making disparaging comments about my Kristen. Especially not a syphilitic tramp like you." Barry released her, walked over to Kristen, and held out his hand. "Shall we?"

Kristen knew she would undoubtedly pay for this later at the office, but right now, she was delighted. Grinning, she took Barry's hand. "Let's."

He helped her up and together they left the bar, all eyes upon them, people whispering as they passed. It was an exit right out of a girl's dreams.

Kristen woke to yummy smells drifting in from the kitchen. She stretched and yawned, exhausted but contented. No, not merely contented—elated.

Last night had been beyond beyond. After escorting her from the bar, Barry led them to Kristen's car and, at his direction, she drove them all over town on a night of unequaled romantic perfection.

First, Barry had her drive downtown, where they waded

barefoot in a fountain. Kristen had always wanted to do that; it looked like so much fun when people did it on TV or in the movies. But she'd always been too afraid of being caught.

But not last night. Barry removed her shoes, set them neatly on the fountain's edge, lifted her as though she weighed little more than dandelion fluff (though her scale at home told a different story). He then lowered her into the water as gently as if he were placing a rose in a vase. She waded tentatively at first, then grew bolder. Finally, they were splashing and kicking water at each other like children. And just like in a movie, a police car came cruising by and they got out of the fountain quickly, laughing as they drove away in bare wet feet.

Barry then told her to drive to the small airfield on the outskirts of town. They parked where they could see the runway and watched planes taking off and landing, car windows rolled down so they could hear the throaty rumble of the engines. They wondered aloud at the identities of the pilots and passengers, who they were, where they were going or where they had been. Kristen was surprised at one point to look down and find herself holding Barry's hand. She didn't remember him taking it, but she didn't pull away.

After the airport, they drove to a park. The sun had set by then and the gate at the entrance was closed and locked. Barry was undeterred, though. He had Kristen pull over down the road a bit, and they climbed the fence and entered the park. Moonlight cast diamond-glitter on a small pond while bullfrogs and crickets called out to potential mates.

It was here, at the edge of the pond, water whispering encouragement, that Barry kissed her.

She knew all the clichés from her romance novels and from the movies every boyfriend she ever had referred to as "chick flicks." But the earth didn't move, her breath didn't catch in her throat, and he didn't touch the core of her womanhood in a way it had never been touched before. Barry's kiss did more than these things. It was as if the moment their lips touched, she was made complete, a partial soul finally reunited with its missing half.

She lost no time getting Barry back to her apartment

after that, and they made love. Barry had been considerate, thoughtful, attentive . . . so much so that he took care of her needs in lieu of his own. She lost track of how many orgasms she had. After the last time, he held her, stroked her gently, asked if she would stay awake with him and watch the sun rise. Unfortunately, that was the last thing Kristen remembered. She fell asleep.

But that was the only flaw in an otherwise absolutely perfect night, the best she had ever experienced in her life. And, unless her nose was wrong, it smelled like Barry was making breakfast. She wondered if he was as good at cooking as he was at everything else. Only one way to find out.

Even though Barry had explored every inch of her body quite thoroughly last night, she still put on her robe. Now that it was daylight, she was more than a little self-conscious about the extra weight she carried. She shuffled into the bathroom, peed, brushed her teeth, attempted to do something about her hair. Not that it helped; she still had a terrible case of bed head. Then she walked down the hall and into the kitchen.

Barry stood at the counter, dressed in the same outfit he wore last night. Kristen wondered if he even had any other clothes. His pants and shirt looked as if they had been freshly ironed, despite the fact that Kristen knew they had been tossed onto the bedroom floor last night. After all, she'd been the one doing the tossing.

Barry was busy chopping a green pepper with sure, deft motions. He'd already sliced an onion and a red pepper, their pieces collected neatly in separate wooden salad bowls. On the kitchen table, an omelet rested on a china plate, a sprig of parsley on the side. A cup of coffee and a glass of freshly squeezed orange juice completed the meal.

He looked up as she approached, smiled. "Good morning, love. There's a ham-and-cheese omelet on the table waiting for you, and there'll be a western omelet, too, as soon as I finish chopping this pepper."

"Those are my two favorite breakfast dishes," Kristen said. "I can never decide between them."

"I know. But today you don't have to decide. You can have both." Barry returned to slicing the pepper.

Kristen felt a sudden hollowness in the pit of her stomach. "You really are Barry, aren't you? *The* Barry, the one from my dreams. That's how you know about the omelets, and that's how you knew I'd love all those things we did last night."

"Yes." He finished with the pepper and reached for an egg. He cracked it on the counter's edge and emptied it into a mixing bowl. He discarded the shell in the sink, then added the onions and peppers to the egg, humming as he stirred. He poured the mixture into the pan, and the omelet-to-be hissed and popped as it began to cook.

Kristen reached for her coffee with trembling fingers, lifted the cup, held it in two hands to keep it steady. "I guess I knew it all along. I mean, I recognized you when you walked into the bar." She took a sip of coffee. It was perfect: not too strong, not too weak, not too hot, not too cold. "But I really didn't think about what it meant. Everything happened so fast . . . I was swept along and didn't question what was happening or why it was happening. It was like—"

"A dream?" finished Barry. He lifted the pan off the burner, tilted it over a plate, and the omelet rolled out easily. He set the pan back on the burner, turned it off, then placed the western omelet on the table next to the ham and cheese. Barry pulled the chair out for her, invited her to sit, and she did. He took the chair opposite her, and she noticed there was no plate for him, no coffee, no juice.

"Aren't you hungry?" she asked.

"I don't need to eat. You didn't dream me with an appetite." His smile held a hint of a leer. "Not for food, anyway."

She took another drink of coffee as she tried to gather her thoughts. "I've been dreaming about you ever since I was fourteen," she said finally.

"Thirteen," he corrected. "You were thirteen years, seven months and eight days old." She must have looked doubtful because he added, "A man doesn't forget his own birthday."

"I dream about you every night. Sometimes we ride horses in a meadow of flowing grass that ripples like the surface of a green ocean. Other times we go for long walks in an autumn wood, the leaves on the trees just beginning to turn colors. And as we stroll, we talk. No matter how trivial the topic I bring up, how silly I sound even to myself, you always listen, always make me feel like the most interesting person who ever lived."

"That's because to me, you are."

He had always been there for her, through a painful acne-scarred adolescence when boys wouldn't look at her, through college when the boys who asked her out did so only because they wanted to get into her pants, and on into an adulthood of diminished expectations—a boring job, disastrous dates, body beginning to sag, hair starting to gray. But none of that mattered when she went to sleep because Barry would be there waiting.

Except now he wasn't *there* anymore, was he? He was *here*.

"How is it possible? Dreams—literal dreams—don't just become real one day."

"They do if you need them to badly enough. You've dreamed about me every night for twenty-one years. Each night you invested a little more of your mental energy in me, until finally there was enough to allow me to cross over to your world."

Kristen frowned. "I just realized something. I didn't dream about you last night. Instead, I dreamed about . . ." She struggled to recall. "Trying to find a parking place at work. I drove for what seemed like hours, but all the spaces were filled, so all I could do was keep driving and looking." She grimaced. "It was so boring!"

"You didn't dream about me because I'm not in your head anymore." He spread his arms. "I'm here." He stood, came around the table, placed his hands on her shoulders, and began massaging. "And I'm going to take care of you from now on."

Kristen thought she might melt under the warm pressure of Barry's hands.

"Now eat your eggs; they're getting cold."

Kristen picked up her fork, took a bite of the ham-and-cheese omelet, chewed while Barry continued kneading her shoulder muscles. She smiled. Maybe this *was* a dream come true after all.

"Aren't you supposed to be paying a visit on Adkins State?"

Kristen jerked awake and nearly fell out of her chair.

Lauren smirked. "Sorry to interrupt your nap."

Kristen turned in her chair to face Lauren, hoping she wouldn't comment on the haphazardly stacked reams of paper that cluttered the desk and floor of her cubicle. "I haven't been sleeping too well lately. I think I'm coming down with something."

Lauren took a half step back. "Whatever it is, don't give it to me. Now, about Adkins State . . ."

"You're right, I was scheduled to visit the sociology department today." She rubbed her eyes. They felt sore and red. She hated to think how they looked; good thing there weren't any mirrors in her cubicle. "But I was feeling so lousy this morning that I decided to stay here and try to catch up on some paperwork."

Lauren glanced at the mountains of paper that threatened to take over Kristen's cubicle. "I can see you've made a lot of headway," she said in a sarcastic tone.

Kristen wished she could come up with a smart comeback, but her brain was tapioca. "I'll try to do better." Lauren had been on her case ever since that night over a month ago when Barry had insulted her. The last thing Kristen needed to do was give the woman any more reason to harass her.

"You certainly couldn't do much worse." Lauren turned to leave, then stopped. "By the way, how are things with you and Barry?"

Lauren's voice was neutral, but Kristen knew what game she was playing. She was hoping to find out that they'd broken up and Barry was available. Lauren was the kind of woman who wasn't turned off by a man insulting her. If anything, it made her even more determined to conquer him. Kristen started to say *Fine, everything's great, couldn't be better,* but the truth came out instead.

"Not so good."

"Really?" Lauren leaned forward, all attention.

Kristen didn't know why she was telling Lauren this. Maybe she needed to confide in someone, needed someone who would listen to her the way Barry used to in her dreams, even if that someone was an enemy.

"Do you think there's such a thing as a man who's too perfect?" Kristen asked.

Lauren laughed. "Honey, if there is, I sure haven't met him!"

"Barry does everything for me. He cooks all my meals, washes the dishes, does the laundry, cleans the apartment—including the bathroom—does the shopping, changes the oil in my car—"

"Good God, and you're complaining? Most women would kill for a man like that. I know I would."

"He insists on going out every night, and he always wants to do the same kinds of things—buy a bunch of balloons and set them free, go to a pet store to see the kittens, ride merry-go-rounds, sip wine by moonlight, take walks in the rain . . ."

"That all sounds very romantic," Lauren said wistfully.

"It is—the first few times you do it. But it starts to wear thin after a while. Sometimes I'd just like to stay home and relax, you know? And he doesn't talk to me; he just listens. He hangs on my every word as if it were a revelation from above."

"I've never had a man who listened to me like that." Lauren's voice was thick with envy.

"It's not the listening that gets to me. He never has anything to say—beyond talking about how wonderful I am, that is. He never has any thoughts or observations of his own to share."

"Some men aren't good at expressing themselves with words." Lauren paused, as if deciding if she should ask her next question. "What about the physical side of your relationship?"

"Boring. It's the same thing every night. He always wants to take care of 'my needs' instead of his own. Don't get me wrong, he's good at what he does, but would a little variety now and then hurt?" In addition, Barry had never climaxed during their lovemaking. Kristen wondered if he were physically capable of orgasm.

"Have you tried to talk to him about how you feel?"

"Of course. But he says he can't help it, that it's just the way he is."

"Then stay home. Tell him to sleep on the couch for a change."

"I've tried. But Barry can be quite . . . persistent when he wants something. He won't take no for an answer."

I can't help it, he'd said once. *I can only be what you've dreamed me to be.*

"Kristen, no offense, but you're certifiable. You've got what every woman fantasizes about, and all you can do is complain. Why don't you tell Barry to dump you and give me a call? I'd sure appreciate him." Lauren turned and walked off, shaking her head.

"I would if I thought it'd do any good," Kristen whispered. She hadn't told Lauren the worst part because there was no way the other woman would understand. In the few hours of sleep Kristen got each night, she still dreamed, but now instead of strolling through an autumnal wood with Barry, she dreamed of stupid, mundane things: trying to fit into jeans that were one size too small, walking along a sidewalk without making any forward progress, trying to read a book in which the letters were all jumbled nonsense. Her dream life with Barry had been her escape from reality, her refuge from the day-to-day banalities that everyone had to endure. But now that Barry had crossed over into the physical world, she had nowhere to escape to.

She couldn't go on like this. She was always exhausted, her work was suffering, and not only didn't she love Barry anymore—if she ever truly had—she was starting to actually hate him. Her dream had turned into a nightmare.

"Hi, sweetheart. How was your day?"

The apartment was immaculate, as usual. Nothing out of place, no lint on the carpet, not so much as even a speck of dust on the furniture. The faint smell of cleaning chemicals in the air reminded Kristen of a hospital—antiseptic, sterile, and cold. Barry puttered about in the kitchen, dressed in the same gray shirt and pants which never needed cleaning or pressing. She'd tried to get him to go out shopping for some new clothes (she was so sick of that damn gray!) but he'd politely refused.

"I'm making stir fry for dinner tonight. How's that sound?"

"Fine." She slumped wearily onto the couch. "Could you come in here for a minute? We need to talk."

Barry responded so quickly it was as if he'd materialized on the spot. "Yes, my love?"

She patted the cushion next to her. "Sit."

He did so, sitting with perfect posture, hands folded on his lap. He looked at her expectantly, his attention completely focused on her. Just once she'd like to see a hint of distraction in his expression—a glance off to the side to check what was on TV, a tightening of the lips as he fought to suppress a yawn.

She felt an urge to take his hands, decided against it. It was best to maintain some distance right now. "Barry, I'm afraid I'm not very happy."

His face clouded over. "What's wrong? Is it something at work? Don't tell me that bitch Lauren has been pestering you again." His hands curled into fists. "I'll go in with you tomorrow and tell her to back off."

"NO! Uh, I mean, it's not work. It's . . . us." She sighed. "Actually, it's you."

"That's not possible," he said simply. "I'm everything you've ever wanted. I exist only to make you happy."

"There's such a thing as being *too* happy. Don't get me wrong, I appreciate everything you've done for me, but I need a little bit of mess and uncertainty in my life. Hell, I'd be happy just to get a good night's sleep for a change. You're smothering me with love and attention. Can't you understand that?"

He looked at her blankly.

Evidently not. She tried another approach. "I miss the way things were before you entered the real world. Isn't there some way you can go back to where you came from? Back into my dreams?"

Barry shook his head. "I may not be exactly human, but I am flesh and blood." He tapped his chest. "As long as I have corporeal existence, there's no going back. But I understand what's bothering you now, and I think I can fix it."

She smiled hopefully. "You do? You can?"

He nodded. "I haven't lived up to your expectations of me. I need to work harder to please you: keep the house cleaner, come up with more interesting things for us to do, be a better lover. From this moment on, Kristen, I will rededicate myself to your happiness. I will shower you with love such as no woman has ever known before!"

Kristen started to protest, but she knew it wouldn't do any good. "That sounds . . . wonderful."

He beamed. "I'm so glad we had this talk." He gave her a hug and a kiss on the cheek. "Now I really must get back to making dinner. I thought we might go wading in the fountain again tonight. We haven't done that for a while."

"No, we haven't." If four days counted as a while.

Barry returned to the kitchen, whistling tunelessly as he began chopping ingredients for the stir fry. Kristen closed her eyes and wondered what she was going to do. What if she told him point-blank to get out? No, he'd probably just rededicate himself to making her happy all over again. She supposed she could not come home tomorrow. She could stay in a hotel for a while—days, weeks, if necessary—and wait to see if Barry left the apartment on his own. If not, she could always cancel her lease and let the apartment manager worry about throwing Barry out. But she doubted even that would get rid of him. He'd found her in the bar, hadn't he? What if there was some sort of connection between them which allowed him to home in on her, to track her? If that were true, she'd never be rid of him. No matter how far she ran, eventually he'd find her, more determined than ever to make her happy.

She thought back to something Barry had said. *As long as I have corporeal existence, there's no going back.* She realized then what she had to do if she wanted to be free. She stood and walked into the kitchen. Barry was slicing a boneless chicken breast into bite-sized chunks on the cutting board.

"How about I help you with dinner tonight?" Kristen asked. "I know you like to do it all yourself, but if I help, we'll be finished and on our way to the fountain that much sooner."

"I don't know . . ."

"It would make me happy, Barry. Very happy."

"Well . . . all right." He smiled. "But just this once."

She nodded as she reached out and drew a long, sharp knife from the butcher block. "Once is all I need."

Three swift strokes later, it was finished. Barry lay on the floor, unmoving, eyes open and staring up at the ceiling. His shirt was torn, but no blood issued forth from his wounds. As Kristen watched, his form grew hazy and indistinct, until finally he evaporated like morning mist in the harsh glare of a summer sun.

*   *   *

That night, Kristen lay alone beneath her sheets.

"Forgive me?" she thought in her dream.

A pause, a sigh, a tolerant smile. *"Of course. I could never stay mad at you."*

Barry took her hand and led her toward a forest where the leaves were just beginning to turn gold and crimson.

It was perfect.

LEGACY

by Roberta Gellis

Roberta Gellis has been a very successful writer of historical fiction for the last two decades, having published about twenty-five historical novels since 1978. Gellis has received many awards, including the Romantic Times *award for Best Novel in the Medieval Period (several times) and the RWA's Lifetime Achievement Award. The six books of her Roselynde Chronicles (*Roselynde, Alinor, Joanna, Gilliane, Rhiannon, *and* Sybelle*) are considered classics. Gellis has also successfully adventured into other genres: romantic suspense (*A Delicate Balance*), science fiction (*Offworld *and* Space Guardian*, writing as Max Daniels), and mythological fantasy (*Irish Magic, Irish Magic II, Dazzling Brightness, Shimmering Splendor, *and* Enchanted Fire*). Currently she is writing a historical mystery.*

HININ and I, Heulyn, were born in the same year, not only on the same day but at the same minute of the same hour in the same room, our mothers sharing a midwife and our father laughing like the madman he was just outside the door. We never could discover how our father had arranged such a thing; as children we both feared him too much to ask him, Hinin's mother vanished soon after the birthing, and mine would never speak a word on that subject. Indeed, she spoke few words on any subject, but she took Hinin to her breast as freely and as often as she took me

and she cared for him as if we had both come forth from
her womb. And so we were raised, living as close as birds
in a nest, sharing everything—until Hinin died for me.

From a child Hinin had been sure that only one of us
should have been born and that, because I was the legiti-
mate child, born of our father's wife, I was that one. He
said at night, when we sat in private by the fire in my
chamber and he could speak of such things, that our father
had bungled some spell he had attempted and set a curse
upon us.

Hinin had been determined to break that curse and came
slowly to the opinion that if he died it would die with him—
but he was not sure. I begged him not to think that way; I
swore and swore again that I needed neither husband nor
lover and was content to be ugly as long as he was with
me; I assured him that he was part of me and I could not
live without him. In this alone, he paid me no mind, and
when he was sure of his power, Hinin seized our father
and, at knife point, asked what would break the curse.

The courtyard rang with laughter as the madman leaned
forward into the knife so that his blood stained it and said,
"When the right husband gives Heulyn what every woman
most desires, she will be free"; and then, stronger than
Hinin believed, he tore free of him, raced to the top of the
north tower, and flung himself from the battlement.

No one tried to stop him, nor can I remember any grief
over his death, not even an exclamation from my mother.
She, however, began to fade and in a month followed our
father to the grave. I wept for her—not so much for my
own loss and loneliness; I had Hinin as for her own gray
and empty life. I had hoped when our father was gone that
she would regain a joy in living, which he seemed to have
leached out of her.

Grief past, I was not sorry to be without father or mother
because the need to protect me and the lands bound Hinin
to life. What our father had told him was useless. I racked
my brains and Hinin racked his, but we could not come
near to deciding how we could find the right husband, how
we could induce the man to marry such a woman as me,
or even what *every* woman would desire most.

Then near dusk one day Hinin came back from driving
off border raiders with a companion, who, for one instant,

made me catch my breath. Sir Jaie St. Croix—Hinin named us to each other before falling into his usual silence—was of a dark beauty that would catch any woman's eye: sable curls only a little crushed by the helm he had removed tumbled over a broad forehead above great eyes luminous with intelligence, a straight nose, and a mouth that would have been too soft if not for the determined chin.

It was only an instant that I froze before I was restored by a reminder of what I was. Sir Jaie, his eyes sliding away from my ugly, raddled face, told me that he and his men had driven the raiders off his land and, seeing they were fleeing into the forest that bordered ours, had followed. There he met Hinin and our men who were lying in wait. Between them, they had killed or captured the entire band.

"Your brother does you much honor," Sir Jaie said. "He insisted that we bring our captives here to be judged."

As he spoke he cast a puzzled glance at Hinin, who was still silent and staring into nothing, and then glanced again at me. Perhaps he was trying to see any shred of similarity between Hinin's profusion of golden hair and perfect features and my thin straggling locks, mean little eyes, piglike snout, and blubbery lips.

"That is my right," I answered. "The lands are mine. My father and mother are dead and I have no full-blood brother or sister. Hinin was a love child and, though beloved of me, has no power to order death or mercy."

Sir Jaie stared at me for a moment, his eyes passing quickly down from my face to my dumpy, sagging body. "You are fortunate to have so powerful and loyal a protector."

"I am aware," I replied smoothly, but I was surprised.

Most men, hearing that the lands were mine absolutely with no father or guardian to oversee my choice of husband, began immediately, despite my revolting appearance, to court me. Some fools tried to belittle Hinin as a protector. This man had not. I was rather pleased at that.

Before either of us could speak again, servants came to light the torches on the walls and the tapers in the candelabra. Since I was hungry for news, I pointed out that it was growing dark and I would be glad to offer the hospitality of my keep. Sir Jaie thanked me for the offer and accepted.

I summoned the steward and bade him see that the pris-

oners were secured and that Sir Jaie's men were quartered
and provided with what refreshment they needed. When
the steward had bowed to me and gone about his duty, I
turned back to Sir Jaie and told him I would go down and
attend to the wounded when I had made him comfortable.
He cast another curious glance at Hinin, who was standing
quietly, smiling at both of us, and then asked me to see to
the wounded at once and not trouble about his comfort.

I knew what that meant, but to my shame this time I did
not feel like laughing because a man could not bear the
thought of my touching him. I only bowed and quickly sent
for the prettiest girl in the keep to attend to him, but I
noticed that Hinin's eyes followed him as he left the Hall.
Shrugging, I went to gather up bandages, needles, silk, and
poultices for the wounded.

Upon returning from the outbuildings in the bailey where
the men-at-arms were quartered, I went above to wash and
comb my hair—for what good that could do me—and
found the maid I had sent to Sir Jaie already waiting. As
she drew over me a fine gown, which was made into a
mockery by my disgusting face and body, she told me he
had not tried to use her. That pleased me too.

When I came down, I saw Sir Jaie by the fire, clad in a
guesting gown from Hinin's store, and could not resist pausing to look at him. While I stood in the shadow of the stair,
Hinin came from his chamber and I shrank against the wall,
gasping for fear we would touch. We passed safely and
Hinin entered the Hall, I following on his heels and gesturing for the servants to bring in the evening meal.

I had ordered a hot meat pasty added to the usual po-
tage, cheese, cold meat, and fresh bread, and took my place
in the high chair at the center of the table. Sir Jaie sat to
my right and Hinin beyond him. Sir Jaie looked surprised,
but I smiled (he had to look away) and explained that a
visitor was precious to us both and it would be cruel to
place Hinin where I would be between him and his guest.

It was also safer. Hinin and I were long practiced in not
touching until we were private, but a stranger at the table
might distract either or both of us and cause an accident.
The placement had another advantage. Because of his need
to serve me, we being dining partners, Sir Jaie noticed less
how silent Hinin was. It seemed natural that I should ques-

tion him and reply to his remarks when he was turned toward me to put food upon my trencher or fill my cup. He kept his eyes on the platters the servants placed before him or on my hands, but he answered my questions readily and was amused by my talk.

Of note to us, I learned that our neighbor, Sir Eric, was failing and that Sir Jaie, a landless younger nephew, had been chosen by the childless old man to inherit. That troubled me for I liked Sir Eric. I said most sincerely that I was sorry to hear of the old man's illness and offered to come and see if I could be any help. In fact, I wondered why Sir Eric had not sent for me or whether he had been prevented and Sir Jaie's beautiful face hid as monstrous a soul as our father's had.

"You will be very welcome," Sir Jaie exclaimed, turning toward me, and blinked and looked away from my face, his expression surprised, as if he had forgotten how I looked. Then he told me how Sir Eric had fallen ill and that he felt it was his fault for not coming to take up the burden.

I said what was proper, pointing out that Sir Eric had his pride. It was natural that he did not wish to sit with folded hands while a younger man fought for him. Now he had had a sign, I told Sir Jaie, and he knew he must accept help. I soothed him, too, over his guilt that he had been amusing himself instead of coming north. Hinin said nothing, only smiling when Sir Jaie spoke directly to him.

Later, when Hinin and I were alone in my chamber with the door barred against any intruder, he took my hand and led me toward my chair. "You like him," Hinin said. "Good. Likely he will do for a husband."

Deep within the emptiness that remained after my substance was sucked away when Hinin touched me, something writhed and screamed. I could find no way to express my fear and agony, however; and, because Hinin was smiling, I smiled too.

"Tomorrow, when you go to Sir Eric's keep, you must look carefully along the road at the cots. See if the women and children run to hide and whether there seem to be fewer than usual cattle and pigs about. In the keep, watch the servants to be sure they do not flinch away from the men-at-arms, and see how the women, especially the young ones, act toward him."

I looked into the fire. What Hinin said to me fell into my empty core without meaning, but I liked to hear his voice and it did not really matter what he said—until he nodded at me and ended, "If you find no fear of Sir Jaie, no sign of deliberate harm done to Sir Eric, it is best you marry him."

Something seized my heart and squeezed it so that I tore my eyes from the flames to stare at him.

He frowned then but held my chin so I could not look away. "There was something . . ." Hinin shook his head. "It was not like our father, not that, but something . . . Yes, he is the right one. I know it."

I gasped and turned away. Black grief roiled in the emptiness, but I did not know why, nor could I speak.

"Now, Heulyn," Hinin said firmly but kindly, "you must not mind that he cannot yet accept your looks. You know how the maids and menservants are, horrified for the first few days and then they grow accustomed and come to love you. Others, too, have grown accustomed; Sir Eric loves you well, and think how Sir Raoul at first sight of you had to run to the waste shaft to empty his stomach and how much pleasure he now takes in your company. Treat Sir Jaie the same way."

By now such a freezing horror had hold of the core of my life that I could hardly breathe. If Hinin noticed, he ignored my distress. Rising and kissing my cheek, he urged me to go to bed and sleep because I would have a long day on the morrow.

When I woke in the morning, I remembered what Hinin had said about Sir Jaie and Sir Raoul and I had to laugh. I do not think any woman, no matter how indifferent to male charm, could have treated Sir Jaie and Sir Raoul the same. Sir Raoul was short and squat, with a broad, flat face, red and freckled, sandy-haired, muddy-eyed. He was a good man, kind to his wife and children, fair to our serfs, quite clever, but coarse and unlearned. Sir Jaie was . . .

I shook my head as I combed my scant, lank locks and pushed them under my veil. Ah, well, Hinin was a man and not likely to understand. But to think of Sir Raoul and then see Sir Jaie . . . My heart fluttered a little and I bade it fiercely to be still. Even if he could accept me after growing

accustomed to my face and, perhaps, fond of my wit, I could
not have him, considering the price I would have to pay.

I found it hard to remind myself of that over breakfast
and during the ride to Sir Eric's keep. Sir Jaie, it turned
out, had been fostered with the earl of Leicester. He knew
poetry and music as well as how to fight. It was such a joy
to talk about things I loved and receive the kind of answer
that showed an equal love that I forgot to watch how the
folk behaved in the villages we passed and I did not waste
time asking the servants questions when we reached the
keep. I went at once to Sir Eric's chamber.

He was resting easily when I arrived, but just his pleasure
in seeing me made his breath come short and hard, and
being helped to sit up against his pillows turned him white
with exhaustion. I scolded him gently because he had not
sent for me while I measured out a draught for him. He
drank the medicine, although he wrinkled his nose over the
taste, but I noticed that he did not ask me when or even
whether he would recover. He knew the answer.

I gave him no false hope, only telling him not to climb
the stairs or ride ahorseback, and warned him that when
he tired, he was to rest, not to push himself to any effort.

"And so he will," Sir Jaie said behind me.

I was looking at the old man's face, and it seemed to me
that his smile broadened and showed true pleasure in his
nephew's coming. We talked for a little while of small
things, but soon Sir Eric's lids grew heavy and I took my
leave. Sir Jaie walked with me to the bailey, waiting until
a groom brought my horse. He lifted me to the saddle with
his own hands, but he did not look at my face when he
thanked me and begged me to come again. Although a sigh
rose in my breast, I gave it no release, only assured him,
as he summoned Sir Raoul and my men to escort me home,
that I would return every few days.

So I came often to Sir Eric's keep. Most times Sir Jaie
was there and on Sir Eric's good days, when he wished to
be helped down to eat with the castlefolk, I stayed to dine
with them. From the first we were comfortable together,
speaking of our crops and the breeding of horses and our
small, hardy cattle, of the raiding Scots. As the weeks
passed, it seemed to me I detected a special warmth in Sir
Jaie's voice, a kind of lingering when he touched my hand.

Perhaps I only desired that and imagined it, but when I thought he showed me favor, my nether mouth would feel hot and wet and my sagging breasts would tingle.

Then he would forget and look at me, and a wary coldness would come over him. Oddly, I did not hate him for that. It pained and grieved me, but he still joined Sir Eric and me when he could easily have found excuses not to do so. And once or twice in every meeting he would forget what I was and the warmth would come back to his voice. Sometimes we were quite merry, making jests and telling harmless tales of our neighbors; it did Sir Eric good to see himself valued for the advice he gave us and to laugh, and it did my heart good to see how Jaie's spirits seemed to lift at any sign his uncle was stronger.

One day, however, Sir Eric was alone beside the fire when I came in. I bit my lip as I approached, seeing how his lips were tinged with blue and his face looked like molded clay. He sighed and beckoned me to pull a stool beside his knee, which I did. I said he should not have come down and he shook his head and replied that he was tired of taking care and was very ready for the long sleep. He spoke of Jaie, then, and praised him. A little silence fell.

"He will not have you, Heulyn," he said suddenly.

I started, for my mind had been on medicines, what new drug I could find to help since I dared not give more of what he was already taking. "What?" I gasped.

"When I received Hinin's letter, I agreed most heartily with it and I told Jaie he should ask for you in marriage. I thought he would, for he talks of you often and I have heard him say that you can lighten a man's day. The lands are perfect, marching together as they do." He sighed. "I suppose it was too soon, that he was not sufficiently accustomed to . . . but he said something very strange, that it was not because you were ugly but because you were two."

"What?" I gasped again, doubly stunned; I had no idea that Hinin had written suggesting marriage to Sir Eric nor that Sir Jaie had somehow perceived that I was more—or rather, less—than only Heulyn.

Sir Eric sighed. "I suppose he is jealous of Hinin."

I seized on that. "He is right, too. I cannot be parted from Hinin and do not desire a husband."

He protested that, but I told him my plans for adopting

a child to inherit my lands, perhaps, if Sir Jaie married and had a large family, one of his; perhaps one of Sir Raoul's brood. Still, after what had been said I could not bear the thought of looking into Sir Jaie's face, and I found a reason to leave. How foolish that was! I never wanted an offer from Jaie; I would have had to refuse the offer if he made one. But knowing he had refused to offer, which should have made me grateful, filled me with shame.

I began to wrack my brains for tasks and duties that would keep me from returning. I told myself I could do no more for Sir Eric, but I knew my company cheered him so conscience warred with inclination. Then, as if to deliver my punishment while my wish was granted, Sir Jaie sent word that a great army had poured out of Scotland into the eastern counties, ravaging the land, and that raiding parties were coming near. Thus I was confined within my keep for safety. That did not trouble me, but Hinin asked if that meant we would go to war, which was strange for him, and I cursed Sir Jaie for disturbing him.

Worse followed. Hard on the heels of that news, Sir Jaie sent a summons from the archbishop of York to join the army that was forming to resist the Scots. Sir Eric, knowing Hinin could not leave me, never sent on such messages. Nonetheless, since a summons could come direct from king or overlord, we were prepared. I was about to order Sir Raoul, who led our forces to make ready, when Hinin stopped me and said he would go himself. At first I laughed and said it was impossible, but that night he explained how he would manage and told me he had been thinking about this since Sir Jaie had refused to marry me.

The next day I sent a message to Sir Jaie asking him to make plain to Hinin that he would be useless as the leader of our troop. I was sure Sir Jaie was well aware of what Hinin was, that Hinin could fight off reavers, but not engage in the kind of battles that required tactics and planning met in a war. Sir Jaie's answer struck me like a blow; he said I should stop belittling my brother, that Hinin would do well without my advice.

Then I begged and pleaded. I wept and raved. All day and even at night I struggled to make Hinin change his mind. He smiled and caressed me; he assured me all would be well, different, perhaps, but well. I wrote again to Sir

Jaie and begged him to tell Hinin to send a deputy, but Jaie did not come and sent no message. By the end of the week it took Hinin to ready himself and his men, my eyes were swollen shut with weeping and Hinin's face had lost its smooth perfection; he was haggard, showing blue-circled eyes and deep lines around his mouth.

I did not even bid him farewell, but locked myself in my chamber the day he left. It was just as well I did that, for in Hinin's absence our father's curse did not wait for his touch but struck me at the moment the first star showed clear in the darkened sky and released me as the sun rose.

With light came thought. I knew then what Hinin planned and though I wept and wrote letters not only to Hinin but to Sir Jaie and tried and tried to think of how to stop him, there was nothing I could do. So then I waited—not in hope; I knew what the end must be. But while I waited, I wondered more and more whether Sir Jaie, who had seen that I was two, had drawn Hinin into war apurpose. The little liking, the flicker of a hopeless love that had nonetheless warmed me, died. Instead I learned to hate.

Just after dusk on August 22 the blow fell. Fortunately I had already closed myself into my chamber and none heard my screams as Hinin was severed from me. The pain was so great, I fell into a black pit in which nothing was real. And when I woke, I faced the ultimate horror. Hinin had died for nothing—I was as cursed as I had ever been.

The next day, when I could speak, I told the castlefolk that Hinin was dead. Although there was great grief, for Hinin had been loved by others than I, and fear also, for he had been a bulwark of our defense, no one asked me how I knew. That was when I understood that the secret of our curse was not truly much of a secret after all.

I suppose I went on living, that I ordered the servants and did what was needed about the keep and lands, but I do not remember it. On the last morning of September, feeling forced itself upon me again. A slow cortege all dressed in mourning hues wound its way across the open fields that bordered my keep and then up the road to my gate. A big man in rich armor and a black-robed churchman rode with Sir Jaie.

Sir Jaie led Hinin's riderless horse and most of the troop that had ridden with Hinin followed him, so they were all welcome. The armsman Sir Raoul sent told me of the arrival and that Sir Jaie and the other men were talking to Sir Raoul in the bailey, but I did not go down to greet them. I sat in my chair of state on the dais of the great hall so wrapped and bound with hate that I was frozen. And what the three men said to me when they entered—Sir Raoul not protesting but looking sorely troubled—nearly stopped my heart.

The big man was Sir Walter, the sheriff of our county; the churchman was the bishop of our diocese. From their expressions of horror and the surprise with which they now looked at Sir Jaie, I was not what they expected to see. Nonetheless, they both seemed to remind themselves that the land was rich, the keep strong, and they swallowed the doubts my horrible appearance raised and spoke their pieces. They had come by the king's command, because Hinin had died with extraordinary valor in the king's service, to satisfy my brother's last request that his dearest friend Sir Jaie marry his beloved half sister, Lady Heulyn.

I stared, mute with shock as the bishop explained that though they were sorry not to give me more time, they understood I was well acquainted with Sir Jaie already. Thus, because this was only one stop of many they must make and because once the knowledge of Hinin's death spread other men desiring my lands might try to seize me, I was to be married to Sir Jaie here and now. In my own chapel. Before dinner, which could serve as a wedding feast. And, in fact, as soon as I was married, they would leave on the next stage of their journey.

I was helped to my feet and led to the chapel by Sir Raoul, who whispered that we could not stand against the king's will and that with Hinin gone, Sir Jaie would be a strong protector. Perhaps as the shock passed, I would have refused my consent, king's will or no, but when I looked at the crucifix over the altar, I realized that God works in mysterious ways, and in a strange way indeed was answering my prayers for vengeance. The person to whom a man is most vulnerable is his wife. As wife, I would have my choice of painful and protracted ways to torment Sir Jaie. I almost smiled as the bishop began the prayers.

My mind being busy with devices dreadful enough to satisfy me for Jaie's part in my loss of Hinin, I do not remember either the wedding service or what followed very clearly. I know I never looked at Jaie or spoke to him and he said no single word to me. If he looked at me, I was not aware of it, and he never touched me; it was Sir Walter who put a ring upon my finger.

At dinner the bishop and the king's emissary sat on either side of me and kept assuring me that my husband wished me no ill, that Sir Jaie had secured my interests in his own despite. I must have smiled at that because the emissary turned away and the bishop closed his eyes. But it was funny that they should think I might be afraid. My hate was hard enough, cold enough, to kill without any other weapon.

When they were gone, to my surprise, Sir Jaie brought me back to my high chair on the dais and knelt down before me. "The blow he took was meant for me," Sir Jaie said.

I had not known that. My breath sucked in, and I really looked at him for the first time. He might have been a man risen from his deathbed, his skin clay-gray, his eyes dull and heavy, his mouth drawn thin with pain. Gone was the easy litheness I had known. He moved like a man still sore with half-healed wounds, but I had no pity for him. He could not suffer enough to satisfy me.

"I could not even bring you his body to inter." His voice was low and harsh. "You will not believe this, but the sheriff saw it, which doubtless added to his eagerness to fulfill Hinin's last wish. Hinin disappeared."

I drew a sharp breath, but my voice was caught in my throat and Sir Jaie continued, "It was not that his body was stolen and his armor and weapons looted. I stood over him myself until the battle ended and Sir Walter and I brought him to my tent, sore wounded but alive . . . he spoke to us. He said, 'You owe me a life, Jaie. Swear you will marry Heulyn. Sir Walter, you must see to it.' Sir Walter asked who Heulyn was and I turned my head to answer, and when I turned back, Hinin had . . . vanished away."

I felt my mouth drop open when he said that, and the iron weight of rage and hatred that crushed me lightened enough for me to remember. That could have been my mother speaking when Hinin asked about *his* mother. "She vanished away," my mother had whispered. "The midwife said she caught you and turned to take Heulyn, and when she turned back, your mother had vanished."

"I have his armor, his shield and sword." Sir Jaie's voice recalled me to the present. "But Hinin . . . he was gone."

He gestured and a man carrying a casket came forward from near the wall where he had been waiting. He set the box down beside Sir Jaie, who opened it. Inside were the weapons and armor I had given Hinin—his rich chain-mail shirt, his crested helm, his jewel-hilted sword and knife, all clean and shining, resting in the curve of his shield.

Then I wept, the tears making their way by crooked paths among the pustules on my flaccid and blotched skin.

"And it was not only Hinin's wish that we marry. Sir Eric, too—" Sir Jaie swallowed hard. "Sir Eric said that Hinin was right, that I must take you to wife. So when the bishop and Sir Walter came, I agreed. I am here to offer myself in your brother's place."

That jerked me upright. "No man can take my brother's place," I spat, "and especially not you! Why did you not tell Hinin you would rather a deputy led my men? You knew what he was. Why did you not send him home?"

Slowly, he shook his head. "I did not know," he whispered. "I thought you made him dull and slow by your cleverness. I thought that away from you he would grow." He closed his eyes. "I did not know you would be my legacy."

I stared at him as tears began to roll down his cheeks.

"I am a murderer twice over," he said. "Sir Eric died on Sunday. It was my fault. I knew how sick he was. I should have taken back the burden of the keep and lands as soon as I came home. Instead I went to bed, to coddle myself, and left him to struggle on alone. Is that not murder? Should I not die for it?"

"Death is too good for you," I answered smiling sweetly—but this time Jaie did not look away. "Why should I stain my soul with murder when you will suffer ten times the torment of death as my husband? Every man in the county knows what I am. Now the sheriff knows, too. Is there one who will not scorn you for taking such as me to wife for my lands? And you cannot be rid of me. No matter when I die, you will be branded a murderer. How could such a wife as I die of natural causes, leaving her husband with everything because she had no blood kin?"

"What you leave me will be at your will," he said harshly. An odd shiver ran through me at those words, but before I could consider that he added, "Whatever anyone thinks, I did not marry you for your land." He drew a parchment from the breast of his tunic and thrust it into my hands. "Read. I know you can. There is your marriage contract."

I had to read the words twice because I could not believe that the sheriff or the bishop had witnessed such a document without setting bonds on Jaie as a madman. This was what they meant when they told me he had secured my interest in his own despite. It was simple enough; my lands were still mine, to rule during my life and to leave to whomsoever I willed after my death. And if Jaie died before me, Sir Eric's lands would come to me also.

Sir Jaie had bowed his head again; there were tear streaks on his cheeks and his eyes were empty of everything but pain. I shuddered and tried to hold my hatred, to push away the knowledge that Jaie had completely misunderstood. "Your cleverness made him dull," he had said. "If he were away from you, he would grow." I could not even hold the conviction that Hinin had died to save Sir Jaie. I knew better.

I knew Hinin had died for me, thinking that would free me from our father's curse. So, if Sir Jaie had murdered Sir Eric because he was too sick with wounds to perform a necessary duty, was I not a murderer, too? Did it matter that Hinin had been unsuccessful or that I had been unwilling? In fact, Hinin had died even more senselessly than Sir Eric, who was at least serving his land. I knew my hatred of Sir Jaie was only a disguise for my self-hatred, my guilt, and grief.

"No," I said at last. "Sir Eric's death was not murder. Sir Eric was doing what he wished to do." Sir Jaie did not raise his head, just looked at Hinin's leavings. After a long pause, I said, "As Hinin did."

The pain of letting my hatred burn away in the fire of truth was almost as great as that when Hinin was reft from me, but I endured.

"But they are both dead," Jaie said, staring stubbornly down at Hinin's weapons and armor.

"Go home and be at peace," I answered. "Sir Eric died

because he was tired of living. Hinin died for me, not for you. Death was his purpose. He was using you, not saving you."

"Using me?" His head lifted to protest, and then his eyes widened. "You are one!" he cried, and stepped forward to take my hand. In the next moment he dropped it, gasping, "Hinin?"

In that instant I became aware that the castlefolk had all drawn back toward the walls and were staring, silent. Some wept, some covered their faces; I stared, too, wondering at them, such a crowd of people. I had never seen such a crowd of people, only Hinin and my mother had ever come into my chamber to visit with me. I heard the man by my chair speak to me and ask for Hinin, but I only stared, and he seized me by the shoulder and shook me.

Sir Jaie gasped again and stepped back and I saw all the castlefolk shivering and clutching at each other because they had seen at last what had only been whispered behind closed doors. That was dangerous, but I could not even fear that I might be called a witch; my mind was frozen on the fact that it had been Jaie's touch that changed me. The right husband, Hinin had said.

"Did I see what I saw?" Jaie cried.

The look on his face warned me that I might be for hanging or burning. "I am not a witch," I protested. "That was my father. Hinin told me he had learned that my father had foreseen that he would have only one child and that a female. That was not to his taste. He decided to conjure a male and cast off the female part into a fetch he would create, but he bungled the spell or was not strong enough. We were two, and when Hinin and I touched, we exchanged forms."

Sir Jaie shuddered. "But there was only one mind, so when you have Hinin's beauty you are as mindless as he was."

"Yes. The fetch form had the mind." Then suddenly I laughed. "But why should you care, for you must be nearly as witless. What sane husband leaves a wife utterly to rule herself and her lands and passes his to her also?"

"I do," he said around clenched teeth. "That is how Hinin lived with you. When I accepted you as my legacy,

I accepted that also." And he came forward a step and laid his hand upon my shoulder.

The strange shiver coursed over me once more, and I knew if I touched my face I would feel smooth, perfect skin, a fine nose, well-shaped lips, thick curly hair. But I was not empty! I was still me—or, more than me, perhaps Hinin too.

Tears filled my eyes. My brother was not lost to me. I could always remember all the things he told me after dark. Now, added to those, were all the knowledge, thoughts, and feelings that he had kept silent within when he wore the fetch's body, knowing my empty shell would not understand. But those had been my thoughts, my feelings also, and we were now one, as we would have been had not my mad father decided he *would* have a son.

I also understood, at long last, what my father's cryptic words meant. I knew what *every* woman desired, what I must have to bind my form to my own will, but the shock of so many happenings, so many revelations, took my power of speech from me and made me gape like an idiot. Jaie, unthinking in his own bewilderment and anguish, touched my now-beautiful face. I felt my body sag into the fetch's revolting form, but my mind was still my own. I had one chance to be rid of my father's curse.

"Well, Sir Jaie," I said, "which of us do you wish to keep, the beautiful idiot or the horrible creature who can think and be a companion to you?"

He stared at me, at my raddled face, my lumpish body, no doubt remembering the beauty with the blank eyes and open mouth. "I do not know," he sighed, tears standing in his eyes, and then he smiled faintly. "That, too, I will leave to your own will, for you must suffer more from either form than I."

A last time the tremor passed over me, and this time not by Jaie's touch but by my own will. I reached out and took his hand in mine and there was no further tremor. Hinin's form and Heulyn's mind were together.

"Since I may choose," I said, smiling into his astonished face, "and my will is now only to please you, my husband, you shall have the best of both, Hinin's beauty and Heulyn's mind and spirit."

TEEL RULES

by Mark Kreighbaum

Mark Kreighbaum's short fiction has appeared in anthologies such as Starlight 1, The Sandman: Book of Dreams, Enchanted Forests *and* The Shimmering Door. *His latest science fiction novel is* The Eyes of God. *He lives in San Francisco, California.*

FIFTEEN Teels waited at Dave's bus stop. They were three-dimensional double exposures, a scintillating blur of variously clothed young women. Glancing around, he saw that he was alone, and was glad. He hated sharing her.

The newspaper-reading Teels wore the pink-tinted glasses that became such a fad for a while after the first few Teels appeared. These Teels, Dave knew, were from the last summer of her marriage to Harvey Lemke, when she was working as a researcher for the school board.

The Teels made no sound, not even a rustling of the newspapers.

Nine of her incarnations were engrossed in a chewed-up copy of a Dickens novel. He could tell these Teels were older versions from the winter of that year because she'd cut her hair, tinted it red, and bought contacts. According to *Who's Teel?*, the magazine her family put out, she'd just gotten divorced and was starting a new job editing a newsletter for Greenpeace.

Three Teels leaned against the bus stop sign looking bored. One of them cocked a slender leg and smoothed out a wrinkle in her nylons. The other two constantly checked their watches.

Since her first appearance, nine years ago, Dave had read endless magazine articles about the phenomenon of Teel. Physicists thought she was a catastrophic effect, a consequence of Chaos Theory. Biologists postulated that Teel was the result of a genetically engineered retrovirus that rewrote a portion of the thalamus of the human brain and dropped dark hints about the military's history of human experimentation. Psychologists hypothesized that she was a cascading mass hallucination generated by profound alienation. Televangelists made enormous sums of money on the conviction that Teel Mackenzie was the herald of the Second Coming.

Dave didn't care about any of these theories. Whatever accident or purpose caused Teel Mackenzie to become a perpetual echo in time had brought one of her past lives to him. He had fallen in love on first sight.

One of the Teels swung around the bus stop pole singing, though, of course, Dave heard no sound. She laughed and sang, eyes squinted behind the pink-tinted glasses, her whole body loose and dancing to some private music.

Dave didn't need his Teel almanac to know when this one was from—the week of September eighth through the fourteenth of the year she'd fallen in love with a con man. This was his favorite Teel. This was the Teel he loved. In six years of searching, he'd found only nine of her.

He loved the color of her hair, melted-down topaz. It waved across her shoulders while the lanky woman whirled around the bus stop pole. The September sun of six years ago ran its fingers through her hair, leaving a trail of reddish gold. Teel wore stone-washed jeans ripped at one knee, battered Reeboks, a pair of big garish earrings that swung with her every movement, and a brand new sweater with a picture of the Empire State Building silk-screened on the front. Her purse leaned against the pole.

Dave knew that she'd just returned from New York where she'd met the con man who would later break her heart. But, poor Teel didn't know that yet. Right now, she was full of love for everything. Four of these Teels Dave loved had been singing when he found them. It saddened him to think of what lay in store for her. A part of him was glad that the man who'd betrayed Teel had committed suicide after she started to appear.

She smiled the way you do when you don't care if the smile's too wide. There was something about that smile, unfettered and full of uncomplicated joy, which captured his heart when he first saw it.

Dave was a lonely man, a thirty-two-year-old virgin, and he knew all too well how pathetic this unrequited love was. In dreams, he imagined meeting her, somehow willing himself into her past and finding her. Most times, those dreams burned with the fire of their coupling, as if they were two halves of the same soul, reunited after centuries apart. But there were many other nights when he dreamed that she spurned him, laughed at his need for her. Those nightmares were the ones his heart most believed.

He watched while she sang. He wished he knew what song it was so he could sing along. Teel loved too many different kinds of music for him to memorize all her favorite songs. Instead, he just grinned and hummed under his breath, and kept a wary eye out for witnesses.

After a minute or two, all the Teels faded away, except for the one singing. Dave was delighted. Normally, when Teels went, they went as a group. He checked his watch nervously. His bus was due shortly. He hoped it wouldn't arrive while this Teel was here. He couldn't stand it when strangers stared at his Teel.

She let go of the bus stop pole and tilted her head to the sky, stretched out her arms, and twirled around like a child. Dizzy, she stumbled, laughing with her whole body. After a moment, her shoulders lifted in a sensuous shrug and she skipped over to the bench. The skip was a cross between a bunny hop and Dorothy's dance in the Wizard of Oz. Dave couldn't help but laugh, even as his heart melted with desire and love.

Teel jerked her head in Dave's direction. Dave flinched. Teel stared at him, or rather, he realized, at something in her past that stood where he was standing. Dave couldn't move. Her gray eyes, wide behind the pink-tinted lenses, transfixed him. He couldn't shake the notion that she saw him. But that was impossible. Still.

"I, um . . . hello?" said Dave.

Teel frowned, cocking her head as if she heard him, but faintly. She leaned toward Dave, then smiled tentatively. It can't be, Dave thought. It's impossible. An ache like a splinter driven into his heart made his breath short and pained.

"Hello?" he repeated softly. And even more softly, "My love?"

Her smile grew until it crinkled the corners of her eyes. She affected an aggressive wide-legged stance, stuffed her hands into her back pockets, tilted her head, and opened her mouth to speak.

Just then, the squeal and whoosh of air brakes broke Dave's concentration, and he whipped around to see his bus coasting to the curb.

When he turned back to Teel, she was gone. His heart hammered. He let the bus go on without him and spent the remainder of the morning at the bus stop. Like Teels, buses came and went, giving and receiving passengers. He hardly noticed the passengers, and they never spoke to him.

She never returned.

Finally, he left the bus stop and spent the afternoon in Prospect Park, feeding unsalted peanuts to the pigeons and squirrels. Teel had never been to this park. He'd checked his almanac to be sure.

As night fell, Dave sat alone in the park watching white moonlight shatter in the leaves of the elms and cottonwoods. What should he do? What could he do? Should he talk to someone about this?

His thoughts whirled like deformed planets around a black sun that he refused to name. He'd read about similar cases, of course. He wasn't the first person to become obsessed with Teel Mackenzie, to think she saw him.

Dave spent much of the night in a bar drinking endless cups of coffee. There was no one he could call who would understand, or care. His parents were not the sort of people who welcomed the numinous and his only friends were Teelwatchers. He could imagine the expressions of the others in his Teelwatchers group if he told them. They often exchanged jokes about the pitiable fools who became consumed by Teel to the point of losing their minds. Dave couldn't stand the thought of being laughed at.

Let it go, he thought. *It's not for you to hold.* It was a small gift from above, a reward. Didn't he deserve some happiness, after all? But his hands trembled, and he didn't want to return to his apartment in a neighborhood where there were always at least half a dozen Teels running ghostly errands. And one of those Teels was a Teel he loved.

Finally, he returned home, flinching from every apparition of Teel that caught his eye.

He spent a sleepless night, suffering from the old hated nightmare—Teel laughing at him, at his body, everything.

The next morning, Dave didn't go to work. Instead, he sat on the windowseat in his living room, looking out on the street below. He spent almost all morning watching Teels.

They appeared and disappeared like lightning flashes. With a glance at his almanac, he could have made a fairly accurate guess as to the errand of each manifestation. No one else on the street below paid her any attention. Other than hard-core hobbyists like Dave, most people ignored Teel these days, though he still saw a lot of graffiti around like, "I'm the Real Teel," and "Teel Rules," and "Teel Heals"—he saw that last one sprayed on churches a lot. Plus, of course, that special Pentagon Task Force was probably still trying to track down the Real Teel. He wondered what they were going to do if they ever found her. Dissect her? Make her queen? The others in his Tuesday night Teelwatchers group were fascinated and excited about the possibility of finding her and learning how she had become a human slide show. They spent hours speculating on her whereabouts and the scientific theories for why she manifested. One or two of them occasionally advanced more mystical notions, but always in the spirit of logical positivism.

Dave faked enthusiasm. Secretly, he didn't care whether the Real Teel existed anywhere, or whether she was ever found. In fact, he didn't even much like the last known avatars of Teel Mackenzie that he'd seen. They were terribly sad, paranoid, and too clever by half.

Later, Dave took a load of laundry to the Lim's Launderland and Coin-Op down the street. It was deserted, except for a pair of Teels doing laundry. Neither of them were his Teel, and he was pleased that he could look at them without qualms. It would be okay. He'd spent too much time thinking about a ghost. He'd spent too much time in a dream of love. But it was nothing new. This was his life, and he wouldn't have called it joyless. Dave had many solitary pleasures. He was seldom bored by his own company. For the most part, he was at peace. It would be okay.

While his clothes were in the washer, he read a free weekly that he found on a folding table by the dryers. It had a pull-out section of book recommendations. Dave pulled up a plastic chair and began to read.

He was so engrossed in an essay about gothic poetry that he almost didn't notice the smell of perfume—*Enchanté*—Teel's favorite. As soon as the scent registered however, he whipped his head up and found himself staring up into the gray eyes of Teel Mackenzie.

Before the confusion, before the fear, his first feeling was one of deep and bitter disappointment. It was one of her later manifestations, not the Teel he loved.

She wore contacts and her skin was tanned. Lines of worry creased her forehead and caged her eyes. Her hair was blonde-streaked and rag cut. A tiny scar arced across her right temple. She'd picked that up while on the run, he knew, just before her images stopped appearing in places where people could find them easily. She cocked one narrow hip against the folding table, as unconsciously sensual as a cat stretching in the sun.

She wore a T-shirt from the American tour of some rock band he'd never heard of. The sleeves were torn off revealing her strong shoulders and muscled arms. Her smile was thin and a little mean. She wore no lipstick, no makeup at all. He could smell her, sweat and *Enchanté*. Her hands were thrust knuckle-deep into the front pockets of her black jeans.

"Hi, Dave," said Teel, in a husky tenor with a Midwestern twang. It was the first time Dave had ever heard her voice, though he'd read so many descriptions of it that it came to him almost as an echo.

His heart beat slow and hard and his hands shook.

Dave looked around the laundromat. He was alone. The other Teels were gone. He rose from the chair and backed away from her, letting the book supplement spill to the floor. She frowned.

"What's wrong?" asked Teel. "What's wrong, my love?"

He ran blindly out of the laundromat and he didn't stop

running until he was utterly lost in a part of town where he thought Teel had never gone.

It was the middle of the day and he felt that guilty strangeness of the child who has ditched school for no good reason. Would anyone at work be wondering about him? He was almost always the one who made the first pot of coffee for the office. He was also the guy who booted up the network, even though that wasn't really his job and most of the other temp workers just used the network's email to send each other dirty jokes, though not to him. He made sure the printer and the photocopier were warmed up so that his fellow workers could copy their morning cartoons right away, the cartoons they never posted in his cubicle. He didn't think they meant to exclude him. When they noticed him, they nodded pleasantly. He was always asked to sign the office birthday cards. He didn't think they were ignoring him deliberately. It was something else. He'd once tried to explain it to Brian, one of the Teelwatchers, and Brian had come up with a good analogy. Dave was like one of the elves in the old fairy tale. You left out your shoes and the elves fixed them. But he was the elf who went for coffee and missed all the excitement. Could he call Brian? Tell him what had just happened in the laundromat? Dave tried to imagine Brian's reaction and sighed.

I'm like Teel, he thought. A thought he'd had many times over the years. After a while, people get used to things and they stop seeing them. He didn't think he minded so much being a ghost, as long as it was on his own terms. If people found out about his . . . encounter . . . with Teel, they'd see him all right, but it would be with pity, or contempt. Hadn't some poet said something like, what a gift it would be to see ourselves as others see us? He'd never understood that idea. To be seen, really seen, would be awful. But wasn't that what love meant? Wasn't that why it was supposed to be so dangerous? He'd never really thought about being seen by Teel. What did that mean, really? Was it possible to be loved in the abstract?

Dave paused to look around. He was a long way from home and he didn't even have his wallet with him. The streets had more people moving on them than he'd have expected for a Tuesday afternoon. Who were all these people anyway? Dave sat on the corner of a stone fence and watched the ebb and flow of humanity. There, a young man walked rapidly north, switching an aluminum briefcase from hand to hand. He was sweating, though it wasn't very hot. He snatched glances behind him frequently. Here, a pair of older women in suits walked together, talking rapidly, seldom listening, but once, the taller one gave the other such a strange look, maybe of hatred, that the smaller never saw. An old man wobbled down the sidewalk on a bicycle, a fierce desperation in every line of his face and body.

How much of all this was imagination? He wasn't sure, but he felt very deeply sad. No matter how carefully you looked, you never saw everything there was to see. Only Teel revealed all of her selves and even she had learned how to hide.

A man, of average height and graying hair, perched on a stone fence, his round face as serene as a Buddha. It was himself, of course, reflected in the glass of a display window by a trick of the light. Do ghosts cast reflections?

A woman entered the frame, blonde rag-cut hair lining a face with too many shadows. She walked with purpose and confidence and grace. She was coming for him, this fierce woman who was only an echo of the one he loved. He glanced to his side and saw nothing, turned back to see that his own reflection had been erased from the window by the setting of the sun.

It was Tuesday. Teelwatchers Night. The meeting was being held across the street, in fact. Should he go? Dave stood up. Destiny was one of those words, like love, that he'd always felt that he understood too well. Destiny wasn't something you knew and followed. It was like coincidence in the Winter, a cold surprise that was, nonetheless, not entirely unexpected.

He was the last to arrive and, as usual, the others had not waited for him. For the first time, the realization upset him. Was he so insubstantial? So Teelish? Brian was having a heated sarcastic argument with Cassie and just from the way they leaned toward each other, Dave suddenly understood that they were lovers. Why had he never seen it before? Just because he thought cruel words made love unthinkable? A sense of loss filled him, as if a sister had died. It was, he thought, the moment of innocence lost at the apex of the roller coaster and the shame of knowing that he had never really looked at any of these people before. Was that why they couldn't see him?

Teel Mackenzie—if she was still alive somewhere, if that woman in the laundromat was not just a mirage made of pity's light—she sees herself all the time, like an echo that refuses to fade. She doesn't have the luxury of blindness.

Douglas and Larry were playing chess with a commemorative Teel chess set of sterling silver and gold plate that must have set Larry back a bundle. Larry's hand brushed Douglas', maybe by accident, and Dave saw that Larry was in love with Douglas and that Douglas was pretending not to know. Was it a kindness, or was Douglas pretending only well enough to wound? Loving someone through one-way glass was exactly the sort of thing a Teelwatcher would do.

Janice was in the corner. She was middle-aged with care-worn features, but she had a sweetness that he admired. She was wearing a gray dress and pink-tinted glasses. She smiled at Dave and waved. But he had the sense, suddenly, that she was waving to someone from another day. So many times, he'd wanted to ask her out on a date, but his courage always failed. Or at least, he'd assumed that it was cowardice. Maybe he was simply being faithful to Teel, in his fashion.

In a moment, they would all notice him and someone would ask if anyone had any sightings. Yes, he would say, but not of Teel. I see you all.

Night had fallen, but the moon was still strong and high. Dave was cold—he'd run out of the laundromat wearing only a T-shirt—but the cold seemed more like a memory than a presence. He wandered the city, waiting for that cold surprise of Destiny. She'd found him before, hadn't she? Where would the living Teel wait for him? And did he want this version of her? How much of love is the delusion of selected moments? Where would she be? He had an intuition that she would not wait long in any place that he would know.

And then he knew.

*   *   *

The moon was nearly gone and he'd visited this place only once. But he found his way easily enough. And there, before the grave of a con artist from New York, knelt Teel Mackenzie. Her eyes glittered with tears in the remnants of moonlight. This was the dangerous Teel, not the one he loved, or would love, or had loved.

" 'The grave's a fine and private place,' " she murmured, her lips quirking into the smile of the Teel he loved. Was he seeing what he wanted to see?

He settled down beside her. She rested her head on his shoulder.

"Why me?" he asked, meaning one thing.

"Why me?" she replied, meaning another.

He put his arms around her and smelled the faint scent of *Enchanté* and felt the warmth of her body. The moon was nearly gone, but enough light remained to pick out the freshly painted graffiti on the gravestone.

"Teel Heals," he whispered. And, beside it, "Dave Saves."

CHURCHYARD YEW

by Andre Norton

Andre Norton has written and collaborated on over one hundred novels in her sixty yeas as a writer, working with such authors as Robert Bloch, Marion Zimmer Bradley, Mercedes Lackey, and Julian May. Her best known creation is the Witch World, which has been the subject of several novels and anthologies. She has received the Nebula Grand Master award, The Fritz Leiber award, and the Daedalus award, and lives in Monterey, Tennessee, where she oversees a writer's retreat.

"YES, yes—well—I'll see—"

It was very plain to Ilse Harveling that her hostess was between irritation and embarrassment, fighting to break into the flow of speech on the other end of the phone line.

"Yes." That came with sharp firmness—Louise was losing control. "I shall let you know." She snapped the phone back on its cradle forcibly. "People! Really—"

Ilse waited for her to return to the small table in the bay window where they had been sharing a leisurely breakfast. *"People!"* she exploded for the second time.

"So—we have people, my dear. And it is plain that something you dislike has been asked of you." Ilse slid the jam spoon back into its pot. The morning sun was bright across the table, it was a good morning—yet—there was a shadowing which was not that from any cloud.

Louise plumped herself into her seat, beginning to fiddle with the dishes before her, moving a plate, a cup and saucer a fraction. So far she had not met Ilse's level gaze. Then her lips pursed as if she tasted something sour.

"It is an imposition. I will not allow it!"

Ilse waited. Louise was more upset than she had ever seen her.

"Marj Lawrence—she wants you to come to lunch at Hex House."

"And this is an invitation which you find so very upsetting. Why is that?"

"Because Marj—she thinks they have a ghost—or something wrong. Of all the stupid things! It's my fault. I'll admit that. I told Marj once about the time in Bradenton when you helped old Mrs. Templer. Jack always does say I talk too much and this time it's caught up with me. But you are not going to be pulled into anything. Of course I feel sorry for Marj and Tom—they invested most of their savings in that place. There were some old stories—but goodness knows that James Hartle lived there all his life and there was never any trouble. It was only when they bought the place and turned it into a bed and breakfast and that lawyer died of a heart attack. Then people began talking—"

Louise pushed aside all the china and planted her elbows on the table, supporting her chin in her cupped hands.

"People," she continued, "have heart attacks all the time in all kinds of places. It was just hard luck for the Lawrences that this Mark Walden had his in one of their bedrooms. The doctor said there was no question about the cause of death. They could just have shut up that room and forgotten about it for a while. Only all the talk started. Just a lot of gossip which should be laughed at. Maybe some of it was even this Walden man's own fault—he was poking around asking questions—seems he thought he had some roots here—of course, with that name—but it's been over a hundred years!"

Louise paused for breath and Ilse took the opportunity to ask: "So there was indeed a story. Why was the house given such an unlucky name in the first place?"

"Well, it was called the Hartle place when the Lawrences bought it. But Marj is a local history buff, and she started to trace its history. So—there you are," Louise said triumphantly. "It is partly her own poking around which must have started the talk. She thought what she found out was romantic! Ghosts!" Louise uttered a sound which was not quite a snort.

"And there was a recent death—it is this, then, that has started talk?" persisted Ilse.

"A man died of a heart attack. Now most of the valley is talking about it and the Lawrences are not prospering. But they are not going to drag you into this, I promise you, Ilse! You came here for a rest, and we have things to do which are cheerful and fun. Tomorrow there is that auction at the Brevar farm and the old lady is said to have just trunks and trunks of stuff which have not been opened for years. We could find some real treasures."

Louise's mouth turned up. She was a collector of vintage clothing and the thoughts of what might be found in those old trunks drew her attention momentarily away from the woes of Marj Lawrence.

"There ought to be some old beaded things—just what you are looking for, Ilse. Mrs. Brevar inherited from her mother and her great-aunt, and her grandmother, and none of them ever threw anything away."

"An outing to be enjoyed, Louise. But for the moment, please, satisfy my curiosity concerning this affair at Hex House."

Louise frowned. "It's about the oldest house around here. The story is that it was built on a direct grant from the king in the old days. You know that the south end of the valley was settled by some odd church people from Austria. Not Amish—but something of the same order— very strict but excellent farmers.

"In that day Hex House was rather like an inn—travelers stopped there. The church crowd would have nothing to do with anyone from the inn. In fact, there was bad feeling. Honestly, Ilse, I really don't know much of the story. It had been forgotten until Marj got her certainly unbright idea of capitalizing on its history. You would have to ask her— Only you are not going to! She is not going to bother you."

"I do not think that the term 'bother' enters into this, Louise," said the other slowly. "It might be well to lunch with your friend and hear what is troubling her so greatly."

"No! Ilse, she has no right to ask you—"

"That is not the truth, Louise. I did not hear your

friend's side of that telephone conversation, but I think you were speaking with someone deeply distressed. I do not believe that there is any thought of publicity in Mrs. Lawrence's desire to speak with me."

Louise was shaking her head.

"You know, dear friend," Ilse continued, "that I have been granted certain gifts. When one is so favored—or burdened—there is also a duty to use those for the relief of others. I think it is wise that we do accept this invitation. Perhaps it is all nothing as you believe, but on the chance that my talent is needed, I cannot say no. And—" Ilse hesitated. She was not watching Louise now but looking beyond her into the garden. There was a strangeness about her stare as if she could sight something of importance if she would try hard enough. "And, if that invitation was for today, then I think it best we accept."

Louise's face was flushed. "I am more embarrassed than I can tell you. I do talk too much and so I am caught— and you with me. All right."

She got up so abruptly from the table that it rocked a fraction and a spoon fell to the floor. Paying no attention to that, Louise went to the phone, dialed with an impatient flick of the finger, and relayed their acceptance.

"At least you'll get to see some of the southern valley," she said when she put the receiver down, though that thought did not appear to cheer her much.

The southern end of the valley did have its appeal as Louise drove slowly along the narrow back roads, ditched on either side, the verges thick with the berry-shaped flowers of red clover and the tall lace-crowned stalks of Queen Anne's Lace. Wild morning glories with their pallid blooms patched the strangling vines clumping on the old fences. Here and there could be sighted a red barn or a low-roofed house.

"Stuben land," Louise waved with a gesture wide enough to include most of what they could see.

"Stuben?"

"That's what the north valley calls it. I told you about those church people who settled here—they kept aloof from everyone, did all necessary communication through one man—Johanus Stuben. So everyone thought of them collectively as Stubens. Oh, here's their church—looks more like a barn, doesn't it? That was part of their beliefs: no steeples, no ornamentation."

Louise stopped the car before a building now sagged of roof, its narrow windows shuttered by weathered boards nailed to shut out time and life. It did resemble a barn but lacked the usual quaint appeal of those structures.

"The sect has died out?" Ilse studied the sober, grayish block. Even the common field flowers appeared to shun its vicinity. Only sun-browned tangles of grass grew sparsely about.

"Oh, a long time ago. The younger generations broke with the strict rules and most of them left. I think there are one or two of the old families that still have descendants hereabouts, but there are no more Stubens. I'll turn back on the highway here, and Hex House is only a short distance on."

It was exactly on the stroke of noon when they pulled into the parking lot of Hex House. Save for a dusty van and a small, aged Volvo, theirs was the only vehicle, which made the space seem almost deserted. Once outside the car Ilse stood for a long moment surveying the structure facing her.

The present parking lot was cobbled, perhaps a restoration of its former paving when this building might have served as a stage station. There were smaller outbuildings on either side, all constructed of the same gray native stone cut from a nearby quarry. The main house was two stories high with deep-set windows flanked by newly painted shutters. A door, which had a shallow overhang as a weather guard, showed the glint of gleaming, well-polished brass at both knocker and latch. There were certainly no signs of dilapidation but rather of careful and knowledgeable restoration.

Yet it was also apparent that the house was very, very old and had settled well into the land which formed its foundation. Ilse's head was up, and more than her eyes were questing. Time, as she well knew, could encase and even nourish that which was not of the daily world. Disturbances of the kind she had met in the past flourished in such places.

"Oh, Louise!"

That polish-enhanced door had been flung open before

they had advanced under the overhang of the half porch. The woman who stood there was of middle years but as well kept up as her surroundings—in a discreet manner, so she made an appearance neither brittlely smart, nor dowdily out of fashion.

Her fine hair was a silver cap cut very short, and she wore a black-and-white-checked shirt crisp from laundering, with well-cut black slacks. Her skin, however, had a yellowish tinge and there were dark shadows beneath her rather prominent blue eyes which even the large-lensed glasses she wore did not conceal.

"Dr. Harveling!" She hailed Ilse in the same nervously enthusiastic voice as that with which she had greeted Louise. "It was so very good of you to come—so very kind—" For a moment she paused, her lips tightened as if she were fighting for control.

Ilse knew fear when she saw it eroding another. She smiled and held out her hand, closing it about the nervously fluttering one of her hostess.

"I am Ilse Harveling, yes. And you are Mrs. Lawrence who has brought this old place back to life."

"Life!" the other interrupted her. "No," it was as if she gave herself an order, not addressed her guests. "We shall have time—Oh, but I am so glad you could come! Eliza is ready to serve us what this locality calls a 'spread'—she has a wealth of old recipes—her mother was from a Stuben family and, if they did not allow any pleasures for the eye or the ear, they did not stint at the table."

She led them on down a short passage into a long room which had once been the kitchen. The huge fireplace still had its spit and pot chains in place. The door to the brick side oven looked ready to be opened for instant use.

There were two settles at the deep arch of the hearth opening. A long dresser with an enticing wealth of old blue-and-white wear stood against the wall. But the larger part of the room was occupied by half a dozen small tables each covered with a blue-and-white-checked cloth, the attending chairs bearing matching cushions.

Ilse and Louise were firmly steered to one of the tables, urged on by the hostess as if they were famine refugees who must be fed at once. As soon as they were seated, Mrs. Lawrence vanished through an opposite door, probably to summon the "spread" before they could really adjust to their surroundings.

Louise's eyebrows rose a fraction. "Well?"

Again Ilse had been studying what lay about her. "Your friend is a badly frightened person. She is not like herself today. Is she?"

Louise shook her head. "I never saw her this way before. And I have been here a number of times. Jack and I often have Sunday dinner here. They've been open for almost a year. It's a treasure house, really. I can't believe that—"

She was silent as Marj Lawrence returned, pushing a table cart on which there were a number of dishes.

It appeared that Mrs. Lawrence was determined to play the part of hostess—during her time away she had once more gained full control—and as they lunched (and very well), she kept her flow of subject matter away from any problem. There was no mention of a shadowed past, and certainly not of any fatality within these walls.

As they lingered over coffee, Ilse quietly guided the conversation with simple questions concerning restoration problems, and she mentioned their having seen the deserted Stuben church. Marj Lawrence plunged in, into what was undoubtedly one of her deepest interests.

"Yes, the Stubens are all gone. Their settlement really lasted only for a couple of generations. Johanus Stuben was a prophet of the old school, and his successor, Rueben Straus, tried to carry on but they turned against him. Rueben was a queer mixture. Look here!"

She jumped up from the table and went to a ledge running across the mantel, to return holding an object she set down before Ilse.

"Now what do you think of that?"

It was a carved candlestick of aged wood, worn a little by years of handling. But its thickly patterned display of intertwined vines and leaves was still in strong relief. As Ilse picked it up and turned it around, she could see minute additions to those vines and leaves which were only visible to the seeking eye. Here was a face peeping from under a leaf—a face which was subtly nonhuman; there a weird insect was in half-hiding.

She cupped it with both hands and closed her eyes for a moment. No, she was not mistaken. Though it had never been used as she first feared, the skill which had shaped this had known secret things. As it was, it held no menace, but that menace could have been called forth.

"This was made by Straus—the pattern is foreign, perhaps Black Forest, perhaps Austrian."

"Rueben Straus made it right here." Marj Lawrence's hand swung perhaps to indicate this room. "He wasn't one of the first Stubens, though they say he was related to old Johanus. He and his sister, Hanna, came later. He was a hunchback and couldn't farm, but he earned his way as a carpenter and by making things like that. Only that one he made specially as a gift for Gyles Walden, the man who owned this house.

"Hanna Straus came to be cook here. By all the old gossip she was more than a cook. Gyles had a roving eye but no wish for a wife. Only the Strauses did not believe that. Hanna worked on filling the dower chest Rueben made for her, and he did what he could to provide her with a dowry.

"But when it came down to the actual calling in of the preacher, Gyles went off on a trip. He came back from the east with a wife—a rich widow—and she soon sent the Strauses packing."

Suddenly Mrs. Lawrence's flow of words slackened. "But all that ancient history can't have anything to do with—"

All her animation vanished as fear again showed in her eyes.

"Please," Ilse said quietly. She pushed aside the candlestick and put her hand gently on Mrs. Lawrence's wrist as the other woman stared at her with an almost childlike plea. "Tell us what you know of the past. It may have more bearing on your trouble than you think."

"But it can't. After all, people who died more than a century ago—"

"And who were those dead?"

"The story is that Hanna drowned herself—she was going to have Gyles' child. And Rueben buried her in the dower chest he had made for her. He quarreled with the Stubens, and they threw him out, saying that he had had dealings with the devil. He was found dead in the woods, and they said he had fought with Gyles. But no one ever tried to find out.

"Oh—" she was flushed and it was plain she was even more upset, "—maybe it is all my fault! I thought it was so clever to go hunting down all the old stories. I wanted to make a booklet, you see—just like those they sell at the old English houses open for visitors. There was the curse rumor, too—"

"A curse?" The quiet question stemmed the flow of words for a second. Marj Lawrence had dropped her eyes and was looking down at the crumbs on the plate before her.

"There was an old letter—we found it while we were cleaning out the long attic. That was a mess, and it took us just days—but the things we found—!" She touched the candlestick. "It was like a treasure hunt."

"The letter?" Ilse drew her back to face a subject it was very plain she did not want to discuss.

"Yes, well, it was sent to Gyles' wife after she had gone to New York. It was almost a threat—all about how her husband had paid, but the price not enough. It warned her against coming back here, but she did—only long enough to sell the house to the first of the Hartles."

"And the price Gyles was supposed to have paid?" persisted Ilse.

"He died—very suddenly—in his bed. Probably a heart—" Mrs. Lawrence's eyes went wide, and she stared at Ilse. "A heart attack," she finished in a voice hardly above a whisper.

"And the Hartles—they lived here for several generations, did they not? Was there any trouble recorded in their day—any stories?"

Marj Lawrence shook her head. "There's been nothing wrong. And we've been here for nearly two years. There have been workmen all over the place since we opened and after—and nothing except the things which always cause trouble: plumbing, heating, leaks.

"I—I didn't go ahead with the booklet idea; somehow I didn't want to. But we did give it the name people called it before the Hartles took over. 'Hex House' was so different. And everything was going so well until that Mark Walden showed up!"

"Mark Walden—Gyles Walden—there was a connection?"

"Maybe. He said something about wanting to see some of the older places around the valley. He was pleasant enough, but there was something about him—he was very reserved and stayed to himself. The police asked questions afterward, they and his partner—where he had gone and what he had done—but nobody had really paid any attention. The partner said he had been engaged in a big law case which had been before the court for a long time, and after it was over he decided he needed a rest. Somehow he ended up here." Once more her gust of speech died.

"Mark Walden . . ." Ilse repeated slowly.

"You know him?" Louise demanded.

"*Of* him. He was a criminal lawyer of standing in some circles. So Mr. Walden died of a heart attack?"

"Yes. He had left a note on the hall desk to be called at seven in the morning, as he wanted an early start to return home. The church fair was the day before, and I saw him there. He bought some old books and a cane— something he certainly had no real use for. When he didn't answer Tom's knock on the door in the morning, we waited a while, but he had been so insistent that we call him that Tom finally used the pass key. He was lying across the bed—dead. Tom called Dr. Albright, and the doctor got the police. They asked questions, but the autopsy proved it was his heart."

"You question that?" Ilse was aware that this volatility had been born of fear. Those hands twisting together, the eyes which no longer met hers, were reactions she well recognized.

"His—his face—" Marj Lawrence swung around in her chair as if to elude Ilse as much as she could.

"The face?" prompted Ilse.

"I—I saw—but Tom says that I just imagined it. I was afraid to say anything afterward to the doctor. By the time he got here it was—changed. Maybe—maybe I did just imagine it. But then why do I keep on having those horrible dreams?"

"You have dreamed? But first tell me what was it in Mr. Walden's face which frightened you so?"

"It looked—he looked as if he had been caught by some kind of monster. Oh, it does sound stupid. But he looked so afraid. And one of his hands had clawed at his own throat. That cane he had bought at the fair was in his other hand, one end of it caught at the top of the bed. But by the time the doctor came the horrible look had smoothed away. Only then the dreams began.''

"Yes, the dreams,'' Ilse said. "What about the dreams?''

"Always the same thing. I am standing in the hallway right outside the door to that room. I have to open it although I am afraid.'' She shivered. "It is dark inside, but still I can see. It isn't a room anymore at all but like a wood of trees with their limbs moving back and forth—reaching—

"I've managed to keep quiet about it, especially around Tom. He'd think I had lost my mind. But I can't keep on!'' Her voice arose shrilly, sliding into hysteria.

Ilse was out of her chair, leaning over the woman, holding both those hands in a firm, restraining grip.

"Louise, in my bag—the small bottle with the silver top.'' Her tone held authority enough to send the other scrambling to obey.

"Twist off the lid and hold the bottle under her nose!''

As Louise obeyed Marj took a deep breath—half choked, as a strong scent filled the room.

"Again.'' Ilse kept her grip on the woman's wrists. "Take a deep breath and hold it as long as you can.'' She watched sharp-eyed as the other followed her instructions. The taut body began to relax. Some of the flush faded from the other's cheeks. The moisture which had gathered in the corners of her eyes formed tears.

"I'm—I'm all right.'' She jerked to free herself from Ilse's grip. A moment later she added, "I guess you think I'm an idiot—dreaming dreams such as that.''

"Mrs. Lawrence,'' Ilse returned quietly, "you were moved to ask me here because of a danger which your spirit sensed, even if your mind cannot identify it. This is a troubled house, and the heart of that trouble must be found and cleansed. You spoke earlier of a curse—such are often a source for scoffing these days but, as with all things, there is often a kernel of truth at the heart of such stories. I wish now to see this room which is the center of your evil dreams and which has already sheltered death.''

Without another word, but as might an obedient child, Marj Lawrence pushed away from the table and led the way into a hall from which a staircase led up past paneled walls polished into life. There was another hall above, and the shut doors of what must be a half dozen rooms faced each other across a strip of tightly woven rag carpet. It was to the last of these that Mrs. Lawrence brought them, throwing open that door but standing aside so that they could enter the room or not as they pleased.

It was not a dark room, nor did it look in any way threatening. The walls had been papered with a pleasing design of green vines, showing here and there clusters of pale lavender flowers. There was a framed sampler on the wall and what might be authentic old engravings of European style, picturing ancient houses and forest-bound castles.

One wall gave center room to a tall, free-standing wardrobe of pre-closet days, the mirror door of which, though polished, was slightly misted by age. A more modern chest of drawers flanked the doorway. By the window in the right wall, which had short drapery repeating the vine pattern, was an inlaid table on which stood a lamp, and a chair, the arms and back of which were heavily carved, cushioned in green plush.

There was also a small bedside table with a very modern reading lamp in place beside a pile of books. Another chair, less impressive than the first, with chintz cushions promising more comfort, was drawn up by the second window, which broke the wall against which the head of the bed had been placed. At the foot of that piece of furniture itself was a dower chest painted with an age-faded pattern.

However, the bed dominated the room. The head, though well above six feet in height, was not solid. Instead, wands of dark wood had been woven like wreaths or vines. Yet there were thicker places where a number of those entwined by some freak of pattern and those portions showed evidence of carving.

The foot was not so tall but was of the same workmanship. And the wood, which showed no evident dust, still appeared overset with a filmy cast.

Mrs. Lawrence made no effort to join Ilse and Louise. And Louise herself stepped in no farther than just within the door. It was Ilse who advanced to within touching distance of the bed.

"You didn't have that here before—I didn't see it at the open house." Louise's voice was almost accusatory.

"It was one of our finds in the attic. We had a hard time cleaning it up. It had just been jammed back in the corner and was covered with dust."

"It is made of yew," Ilse said as if she had been paying no attention to them. " 'Churchyard yew' they used to name it, for it was mainly planted there."

Delicately, as if her touch might disturb something better not alerted, Ilse's fingers continued to trace the curves and hollows of those wands. Her head came up a fraction; she might have been questing as a hunter for a scent.

"There is something here, yes. Rage, hate, fear. But it sleeps."

Suddenly she drew back the hand which had rubbed the ancient wood. "By the same hand—this was also made by Rueben Straus. His mark is graven into this wood even as it stamps the candlestick and—something else—"

Ilse moved now to the head of the bed. It was made up ready for use with an intrically patterned quilt for coverlet. Ilse slipped off her shoes and climbed close to that billow of quilt marking the hidden pillows, bending her head very close to the carving. Once more she raised her right hand and finger traced a path of weaving.

"A wedding bed." It was more as if she murmured to herself than addressed those with her. "Symbols for good fortune, for fruitfulness, blessings—all here." She shook her head. "This was meant to bless, made by one who had knowledge, old, old learning. This," she moved a fingertip across one of those knotted spots, "is the moon waxing, bringing life. Here is the heart wish in full. Yes, this was meant to bless, not to blast."

She moved back a little but still knelt facing the head-board. Now she raised both hands to her temples, her eyes closed, her body tense. Then, as if a finger's snapping had aroused her she turned to the two at the door.

"A blessing which is poisoned by a curse—so twice potent. There is something locked here which I cannot reach without deep seeking. Mrs. Lawrence, is the room exactly the same as it was on that night of death? What changes may have been made?"

Marj Lawrence came reluctantly into the chamber and looked around.

"Everything is the same—except his things are gone, of course. And the bed linen, that was changed." She gave a small shiver. "That quilt I bought at the Kellermans' sale last spring, and it was the right size, so I put it in here. We had not used it before."

"Otherwise all is the same?" Ilse persisted, sliding down from the bed.

"Quite the same."

Ilse's right arm moved; her hand, palm flat, was held out before her as if to sense some energy arising from the floor. She had reached the wardrobe and stopped, in mid-step, her hand swinging as if it had been ensnared by a cord and jerked in that direction. In a moment she had the mirrored door open and was looking within. Then she went down on one knee to feel along the floor. There sounded a rattling and she brought into light a cane.

The length of most of its surface was smooth, but the top had been carved into a twist of vine. As Ilse swung her find into a patch of full sunlight they could all see a small head which was nearly concealed by a curve of that carven vine.

"Made with love," Ilse said softly, "made for a gift with love and admiration. She who wished it loved deeply. Then—" she frowned. Her finger pointed but did not quite touch the shaft immediately below that carved head, "This!"

"What?" Louise pushed forward to look over her friend's shoulder.

"Something of the dark—perhaps meant as a warning—or a threat—"

"But that is the cane Mr. Walden bought at the fair—at the white elephant table!" Marj joined them. "How did it get here? I thought we packed it with all his other things. He was quite taken with it—told Tom it was a real bargain. It must have fallen down in there and been forgotten."

"This was in his hand when he was found?"

"Oh, yes. The top of it was caught in one of those twists of vine on the headboard. He must have been looking at it when—when—" her voice dwindled.

"Yes—when. Now I must tell you this, Mrs. Lawrence.

In itself there is only a hint of darkness about the bed, in this cane. Together—together there could be a change. So—we shall see. I must spend the night here and, with what I know, try to find the core of this evil."

Louise protested at once and, more slowly, Marj Lawrence offered some token opposition which Ilse swept away. It was decided that she would return later and check into the disturbed room.

"Tom wants to just shut it up," Mrs. Lawrence said. "But it is better to know the truth, isn't it?"

"Evil is as a spot of rot upon an apple," returned Ilse. "Unless it is cut away, it will spread. You do not want to merely lock the door upon something which may taint your whole house."

Louise continued to protest as they drove back to her home until Ilse said firmly: "I told you, my dear, those who are gifted must return what is asked of them. Now, if you really wish to be of service to me, let me ready myself for what is to be done."

She helped herself to the contents of various herb containers, many of them her own gifts to her hostess, and brewed a pot of a dark liquid which she strained and drank at intervals during the afternoon. She chose only a small portion of fruit for her supper before she refused Louise's offer to accompany her back to Hex House. Marj Lawrence welcomed her eagerly.

"We have no guests tonight, and Tom is at a lodge meeting. I'm all ready—"

"No, Mrs. Lawrence." Ilse spoke with authority which could not be questioned. "This I must do myself. If you wish, you may remain in the hallway, but otherwise it is not safe. This is a force which is malign—it has already killed."

She turned on the lamp by the bed, focusing it directly on the pillows where she folded back the quilt. On the sill of each window she placed a small packet. Then, from her overlarge tote, she brought out a pair of blue candles which she set in holders Marj Lawrence provided and placed on the dower chest at the foot of the bed.

Having made a minute inspection of the now-bared sheets and pillows, Ilse lifted the cane which she rubbed for its full length with a rank smelling cloth. Now she again busied herself with the bedclothes. The pillows she put in a straight line lengthwise down the bed and then pulled the sheet up over them.

The cane was laid carefully beside that semblance of a body. From the tote Ilse brought out a small tightly closed flask. She wet her fingertip with its contents and brushed across the top hump of pillow which might be a head.

"By the White Way, The Light Way, the Right Way, here rests one Walden. So be it by all that stands against the Dark!"

A snap of light switch and the only illumination now came from the candles. Yet it was enough to give full sight of what was happening.

Ilse had withdrawn to stand at the foot of the bed squarely between the candles. She could only improvise, and she had. But now she centered all her inner consciousness on what lay before her. Almost in the subdued light it did seem a body rested there.

She shut out the thought of time. Time was born from the acts of humankind—it might mean nothing to what lurked here. *Lurked*—yes. She was right—there was building that feeling of another presence, of age-tattered but still-strong emotions: fear, rage—hate?

The cane sprang like a piece of iron seeking a strong magnet. Its head clicked against one of the knots in the headboard. Then—down that connecting rod speared a thrust of darkness—as thick as one of the wands from which it had been born.

It struck against the top pillow and at the same time there belched forth a stench of old rottenness, a wave of unhuman menace beyond all bounds of sanity.

Ilse's lips moved in words as old as time's meaning could be measured. With both her hands she raised the old christening flask to her teeth and worried out the stopper. Then, holding the bottle in a fierce grip of fingers laced tightly together, she threw its contents at the heaving mass on the bed.

There came such a burst of flame, such a roaring in her head, as if not only in the room—such a scream of heart-piercing anger as made her sway with its force.

That threshing on the bed stopped; the cane lay across the rounded covers. What had been here was gone.

"What was it? Will—will it come again?" Marj Lawrence crouched by the door.

"It was the murderous will of one who had black knowledge and sought to use it in revenge. Rueben Straus made these: the bed for his sister's wedding, the cane perhaps for her gift to her lover. But since Rueben had some glimmer of mistrust in him, he put in also a demand for justice if there was any sorrow for the one he loved. Instead of gifts these became curses.

"Mark Walden could indeed have been blood-related to Gyles, or else perhaps he only shared some deviousness of spirit. So Rueben's hate made a trap . . ."

"But—but it is gone?"

"I only banished this manifestation." Ilse was very tired. "Fire cleanses best. You must see that this bed, the cane, are burned and the ashes well scattered. This doorway must be so closed."

"Yes, oh, yes!"

Ilse, looking at the other woman's drawn and haggard face, believed her.

MUSHROOM TEA

by David Bischoff

David Bischoff is active in many areas of the science fiction field, whether it be writing his own novels such as The UFO Conspiracy *trilogy, collaborations with authors such as Harry Harrison, writing three* Bill The Galactic Hero *novels, or writing excellent media tie-in novelizations, such as* Aliens *and* Star Trek *novels. He has previously worked as an associate editor of* Amazing *magazine and as a staff member of NBC. He lives in Eugene, Oregon.*

His coffee mug squeaks.

Kromcek's been trying to access a particular webpage without much success, hunkering over his computer in his little RomTech cubicle, when he hears this strange little high-pitched sound. His CPU? Ear against metal shell. No, nothing in the machinery. He leans over and checks below his feet. Has some mouse of the biological persuasion somehow invaded the neat halls of this computer company and now is lying amidst the cables below his feet?

He sees a pair of shapely legs below the partition. Cynthia Adams, across the way from him. She's worn a dress today for some reason. Maybe a hot early dinner at Xenon's after work or something. Lucky guy.

No sign of any rodents.

The squeak again. Startled, Kromcek hits his head on the desk bottom, making an awful noise. Cynthia Adams looks under her desk.

"You okay, K?"

"Yeah. Just thought I heard a mouse down here."

"Okey doke. Good hunting," she says, blonde hair spilling and a 'yeah, right' look in her eyes. She goes back to work, but makes sure to cross her legs and sweep her dress down over her shins. Oh, great, Kromcek added to his inner monologue. Now she thinks I'm not just a geek, but a geek that wants to look up her dress.

The squeak again, this time from up above again, and Kromcek doesn't hit his head. This time, he gets up, checks around his desk and as calmly as he can, determines the direction the squeak is coming from.

His coffee mug.

Squeak, it says. And, perhaps even just a little less audible:

"Help me! Help me!"

Warily, he takes the drink by its handle.

It is one of those plastic thermos Dunkin-Donuts-thermos-style mugs you can refill cheap. Big. He saves ten cents a cup at Safeway by not using their paper product, gets a twelve-ounce supply of coffee and then fills the rest to the brim with skim milk. Only problem with the thing is that it's hard to keep clean. Light brown stains mar the face. The decal is half worn off, making it look as though it reads: DU DO.

And now his thermos mug seems to be speaking to him.

Of course, it's just imagination. Words do not come from coffee or their containers. Words come from tvs. Words come from computers. Words come from radios. Words come from CD players. Words come from telephones and loudspeakers and sometimes from cars when people hook up loudspeakers to their horns to be obnoxious. Words come from certain kinds of birds.

Oh, yes, and they also come from talking dolls.

Um, and biological-type people, too.

Not from thermos mugs, and not squealing "Help me, help me!" like the guy from that Vincent Price '50s movie, *The Fly*.

"No, you're not imagining things, Kromcek, I am speaking to you, and I am your thermos. Would you mind turning off that webpage? I find it particularly creepy and I think its peculiar radiation emissions are messin' with my brown matter. That's coffee to you, and the equivalent of your gray matter, only much more temporary."

Kromcek looks around, to see if anyone else is hearing what's going on here. No. Everyone else is in their booths, doing office stuff or answering phones or explaining to people how to use the software that's stuck.

He looks back down at the mug and the very fact that he accepts this, tells you something about his personality.

"Okay," he says. "I don't care much for women dressed in rubber anyway." With the mouse and its attendant pointer he clicks the off area of the WebCrawler Web-Browser. Mr. Cartoon Spider disappears with a 'Slinging off' stutter from the voice box on the computer and Windows grows again on the monitor, like some graphic garden.

"That better?" he asks.

"Ahh. Yes. *Much* better," says the thermos. "Thank you."

Kromcek has always hoped for some inanimate, unexplained object to speak to him. People were so frightening when they talked, and objects . . . well, objects were so much more a part, it seemed to him, of some matter/energy matrix that *really* had its earlobes pressed against the pulse of the universe. Inanimate objects could maybe tell you secrets. Besides, they were always weird smart asses in comics or cartoons or stories, and Kromcek has always wanted to speak with one.

"Let me get this straight," he says. "When you have coffee in you . . . I mean, you're saying that at that point you're a sentient being."

"Uhmm . . . Yes. IQ entirely dependent upon the grade of coffee. Up till now I've been a proverbial moron," said the thermos coffee cup. "Now I'm your very own ET. Your alien pet, sir, at your service. Here to befriend and guide you."

Generally he fills the cup from the industrial strength generic brand favored by the brewers in the backroom of RomTech if not at the other place. Today, however, he stopped at the top place in Eugene, Full City Coffee, and treated himself.

"Yikes—you mean I've been drinking your brains?" says Kromcek.

"You think in human equivalencies. Not really appropriate," says the coffee cup. "Hmmm . . . Suppose I compare the interaction to . . . Umm . . . No, that analog is inappropriate. Yes! How about . . . Drat. No, that's silly. Look, if I had shoulders I'd just shrug. Just take my word for it. It's no problem. My particular space of being, my consciousness is just not comparable. You just enjoy yourself, okay? Drink up whenever you care to. I'm sorry I even spoke. This is very awkward. We're not supposed to, you know. That website was really, really annoying me and maybe the particular blend of milk and coffee and sugar you placed in me makes me . . . well, a little peevish."

"Look, no problem. Long as I've got you, though—there are maybe a few questions I have for you."

"Questions? Sure. Why not? I guess the cat's out of the bag."

"You must know secrets of the universe. I mean, being plastic and everything . . . you must see how matter and energy intertwine and relate and maybe you can tell me some stuff."

"Oh. You want faster than light drive? The secrets of time travel?" The coffee cup ruminated. "No . . . Wait. I know. You want the secrets of consciousness. You figure, heck, a self-conscious Dunkin Donuts coffee cup should know some of those sacred, esoteric secrets that elude the grasp of peoplekind like a wet bar of soap."

"I am self-conscious," said Kromcek. "I'm an awkward boob. That's my problem." Absently, he picks up the coffee cup and sips thoughtfully.

"Ah! My frontal lobe!" squeaks the Du Do cup.

"Sorry."

"Look, no problem, brains come and go. But if you want this configuration to remain more or less the same for now, lay off."

"Nervous habit."

"Tell me about it. Every day I get tipped more than the hottest topless dancer in the country. Sheesh."

Kromcek feels better. Snappy dialogue. Just like in one of those cool stories.

"This is it," says Kromcek, leaning forward hopefully toward his stained cup. "There's this girl . . ."

* * *

KROMCEK'S DIW (Desert Island Women)
Cindy Crawford
The Women on that show Friends (except for the ugly
    one)
Claudia Schiffer
Pamela Anderson
Marilyn Monroe (age 29)
Caroline Monroe (circa *Kronos, Vampire Hunter*)
Veronica Carlson (circa *Dracula Has Risen From The
    Grave*)
Betty Paige
Kristy Moore.

"One Northwest Life Bitter," Kristy Moore puts his pint
of beer down before him with a tart smile. "T.G.I.F. huh,
Jimmy?" She pulls out her waitresses' pad, scribbles, and
puts the paper down.

"Uh, yeah. Right. Thanks, Kristy."

She's off to help someone else out in the Oak Street
Brewery and Cafe. She's about twenty-five, Kristy Moore,
and she's still chipping away at a degree at the U of O,
supposedly. However, slacker life is such in Eugene, Oregon, that time has gotten unstuck in a post-Grateful Dead
kind of way, and somehow, when there aren't all that many
good jobs out there anyway, life just kinds of flows like
LSD molasses. Kromcek knows this, but then Kromcek has
always had a way with machines and tests and stuff and
Kromcek therefore whizzed through school, got himself an
okay job and now is just rotting in the stasis of his mental
and endocrine juices and the radiation of his computer
screen and television and stereo.

This is Kristy Moore. Long brown hair. Large hips and
large lips. Close-fitting clothes. Killer perfume. Deep dark
eyes and pouty lips that make her look deep and sad and
bedroomy when in repose. When smiling, just sparkling and
full of life and wonder. Kristy Moore is witty, funny, hip,
quixotic, nutty, sharp, deeply feminine, and best of all she's
nice to Kromcek.

True, she works here, and this pub is a part of a chain
that trains its people to be casual Northwest friendly, and
gives them the kind of benefits and flexible hours that keep
the sparkle in their bon mots. Kristy is part of the well-

educated, underemployed, Generation X, products of a gene pool unblemished by war, pestilence, or disease and growing healthy, TV-suckled sharpies to flap toward the turn of the New Millennium like spawning salmon. . . . Only mostly just hanging around, smoking dope and drinking beer in easier waters.

Kromcek is nuts about Kristy Moore, and now, he thinks: T.G.I.F? He looks down at his beer.

Thank God it's Foamy. Damn. That's what he should have said. Something witty, something quick. She wouldn't think he was such a geeky slug then. No, that's not the problem really, he remembers. He's really not a geeky slug, he just *feels* like one sometimes. He gets all goofy and tongue-tied when he tries to talk to her. Odd, because it's not like he hasn't had a girlfriend before, down in California. He even dated some back in college. Hell, even though he's single, he even dates some now, although it's not like there are a whole lot of single women who aren't either too young or too lesbian here in Green Eugene.

He sips at the beer and it bites back, with the strong sour taste *all* these beers have, from stout through ale through lager. In fact, he doesn't even really *like* these beers super much, there are much better breweries in town, no question. He just likes the atmosphere. Homey and oaky. It's in an old house with a fireplace and it looks, well, comfy and hospitable, unlike his own rat's nest of an apartment where he mostly hangs out, reading or watching videos or listening to his CD and vinyl collection or logging in on the Net, or playing games or any of the other avocations of his rich, rich life.

"It's simple," his alien pet coffee mug's words ring in his mind, clear and plain. "Try."

"Try?" he'd answered, baffled.

"Yeah! You think that's not a turn on for women? Look, what we've got here is a classic boy/girl thing. You know, this has been going on for hundreds and thousands of years and you know what, it still hasn't gotten boring to humans. But if you just sit there like a dunce, slurping the beer or chomping burgers . . ."

"I usually eat soup and a tuna sandwich. And the fries there are just amazing."

"Whatever. Just let her know you're interested, get her

to think of you as a guy who likes to do what she does. I mean, what do people like her do after work in this town?"

"I'm not sure."

"Well, find out! Info, info, info. Data, data, data. The more you know, the more you don't blow. Fact gather. That's the secret. Now . . . before my thought medium disappears down your gullet for now—and mind you, that's no problem, that's the nature of reality . . . in fact it may just give you the caffeine kick you need to send you on your way for a finally fulfilling love life . . . before you drink me . . . do me a favor?"

"Uh, sure. . . ."

"Think of me like the Scarecrow in Wizard of Oz. I need a brain. Quality arabica beans, no robusto. I prefer South American . . . of decent pedigree. . . . I mean, home's fine or brew it here, but if you really want to help me out, Starbucks' at the very least. And by the way. You need some really fulfilling answers? Try filling me with that fungus tea."

"What?"

"Just ask any hip health store clerk. They'll know what I'm talking about." The coffee thermos mug quivers a bit. "Oh, whoa. Fungus tea. I hear *that's* a trip!"

He'd nodded then, but it hadn't been easy to drink that coffee, even though it never even squeaked once while he'd sipped it while poring over the program he was supposed to do documentation for by next week. He felt bad because he far preferred systems analysis, but right now, that's what they needed him for. That and sometimes answering the phone. That was the kind of company this was, only a few people were specialists, most were barely functional and *all* were *dys*functional.

The beer goes halfway down by the time Kristy Moore returns with his Clammy Clam Chowder and Sea Breeze Tuna on Rye. She leans over and her hair falls like a whisper of magic.

"Kristy," he blurts.

"Yes?"

"You know I tend to stay home a lot."

"Except when you're off at the Bijou Theater, I guess, huh? A guy with your cinematic knowledge must take in a lot of video."

"Oh, oh, yes. A great deal. Too much probably. I should get out and meet other people. Like, if you would want to go out with friends after work, where would you go."

She shrugged. "Larry's Loft. That is, if I don't go home and crash. Probably where I'm going tonight with these loons." She gestures at her coworkers, young men in loose clothes, long hair tied behind their backs with arts-and-crafts binders. "Friday night is Long Island Iced Tea night."

"Oh, right," says Kromcek. He's heard about Larry's Loft, but for some reason, he's never tried it. It's a slacker place, open late, that's fashionable with college students of age—and, given a good fake ID . . . "Thanks."

She's off again. The nice thing about Kristy, and one of the reasons Kromcek thinks about her in a wankingly romantic way is that when he can sit in the bar area, if she's not busy she'd stop and yak a little bit with him. Tonight's busy though.

But . . .

Bingo!

He's got the info.

He looks at his beer and wonders what would happen if he filled his thermos with Thunderbolt Stout.

KROMCEK'S TOP TEN SO-BAD-THEY'RE-GOOD
B MOVIES
1. BRIDE OF THE MONSTER
2. THEY SAVED HITLER'S BRAIN
3. BLOOD OF GHASTLY HORROR
4. THE GREEN SLIME
5. YOR, HUNTER FROM THE FUTURE
6. DR. BUTCHER, MD
7. EROTIC RITES OF FRANKENSTEIN
8. CLONES OF BRUCE LEE
9. SLAVES OF THE CANNIBAL GOD
10. KROMCEK DOES KRISTY

EXT. HARRY'S SODA SHOP—DAY

This is CLARKSTOWN, an average midwestern town of the early sixties. A group of TEENAGERS, mostly female with bright haircuts and scarves around their necks, wearing tight jeans and blouses, are hanging around, lovingly sip-

ping sodas through straws and cherry-lipsticked lips. In the
background we have Dick Dale Surf Music.

CLOSER—FAVOR JUDY AND KRISTY
Two luscious chicks, a blonde and brunette. They stretch
languidly, showing off their curvy figures.

JUDY
This town is just so *boring*.
When are the sixties ever gonna get started?

KRISTY
Tell me about it. What I need are some drugs and loose
clothes and Beatles music . . .

JUDY
Yummy yummy yummy
I've got love in my tummy.

KRISTY
(snaps fingers)
Uhm, more like . . . Inna gadda da vida
or something cool like that.

NAMELESS TEEN QUEEN
(pointing)
Hey, look, guys . . .
Isn't that the Amazing
Colossal Man? Wonder's what he's
like to make out with?

JUDY
Don't bother. He's
already going steady with
the 50-Foot Woman.

KRISTY
(getting all animated)
Wow . . . Look . . . a guy on a motorcycle.
Keen! He's coming this way.

POV—MOTORCYCLIST

He's pulling up to the SODA SHOP. He STOPS and looks
at the teenager.

CLOSE—MOTORCYCLIST
It's KROMCEK. He's riding a Black Lightning. He's lost
about thirty pounds, he's got big shoulders and he's not
wearing a helmet, just real cool Ray Ban sunglasses.

KROMCEK
Hey, kids. How's the suds here?

JUDY
No beer here. It's a soda shop.

KROMCEK
Gee—that's too bad. I've got
a couple cases back in my pad, coolin'
off. Got some keen platters I just bought . . .
And some M, if you like that kinda thing . . .

FULL SHOT
The girls like it a lot. They wave their hands eagerly in a
Me, Me, Me! kind of way.

JUDY
Gee . . . aren't you Jimmy Kromcek, the
star of *Teenage Vampires, Hot Rods
From Hades,* and *High School Werewolves.*

KROMCEK
Yep. But that's just for fun.
Mostly I play sax in a hot new group
called the EXOTIC SOUNDS OF JIMMY KROMCEK.

CLOSER
He takes off sunglasses. Beautiful Paul Newman blue eyes
shine. He smiles and his white, white teeth sparkle.

KROMCEK
Say, aren't you Betty Paige's
kid sister?

KRISTY
I don't have any idea who
Betty Paige is . . . but I sure
do dig a crazy sax. Would you play
a song for me, while I drink some
underage beer and look at your extensive
record collection?

KROMCEK
Um . . . I dunno . . .

The other women stand and bounce like healthy cheerlead-
ers, waving their hands enthusiastically.
GIRLS
(Me! Me! I'd love
to go!)

KRISTY
Bats her beautiful green eyes. She undulates provocatively.
I truly *dig* sax.
(She picks up a purse and digs out a rubber from it, wig-
gling it.)

KROMCEK
Well—okay. Okay,
hop on.

KRISTY GETS ON CYCLE
Hugs up close to Kromcek.

EXT.—MOUNTAIN TUNNEL

Motorcycle holding Kromcek and Kristy speeds along and
enters dark hole of tunnel.

KRISTY
Weeee . . .
KROMCEK
I'm spinning out, babeeeeee. . . ."

  Kromcek burbles awake.

"Babeee . . ." He murmurs to himself, hazy and momentarily having absolutely no idea where the hell he is.

Woozily, he pushes himself up.

He's in his living room, on his blobby couch. On the coffee table nearby are strewn copies of *Scream Queens, Psychotronic Video,* and other fringe movie magazines, book and video order catalogs, *Locus* and a batch of old ACE doubles he purchased recently and has not yet placed in plastic bags (the GOOD ACE doubles, mind you, from '56 to '65 or so). There's an *X-Files* comic book winged open, and a stack of *Inner Sanctum* videos he's just received from Foothill Video, in Tujunga, California.

The TV in front of him is playing out the last few minutes of *Weird Woman,* the first of three film versions of Fritz Lieber's *Conjure Wife.* Lon Chaney Jr. is in all these *Inner Sanctum*s, and he's just as wooden and bad in this as the others.

Beside Kromcek is his coffee mug. Only now, the DU DO container is half-filled with Thunderbolt Stout. Experiment. He's bought a half-gallon bottle from the brewery and has drunk a good deal of it.

The movie is almost over, which means he's been asleep for close to an hour now. This is good, since it has given him a chance to sober up some.

"Shoo . . ." says the alien mug. "Finally awake, huh?"

"Some dream," he says, shaking his head to clear it. This has not been an unusual dream, however, since Kromcek often dreams in cinematic grammar. His dreams are always like movies and once, when he picked up a copy of a book called *Lucid Dreaming,* he actually attempted to script out a series of spectacular scenarios linking him to some of his top ten movie stars. Alas, what he got instead were falling dreams, his least favorite, and he ceased and desisted from those particular dream endeavors.

"Wouldn't know what the shit you're talkin' 'bout," said the mug. It is clear that the mug is drunk. This is not an unsurprising result, but still the very fact that it's a talking mug is still significant and not a matter to be sneezed at. So far its advice has been sound.

Kromcek sits up. He looks around. All about him in the room is decorated in movie posters. Bookshelves bulge with albums, CDs, book collectible and otherwise. This is artful trash clutter, fringe culture effluvia. Vinyl and chemical and papery secretions of passions. Waltzes of mind with celluloid, polkas with vinyl, mambas with tape, boogies with magazines and foxtrot with books. This is the clutter of thousands of joyous moments in a frieze of alphabetized history. This is the shell-mind of Kromcek, in stuporous repose.

"I was wondering if it would just be coffee," he says, almost to himself. "I'm not sure I like the result of this particular blend, though—"

"Yep." The alien pet mug hiccups. "Lasht time, we talked, I believe we discussed . . ." Pause. A burp. "Some female or another."

Some female all right.

Kromcek suddenly feels very depressed.

Here he is, his brain filled with beer, talking to a thermos mug named DU DO whose brains *were* beer.

It seems, somehow, less a plot point in a story than a mistake. Here he is, back in his apartment, hip deep in his comfy sofa, the effluvia of his life teetering over him from every corner and shelf, and he has none of the particular forward momentum that he'd obtained from simply asking Kristy where she hangs and getting an amazing answer. The simplicity of speaking to her, as Mug-with-Coffee-Brains suggests, in a neutral environment is appalling. The medium is perfect. He can obliterate his nervousness with beer, and thus achieve a beatific attitude—enough to let his true spirit shine before her, and thereby commingle with her non-waitress essence.

True, he realizes as he examines his Mickey Mouse watch, it's not like she's precisely *there* yet at Larry's Loft. Hell, there's time, in fact, to watch two more of these *Inner Sanctum*s, read an article in *Draculina* and finish his *X-files* comic to boot. However, his inertia seems painfully eternal. He feels as though he will *never* be able to leave this couch. He senses that he is somehow stuck here, morally and spiritually, and though he might be able to pull himself into work from day to day to pay the rent on this couch and the food it devours and get away long enough to run the errands that pay for a roof over his couch and the electricity that runs its toys, he is doomed to linger here in its grasp, its invisible Chthulu tentacles wrapped around him lovingly and possessively. He fears—indeed, this is one of his nightmares—that he shall have to purchase a very large cemetery plot so that, when he dies, the couch can be buried with him.

"I dunno," he mutters. "Maybe I should just get a dog or something."

"Nonshense," says the mug. "Why get a dog when you got me? Now where were we . . . Woman. What the hell do you want with a woman anyway, Kromcek?"

He's not entirely sure. It's not like he's happy when he does have a girlfriend. He's read plenty of psychology and checked out his share of self-help books from the library. Trouble is, he simply cannot relate to them. He was never abused as a child, he's in fairly good health, he's got no problems with siblings or parents, he's on a perfectly even keel, employmentwise—he's on just the right upward curve. . . . And, dammit, even though he feels depressed now, he knows something about life that many don't. He's felt and seen things that your average guy never even dreamed of . . . he loves his books and movies and television, his life is full and vibrant with goals and enthusiasms . . . And yet . . . and yet . . .

He yearns.

There is something about Kristy Moore. He just knows that if, in some way, he can get more intimate with her that all the stored wisdom and passion in his life will simply explode and hurtle him into the dimensions beyond.

"Shut up," he says to the mug.

And he drinks down its brains in several gulps and starts building up his courage.

KROMCEK'S DESERT ISLAND DISKS

1. *Songs for Sinners*—Rusty Warren
2. *Kapa*—Exciting Sound of Milt Raskin
3. *Mondo Cane and Other Horror Music*—Ugella and the Viking Pops Orchestra.
4. *Voice of the Xtabay*—Yma Sumac
5. *Orienta*—The Markko Polo Adventurers
6. *Hot Rods and Dragsters in Hi Fi*
7. *Music to Be Murdered By*—Alfred Hitchcock
8. *Afro-Desia*—Exotic Sounds of Martin Denny
9. *Taboo V.2*—Arthur Lymon

10. *I Put A Spell on You, Kristy*—The Blues Thing featuring James Kromcek

This is the music that fills Kromcek's soul as he enters Larry's Loft.

It is quirky music, it is bizarre music, and it is the music of a life of quiet pleasures and gentle epiphanies. Individuality is all here in this music hall, and the melodies and counterpoint that intertwine do so in unique and odd ways. Most of all, it is music from Goodwill bins, shunned music, spat upon music, persecuted music, forgotten by the ramming guitars of muddy Grunge-Rock and loopy fripperies of Mainstream AOR Alternative.

It is the music that Kromcek identifies with now, and he uses it to soothe his fevered id.

Play that funky Xylophone, Martin D!

He understands that Lawrence Welk may be the next avenue he has to explore, but he is doubtful. He's never liked bubbles and polka much, and he associates Welk with his dead German grandmother, who never missed a show and who would feed him strudel as Welk intoned "Wunnerful Wunnerful."

He's not drunk, but he knows he shouldn't drive, so he's walked here to Larry's Loft, his B-movie fantasia of Kristy altering to hip noir. In this, he is a private detective, cool and competent. Alan Ladd plus a few inches. She is Virginia Mayo, spunky and challenging. Together, they track down the secret of the Maltese Godzilla. Boris Karloff, Peter Lorre and Bela Lugosi make guest appearances. Their dialogue is written by William Faulkner, Raymond Chandler, and Leigh Brackett with a score by Max Steiner. All tasteful, crisp black-and-white, mind you, a masterpiece in thirty-five millimeter.

Eugene at night seems to echo this noir frame of mind, grim and tattered. Steam rises from sewer grates and the sour smell of sawmills hangs in the air. I want to sleep in a city that never wakes up, thinks Kromcek. It is hard, however, to think of Eugene, Oregon, as a *bête noir,* let alone *noir.* It seems too bland, too harmless. He's never felt afraid to walk the streets at night, and he has no fears now.

Larry's Loft is a tacky little place adjacent to a Chinese restaurant. After nine, when the Chinese joint shuts, it rents out its booths to overspill from Larry's. It is 1:30, and the place is crowded. The air is blue with cigarette smoke. Kromcek coughs. He checks this room and the other room. There is no sign yet of Kristy. He takes off his beige raincoat and somehow finds a dinky deserted table, where he sits down, keeping his eye on the door.

Eventually he waves down a waitress. He orders a beer . . . and what kind of coffee did they serve here? She doesn't know, but he orders two cups. When the order comes, Kristy has still not yet arrived, although surely she has finished at her work. He takes a sip of the beer, pulls out the mug, and places it on the counter. He pours in the coffee and the milk and some sugar and then starts talking to the mug. Nothing happens except that the people next to him, playing darts, give him an odd look.

Hmm. Cheap coffee.

For a moment, he feels panicky. He feels abandoned. There is no one to get advice from. He drinks his beer and sits, keeping an eye on the door.

The blur of the cigarette smoke seems an omnipresent, omniscient thing, connecting all the people here, talking in a stirred grumble, into a kind of mass mind. He fancies he sees ganglia growing between nose-rings and shaven scalps, glittering and crackling with chemo-electrical impulses. He wonders what kind of consciousness might erupt from this mind-meld, what slacker Super-Being might rise up and slouch toward Seattle to be born.

Pshaw. Nonsense. Now, drinking, and looking at his mug, he's afraid that this has permutated from a Borges-scape, degenerated past a mere Philip K. Dick story and devolved into a mere Hollywood geek-meets-girl sub*Twilight Zone* goof. Reality, after all, is an elastic thing, and twists are the norm. He wishes his mug could comment on all this, but the mug stays mute and even the beer sags in his heart.

A few minutes past this nadir, however, Kristy walks in. She is with a group of five people, men and women, but doesn't seem particularly attached to any of them. And, more miraculous than a talking alien pet coffee mug: she sits with them at a table next to his, which has just cleared of people.

She doesn't notice him. In fact, she's not doing much, just kind of staring out of glassy eyes. Hard day, probably.

He knows what that's like. The group orders their drinks and Kromcek waits until Kristy sips some of her Long Island Iced Tea before he approaches her. It's not that this is some sort of plan, though—it just takes that long to build up his nerve. He's got no coffee mug to kick his butt. This is all Kromcek.

"Hi."

"Oh. Jim. Hi." Kristy's a little monotone.

"How are you?"

"Kind of spaced."

"Hard evening?"

"Yeah. You could say that—"

The others are busy chattering about something, leaving her a Kristy satellite, wobbling about a GenX planetoid. She's wearing the same jeans and blouse outfit she'd been wearing at the brewery, only she's got a coat over it which she wraps around herself now as though the place is cold, although it's really pretty warm.

This is it. The moment. He could bug off, get out, just forget the whole thing. Or . . .

He dips his 'or' in the water.

"Mind if I sit down."

Whew! Man, what a rush. He's done it, he's asked without prodding. This is better than the *Outer Limits*. He has control of transmission! He is controlling the vertical . . .

"Sure. Why not?"

Okay, she isn't exactly playing Lauren Bacall and inviting him to put his lips together and blow, and gee, she is about as lively as a stump. But he's asked, and now he can park himself beside her and A: get to know her casually and socially and B: try to be himself and let his true personality shine forth so, as the mug had pointed out, she could see him as more than just a gullet to dump beer down, a French-Fry John.

He sits down by her, and waits for his next *bon mot* to float up. When it does not appear, he forces himself to say something, anything:

"Kind of smoky in here, isn't it?" Oh, God, why didn't he get the mug to shoot out some fancy one-line conversation goosers.

She barely looks up. Her eyes gleam with a dull cast. "Yeah. You gotta cigarette?"

"Uhm . . . no. Sorry. I don't smoke."

No one else at the table volunteers to offer Kristy a cigarette.

"I think there's a cigarette machine over by the entrance. Can I get you a pack?"

"Hey, would you? That would be real sweet of you, Jim."

Fortunately the machine takes dollar bills. He feeds them one by one, and pushes the button for filtered Camels.

Inside, the machine makes gurgling noises. It clanks and whirs and whistles. There is the sound of a bomb falling, and an explosion. A creaking door, a spooky wailing.

However, fortunately, the cigarette machine does not speak to him. The soft pack flops out, along with a pack of matches advertising cheap mailing labels.

Judiciously, he plucks both out of the metal tray maw. No teeth, fortunately, clamp down.

"Could you open them for me?" says Kristy when he puts them in front of her. "I'm just rotten with cellophane."

"Yeah. I know what you mean. The new style CD packaging has been giving me trouble. So I got this." He hauls out his key chain, upon which depends a nail clipper. He uses the miniature file herein to tear at the package.

He lights the cigarette when it is in Kristy's mouth with the match that he's almost burned himself igniting. The smoke drifts up to link up to the drifting mass-mind.

"Thanks." The cigarette hangs from the corner of her mouth. "Glad you're here, Jimmy," she mutters. "This is good. This is real good. You and I . . . We get to talk now. Never . . . really . . . get much of chance . . . You can . . . tell me . . . some more about yourself . . ."

He can't believe his ears. Oh, joy! It's working, he thinks. However, he checks himself. He remembers that book he read last year, *Women Who Don't Like Men Much, And Why,* which said that it was a turn-off to women if you just blathered on about yourself, so calm down and make sure *you* ask questions, too, Meathead Male.

"Actually, you know, I'd be interested in hearing about you. How's school going . . . ?"

"Oh, wow, Jim, I, like can't talk much at the moment, know what I mean? I know it's not like me, old motormouth . . . but . . . I just can't . . . seem to get much out at the moment."

Well, that certainly put the ball in his court. He isn't quite prepared to play this way and Kromcek's a bit flustered. He's certain that she doesn't really want to hear about his video or record collection. He's already talked a little about that before, and whenever he's in on a lazy Saturday afternoon, sipping a beer, she asks for his recommendations for Oddball Video.

She prompts him. "What . . . is it . . . that you want out of . . . life, Jim?"

Her eyes are still vacant when she asks him this.

He thinks about this for a moment. Everything has been so overwhelming in his thirty-some years, he's never been able to actually put all this together. And if he did put words onto it, summarized things into those words (what . . . peace of mind, a happy family, world peace, the doll butcher cover of the Beatles 'Yesterday, Today and Tomorrow' album?) it would all seem so cheap and abbreviated.

Troubled, he realizes that there is a way around this:

"Okay," he says, suddenly and inexplicably articulate. "Here are Kromcek's Desert Island Top Ten Wants Out of Life.

1. A complete run of *Weird Tales*.

2. To give my father a hug and say that I love him without feeling strange.

3. To own a successful computer software company and program what I care to, when I care to.

4. To stop feeling bad about my mother dying.

5. To have a house big enough to hold a lot of collectibles.

6. To forget about my cat who died last year, so I can get another one.

7. Enough money to buy all the collectibles I want . . . but only in delectable increments.

8. To meet God and get things entirely straight about this universe.

9. Air-conditioning and a pool on the desert island.

10. Dinner with you on the Desert Island, Kristy. With an option for more."

He's delivered all of the above in a low, unsteady but very clear voice, not looking at Kristy, but looking at the wall. Looking at Kristy, he knows he will not be able to say what he feels because what he feels will be nervousness.

When he is finished, he realizes that he has been very imprecise. If he had enough money to buy all collectibles, after all, he would be able to get a copy of the complete run of *Weird Tales*. So number one should be changed. Nonetheless, he feels he's said what he felt, and that Kristy will get the idea in what is, after all, a format that is not only a clever pitch for a date, but enough of him to make her know who he is.

He looks at her.

She is slumped on the seat, head tilted on her shoulder. Her cigarette has fallen out and is smoldering on the rug. A dollop of drool is running from her lips onto her coat.

"Kristy!" he says. He stomps out the cigarette, and moves to shake her awake.

"Hey, guy," says one of the other table mates, for the first time acknowledging his existence. "Leave her alone. She's just a little numbed out, that's all."

The women laugh and whisper to each other. He hears a number of heavy duty drugs mentioned. The women giggle and their eyes glitter.

"Are you sure . . . I mean, this isn't—"

"I'm telling you, she's fine. So just don't worry about her okay? Drink your beer."

"I—" he begins, but he's interrupted by a clatter on the table that he abandoned to sit here. It's the coffee thermos mug, and it's *moving*. It's clattering up a storm, and in its squeaky little voice it's calling out his name.

"Get your butt over here!" says the mug.

He looks around. The others don't notice the mug's antics. Kristy is still out of it, but it doesn't look like she's going to hit the floor or swallow her tongue or anything dangerous.

He goes over to the table. "What's the matter with *you*?" he wants to know.

"Get me out of here!" chirps the thing desperately. "Man, this is a Nest!"

"What are you talking about . . . ?"

"Yikes, Kromcek. If I'd known what this place was, I sure wouldn't have let you come here, heartthrob or no heartthrob."

"You're crazy."

"Am not. Look at them. They . . . they . . . oh, God, I can't watch!"

Kromcek turns around. He is so stunned he falls back into his chair.

At the table across from him, the curly-haired head of a young collegiate-looking man is slowly peeling open. From moist brains an alien Tinkertoy-like apparatus lifts out, unfurl in double jointed, oily wonder and reaches out with tentacled talons, questing like radar. His drinking buddy's nose falls off, and a metal proboscis telescopes out, questing. The new limbs meet spark and begin to curl like mating snakes.

Across the room, these dances are being emulated but by no means imitated. The odor of smoke and alcohol are pushed aside by a bitter smell, a briny pungent something. . . .

"Take me out of here!" cries the mug.

"But, Kristy."

"Don't you get it, Kromcek. They want to make her one of them. Hurry up! Our lives are at stake."

Confused but panicking, Kromcek picks up his mug.

He starts to head out the doorway of Larry's Loft, but the pain inside him hammers so horribly, he stops.

"No," he cries out inside the din. "I won't leave you here, Kristy!"

"Hey! What are you? An idiot?" cried the mug. "Don't—"

"Shut up!"

He goes back in to save his beloved.

Saturday afternoon.

It's raining outside. The sky is low, gripping the mottled landscape like a soggy fist.

The layer of fungus rides the tea, white over black.

Kromcek's been brewing it for a week now, and it's happening just like the health food friend at Sundance Organic Food said it would, after selling him the "baby" fungus that started the growth.

Kombucha tea.

Manchurian mushroom tea.

Sounds exotic, like something inscrutable from a Sax Rohmer novel—and therefore quite appealing to Kromcek.

The white stuff is a symbiotic colony of yeast, lichen, and bacteria, technically a part of the fungus family. This ferments the sweetened tea below even as it thrives on it. The process is supposed to create "glucuronic acid" which helps break down toxins in the body. This doesn't mean much to Kromcek. He just likes the weird ring to the whole proceedings.

He has labeled it neatly, black magic marker on canning paper: SHUGGOTH FUNGUS TEA.

Now is the moment. According to the book he bought, the tea should be properly fermented now.

Kromcek pours it gently through cheesecloth into his coffee thermos mug. He takes the filled mug from the kitchen to his living room. The television is off. Several candles are lit here and there and they flicker against his records, CDs, and books. The air is filled with a vanilla-and-candlewood smell. He feels pleasantly relaxed, yet expectant. The German electronic group Tangerine Dream is playing through the speakers.

Kromcek puts the filled mug on the coffee table, which he's cleared of his latest catalogs and other junk. He sits on his couch and peers expectantly at the coffee mug.

"Hey there. Anything going on I should know about?" he says after a few moments of silence.

The thermos squeaks.

The squeak softens into a sigh and then a soft song. It sounds liltingly Arabic, mournful and yet prayerful. Then the song becomes a voice. "Behold," it says. "I am the Sacred God of the Mystery Cult."

"Hi there," says Kromcek.

He feels as though he's been waiting for this moment all his life. If there was ever a soul that needed salvation, it is his. If there was ever a person that needed redemption, it was him.

Here, finally, is hope.

"I've called," continues Kromcek, "because I need help."

"Of course, my son," says the alien coffee mug. "I have come to redeem the benighted of this dreary world. Drink me and be saved!"

Kromcek picks up the coffee mug.

His front doorbell rings.

Kromcek puts down the coffee mug, which squeaks disconsolately. He goes to the front door. Out front, her long skirt rippling a bit in a spring breeze, is Kristy Moore.

"Hey there, Jimmy!"

Kromcek's heart lightens. "Kristy!"

"Can I come in?"

"Um . . . sure." He lets her into the apartment and clears a space on a chair for her to sit down.

"I just wanted to thank you again for the other night." She looks down at her neatly tied boots. "I was really out of it. The gang shouldn't have been doing that stuff we had . . . You taking me home—well, I guess I could have gotten into a lot of trouble if you hadn't."

He smiles shyly. "I wonder if I should have butted in?"

She flips a hand nonchalantly. "Those bozos— Don't worry about them. What's the psychological term? Boundary problems?"

"That and alienization, maybe," he says.

"Oh, yeah. So much so! Aliens from inner space!" She looks over at his shelves of books and video tapes. "What a collection! You weren't lying."

He smiles. "Thanks."

"Smells like you're brewing some sort of tea."

He laughs. "Yes. Mushroom tea."

"No! That's supposed to be very healthy."

He looks down at his mug. He wonders if he dares— Sure. Why not.

"My mug says it's a sacred tea. Great for salvation and redemption."

Kristy blinks.

She looks down at the mug. Then she looks at Kromcek with astonishment, almost disbelief.

"Oh, my God."

Kromcek panics. He has let too much out. Surely now she thinks he is insane. He should have kept his mouth shut! He has said far, far too much!

He is about to retract everything, when she continues.

"You've got a talking alien pet mug, too?"

"Well . . . it . . . um . . . squeaks . . . that is."

"Yes, of course it squeaks! But that's not what I'm talking about! You said it talks to you . . ."

The actual nature of what Kristy has said begins to sink in. "Your Dunkin Donuts cup speaks to you . . . ?"

"Intelligently, if it's got good coffee!"

He smiles.

She begins to smile as well.

"You know, I was thinking about having a relaxing afternoon watching an old Vincent Price movie."

She brightens further. "Oh, I love Vincent Price movies. Especially his forties movies you don't see so often! Did you know that he played The Saint on radio?"

"Yes. I've got a few on tape."

"Really!"

Tingles of excitement pass over him.

Sometimes it is healthy living in a universe of metaphors, thinks Kromcek. And other times it is healthier to just keep them in your fantasies, celluloid, bookish, *fungoid*—and otherwise.

"Kristy?" He pauses and then blurts his question. "Would you like to watch a Vincent Price movie with me this afternoon?"

"Sure!" she responds, "As long as I can have some of your new sacramental mushroom tea!"

Thus, Kromcek is redeemed.

Thus he is saved.

And by the end of the Vincent Price movie, not only is all the tea gone and the alien pet mug silent once more.

But there has come into being:

Kristy and Kromcek's Top Ten Favorite Vincent Price movies.

THE ENCHANTED GARDEN

by Deb Stover

As a child, Deb Stover wanted to be Lois Lane, but once she discovered there was no Clark Kent, let alone Superman, she turned her efforts to fiction. Her unique time-travel novels have received Reader Favorite Awards, Reviewer's Choice, and Career Achievement nominations. Deb was selected as the 1997 Pikes Peak Romance Writer of the Year. Visit Deb's home page at http://www.debstover.com/ for more information.

THE Scottish Highlands.

Glendon didn't see the bee until it was too late. He tried a diversionary tactic, but the insect's wing caught him square in the jaw and sent him spiraling toward the nearest flower.

Heather. Just my luck.

The pollen would cling to his wings and make him smell like a pillywiggins for weeks. But he consoled himself by remembering his destiny.

Fate had smiled on him. What was a little pollen on a sunny day? A smug smile tugged at his mouth. As the new king and only remaining male of his race, his responsibilities would include ensuring the propagation of his species.

Twenty virgin brides awaited him.

Releasing a ragged breath, Glendon flapped his wings and attempted liftoff, but too much residue remained. Until the pollen dried, he was grounded.

It was a fine day for an afternoon nap, but he'd best find

a different flower. A lone violet caught his eye. Growing near the ground, as violets will, the plant provided seclusion and cool shade. He leaped to the ground, then climbed the violet and found a likely leaf. With a sigh, he settled himself for a well-deserved rest, and closed his eyes.

A short time later, a vile stench jerked him from his dreams, and breathing eluded him for a few agonizing moments as he came fully awake. Coughing and sneezing, Glendon blinked and tried to rise, but the cloying scent pressed down upon him. He was trapped.

Paralyzed.

"You ain't supposed to harvest there, Ian," a voice boomed.

"But them Yanks pay dearly for these weeds."

Both voices joined in raucous laughter. Footsteps came dangerously close. A giant bent toward the flower. Toward Glendon.

A human.

"Let me get this straight, Lisa," Penny Basinger said. "Organic flower fertilizer? Isn't that called manure?"

Lisa scowled. "Go ahead and laugh." She reached for a piece of celery. "I'm dying to know why you— the original human herbicide—are suddenly interested in flowers."

Penny gave her friend a crooked grin. "Sometimes it's hard for me to remember how serious you are about all this stuff."

Lisa sighed. "Try harder, because I *am* serious, and you're stalling."

"And I *did* ask for help."

"So how'd your talk go with your dad?" Lisa asked.

"Same old stuff." Penny replied. "A mere woman can't run the ranch, degree in animal husbandry or not."

Lisa stared, celery poised in midair. "The Lazy B's been in your family forever. He should want you to help run it and keep it in the family."

Penny sighed. "Yeah, I mentioned that."

"And . . . ?"

"He came up with something screwier than even I expected." Penny used her fingernail to trace water droplets down the side of her glass.

"What?"

"He . . . issued me a challenge."

"Uh-oh," Lisa said.

"You know my dad too well."

"I know *you* too well."

"That, too." Penny met her friend's gaze. "Okay, here's the deal. If I win the grand prize at the Garden Society's annual—"

"The one your grandma always won?" Lisa asked.

"Any other flower shows here in cattle country?"

"Good point."

"Well, ever since Grandma died, Dad's talked about getting the Society to name the award after her, since she won every year for the last twenty." Penny couldn't believe she was even considering this. "Cecelia Winston is the director, and—"

"The one who always came in second to your grandmother?"

"Yeah." Penny said. "She's the president now, *and* she knows I didn't get Grandma's green thumb."

"Uh-oh."

"Bingo." Penny bit into a carrot. "She's using me to get even with Grandma."

"I'm sorry."

Penny blinked and swallowed the blob of carrot stuck in her throat. "I *have* to win."

"But you murder anything with chlorophyll," Lisa said.

"Gee, thanks." Penny knew she was a plague on the flowers of Kansas. "But if I win, they'll name the award after Grandma, and then . . . Dad'll change his will."

Lisa gave a low whistle.

All this agony, just because of pride and chauvinism. "We both know I'm rotten with flowers, but *you* aren't."

"True."

"I've ordered some flowers from Scotland. They'll be delivered this afternoon."

"This'll be a nice change for you." Lisa flashed a smile. "And we can test the new fertilizer."

"Does this mean you'll help me?"

"Of course." Lisa stirred her tea.

"You're sure this magic fertilizer of yours isn't cow, horse, or sheep poop?" Penny asked.

"No," Lisa said. "The ingredients are things you already have. We mix it up and burn it in—"

"*Burn* it?" Penny straightened. "Waitaminute. Not in this dry weather, we don't."

"Ha. Ha." Lisa shook her head. "In your *fireplace,* then we mix the ashes with the soil. For extra zing, you spray it on, too." Lisa cleared her throat. "I do have one condition. . . ."

Penny eyed her friend suspiciously. "No blind dates."

"Not that." Lisa said. "No chemicals. This stuff is still experimental, though I've been getting some blowout results. I'm not sure what would happen if you mixed it with something else. Promise?"

Penny leaned back in her chair. "I might as well surrender now."

Lisa reached into her huge canvas bag. "Here's the formula." She retrieved a folded piece of paper. She continued digging, and pulled out a deck of cards, as well. "I think you need another reading."

"Keep those cards to yourself," Penny said. "Last time you said I'd meet a man."

"I only read the cards, Pen. Now about that fertilizer . . ." Lisa unfolded the piece of paper.

"Okay, let's hear this recipe."

"Formula."

Penny sighed. "If you insist."

Lisa flashed a smile. "I do. This is science, remember?"

"Fine." Penny stared at her friend. She'd known Lisa since kindergarten. They'd been through everything together—school, Girl Scouts, puberty, proms, and college. Penny watched Lisa read the recipe—formula, rather—while she considered the possibilities of her friend's obsession with woo-woo stuff. At what point had Lisa forsaken cheeseburgers and embraced sprouts? And, more importantly, why did that bug Penny?

When it came to her, the answer shocked her, but she couldn't deny it. This was the first thing in Lisa's life Penny hadn't shared. "Lisa?"

"Hmm?" Lisa looked up. "What?"

"Does this new lifestyle of yours have room for a carnivore like me?"

"You know better than that. What's a little animal protein between friends?"

"Good." Penny smiled.

"You need a man," Lisa announced.

"Where'd *that* come from?" Penny asked, then considered her actions the last few months. "Okay, so I'm a little tense lately. But it's not any man I need—it's the *right* man. And we both know there's no such animal."

"Not . . . necessarily." Lisa absolutely glowed—it was disgusting. "I'm seeing someone."

"Oh?" Penny asked. "Details?"

"He's wonderful." Lisa's smile shouldn't have been able to get any wider, but it did. "He's kind and gentle, in touch with his feelings, and he understands his connection to the universe. Are you sure you want to hear this?"

"I do, and I want to meet him, too."

"I'm not sure—"

"Dad's out of town, so bring him over for dinner tonight."

"He's . . . different, Penny," Lisa said.

"Different *how*?" Worry slithered through Penny, while visions of biker drug lords danced through her head. "I mean, different how?" she repeated more pleasantly.

Lisa laughed. "You're hopeless." She squeezed Penny's hand. "He owns the New Age store in town."

"Oh," Penny said. She kept a smile plastered on her face. "A business owner. How nice."

"That's right—a successful business owner. The shop's in one of those old Victorians over by the college."

"Not next to the Feed and Seed so the ranchers can stop in?"

"Very funny. The college kids provide a steady business, and I'm working there part time." Lisa's cheeks turned red. "He's the best thing that's ever happened to me."

"You couldn't have known him very long. Are you sure?"

"Very."

Penny couldn't spoil her friend's happiness. "I just want what's best for you." *And that's the truth.* "If you say he's wonderful, he's wonderful, but I still want to see for myself. Okay?"

"Okay," Lisa said. "I can't tell you how glad I am that's over. What time do you want us for dinner?"

"Seven?"

"Sure. By the way, Fred's a vegetarian, too."

"Fred?" Penny grinned for real now. Fred was such a nice, ordinary name. "Not Rathmel or Sajid or . . . ?"

"Nope, just Fred Simon."

A vegetarian named Fred. She could hardly wait to meet him. Penny pointed to the paper on the table between them. "Now tell me about this recipe—I mean, formula."

Lisa's smile lit her whole face. Fred, it seemed, had a magic touch with Lisa. Good—maybe some of the magic would rub off on Penny. She needed something—she'd missed out on the Basinger family's green thumb.

Maybe she should check Grandma's cedar chest for it. . . .

Glendon remained hidden, holding the stem of his violet as if his life depended on it. Well, it probably did.

Most of the heather pollen had dissipated, but some lingering effects of the human's foul concoction remained. His ability to move had returned, though his wings sagged miserably. Uselessly.

He shuddered. What sort of faerie king couldn't fly? He'd be a laughingstock. A failure. Even the thought of twenty virgin brides couldn't raise his spirits . . . among other things.

No one had touched the violet since uprooting it and dropping it, and him, into a box with hundreds of other flowers. All he could do was hold on, though he had managed to find a weapon by breaking a thorn off a neighboring shrub.

The humans had transported him a great distance. He'd even felt as if he was flying, though not with the wind-in-his-hair joy to which he was accustomed.

Now the box that had become his sanctuary sat forlornly beneath a huge tree. Tufts of white fluff flew from the tree and blanketed the grass, and the wind was the hottest he'd ever encountered.

He heard a sound and reached down to retrieve the thorn from where he'd stuck it in the soil. Sword firmly in hand, he looked beyond the green leaves overhead. Something peered through the foliage at him. A furry face.

A cat!

Pressing himself closer to the stalk, Glendon tightened his grip on the thorn and girded himself for battle. A white paw, claws extended, batted through the foliage and barely missed him. Glendon held his breath and waited—the beast's nose pushed through the leaves and sniffed.

The paw came in again, but this time its claws weren't visible. A nonthreatening rumble emitted from the cat's furry chest.

"Here, kitty, kitty."

Glendon relaxed somewhat, though he held his breath again as his feline visitor withdrew.

"There you are, Samantha."

The human's voice was definitely female, soft and lilting, almost soothing. Glendon wanted to see her, but decided not to leave his hiding place just yet.

"You leave my flowers alone," the voice continued. "Don't look at me like that. Yes, I said *my* flowers."

Glendon begged to differ. If these flowers belonged to anyone after this day, it was him.

"Lisa's going to make me some kind of organic woo-woo dust, so we don't need any kitty fertilizer to go with it. Got it?"

Curiosity tugged at Glendon. He released the stalk and climbed onto a leaf, craning his neck for a better view.

The human female stooped beside the cat, stroking its white fur. Her voice continued in that soothing, musical tone, easing his fears, though suspicion remained. The siren could very well be baiting a trap.

"Let's get these flowers into the greenhouse before Lisa and her new boyfriend get here. The sun is wicked." She straightened and approached Glendon.

He leaped down from the leaf and resumed his grip on the central stalk just as she lifted the box and started walking. The jarring motion shot through his bones, forcing him to clench his teeth to prevent them from rattling in his head.

She entered some sort of shelter, put down the box, and started pulling plants from inside it. Glendon waited, terrified. Would she crush him with her huge hands?

He watched her gloved hand hover over him—he gripped the plant and his sword with all his strength, poised to attack. But instead of smashing him, she gently lifted the plant from the box. With a thud, she dropped it into a container and pressed dirt around its base.

'Tis my fate to be buried alive?

Glendon heard the cat's voice and saw its white fur through the leaves. The beast placed itself between the plant and the human. Deliberately? Glendon readied his weapon again.

Laughing, the woman nudged the cat away. "Samantha, move." The human pressed more dirt around the violet, then stood and walked away. She returned a moment later.

"I hope I know what I'm doing." The end of a snakelike object appeared on the soil beneath him, spewing water from its mouth. Hoping to avoid the flood, Glendon climbed to the next leaf.

She walked away again, leaving the spitting snake behind. After a moment, the water stopped and the human returned.

"There, that should hold them until Lisa casts her spell— I mean mixes her formula. Of course, I'd love to use some *real* fertilizer, but I promised." She sighed. "I'd better wash up and check on the lasagna."

Glendon stared after the human's retreating feet and the cat's bushy white tail as one of the words he'd heard became agonizingly explicit to his muddled mind.

"Spell?" he whispered.

"This is crazy," Penny repeated as she watched Fred mix the concoction. "You call this fertilizer? Toss in a little oil and vinegar and you might have a pretty decent salad dressing."

Lisa looked over Fred's shoulder and shook her head at Penny. The silent communication came through loud and clear: *Shut up, Penny.*

Mr. Wonderful was a nerd in hippie skin. Penny'd bet her last dime that he'd traded in a slide rule for his tiger-eye pendant. The amber-colored stone, she'd been informed, was Yang—male and active.

So from that bit of evidence she'd completed her appraisal of Fred Simon. He was a nerd-turned-hippie—Rush Limbaugh in John Lennon's clothing. A man who preferred spinach to meat in his lasagna.

Lisa's rancher-father would've at least considered shooting Fred on sight.

Penny didn't object when Fred asked for a book of matches and headed for the fireplace. Weird as he was, this man clearly loved Lisa. Penny'd happily set fires in summer for the man who adored her best friend.

Within a few minutes, they were all seated in the living room with a small fire burning in the hearth. Outside it was only ninety in the shade.

She turned her attention to Lisa and Mr. Wonderful.

"So the formula works with the soil's nutrients?" Penny asked.

"Right, with a little compost and some earthly assistance." Fred pushed his wire-rimmed glasses higher on his thin nose. "After this blaze burns itself out—"

—and raises the temperature twenty degrees in here—

"—we'll gather the ashes and mix them together."

Penny watched Lisa slip her hand into Fred's and beam at him. They probably wouldn't react well to being told they were adorable. Giving herself a mental pat on the back for not saying it, she took a step closer. Thankfully, the fire was already dying. Fred swept the ashes into a bucket.

"We'll have to be careful of the hot embers," he said. "And we'll need some gardening tools." Fred carried the bucket into the kitchen and out the back door.

Penny followed Lisa, Mr. Wonderful, and Samantha out to the greenhouse. She retrieved her grandmother's gardening caddy.

Fred and Lisa stood there holding hands, the special fluorescent plant lights bathing them in silver. They looked like Druids or something.

Get a grip, Penny.

Fred took a shovel from the caddy. "I'll just put a little of the mixture in the soil around the plants."

Penny decided to take the first step in growing her Highland wild flowers. "I'll do this part. After all, I have to learn sometime. Tell me if I'm doing something wrong."

She took the bucket of vinaigrette fertilizer and the shovel. Kneeling beside the planters, she loosened the dirt and gently mixed in the ashes. With any luck, the damp soil would smother any hot embers. Behind her she heard Lisa and Fred intoning benedictions to the plants.

I can't believe I'm doing this.

"Save some ashes so we can mix a spray," Fred urged. "This formula's new and we've been getting impressive but wildly varied results, so watch how much you apply. This is science at work."

Yep, a nerd. Penny put her shovel full of hot ashes back in the pail.

Samantha stuck her nose in a small violet and purred. "Come here, fur ball," Penny said. She didn't want her pet to get burned or drenched in vinaigrette gone amok. Holding the cat, she straightened.

"All right, I've saved enough for a spray. Let's do it." She reminded herself this was all perfectly harmless now that the burning part was history.

"Take a look, Penny." Lisa pointed at the violet Samantha'd been exploring. "I think that puny one looks perkier already."

Perkier? How scientific. Somehow, Penny had trouble thinking of imported wild flowers as perky. She retrieved the sprayer, emptied the last of the ashes into it, then filled it with water.

"So I'll spray the same plants I treated the soil around," she said. "We'll compare them with the unsprayed plants in the greenhouse next week. How's that sound?"

"Perfect." Lisa was still holding Fred's hand. "Like Jack's magic beanstalk."

Where do I find the blood of an Englishman?

Penny swirled the spray bottle to distribute the last of the ashes, then gave the "puny" violet an extra good dose. Now all she needed was a giant to go with the beanstalk.

Or maybe a goose that lays golden eggs?

Smiling at her own foolishness, Penny straightened and turned to face her guests. "All done. Now we'll just wait to see what happens."

"Right." Fred looked down at Lisa and smiled. Looking at them, Penny could almost see time stop as they gazed at each other.

Penny turned away, letting them enjoy the moment. It was clearly time to send them home. They were starting to quiver like compass needles seeking magnetic north.

She put away her tools, then faced her guests. "Thank you both for coming to dinner . . . and for the fertilizer."

Penny escorted them from the greenhouse to Fred's car. A VW Beetle—she wasn't surprised. The security light on the front of the house made it impossible to pretend Penny hadn't seen the question in her friend's eyes.

Penny gave Lisa a thumbs-up sign. It was incredible, but after that Lisa looked even happier. And Penny felt at peace—her friend had chosen well. Fred was strange, but he seemed to be a good man and he adored Lisa. Nothing else really mattered.

Penny returned to the greenhouse to make sure nothing was on fire. Samantha's fascination with the puny violet continued. The cat buried her face in the plant again, then howled, leaping back as if something had bitten her.

Or burned her nosy nose. "That does it." Penny retrieved the garden hose and put the fan sprayer on the end to make a gentle mist. After turning the water on low, she dragged the hose over to the planters and started to sprinkle all the flowers, including those that hadn't been fertilized.

Whatever happened to plain, old-fashioned manure? That used to be enough to pacify the organic gardeners, and they had plenty of it right here on the Lazy B. Lisa hadn't said Penny couldn't treat the other plants with manure. Now *that* was natural. Penny moved to the other side of the planter, giving the violet Samantha'd been exploring an extra good dousing.

A rumbling, cracking, groaning sound suddenly erupted. Penny took a step back, still clutching the sprinkler. She stared into the darkness, watching the fertilized plants shoot toward the top of the greenhouse like a special effects scene from a cheap '50s SF flick.

Heather and lavender spiraled upward. Penny took another step back as a vine snaked toward her with spindly green fingers. Swallowing hard, she held her breath.

Something shiny and orange crawled from the jungle—strangely familiar black spots covered its back. It was a ladybug the size of a respectable turtle. The hair on Samantha's back stood on end, then she wisely retreated through the open greenhouse door.

Penny dropped the sprinkler. This couldn't be real.

"What in the name of all that's Fae has befallen me now?"

Penny blinked. Forget the mutant ladybug. The organic fertilizer. The cat. The giant flowers. She stood there, frozen to the ground.

A *man* stepped from the myriad of vines and blooms, shaking water from his hair. He paused a few feet away, glowering down at her. He, at least, was normal-sized.

The plant lights formed a golden halo around his head. He was beautiful. Muscles rippled along his arms and shoulders; taut golden flesh stretched across his abdomen. She jerked her gaze back to his godlike face. "Wh—who are you?"

He placed a fist on each bronze hip and straightened— tall, imposing.

Naked.

Terror surged through Glendon as he stood soaked and staring at the beautiful witch. *He* was proof of her awesome power.

Most faeries possessed the ability to achieve human form for limited periods of time and with much deliberation. But this time, he hadn't initiated the process. He was trapped.

"What have you done?" He took a step toward her. Her wide blue eyes were filled with fear.

"N-nothing." She shook her head. "Who . . . ?"

"Prince Glendon," he replied.

"Prince?"

"Aye." Something didn't feel right and he reached behind him. His wings! Fury replaced his fear. "What evil sorcery is this? *Why*?"

"All I did was—"

"Reverse the spell." Glendon glowered down at her. "Reverse the spell."

"Spell?"

"Where is this place?"

"Kansas." Her voice was soft and lilting. Deceptive. "Who *are* you?"

"Prince Glendon. I told you that."

"How did you get here?" She lowered her gaze. "Naked?"

Unashamed, Glendon lifted his chin. "Faeries don't embrace the cumbersome—"

"Faeries? Did you say faeries?"

"Aye." He placed his fists on his hips again. "I require your name, witch."

"Penny Basinger, and I'm *not* a witch."

A witch would not have given her name so easily, unless she was certain of his helplessness. Glendon grabbed her arm and pulled her hard against him. The shock of her softness meeting his body stunned him. For a moment, all he could do was gaze into her beautiful, deceitful eyes.

Magic, he thought. He placed some distance between them, though he didn't release her. She was powerful, and he had no doubt her spell had made him respond to her. Why else would he ache so to touch her? *Why* had she summoned him here and made him human size? He swallowed—only one reason made sense.

She wished to mate.

Penny's life was out of control. How many women had greenhouses boasting giant flowers *and* faeries, after all? Not to mention the mutant ladybug.

I don't believe this.

The naked hunk said he was a faerie. A faerie prince. *Get real.* But she he couldn't drag her gaze from his magical green eyes, nor could she deny the hunger she saw there. Well, she hated to burst his bubble, but she didn't sleep with strangers.

Faerie or no.

She looked beyond him at her colossal flowers, replaying the evening's events. Lisa had said something about "Jack's Magic Beanstalk." *No kidding,* Penny thought.

She looked the faerie prince in the eye. "Jack?"

"Glendon," he corrected.

"You're hurting me."

"Forgive me." He dropped his hands to his sides and genuine remorse filled his eyes. "But I must know what happened."

"That goes for both of us." *Anything to make the naked faerie prince go away.*

"You refuse to reverse your spell?"

Penny threw up her hands. "I'm *not* a witch." She blinked several times. Could Fred have cast a spell?

That was ridiculous. Faeries and giant ladybugs didn't exist. This was nothing but a bad dream, a waking delusion. In the morning she'd laugh about it.

Except for Glendon. He was no laughing matter.

"Tell me what happened, and maybe I can help," she said, no longer frightened. "And maybe you should put on some clothes." She couldn't think straight until he did.

He reached behind him, plucked a giant leaf, and wrapped it around his waist. "Better?"

No. "Yes, thanks." Penny cleared her throat. "Why don't you come to the house?" She led her uninvited guest to the back door. "I don't know about you, but I think *I* need a cup of tea."

Glendon followed her into the house, squinting up at the bright kitchen light. He walked around the room, staring at appliances, and flipped the light switch on and off several times.

"Have a seat," She hurried around the kitchen. "Would you like tea?"

"I prefer milk and honey, if you have it. No tea, please." He stopped playing with the lights, sat in a chair at the table, and watched her fill a cup. "What kind of milk is that?"

"Kind?" Penny said, confused, as she handed him a squeeze bottle of honey from the cupboard. "Cow, of course."

"Many thanks." Glendon upended the bottle and squeezed the substance into his hand, where he tasted it with his tongue. "Ah, clover."

The sight of his tongue lapping honey from his palm made Penny tingle. All over.

"Mercy," she murmured, turning to grab a silver spoon. She'd heard tales of faeries and their reaction to cold iron. No sense taking chances with Glendon and the flatware. She placed the spoon in front of him, taking the honey away before he could entertain her any further. She couldn't handle it.

She squeezed honey into his cup, then put the spoon in to stir it. Finally, she sat across the table from him and watched his eyes widen with wonder as he lifted the spoon from the cup to examine it as though it were alien technology. He was beautiful, and if he was real, he was nuts.

Certifiable.

But how had he appeared in her greenhouse? "Can you tell me what happened? How you got here?"

Glendon lifted the cup to his lips, then hesitated, watching her over the rim. "You are not a witch?"

"No," Penny said.

He took a long drink. "Very good. Thank you."

"Okay, spill."

He frowned. "You wish me to spill the milk? Why?"

"No, tell me what happened to you."

"This morn I was flying through the flowers and encountered a bee—"

"Excuse me?" Penny said.

"Do you wish to hear my tale?"

"I'm sorry." Lisa would love this.

"I crashed into some heather and the pollen grounded me."

"Go on." Penny watched his expression. He *believed* his madness.

"Humans sprayed poison and harvested me with the flowers. Then someone nearly drowned me, cast a spell, and made me big."

Size matters. She put her head in her hand. *Bad girl.*

After a moment, she faced him again. "There was no spell. Get that straight."

"Something paralyzed me, then made me grow with the flowers." He glanced over his shoulder. "Except for my wings."

Penny jumped to her feet and rushed around behind Glendon to examine his magnificent back. His skin glistened like bronze. "I don't see anything," she said a bit breathlessly.

"In the center," he replied. "Please look closely."

Penny leaned closer and saw two small protrusions, almost transparent, in the middle of his back. She touched one of them and felt it move. "They *are* wings."

He sighed. "I fear this day has sapped my strength."

My God, it's true. Penny recalled the scene in the greenhouse, the way he'd appeared with the giant ladybug. His story made sense in a twisted way. Could the presence of an actual *faerie* have caused Fred and Lisa's potion to mutate somehow? Assuming faeries existed, of course.

She walked slowly back to her chair, trying to sort through everything. "You were harvested with the violet in Scotland, we fertilized you . . . and you grew."

"Aye." He sounded so tired. "If you are not an evil witch, will you help me?"

His sincerity touched Penny. "Of course."

"Thank you." He smiled weakly. "Now I must rest."

"I'll show you the guest room." How would she ever explain him to her father?

"Nay, I prefer to rest among the flowers."

"Fine. I'll grab a blanket and pillow."

"I require neither." He stood and walked to the door, pausing to look back. "You did not summon me for . . . anything?"

The expression in his eyes stole her breath—suggestive yet weary. He looked tired. Lost. Would he die? Guilt pressed down on her. Her actions could cost this man— yes, man—his life.

"Are you all right?" She walked toward him, reaching up to brush her fingertips along his cheek. He felt real and warm. "I'm sorry."

"You are good and beautiful, and I regret calling you evil." Gently, he took her hand in his. Desire shot through Penny, sweet and fierce.

He pulled away, turned and walked slowly toward the greenhouse. Penny watched, vowing to see the situation righted.

An idea blossomed in her mind and she raced for the phone. "Hey, Lisa, I need you and Fred back out here tomorrow morning," she said. "Bring every book you've got on faeries."

She *had* to help him.

Penny watched Fred pitch the tent at the back of the greenhouse, wondering how she'd survived this past week.

At least she'd managed to convince Glendon to wear shorts and a T-shirt. Not typical ranch attire, but enough to convince her father he was an expert who'd accompanied the wildflowers. After mumbling something about his late mother's eccentricities, Big John Basinger had turned his attention to other matters.

Whew.

"Your friends are kind," Glendon said, giving her one of those looks of his that made her blood turn molten.

Penny shivered, despite the soaring temperatures inside and out. "If anyone can help you, they can." Glendon made her want things she hadn't experienced in far too long. Time to think of something else . . .

"Did you really talk to the cows?" she asked.

"Aye, and their plight distresses them. And me."

"Glendon . . ."

He lifted an eyebrow.

"I'll speak to my father about dairy farming," she said. *Eventually.*

"Good." He took her hand and squeezed it.

Penny looked up and saw Lisa's smile. Her friend insisted Glendon had been sent here for Penny. Fate.

"I saw a dog this morning," Glendon said, jarring Penny from thoughts of hand-holding and fate. "Yours?"

"Maybe." She didn't want to try to explain hunting dogs to Glendon, or to dwell on the fact that he was still holding her hand. "We have several."

"Small and white with curly hair?" Glendon squeezed her hand, then released it.

Penny suppressed her disappointment. "Must be a stray."

"I thought, for a moment . . ."

"What?" The worried tone in his voice was unmistakable. "Thought what?"

"Ah, 'twas nothing."

Uh-oh. "All right, let's see how Fred and Lisa are coming with the chamber." She took a step, but felt Glendon's hand on her shoulder.

Penny turned to face Glendon. "What is it?"

"If this works, I'll . . ."

"What?"

"I'll miss you."

The confusion in his eyes gave way quickly to what could

only be called genuine regret. He *cared,* and that knowledge made her want to throw herself into his arms.

"I'll miss you, too," she whispered, blinking back the stinging sensation in her eyes.

"Come on over, so I can show you this," Fred said, shattering the moment.

Penny wrenched herself away from Glendon's gaze. "Okay, how does this work?"

Fred grinned. "It's just a tent with a vaporizer."

Penny couldn't imagine anything this simple restoring Glendon to his faerie state, but something equally simple had made him human. Who was she to argue with faerie magic?

"Glendon, you'll sleep in here every night, and Penny will fill the vaporizer with a new mixture we've concocted."

"Will that work?"

"We'll find out soon enough. If it doesn't work, we'll just keep trying until something does."

How could Fred possibly know anything about faeries? Then she reminded herself that her friends were trying their best to help.

"Thank you." Glendon stepped forward and extended his hand the way Penny'd taught him before he met her father. "I'm most grateful."

"I'd love to hear more about your world before you leave us," Fred said. "Humans have much to learn about living in harmony with nature."

"Aye." Glendon looked at Penny.

All eyes turned toward Penny. "So did you write down what I'm supposed to put in the water?" she asked evasively.

"Yes, right here." Fred handed Penny a recipe—no, a formula. "Fill the vaporizer every night."

"Thank you both for everything." Penny squeezed Lisa's hand. "I owe you."

"I'll be back tomorrow to help you choose the flowers for the show." Lisa looked over Penny's enchanted garden and whistled. "You're definitely a contender."

"Thanks to you, Fred, and Glendon," she said.

"We'll check back tomorrow." Fred and Lisa walked to the door. "Page us if anything weird happens."

"Weird?" Penny said as the door closed behind them. *Weird*? "Cowards."

"Cowards?" Glendon placed his hand on Penny's arm. "Not so. Your friends are good and brave."

"They're the best." Heat radiated from Glendon's hand and into her. She wanted him to kiss her. Desperately.

"You are good and brave, too," he said.

"Me?" she whispered, wondering where all the oxygen had gone. This was crazy—she barely knew Glendon, and he wasn't even *human*. Yet, in many ways, he was more human than anyone she'd ever known. And she wanted him. Now. *Her* faerie prince.

She pulled away to gaze into his eyes. Naked desire burned in their depths, mirroring everything she felt. He could be gone by morning. Penny made her decision. If morning took him from her, she vowed they would have this one night together.

A night to last forever.

Glendon opened his eyes in a fragrant fog, slowly remembering where he was, and with whom. His heart slammed against his chest as he gazed down at the warm, beautiful female curled against him.

Feelings washed through him. Intense feelings. Then he realized the full impact of his actions. They were mated for life.

He gazed upon Penny again and her eyes fluttered open. A slow smile appeared on her face and love crowded his guilt aside again. For now.

"Good morning," she whispered.

Glendon's breath caught as she moved against him, warm and naked. "Good morning." His voice sounded husky, foreign to his own ears. Of course, he was no longer the virgin faerie prince awaiting marriage to twenty virgin brides. He swallowed hard.

"You feel good." She buried her face against his shoulder.

"Penny," he whispered. If he could never return home . . . He wrapped his arms around her and just held her. How could this be wrong?

A sound came from the greenhouse door. "Oh, no."

Penny leaped to her feet and pulled on her discarded clothing. "My father."

Glendon pulled on the clothes Penny had brought him. He followed her through the jungle of giant flowers. Seeing the ladybug reminded him they'd forgotten to put it inside the tent last night. Of course, they'd been distracted.

Penny fluffed her curly hair, then grabbed a gardening tool from the cupboard near the door. "Look busy," she whispered, then opened the door.

But instead of Penny's tall father, a small dog—the dog Glendon had met yesterday—trotted into the greenhouse and sat up on its haunches. Glendon stared deeply into its eyes. A curious spark of green flashed in the canine's honey-colored eyes, then a shower of glittering dust surrounded the white fur.

"What the—" Penny couldn't believe her eyes.

Glendon recognized the faerie before her transformation was complete. "Mother." Her crown was slightly askew, but he'd know her anywhere.

"Your mother?" Penny repeated, still staring.

"Aye," Glendon said.

Penny's eyes grew wider as his mother transformed herself to human size.

"Shape-shifting is a skill only very powerful faeries possess." Glendon knelt before his mother and kissed her hand.

"Rise, Glendon."

As he straightened, his gaze met hers and he realized she knew. A hot flush crept into his cheeks.

"Turn," his mother commanded, and he obeyed.

She lifted his T-shirt and examined his wings. "I'm not too late."

"It is too late, Mother."

"The female?"

"Aye." Glendon turned again to face his mother. "What will become of our race if I cannot—"

"Does she know?" His mother looked at Penny.

"No." Glendon reached for Penny's hand and drew her closer. "I love her," he said, and meant it.

Penny looked up at him, her eyes glistening. "You do?"

"Aye."

She pressed her fingertips to her lips. A tear rolled down

her cheek. Glendon captured it on the tip of his finger and held it out to the morning light. "Beautiful." When he met his mother's gaze, he saw tears in her eyes as well.

"My son," she said. "Even if I restore you to faerie, you'll be unable to wed in our manner. You've chosen this woman."

Glendon lowered his gaze, saddened about the fate of his race. "Is there no way . . . ?"

His mother's lower lip trembled and she drew a deep breath. "It is within my power to strip you of all that is Fae, and to return your faerie dust to our burgh."

Glendon's sighed. "And the pollination can commence without . . . ?"

His mother nodded. "Since you've chosen a mate, you cannot wed your twenty virgin brides."

"Twenty . . . ?" Penny said. "Virgins?"

The queen smiled at Penny. "It is our way, but the pollination can commence without Glendon."

"Pollination?" Penny lifted a brow. "Let me get this straight. We're talking faerie sperm bank here?"

His mother shook her head. "I do not understand your ways." She looked at Glendon again. "With your faerie dust there will be more babes, and we will survive."

Glendon swallowed hard. "And I can remain?"

"Aye, but you will be *human,* Glendon," his mother warned.

"Glendon." Penny's voice quivered. "I don't want you to make this sacrifice."

He smiled and cupped her cheek. " 'Tis my wish."

"As much as I love my son," his mother said, "this is for the best. If he were to return, he would live in solitude. He could never mate in the true sense. If it's permitted, I should like to return to visit my son and grandchildren."

"Grandchildren?" Penny said, and smiled. "Of course."

Glendon met his mother's gaze. "I am ready."

Penny placed her trophy in the case beside her grandmother's numerous awards. Her father loomed behind her.

"I'm proud of you, Pen," he said, handing her a long envelope. "My will."

Penny took the envelope. "You couldn't have had time to change it."

He grinned and put his arm around her shoulders. "Honey, that was just me spoutin' nonsense. You've always been my heir."

"What?" She stared at him. "All this was an elaborate joke?"

Glendon walked into the room before her father could reply and her eyes blurred. It was a joke that had changed her life forever, showering her with love and magic. How could she complain? The award was now named in Grandma's memory, and Penny had Glendon.

"Is Lisa bringing that weirdo to dinner?" her father asked. "I kinda like old Fred, and that Glendon fella, too."

"That's good," Penny said, stepping around her father to bring Glendon into their conversation. "Glendon's staying."

John Basinger's brows met his receding hairline for an instant, then he smiled and gave a nod. "Fine. I'm planning to put more acres in alfalfa. We could use a good man."

Penny took Glendon's hand. "What would you say about converting part of the operation to dairy—?"

"What?"

"As a trial?" Penny finished.

Her father drew a deep breath, then he nodded. He took a long look at Glendon. "Your idea?"

"Aye."

John narrowed his gaze. "You're one of them tree-huggin' types, too, aren't you?"

"Tree-hugging?" Glendon blinked and cast Penny a questioning glance.

"I don't know about tree-hugging," she said, "but I know for a fact that he's an expert on cross-pollination."

Glendon cleared his throat.

"We're . . . seeing each other, Dad. It's serious."

"I got eyes." John put his hand on Penny's shoulder. "I wish your mother and Grandma were here."

"Me, too." Penny smiled.

John gave her a hug, then shook Glendon's hand and excused himself. Penny pressed her cheek against Glendon's shoulder.

"There's much for me to learn," Glendon whispered.

"And we'll have to hire a forger." She bit her lower lip. She'd do whatever it took to make Glendon "legal."

"Forger?"

"Don't worry. I'll explain later," Penny said, snuggling against his shoulder. "I have a lot to learn, too."

Glendon tipped her chin upward and covered her mouth with his. After a moment, he broke the kiss. "Such as?"

"The finer habits of birds, bees, and faeries."

AT ETERNITY'S GATE

by Gary A. Braunbeck

Gary A. Braunbeck writes poetically dark suspense and horror fiction, rich in detail and scope. Recent stories have appeared in Robert Bloch's Psychos, Once Upon a Crime, *and* The Conspiracy Files. *His occasional foray into the mystery genre is no less accomplished, having appeared in anthologies such as* Danger in D.C. *and* Cat Crimes Takes a Vacation. *His recent short story collection,* Things Left Behind, *received excellent critical notice. He lives in Columbus, Ohio.*

LUCINDA turned her wheelchair away from the painting, adjusted her belly-bag, and decided that sadness was the color of rain. She knew that rain had a color—hidden though it was—for she had spent many hours studying it from behind her hospice window. Rain and sadness were the same pale shade, their source lying just beyond the darkspace that always swallowed her before a seizure. She'd been having so many damned seizures lately—

—boosted from her body, her thin flesh shed by her shadow, floating down that hazy corridor surrounded by faces with unreadable expressions—

—and none of the doctors could tell her why.

She looked over her shoulder at the painting, realized she was too tired to continue working on it today, then leaned back her head and closed her eyes.

"I'm guessing that's your subtle way of telling me that you're finished for today?" said Jordan, the volunteer art instructor.

"I'm tired and my bag's almost full."

"Do you want me to call a nurse?"

Lucinda shook her head, forcing back the liquid numbness trying to envelope her torso—the first warning sign of an oncoming seizure. It was so tempting, that numbness, so benevolent and tender, promising her flight if only she would accept her vulnerability and submit, submit, submit. She often wondered if she wasn't subconsciously going through the Kübler-Ross final stages of death and her body was accepting what her mind didn't want to think about.

Jordan came over to her chair. "Are you sure you don't want me to—"

"No. The nurse'd only give me a shot—not that I mind. Sometimes, even when I'm not in all that much pain, I ask for one, just so I can sit very still and feel the drugs blossom inside. It's like your first cool drink on a really hot day, an ice-bird in the center of your body spreading its wings wide." She laughed. "All of which probably means I'm a junkie by now, but . . . what the hell, you know?" She opened her eyes and saw Jordan standing in front of the painting.

"This is really quite splendid," he said. "You've come a long way in a very short time. I feel like I might have actually taught you something."

"You have, you know that. Fishing for a compliment, are we?"

He smiled at her, a perfect boyish smile from the hairy face of a bear. He seemed so much larger and more powerful today; he filled the room.

The numbness spread upward into her skull. Everything was slowing down. The darkspace opened up to her, revealing the pinpoints of light hidden behind the pale scrim of the rain. She felt weightless and freed and very much afraid.

". . . ohgod . . ."

Jordan was next to her, taking her hand. "What is it? Is it happening again?"

". . . yes. I d-don't want—"

The pinpoints tumbled toward her, each one becoming a face that sped past with astonishing momentum, leaving only emptiness and longing in their wake, the last of them becoming a sphere as it approached her, folding in on itself until

it was the very absence of space; then it flashed, an eye wink-
ing, blossoming and segmenting into a maelstrom of kaleido-
scopic images: A ramshackle windmill, a group of miners
emerging from the pits, a dusty country road, a field of sun-
flowers, boats in a harbor, a billiards room that remained
before her gaze, expanding, solidifying, emitting sounds, vi-
brations, scents of wine and smoke and fresh-baked bread
and sweat . . .

. . . She sat at a table near the entrance. The table was
part of the billiards rooms, the room part of a tavern, and
the tavern was overflowing with people, some festive and
gay, others pensive and melancholy. Smoke drifted past her
face in thin, spicy wisps. The music was muffled and somewhat discordant but appealing, nonetheless. More scents
came to her: Coal dust and drying mud, hot beef and gravy,
dying flowers and damp wood. She liked it very much.

Across the room two men were sitting at a scarred oak
table, an opened bottle of wine between them. One of
them, a great bull of a man who reminded her too much
of Jordan, was laughing boisterously while his companion
sat intensely—almost *deathly*—still, glowering with narrowed eyes and chin pressed down against his collar. He
wore a tattered, wide-brimmed hat of woven straw; his
beard was scraggly and auburn, his eyes bloodshot and be-
guiling. After a moment, he raised his head and spoke to
the bull.

"I should have known better than to tell you about it,
Paul. I despise you when you get this way. Everything has
to amuse you or you don't want to hear about it."

"Ah, my dear friend—if only you would *listen* to yourself
when you these moods come on you!"

"I find I can still recognize my own voice, thank you."

The bull named Paul leaned onto the table. "But if you
could hear yourself—it isn't so much what you say, it's how
you say it. Your words are often more colorful than your
paintings." He sat back, brushed some hair out of his eyes,
and launched into an over-ripe imitation. "I tell you *it fol-*
lows me! I hear their *keening,* I see their *faces!* And I float
there, trapped, frightened—" he dramatically placed his
hand against his forehead " '—*oh, so frightened,* so frightened and *aloooooooone!*' "

Merrymakers at nearby tables laughed, a few of them applauding in thanks for the entertainment.

"What?" said the Bull, looking at his companion. "Did you find my performance less than satisfactory?"

"You wail like a woman in childbirth."

"I consider that a compliment."

"I thought you would understand," said the auburn man. "To feel that you are bodiless, unbound. I am more than just myself in that place, I am some idealized form of myself. I know there is a way out, you see, and I know that it's very close to me. I can *feel* it but I cannot get near it. And the crying, it follows me even after I waken. I go to my window, I look out, but there is no light to be seen in any of the houses, there are only those in the sky above, and I know that those lights contain the source of that soul-sick weeping, and I feel a force—"

"—you feel the force of drink, my friend," roared the Bull as he lifted the dusty wine bottle. "Perhaps a taste more of this will satisfactorily deafen you. If not, I can at least promise that enough of it will leave your soul too drunk to wander from your body while you're sleeping."

Lucinda felt her body go rigid; this was all very familiar, too much so: As if she had heard the echo of a sound that hadn't yet been made.

The auburn man grew suddenly furious at the Bull's words, and with a violent swing of his arm flung the wine bottle to the floor. "Isn't it enough that you perpetually mock what we do, you and I? You wear your hypocrisy like a priest donning his robes for mass. When the nobility dangle their wealth in front of your face like a scrap of meat at the lips of a starving dog, you loudly proclaim that there's such divine, moral, ethereal passion at the heart of your work—'It is the soul in conflict with itself that is the most important thing of all'—yet you feel no remorse when you strike away the hand of a beggar in the street. How can you do that? Tell me. Make me understand how you can profess such compassion and yet continue to deny that there *is* truly a measure of pain in the universe that is born into each of us, one that cannot be eased and follows us through every moment of our existence and perhaps even beyond? Make me understand how you can go on gorging yourself on meat and wine and sleep in a sad whore's stained bed, forever turning a blind eye to the misery of humanity when you know damned well it's in your grasp, your gift, to ease part of that misery!"

"You never were any fun once the drinking started. I think—"

"Goddamn you, Paul! How can a man so brilliant be such a filthy, arrogant shit?"

The Bull's face turned into a slab of granite. "How dare you lecture me about compassion. Christ!—how many times have I listened to you bemoan the rancor that chokes you when you think of the way your fellow men treat one another? Are you telling me that it is permissible to disdain mankind as a whole yet admire individual dignity? Or are the poet and composer the same to you as the aristocrat and anarchist—deserving of scorn until they have suffered enough that you deem them worthy of your caring? For someone who purports to be a man of the people, my friend, you have a curiously selective heart."

The auburn man's eyes seemed to slide back into his skull. "I think . . . I think. . . ." He grabbed the edge of the table, shuddering.

The Bull looked suddenly terrified. "Is it happening again?"

"Not for love . . . not for any woman's love or the love of a people . . . just . . . let me awaken once with silence surrounding me . . . just once let me not hear it!" He flung himself off the chair and into a waiter, knocking them both to the floor as he kicked and moaned and flailed his arms, a thin trickle of foam crawling from the corner of his mouth. The Bull leaped to his feet as the auburn man thrashed to his knees and reached for something on the table, then all too quickly a crowd gathered around the scene, laughing, shouting, pointing—

—Lucinda could catch brief glimpses of frenzied, violent movement—

—then came a crash and the howls of laughter turned to gasps, then cries of fear and disgust. The mob quickly dispersed. A gust of cinnamon smoke drifted against her eyes as she rose to see the two men.

The Bull, the man called Paul, was sitting at the table, roaring with black laughter that threatened to become a snarl through his clenched teeth and tears. The auburn man was on his feet, pressed face-first against the stone wall, pounding it with his fist, scraping flesh and blood over the stones with every blow. He clutched the left side of his head with his other hand, blood streaming from between his fingers. A rusted knife lay at his feet.

The Bull rose, grabbing something small and blood-sopped from the table and flinging it at the auburn man. "Here, goddamn you: Take it! Take this proof of your bloody magnificent suffering that you value more than anything else in your pathetic life! Take it and put it on your tongue and taste it and swallow it and gag on it!" He slammed his chair into the wall, splintering it into kindling, then stormed out the tavern door. The auburn man sank down, trying to pick up the severed lobe with trembling and blood-slick hands. After a moment he snapped his gaze up to Lucinda's face.

She had never seen such haunted, haunting eyes.

"Did you understand?" he whimpered. "Did you?"

She could find no words. She knelt beside him, took the earlobe from the floor, and gently placed it in his hands.

His fingers closed around her wrist. Lucinda touched his cheek, feeling an affinity for him that she'd never experienced before.

His voice was the whisper of a child lost in the darkness: "Have you ever felt it?"

She wanted to answer him, to say that she had, she was, but the numbness had returned and was seducing her, drawing her back through the darkspace and into the pale shade of rain; a surge of suffocating pressure.

The auburn man spoke her name, his image dwindling.

"Lucinda?"

She reached toward him, but he was mist.

"Lucinda?"

Shaking her by the shoulders. Her head lolled to the side and she opened her eyes to see Jordan kneeling in front of her wheelchair—

—no, it was there, on the other side of the room.

She was in her bed, her head cradled by pillows, and Jordan was sitting on the edge, holding her hand. She blinked, saw the clear tube rising from the bandage on her arm, snaking up to an IV drip. She drew in a short, sharp breath that filled her torso with fire. She touched her belly-bag; it was empty.

"Jordan." She felt a smile. "Is it morning already? I don't remember when I—"

He rose to his feet, stepped away, and turned her painting toward her.

"Jordan? What are you—?"

The words caught in her throat.

The painting was finished. She could clearly see that it conveyed everything she had intended; the gulls seemed to shimmer as they soared toward the morning sun, the sands had a life all their own, shifting and scattering and drowning under the foaming force of the ocean.

Not looking at Jordan, she whispered, "How . . . how long have you been here?"

"A day. A day and a half. You don't remember?"

She shook her head. "All I can remember is feeling the numbness right before the seizure, hearing the sounds of someone crying . . . a lot of people crying, then . . ."

She closed her eyes and breathed slowly, steadily, her mind grasping at the remnants of images, finally focusing on that of a scarred table top—

—and she remembered what had happened to her beyond the darkspace.

Opening her eyes, she asked Jordan what he had seen and heard.

"You had a seizure. I called for the nurse. We took you from the chair and put you in bed. I wanted to stay, but a doctor came in and ordered me to leave. I came back early the next morning. They told me that you were fine, that you were conscious and were working on a painting. I came in and found you. . . ." He gestured toward the easel. There was a deep, drying stain on the carpet. Lucinda blanched; once before, after she'd first arrived at the hospice, she'd tried to stand while her belly-bag was full, only to have it burst and slop down her legs, filling the air with a stench so overpowering and rancid it caused her to faint. Standing was, had always been, would probably always be, a nearly insurmountable task, requiring reserves of strength she couldn't sustain. So weak, so damned weak and sickly ever since childhood. She had firmly believed that she wouldn't live to see seventeen, let alone twenty-eight. She used to

imagine herself just snapping off one night, doing a Granny
Weatherall and clicking out, not living long enough to
watch her life grind to a halt in a series of repulsive, sput-
tering little agonies. She never thought her last days, weeks,
months—however the hell long it was—would be spent like
this. She looked at her tutor and felt a pressure in her
throat.

"How did I—?"

Jordan placed his hand against her cheek. His touch was
satin. "You spoke almost constantly. In French. Why didn't
you ever tell me that you spoke my native language?"

"I . . . I don't. I flunked French in high school. I picked
up one or two phrases, a half-dozen words, but— "

Jordan shook his head. "No, this wasn't textbook French
spoken in a mock accent. You spoke it as fluently as if
you'd been speaking it all your life. You used slang idioms
I haven't heard since I was a boy in Asnières."

"But . . . how?"

He only stared at her.

"I was standing? Moving?"

He gave a slow nod of his head. Lucinda suddenly felt
exposed and vulnerable and angry for that vulnerability but
leaned toward him anyway, burying her face in his chest,
feeling his massive arms enfold her as they would a frightened child, her fear and confusion temporarily held at bay
as she filled herself with the scents of his body. The smell
of a man, she thought. The nearness. She felt something
trickle into her belly-bag, and once again silently railed
against nothing and everything for her condition, her heart
aching at the memory of the auburn man clutching his
bleeding head.

Jordan pulled back and cupped her face in his hands,
staring into her eyes. "The man you spoke of, the 'auburn
man.' Would you know his face if you saw it again?"

She thought of his eyes that haunted, and whispered,
"Yes." Jordan smiled at her, the same smile he gave her
when a painting was going well. She adored that smile.

He turned away from her and picked up a large book
from the bedside table, a thick, heavy volume whose pages
held photographs of various artists and their work.

As he flipped past pictures and biographies of Frans Hals
and Michelangelo and El Greco he said, "It never occurred

to me that I should educate you about various styles or artists. It was so rare to find someone like you, someone who was born with a natural aptitude and had never been exposed to fine art in any way. The minute I saw your work I knew that yours was a genuine talent. All my life I've waited for a student like you. I—" He sighed. "I'm sorry. I was going to make a point with that, but I seem to have lost track."

"You get used to it."

He looked up. "Do you know how much I hate it that you're so sick? Do you have any idea how—"

"—please don't. Please."

He reluctantly returned his attention to the volume on his lap.

Lucinda felt weaker than ever, and wondered if the seizures would ever stop—or, at the very least, lessen in their intensity, fade away as Jordan was now, as if being swallowed by a fog.

Jordan turned the book toward her, one beefy finger resting next to a portrait. "Is this the auburn man?"

"How did you know?"

"Is it him?" His voice was glass.

"Yes." She felt her body tugged forward as the fog cleared and the darkspace emerged from behind, creeping toward her, its silvery pinpoints blinking.

"Arles," he whispered. "You were with Vincent at Arles. Dear God."

She wanted to hold his hand, but he was now an intangible and she was cascading on the pale shade of rain down a hazy corridor, flying past faces, then drifting, finally feeling her feet touch the cold marble floor of a long hall. She walked haltingly until she arrived at the section where he waited for her. Standing at the doorway she could smell the stench of human waste, could hear the wretched outcries of the other patients. She moved through the doorway, tripping over an emaciated woman lying naked on the floor, shuddering violently, the soles of her mangled feet smacking against the wall with a moist, raw sound. Lucinda stepped aside, staring in muted horror as vomit dribbled from the woman's mouth, then flew out and up in a sickening spray as she began to thrash about, clawing at her throat.

The patients were roaming everywhere, staring, singing to themselves, weeping. Their voices rose to the ceiling, the echoes expanding, touching, coalescing, then crashing down on her head; it was the sound of a million babies doused with gasoline and set aflame, the cry of a million broken-hearted men shrieking their anguish into the black, uncaring night, the keening of countless ages of affliction all come to rest in this spot, at this moment, searing her to the core.

She felt disgusted by it, sorry for it, yet at the same time an intricate part of it all. She watched the patients slide down the clammy marble walls like flies struggling to break free of a spider's web, writhe deep inside cement bathtubs, squat in corners relieving their tortured bowels, cover their heads to protect themselves from blows delivered by invisible assailants, all of them muttering in low, hoarse, lunatic voices.

Then she saw Vincent.

He was sitting on his bed next to a large barred window, and he was sketching.

Occasionally he would stop, stretch, and scratch at the bandage on the left side of his head. She watched him for several moments until he at last noticed her, smiled, and gestured for her to join him.

"What are you drawing?" she asked as she sat next to him. He pointed out the window.

Down in the yard Lucinda saw other patients, these wearing flowing white gowns, walking around a large stone fountain as if it would take them elsewhere.

"Look at them," muttered Vincent. "You and I should know such contentment." He blended a shadow with his index finger, put the sketch down, and turned to her. "Everyone suffers here—be it from madness, disease, loneliness or pain—everyone suffers. We understand each other like members of the same family." He took her hands in his; his palms were rough and callused, but they felt like a rose cradled in her grasp.

"When will you leave this terrible place?"

"Soon, if I am to take Dr. Gachet for a man of his word. I will visit with Theo for a while and then, I suspect, I will go to a place I have often dreamed of retiring to."

"Where."

"Auvers-sur-Oise. God speaks through its landscape. There is a field there I have always wanted to paint."

Lucinda moved closer, kissing him on the cheek. "May I come to be with you there?"

"Yes. I need you by my side very badly. Once I feared that all my tenderness had died with Margot, then you—" He pulled her to him. "You have given me back something of myself I thought long dead."

"I do so want to be with you. It's been two months since you came here, yet this is the first time I've been allowed to see you."

"Oh, my lovely lady, why is that so important? You must have known that I would come to find you after my release. Why come to see me in this . . . this squalor?"

"Because I know what you meant now. In my dreams I, too, see the other faces. I hear their weeping and when I wake I can spare little thought for anything else. You are not a madman, you are not possessed."

"Then, you feel it, too? That sense of being . . . lost within those cries? Abandoned?"

"Yes."

He grunted, released her hands, and turned away. "All colors are ones of despair," he whispered. "Red is man's rage, yellow his lust, blue his reason and gray his conscience. Green is his spirit, shit-brown his heart, and all of them are moving toward the same place, a place where they will unite into blackness and . . . unimaginable nothing." He wiped something from his eye, peered out into the courtyard, and began shaking.

"Once, when I was in the Borinage, I painted the miners there, and the colors seemed so majestic when used for them. It was one of those times—all but lost now—when I felt as one with the colors. I used to think red was the color of love, after all—be it sentimental tripe or not; a rose awaiting the touch of the sun so it might fully blossom, then be plucked from its stem and held in the hands of a beautiful woman." He arched backward, gasping in harsh breaths, one hand pressing against his chest.

"But no matter how hard I try, the colors come out their darkest now. And nowhere are they darker than in my dreams. It terrifies me. Not only do I feel that I have been abandoned among those weeping faces, but each time I sleep now, I feel as if I'm getting closer to the moment when that unseen exit will close behind me before I can return to my body and awaken, and I will be trapped in there forever." He smiled a crooked grin. "Shall I tell you my greatest fear? The one that is always in the front of my mind, compelling everything I do? It is that I will never live long enough to paint all the pictures in my head. And do you know why? Because I have betrayed the colors, and they are punishing me by putting me in that unknowable place between the mind and soul every time I sleep. I don't want to go back, do you see? It is so . . . so lonely there."

Lucinda reached out to touch him, but before she could, he leaped from the bed and grabbed the bars on the window.

His cry was filled with rain.

"When the day is over, will you weep at the passing of the sun and all it has given you to see? Will you rejoice when the dawn arrives at all the chances it offers? Will you take the hands of a ragged one, an odd, damaged, discarded one? Will you bring them mercy and comfort, tell them that this madness and loneliness will pass?" He began pounding against the bars with an open hand. In the distance Lucinda could hear the attendants running down the hall. She rose from the bed and once again tried to touch him—she knew she was trying because she could feel her limbs moving— yet she was suddenly outside herself, staring down, watching herself remain motionless.

Vincent began ramming his head against the bars. "No! No, you will not! You shall drink and laugh and close your eyes to all of it. You shall mock the lost and lonely ones, spit on the poor, and in that lonely place where my dreams send me there shall emerge another face twisted in pain! YOU WILL FORGET! YOU ARE DEAF!" The attendants fell on him, dragging him to the ground and strapping his arms behind his back. One of them tore his bandage as they dragged him down the corridor and Lucinda rose, only to be wrenched away and hurled into the darkspace, and there she saw the faces of others lost in dreams and agony, trying to find their way back to bodies long since dead and buried and rotting under the earth. Their mouths opened to release wails of misery; their eyes shed tears that became starlight pinpoints, ebbing away from her, and she lurched forward, dropping her palette and gasping for breath.

Jordan was sitting on the floor in front of her chair, drinking a glass of beer and leafing through a book, one of many that were scattered around him. His eyes were red from lack of sleep.

Then she saw her new painting.

An old, emotionally broken man, sitting in a small, weak chair, his head buried in his thin, callused hands. The room surrounding him was bare and decrepit, its sole window looking out on a golden field and blue sky. Across from the old man she could see the traced outline, barely discernable, of another chair yet to be painted. The scene was one of breathtaking beauty and melancholy, and though the brush which had composed the scene may have been held by her hand, another's had guided it.

The colors were not applied with her usual smooth strokes but, rather, an uneasy yet oddly effective combination of her strokes fused with violent, almost frenzied slashes; the picture seemed to vibrate.

"Four days this time," said Jordan. "You refused to remain in your chair, but your bag didn't leak."

She looked down at her belly-bag and saw that it was empty. There was no discomfort now. She felt the pale shade fading, the darkspace moving farther away.

"Was I still speaking in French?"

"Yes." He stared at her. "You know who he is now, don't you?"

"Van Gogh?"

"Van Gogh." He poured a glass of water and helped her to hold it while she drank. She smiled her thanks, he covered her with a blanket, and she eased back in the wheelchair.

"It's not like a dream at all," she said. "I am there. I make a difference."

Jordan tried to smile and failed miserably. "There's a lot I need to explain to you. *Try* to explain, anyway. I'm not sure I understand some of it myself." He shook himself and took a deep breath, then pointed toward the new painting.

"This painting is based on a sketch Van Gogh did entitled *Worn Out: At Eternity's Gate*. He remarked once in a letter to his brother Theo that he couldn't begin the actual

painting until he found the right color scheme. He said that
if he could realize the proper balance and light composi-
tion, then he'd know what was missing from the picture.
He believed it might have been the fruition of all he'd been
striving toward in his work."

Lucinda could not, did not want to, grasp what he was
saying. "And you're telling me that this is . . . this is the
way Van Gogh wanted it done?"

"Yes . . . and no. There's as much of you in this as him."

She shook her head. ""How could I have—"

Jordan took hold of her hands. "Listen to me. I've been
thinking back to when I was a boy. When I was eight, I
came down with a serious fever that lasted nearly ten days.
The doctors thought I would die. During that time, whenever I fell asleep, I would have these absolutely terrifying
nightmares. One night I woke up after a particularly scary
one and found my father sitting at my bedside. I remember
the way he stroked my hair and sang to me, the way his
hands felt when he placed a cool, moist rag over my
forehead . . . he was a very kind man and I miss him . . .
anyway, on this night, I refused to go back to sleep.

"He told me, then, about the tunnel that our soul flies
through whenever we dream, that all souls travel through
this tunnel, even those of people who have died and are
on their way to God. Somewhere along the way, this tunnel
separates into two branches—the dead take one branch,
the dreamers take another. But sometimes the dreamers
and the dead get confused along the way and don't know
which branch to take once they arrive at that point. A
dreamer has the luxury of simply turning around and going
back, but the dead have to remain there, alone and afraid,
and that's what causes us to have nightmares—that fear.
The lonely fear that the dead have."

"The Lady or the Tiger?" said Lucinda.

"Something like that, yes. As I grew older, I developed
an interest in dreams and did a great deal of reading about
them. I also read about astral projection, fever-dreams,
what happens to the mind of someone who is in a coma or
experiencing a seizure—and, of course, near-death experiences. In almost every account I came across, the people
described a long corridor, or road, or tunnel, and each saw
a light at the end. I began to wonder, What if it's true?

What if there is a place out there along the path of dreams where the road—the tunnel—branches, and there are countless frightened spirits—spirits of the dead—just standing there, uncertain of which way to go?"

Lucinda shook her head. "I still don't quite—"

"Let's just say, for the moment, that it is true, all right? And let's say that, eventually, one of these spirits of the dead decides, to hell with it, and chooses a branch, only it turns out to be the wrong one. Think about it. What would you do?"

Lucinda felt a familiar ache in her chest. She tried not to think about the moment of her approaching death because it would come soon enough. "I don't know. I . . . I guess that I'd try to find my way back to the branch."

"And if you couldn't?"

She bit her lower lip. "I don't want to talk about this any longer, Jordan, please? Why are you—"

He snatched another book from the floor, opening to a previously marked page. "This is an excerpt from a letter Van Gogh sent to Theo in July of 1883. He was talking about what he experienced during his seizures. Listen to this: 'When I am at work I feel an unlimited faith in art and in its healing powers, yet I must take care that I carry that faith with me into the opaque blackness when it enfolds me, as it so often does these days. It astounds me, this *dark space,* for as it swallows me it releases me, also, and I feel weightless, as if being carried away by thousands of glittering pinpoints of light to a place where everything in this tiny universe convenes, a place where life and death meet for a while to tell each other their stories. I believe when I arrive at this place I will find the answers that have been missing in my life. Only there will I be freed to paint as I always should have, to bring my work to fruition, to perfect that one last image which has eluded me for all my days and dreams. I know such things are pure fantasy, for even if it is true, I will be among the bodiless then, the brush forever out of my reach. But I grow weary and the words on this page blur, so I leave you for now." He snapped the book closed and stared at Lucinda.

She swallowed, once, painfully and said, "So you think that . . . that—"

"I think that when Van Gogh died his spirit took the

wrong branch. I think he was lost there until you came along. I think that during one of your seizures your soul met his in the dream branch, and he recognized you for what you are. He knows that he is dead and that you—" His voice cracked on the next two words. "—are dying, so he's . . . I think he saw in you his chance to come back into this life long enough to bring his work 'to fruition.' "

Jordan's eyes filled with wonder. "All their lives artists wonder where it comes from, their gift for creation. You've said yourself, and I've experienced it, too, that there are times when a work seems to be creating itself and is only using you as a conduit. Look at the painting. It's your style, yes, but it's evolving at an incredible rate."

"But—"

"Don't you see? This painting was to be Van Gogh's summation of all he'd done, but he never figured out what was missing from the sketch. He's finishing the work not only through you, but with you, as well. Your two styles are merging into one."

He dropped the book onto the floor.

It took a moment for the full impact of everything to hit her; then Lucinda began shaking. "But . . . why me?"

"Because you share his loneliness, his pain and isolation." Jordan knelt down and held both her hands.

"Tell me, the first time in the tavern, is that when he mutilated himself?"

"Yes."

"Gauguin was there, that's right. October of 1888. And the second time?"

"An asylum."

"That would be Saint-Remy. May, I believe, 1889."

"Why are the dates so important?"

"Because after Van Gogh left the asylum, he retired to—"

"Auvers-sur-Oise?"

"He told you?"

"Yes, I promised to meet him there."

The blood drained from Jordan's face.

"What is it?" asked Lucinda.

Jordan shook his head. "I don't want—"

"Say it."

His eyes met hers. "If this is what's happening, if all he

wants is for the two of you to finish this last piece, then why are you going back into his past? Why is he sharing only certain moments with you? There's no need."

"Why does that scare you?"

"Because on July 27th, 1890, Van Gogh shot himself in the chest in the field outside Auvers. He died thirty-six hours later."

Lucinda was transfixed. "He mentioned a Margot?"

"A neighbor in Holland when he lived there in 1884. Margot Begemann. He loved her dearly, but both families were bitterly opposed to their love. She committed suicide after several failed attempts. It was shortly after that he began his 'crises' periods. That was when those violent slashes became predominate in his work."

"His 'crises' . . . were those his own seizures? Like mine?"

"I'm almost positive."

"But why are my seizures so . . . so unrelenting now?"

"Because whatever it is he needs to do through you needs to be done soon. When was the last time you looked at a calendar?"

"I don't remember."

"Today is July 27th."

". . . and the painting still isn't finished? Is that what scares you?"

Jordan was a statue. "No. What scares me is the thought that goes through my mind when I try to see this from his point of view. I love life, and I love my work. I think I would be willing to do anything to ensure that I could keep on creating for as long as possible."

Lucinda rubbed her eyes and exhaled impatiently. "I wish you'd tell me what it is that's—"

"What if he's decided that a few more months of life, even life in a sick body, is better than staying where he is now? What if he's taking you back into his past, to places you have never seen before, in order to—Christ, I can't believe I'd think this of him—in order to leave you there so he might use your—"

"Whoa," said Lucinda, holding up her hands. "Stop right there. Now, I will admit that this is all quite . . . extraordinary. We both know that something is definitely going on here, but when you start saying that Vincent is trying to trick me out of my body so he can move in for a little while, it's crossing the line into something too weird, Jordan. Do you understand? I'm not totally naive about people. I think I'm perceptive enough to know when someone has a hidden agenda and I truly don't think he does." She was shaking. "I really can't talk about this anymore, at least not right now. I don't feel well, I really don't, and I'm sick of it. Okay? I know that I insisted you tell me what was bothering you, but now I'm sorry I did because you're right, it's kind of scary, so can we just drop it for a little bit? Can we just stay here and enjoy each other's company?"

He leaned forward and kissed her—gently, warmly, compassionately.

Lucinda felt her bowels shift. A thick, wet gurgle filled the air as something leaked into her belly-bag. She looked away from Jordan. "You must find me repulsive."

"Far from it. Even the colors of autumn cannot compare to your eyes. Oh, Lord—I can't believe I said something that corny."

Lucinda began weeping. The smell from her belly-bag reached her, causing her to cough and weep all the more; for all the days of her childhood spent alone in her room, a sketchbook her only companion; for all the times she'd sat listening to the other children playing outside her window, laughing and shouting as they rode their bicycles and played sandlot baseball and argued whose turn it was next on the swing; for all the moments when she looked up from her work long enough to realize that she would never be a part of it, and there was no self-pity in these tears, only an aching resignation which was as much a part of her as her flesh and shadow. Just to have one of those days back, to be a normal healthy child for just a few hours, to have known the joy of jumping into a pile of leaves, a mud fight, a quick, silly game of hide-and-go-seek.

Then the regret blossomed and matured, meeting her at this point in time, making her wish that she were sitting here a whole and desirable woman, one who didn't rage against the frailty that entrapped her, one who didn't have to resort to the humiliating recourse of tears in order to grapple with the cold equations that equaled her reality, a woman who—

—she took a deep breath and began to calm herself. She

felt Jordan release the brakes on her wheelchair and begin pushing her toward her dresser. In the mirror her hair looked tangled and lifeless, not the bright, glowing stream of copper that it was when she was freshly showered.

Jordan smiled at her reflection. "I can see why he is so taken by you. If I were in his position, I wouldn't hesitate to travel across time for you."

She wiped her eyes.

Jordan picked up a brush and ran it through her hair. "See?" he whispered. "A countess is born."

"You may kiss my ring, good sir."

Jordan laughed his roaring Frenchman's laugh, filling her with a sense of need and being needed; a sense of place and comfort.

Then he turned her chair around and kissed her again.

She felt herself grow warm; she could barely contain the excitement his touch brought to her. She gently put her arms around his neck.

"I have been alone most of my life," he said, never looking away from her eyes. "Children mocked me because of my size, my face . . . I've had little need for any companionship aside from the easel, canvas, and brush. After I turned forty I realized that something was absent from my life, so I volunteered to give free art classes at various grade schools and hospitals and . . . well, that's how I came to be here. I look at you and feel the heat of a thousand secret flames. Your breath is a song to me, whispering promise. I feel as if the arc of my life has been pointing toward this moment for all of my days. And sometimes, when the light comes in through the window and you turn to look at it, your eyes sparkle and I imagine I know what God must have felt like the first time He gazed upon the creation that was woman . . . or maybe I'm just full of shit and you happen to be beautiful but can't see it and I've been in love with you for a long time."

Lucinda pulled him to her and kissed him once again. Then, suddenly, as she lay her head against his shoulder, the effects of the last several days draped over her; she felt the sweat, the pain, the time.

"Jordan, I . . . I'd like to take a bath but I don't . . . oh, God, this is harder than I thought it would be. I don't want you to call the nurse to help. I hope you don't—"

He picked her up out of the wheelchair and carried her into the bathroom.

As he gently bathed her body, he took great care not to jostle her belly-bag. "I want to tell you one more thing," he whispered. The water seeping from the cloth in his hands massaged her with warmth, easing the strain. "I know, now, that I was meant to be here for you. Shhh—don't say anything, just listen. It used to be, when I told someone the story of my life, it would stop there. But since I've met you . . ." She closed her eyes and Jordan kissed her wet hair and placed another warm, soaked cloth over her face. "Since I've known you, I have told you the story of my life, and you've asked to hear it again . . . and I find, now, that when I tell it over, it's no longer my story. It's *ours,* and I will protect that with sword and shield." The diamond droplets of water trickled down her cheek, glided over her chin, slipped down her neck, and slid a moist path between her breasts; then his hand was there, the soapy washcloth rubbing gentle circular patterns, moist and creamy, lilac-scented, and she stretched, arching her back, sighing as the washcloth dropped away and his lips began trailing down her neck, pausing at her shoulder, then to the slope of her breast, then he delicately cupped one breast in his hand, his thumb stroking her nipple until it became firm. His lips covered her nipple, drawing it into his mouth meekly yet hungrily, and she closed her eyes all the tighter, hearing a low growl rise from deep in her throat, emerging as a sigh, and the slowly drifting lights behind her closed lids separated, shimmering in rhythm with the spasms below her waist, becoming thousands of bright pinpoints that seemed to surge from somewhere in her center as she reached out and clutched the back of his head, guiding his wonderful lips to her other breast, feeling him take the nipple in his mouth as the fire and lights within her intensified, caressing her, moving her, rocking her, tickling, rolling, arching her toward him, and she felt the softness of the bed beneath, the satiny brush of the sheets, his firmness inside her, pulling back teasingly before plunging in again, and she held him close, pulled him into her until she thought he was buried inside up to her throat as she shuddered and pulled her legs against his pressing hips, digging her fingers into his shoulders, forcing him deeper as she threw her head back and cried out—

—then he kissed her neck again, whispered something she didn't understand, and moved away.

She blinked, rolled over on the bed, and saw Vincent staring out the window. His face glistened from the lights in the street below. The echoes of music and laughter drifted into the room on an intoxicating midnight breeze.

He seemed so weary, so worn-out.

"What is troubling you?"

"I am so very happy that you are here with me," he said.

She rose from the bed and quickly dressed, then joined him by the window, feeling somehow detached from everything, as if part of her had remained trapped in the dream branch.

"Something is wrong," she whispered.

"Did you know that you talk in your sleep?"

"What do I say?"

"You talk of strange people and places. Who is this Jordan you keep mentioning?"

A great jolt tore through her, pulling her out of herself, allowing her to hover above the scene for an instant, then spiraling her back down to Vincent's side.

She felt dizzy and disoriented. Van Gogh put a hand on her shoulder. "Are you all right, my dear?"

"Yes, fine . . . thank you." Something felt . . . felt—

—then Van Gogh was leading her toward the door. "Come. Walk with me. I want to show the field. I want you to be with me at . . . I want you there. I need for you to be there with me. I've a gift I wish for you to take."

She thought she detected the echo of someone else calling her name.

"You should sleep," she said. "You've not been well and—" He touched her lips, and she was silent.

"I mourn for many things, my love. I mourn for the damage we have done to our souls, I mourn for the starving and the lonely and the madness in us all, the loss of our wonder . . . but when all is said and done, no notice is taken. I cry and lament, I rage at friends and strangers, I do myself harm, but in the end, as ever always, I go out at night to paint the stars."

Once again Lucinda was jolted from her body, and as

she hovered this time she saw the many darkspace faces clearly, though she recognized none. Looking down she saw not Van Gogh but Jordan, holding her in his arms, his words a dim echo in the thick air.

". . . he can't have you, I won't let . . ."

Then she was plunging down to a field upon which the moon and stars cast an ethereal glow. She glimpsed the hunched shadow of man, heard the great, unmistakable crack of gunfire, and cried out.

The darkspace came to her again, but this time only one face passed her, a face she recognized, but then there was nothing but the wind, wrapping its arms around her. She began walking through the field. Her foot brushed against something. She knelt to pick it up.

A smoking pistol.

A great pain took possession of her core. Slipping the pistol into her pocket, she stumbled out of the field and through the mazelike streets back to Van Gogh's flat. She opened the door and crossed to the bed, then lay down, the pain finding fiery focus in her chest.

She closed her eyes and saw windmills and dim pool halls, noble miners marching out of caves, shimmering trees under starry skies, an old man sitting in his chair, hunched over, his face buried in his hands—

—and realized that something about this last image was different from the painting at the hospice. Before she could discern what it was, someone jostled her arm.

She opened her eyes and saw a stranger looking down at her. His eyes were gray and his face deeply lined with worry. He brushed some hair out of her eyes and dabbed at her forehead with a cool, wet cloth.

"Shh," said the stranger. "Do not try to speak. The doctor will be here soon." She looked slowly around; she was still in Vincent's flat. Something was leaking from her belly-bag—

—no, not her bag, not at all, so what—

—she looked down.

The center of her chest was pulp; bleeding and painful.

"What is . . . who are . . ."

The voice issuing from her throat wasn't hers but she recognized it, nonetheless.

"Don't you recognize me, brother?" whispered the

stranger, wiping tears from his eyes. "It's me, Theo. Please, Vincent, say that you know me."

Then she knew.

Jordan had been right.

And, quietly, she resigned herself to die in Vincent's place.

"No one will ever know," she whispered. "And if they did, no one would ever believe it." She wondered how long it would take before Jordan realized that the person living in her body and speaking in her voice was not her, but Van Gogh. She wondered what they would do, how they would react, whether or not they would dare to tell anyone.

Theo's face became a fleshy blur as he picked up a pillow.

"I wish I could die now," she said in Van Gogh's voice.

And was answered somewhere in the darkness by an echo: *Only a moment longer, my love, my friend. All I wished was just a few moments alone with the image, nothing more, and then I shall give to you all the pictures in my head that I never lived to paint. Forgive me for my selfishness but I had to see for myself what you have done with my sketch, how you took the base and built upon the image I was no longer worthy to express. I am sorry for frightening you, but I will leave you now—but know this one last thing to be true: I treasure you.*

Don't you know that I would never abandon you to darkness?

There is no image worth the price of a soul.

Then the pillow was pressing against her face, pushing down, cutting off her breath. She became aware of the darkspace, the tunnel, the faces and bright pinpoints, and her heart ached for the loss of Jordan and what time might have remained for them, and suddenly, as she felt herself slipping away one last time, she wanted to be with him again, not here, not dying in Vincent's place, and she raged against the darkspace, choking, her mind screaming out Jordan's name as her hands began flailing against the stone-heavy pillow—

—*remember me to your Jordan, my love*—

—which suddenly was pulled away.

Her chest hitched, and she coughed, blinking her eyes against the light.

Two beefy hands cupped her face.

"Lucinda?"

She opened her eyes and saw him leaning over her.

"Jordan?"

He pulled her into him, embracing her and weeping. "I'm sorry," he said, throwing the pillow aside. "I could think of no other way to force him to leave, to make you return to me. I would have hated living from this moment on without you."

As she lay her hand against his shoulder, whispering, "We were wrong about Vincent, my love," she saw the painting, complete at last.

The old man was no longer alone.

Across from him sat an elegant, aged woman who was looking at him and laughing. She was the ghost of an errant wish—that a woman might never lose the radiance which crossed her features when a suitor came to call, never see her beauty dissolve little by little in the unflattering light of each dawn, and never know a day when the scent of roses from an admirer did not fill her rooms. She was every night you sat alone and lonely, wishing for the warm hand of a lover to hold in your own as autumn dimmed into winter and youth turned to look at you over its shoulder and whisper farewell: all this was in her face, accentuated by a benevolent resignation that told you she was happy, here in this room with this hunched old man who, Lucinda could now see, was not weeping into his hands but, rather, laughing at a joke just told to him by the woman. The scene shone with quiet joy, well-earned repose, and a sense of home; at the last, a home finally found.

As she wrapped her arms around Jordan, she smiled, part of her mind wishing Vincent peace.

I will paint the stars in your memory, she thought.

Outside, it began to sprinkle, and Lucinda decided that she'd had it all wrong; after so many years of staring out countless lonely windows, after so many years of daydreaming among the raindrops that whispered against the glass, after so many years of wishing for a home and the tenderness of a loved one, she finally realized that it wasn't the color of sadness, after all . . .

Rain was very, very pretty.

DREAMSTITCHING

by Kristin Schwengel

Kristin Schwengel is a romantic at heart. A recent graduate of the University of Wisconsin at Green Bay, she lives in Milwaukee, where she works in a bookstore. Her work has appeared in the anthologies Sword of Ice and Other Tales of Valdemar, Legends: Tales from the Eternal Archives, *and* Black Cats and Broken Mirrors. *And yes, she has done elaborate embroidery.*

A gray mist engulfed her and she stood for a moment, staring around her in amazement. Only moments ago she had been working her embroidery, her mind drifting as it often did when she concentrated only on the stitches. Now it seemed that she had drifted into this no-place of dank clouds. The air was heavy, full of portent. Confused but curious, she moved forward, unsure if she moved out of the mist or deeper into it. Then the air lightened. The mist thinned to a fog and she saw trees taking shape in the gray around her, great pines with branches whose needles pulled at her clothing and whose tops were buried in cloud.

The forest was silent, bereft of bird calls and animal noises. Even the trees were still, for no breeze brushed her cheek or whispered through the pines such as she knew from her walks in her own gardens. She frowned, realizing that her stitchery had disappeared from her hands, but she had no recollection of having dropped it. Everything was so strange here, she thought, in this absolute stillness that held only her, the trees, and the mists.

Though she knew not where she was or how she had

arrived there, she was not frightened. This forest land intrigued her, and she wandered deeper into the trees. She discovered nothing but more trees and fog, however, and soon grew weary. Sitting beneath a great pine, she leaned back against its trunk and closed her eyes, breathing deeply the spicy tang of the fir's pitch. As she relaxed, she heard a faint sound, like whispering, and a strange sensation pressed against her temples. She felt the muslin of her embroidery between her folded hands and knew that, somehow, she had returned home. She could even make out the sound that had drawn her back from the strange place— the conversation held in undertones at the opposite end of the hall.

"What are we going to do with her?" Queen Lizaveta whispered to her husband, nodding across the room at their eldest daughter.

King Beren stroked his beard and followed his wife's gaze.

"She's always doing that embroidery, and she never says a word," the queen fretted. "And you know what the prophecy said about one of our girls, but no mention was made of the other. I wonder what that means for her." She frowned down the distance of the hall at Shalyssa, whose eyes never left her stitchery.

The king nodded sagely for his wife's benefit. His heir perplexed him, as well, but he failed to understand his wife's concern. Who could worry so much over the vagaries of one when such a grand future was foretold for the other?

"Does she ever even finish anything?" that other daughter now hissed, stepping up to her mother's side.

King Beren turned back and gave his younger daughter an indulgent smile.

"Well, Lynore, I, for one, have never seen her finished work," the queen responded, taking her youngest child's hand and patting it.

Lynore pouted. "It isn't fair that we should never see anything of hers. Why can't we even look at it?" Her voice rose as she spoke, and Beren frowned at her, not wishing her to draw the attention of either her sister or the courtiers.

Shalyssa tried to ignore the whispers, but found it near impossible. Her mother's complaints and confusion and her father's noncommittal comfortings were a fixed constant in her life.

Until recently, she had been able to dismiss them, but now the suitors were coming and complicating matters. When she and her twin sister Lynore had been born, the faery Athwynna had been present and had foretold that one of the two princesses would wed the King of the Silver Mountain. King Beren and Queen Lizaveta had looked at their offspring and had drawn their own conclusions.

Shalyssa, with her raven hair, pale skin, and large eyes, had been disregarded. But they decided Lynore, blonde, rosy-cheeked, blue-eyed, would be just the sort to appeal to this unknown king. In fact, they named her to reflect their conviction, for 'lynore' meant 'silver' in an old, half-forgotten language of the north.

As the girls became older, their characters were shaped by the pronounced disparity in their treatment. Lynore became the image of her mother in personality as well as looks, for Queen Lizaveta, too, had been the pampered darling of her royal family. Shalyssa, always quiet, retreated even farther from her family, studying her books and working the intricate patterns of her stitchery.

Shalyssa gave a small, secret smile and turned to the book at her side—a small leather-bound volume of old and forgotten lore that she had uncovered from the dustiest corner of the library a few months earlier. The book described some of the connections between dreams and reality—and how one could sometimes bring dreams to life. She had no idea of how one could do so, but she often longed for her daydreams to become real, and of late it had seemed that they were. She bent her head to her embroidery, concentrating with such intensity that her surroundings fell away from her and she was again in the misty no-place.

Her needlework disappeared from her hands as she walked through the fog. Shalyssa had been here before, but each time she explored a little farther, saw a bit more. Each time she came here, the lands seemed to grow more real. The heavy air oppressed her breath at first, but that passed as she walked, until she emerged from the mists into the forest. Although she had explored here before as well, the atmosphere was different today. It took a moment for her to realize that the change was sound—she heard hints of a rustling breeze as she walked, and the dimness of the forest faded until she was sure she would soon see the sun slanting through the pines. She moved forward, eager to explore further, until she nearly ran into a high stone wall. She followed the wall, seeking an end or an entrance. Rounding a corner, she came upon a wrought-iron gate that stood slightly ajar. Peeping through, she saw a beautiful garden, well-tended and full of flowers that filled her eyes with color and the air with delicate scent.

Shalyssa pushed the gate open a little wider and slipped inside, following the cobblestone path around the outskirts of the garden, pausing often to admire the exquisite blooms. It had taken her only a moment to see that this garden was far larger than her own at home, and that it held a greater variety of plants and flowers. At every step, some new shape or color caught her eye, each planted among foliage that enhanced its beauty. Whoever tended this park was very skilled, and she smiled in delight, reveling in the exquisite arrangement. The colors of the blooms were blended to create an artist's palette of light and shadow, drawing the viewer along the cobbled path. Shalyssa followed the pattern, hoping she could recall some of the settings to use in her own garden.

One flower in particular attracted her—a kind of lily that grew in profusion everywhere. She stopped and bent down to admire one, a graceful ivory cup that gleamed against the dark green foliage. Reaching out, she brushed her fingertips against petals as smooth as the silk threads of her embroidery. A smile touched her lips.

"Those lilies are my favorites, too."

Shalyssa leaped to her feet and whirled to face the speaker. A man only a little older than she, he had one hand outstretched as though to assist her to stand. She had a vague impression of dark hair and lean, even features before she dropped her eyes, ashamed of her invasion into his lands.

"My lady, I did not mean to startle you. Please don't go," he added, for she had half-turned and her eyes were seeking the gate as if to flee. His voice was gentle, holding an anxious note that stayed her feet, though her mind insisted that she must leave.

"Please," he said again, softly, and she turned her eyes back to his.

"I am sorry," she whispered, a hint of fear still in her eyes. "I did not mean to trespass in your private gardens—I did not know."

" 'Tis only what I deserve for leaving the gate open, is it not?" He laughed. "Come, let me show you the gardens." The way his warm hazel eyes lit up when he smiled sent a strange chill coursing through her veins, a chill unrelated to her earlier fright. He raised his hand to her again, and Shalyssa could see a faint shadow of earth underneath his nails. Somehow, the proof that this handsome man clad all in black was both owner and gardener comforted her, and she smiled slowly in response to his infectious laughter.

Taking his outstretched hand, she said, "I am called Shalyssa," in a voice soft with disuse.

"And I am Dirreth," he responded, tucking her hand in the crook of his arm and leading her down the winding path. At his touch, a flood of warmth filled her blood, following the course of her chill.

"All this . . . is yours?" Her voice was tentative, unwilling to shatter the peaceful calm of the silence.

He nodded.

"Is the design yours as well?"

"This is how I pass my spare hours," Dirreth explained, gesturing around him.

"The gardens are beautiful," she said. "So many plants I have never seen before! And they are put together so perfectly, to have such a wonderful effect. I could never hope to recreate such a sight in my own gardens, no matter how I tried." She stopped speaking, embarrassed by her effusiveness.

Dirreth paused in the middle of the path. "You do not recognize some of these plants?" Shalyssa shook her head. "Come. If you would like, I would be happy to teach you what I know." At her nod, he led her closer to the flowerbeds. "Tell me what you do not have in your own gardens."

For some time they walked more slowly, for Shalyssa often pointed out a bloom or foliage plant that was strange to her. Dirreth named all of them, listing their properties and sometimes even telling legends associated with one or another.

When she grew weary, Dirreth noticed without a word being spoken. He led her over to a stone bench tucked among some sheltering hedges and seated himself beside her. As they sat in silence, Shalyssa darted sidelong glances at her mysterious companion. They had spoken of much this afternoon, but what did she really know of him that made her so comfortable in his presence?

He knew a great deal of herb-lore, that was certain. None of the other noblemen she had ever met cared anything about flowers beyond having their squires bring gaudy bouquets to the objects of their affections. She wondered what sort of bouquet this Dirreth would bring to his lady, and was startled by the intensity of her desire to be the recipient. She had met him moments ago, and yet something about him was so familiar. It was as if they had already known each other, impossible though that was, and on meeting it was just a matter of recognition. It could not be so, and yet it made sense.

"Why is it," she said, breaking their companionable silence, "that I feel I have known you for a long time, though we have just met?"

Dirreth turned to her, and she felt a shock pass through her at the unnamed emotion in his eyes. "You feel it as well?" he asked in return.

She nodded. "But why?" she pressed.

A shadow crossed his face, so faint she doubted that she had seen it. "If I could, I would explain it," he said, smiling to dismiss her query, "but I know only that I have been waiting for this."

"What do you mean?"

"I cannot truly explain," he said again, laying his hand over hers on the stone bench. Another jolt ran through her at the gentle touch.

Shalyssa frowned, dissatisfied with his evasion, and would have persisted in her questions, but the mists rose up around her and she was pulled back to her own solar. A peculiar sense of loss haunted her, and the young man's image passed before her mind's eye. The sound that had brought her back, a rapping at her door, ceased, and the door opened to reveal her sister.

"Another one has come, Shalyssa," Lynore said, her voice taunting. "Father says you are to come down to meet him." She smirked, delighting in interrupting her sister's work. Stepping further into the room, she approached Shalyssa, who carefully finished the stitch she had been setting.

"Come, let me see," Lynore begged in a wheedling voice, taking another step forward.

A slight frown creased Shalyssa's brow and she shook her head, still absorbed in her work.

Lynore pouted and her voice changed from begging to demanding. "I want to see! You're always working on that and no one ever gets to see it! It's not fair." She darted forward, reaching out to snatch the muslin, but Shalyssa folded the fabric in half to hide the design and hugged it protectively to her chest, glaring at her sister. The fierce anger in her eyes startled Lynore, who backed away but did not end her tirade.

"It's just not fair!" she repeated. "All the handsome ones come for you, too, even though you just ignore them. Only when they get tired of that do they pay any attention to me."

Shalyssa blinked, surprised by her sister's outburst. It had seemed logical to her that suitors would seek her out first, for her sister could not wed until she did. As heir to the kingdom, too, she would be considered a fine prize. Never for a moment did Shalyssa think that any of them truly wanted her, only her position and what she brought them. The young princes did not care for her silence, and so they turned to Lynore, who laughed and talked and promised nothing. This only strengthened Shalyssa's conclusions about the sincerity of their affections. She could not fathom how her sister could see things so differently.

Lynore glowered at her, then heaved a great sigh. "Well," she snapped, "I'm just glad Father has to marry you off to one of them soon, before the King of the Silver Mountain comes for me. Now hurry up— Father's waiting." She whirled and flounced out of the room, waiting in the hall for her sister to follow.

Still stunned, Shalyssa locked her embroidery away in its casket before joining Lynore and hastening down to the audience chamber, where their parents stood talking with a handsome young man.

"Ah, daughters, you have returned. Come, Shalyssa," her father said, gesturing to her. She stepped forward until he took her hand and pulled her to his side. "This is Prince Rolff, heir to the kingdom of Ixantria. Rolff, this is my daughter and heir, the Princess Shalyssa."

Rolff took her hand and bowed over it, placing a courtly kiss on the tips of her fingers, then stood and smiled at her. She smiled back, surprised by the warmth in his eyes, so different from the cold calculation she was used to seeing in her suitors.

Lynore pushed forward next to Shalyssa, not quite hiding her anger at being slighted in the introductions.

"And this, Prince Rolff, is my younger daughter, Lynore," King Beren said, laying a fond hand on her shoulder.

Lynore smiled, batting her eyes as she extended her hand for the new prince to take. As etiquette demanded, Rolff bowed and kissed her fingertips, but Shalyssa saw a shadow of emotion in his eyes as he did so, one that she could only name scorn. She was surprised by how pleased she was to see it.

'When one seeks, one must know and focus on that which one seeks. One must see it, or that which represents it, to have true results.'

Shalyssa smiled and closed the little book. The lines had made little sense to her before, and so she had concentrated her efforts on the border of her embroidery. But now she understood, and took up her pen to draw what would be at the center of her stitchery—a delicate lily, to be worked in ivory against her ivory muslin, with only hints of the palest green at the center.

The first stitches of the lily were barely set in the fabric when she felt the now-familiar abstraction come over her. The walls of the great hall, where she sat in a corner by the largest window, disappeared to be replaced by the heady mists. She paused for only a moment before walking through the gray fog. She took the direction she believed was north, the same direction she had taken when first she had found the lily garden and Dirreth, the same direction she believed she had taken every time since.

Only moments passed before she was striding through the pines, brushing away the overhanging branches. Quickly she came upon the great stone wall, which she again followed to her left. When she came to the wrought-iron gate, it stood wide open in anticipation of her arrival.

And Dirreth was there, clad all in black as was his wont, holding out a fresh flower for her. Their fingertips brushed as she took the rose from him, and she blushed pink as the flower's petals as, with trembling hands, she fixed the delicate bloom onto the brooch she wore over her heart.

He smiled, his eyes teasing her with gentle affection, then took her hand and tucked it beneath his arm as they walked.

"Come," he said in his rich, warm voice, "I have something new to show you." Shalyssa heard the anticipation in his voice, along with a hint of nervousness, and wondered what could be causing it.

"Have the young buds bloomed, then?" she asked, eager to see what new colors might be revealed in the unfolding petals.

"Yes, they have," he answered, "and you wear one today—though it is as nothing so close to your beauty."

Shalyssa blushed again at his compliment, though her heart thrilled to it. He smiled slowly at her and they stood still, their eyes holding each other for a long moment.

It was Dirreth who glanced away first and began walking again, leading her into a new area of the gardens. She looked around her, studying the flowers and landscape. There were fewer blooms here, and more greenery. The hedges had been trimmed into a stern regularity much unlike the freer shrubbery that lined the rest of the garden.

"We are almost there," he said, stopping abruptly in the middle of the path, "but first, you must listen."

Shalyssa had grown accustomed to the near silence of this place, save for the gentle winds, and so it took a moment for her to recognize the light noise she heard. Wonder dawned in her eyes as she turned to Dirreth and her face lit up.

"Water!" she exclaimed, laughing aloud.

He grinned like a young boy, her excitement catching hold of him, and continued forward, leading her around a high hedge, behind which was laid out a beautiful water garden.

Shalyssa gasped and stepped a few paces ahead of him, delight glowing in her eyes as she admired the lush, dark greenery and the white flowers.

"Only lilies," she whispered, walking to a small pool and seating herself on the stone ledge around it. She reached out with the lightest touch to trace the curve of a lily that dipped dangerously close to the water, as though it sought to touch its own reflection.

"I designed it for you," Dirreth said. "Do you like it?" he asked, his concern over her reaction evident in the anxious tone of his voice and the wrinkling of his brow.

"It is wonderful," she sighed, "exactly as I have dreamed of planning a water garden." She realized the truth of her words only after she had spoken them—he had planned his garden for her just as she would have done for herself. "It is perfect," she added, smiling up at him. The emotion in his eyes caused her heart to leap.

He moved to sit beside her and she gazed up at him in anticipation. His hand gently traced the curve of her cheek down to her jaw, lifting her chin. He bent toward her and her eyelids fluttered closed. She couldn't seem to breathe, though her lungs felt near to bursting.

Then, just as his lips began to brush against hers, she felt an all-too-familiar sensation, the pulling away of her awareness from him and the gardens.

"Why can we never stay together more than moments?" she protested as the mists closed over her.

"Soon," he said, "soon, my love." He disappeared, his voice replaced by that of another. Shalyssa blinked, only to discover her father looming over her.

"Soon," he raged, "soon, you must make a decision! We cannot wait on your whims, daughter. The fate of this kingdom must be settled. As the heir and the eldest, you must wed, else your sister cannot. The law is clear on that. Further, you must wed before the next moon turns, or the faery Athwynna's prophecy will come to naught."

Lynore's golden voice rang out from the far end of the hall, where she sat at their mother's knee. "You cannot think to wait for the King of the Silver Mountain as well," she laughed, "for surely he will soon come for me."

In an expression so faint that none of her family noticed it, Shalyssa frowned. What cared she for this king, for the prophecy of the faery Athwynna?

"You must be ready to wed by now, daughter," Queen Lizaveta said. "Why, I was wed and a mother when I was yet younger than you."

Shalyssa shook her head slowly, still stunned by the suddenness of her return from the gardens. Her chest tightened at the thought of what her family had interrupted, and she longed with renewed intensity to be able to stay in the garden with Dirreth.

"Well, get ready!" King Beren snapped, misinterpreting her response. "You know that Athwynna's prophecy was to be fulfilled by the turning of the moon that would come on the twenty-first anniversary of your birth. Less than a fortnight remains. You must wed before then to leave your sister free.

"Shalyssa," her father continued in a softer voice, "the suitors come day and night to ask for the hands of the fair princesses. Does not one of them appeal to you?"

The image of Dirreth flashed unbidden before her eyes, and she knew that none of the princes who came could ever compare to him. She shook her head at her father and folded her embroidery, returning it to its place in the silver casket at her side and locking it tight with the silver key that hung on a chain round her neck. She picked up the casket, gathered up her books, and left the hall.

Stitch by careful stitch, the lily in the center of her embroidery took shape. Shalyssa frowned and closed her eyes, leaning away from the work and relaxing her hands and arms. She longed to escape, but found it difficult, for the abstraction that took her away into the misty no-place was long in coming. Taking a deep breath and clearing her mind of her fears, she returned her attention to her needlework. Finally, the great hall melted from around her and she was surrounded by the gray mists. They were darker than ever before, thick and dank. She hurried through them, but was unable to break free from them and found herself standing at the edge of the pine forest without the energy to continue.

She sat down and buried her face in her arms, breathing deeply to control her mounting frustration.

"Shh, 'tis not so bad as all that," a familiar voice smiled behind her.

"Dirreth!" she cried, lifting her head and turning to look in wonder at him. "But how came you here? I cannot find the garden, and I thought . . ."

"I am not tied to the garden," he said. "Or at least I am not so any longer. Your soul called to mine, and I come," he continued, then stopped at her curious look. "Suffice it that I am here and would not willingly leave you." He sat beside her and took her hands. "Remember that."

She nodded, though she did not understand, and the mists closed around her even as she would have asked him more.

"Ah, lady, you are cruel. Your silence wounds me," he protested, clasping his hands to his heart, his eyes sparkling.

Shalyssa smiled despite her exasperation and shook her head at the handsome suppliant. Rolff, unlike all the others, was not dismayed by Shalyssa's silence. Rather than turn his attentions to the flirtatious Lynore, he continued still at Shalyssa's side, wooing her with all the wit and patience he could command. Today they walked in the royal gardens, and she had been surprised by his extensive acquaintance with plants and herbals. Now it seemed he chose humor to please her rather than knowledge to impress her.

Rolff took her hand and guided her to a stone bench near the hedge, seating her with care. Though his eyes were warm and his touch gentle, she felt none of the spark that she did when in Dirreth's company, and bit back a sigh.

Satisfied that she was comfortable, Rolff took a step backward, standing in the center of the sandy pathway.

"Now, my lady, allow me to entertain you as my father's fool does the court." Pinching the bridge of his nose, he gave a credible imitation of a pompous steward announcing the guests. "And now we present a comedy in one act, a farce entitled 'The Wooing of the Lady Shalyssa.'" He winked at her and stepped forward, plucking a rose from a shrub beside him, holding it out to an invisible other.

"Ah, lady, please accept this bit of beauty, though it can-

not compare to thy own." His voice was his own, his expressions those she had seen often since he had first come
to her father's palace.

Turning around, he assumed a haughty pose, one hand
outstretched as if in disdain of the sorry gift. "It is true, no
rose can ever compare to the blush of my cheek." He spoke
in a high falsetto, mimicking Lynore's manner perfectly.
"And roses have thorns, do they not?" He pouted. "I
would not have it said that I am harsh."

Rolff turned again and became himself. "A tulip perhaps,
with petals soft as my lady's hand?" He proffered another
bloom, then with lightning speed became the lady refusing it.

"A bloom of the spring will not suit, for it fades too
soon, and I would not have my beauty pass."

"A carnation, fair lady?"

"Ugh! Far too common. Perish the thought."

"Perish the thought, indeed. Perhaps forget-me-nots?"
His steps edged closer to Shalyssa, where she sat on the
bench and smiled openly.

"As if anyone could ever forget me!"

"So, then," he mused, "what flower befits my lady?" He
turned and scanned the flower beds, and Shalyssa realized
she was enjoying the farce. He was pleasant company,
though he was not Dirreth. Perhaps 'twould not be so
bad—she censured her thoughts, appalled that she could
even consider the idea.

"Ah-ha!" Rolff cried, interrupting her thoughts. "Here
is the flower for my lady!" He bent over and plucked a
bloom, hiding it from her as he stepped forward. "As fair
and delicate as she, graceful and fragile—true perfection,
as is my lady." He dropped to his knee before her, forgetting his charade, and raised his hand, on which rested a
single ivory lily.

Shalyssa stood and fled, ignoring Rolff's calls to her,
reaching for the chain around her neck even as she hurried
to her solar, where the silver casket awaited.

Shalyssa raised her embroidery to the light, turning it
and examining it with an appraising eye. The flower in the
center was finished, and all that remained was to finish the
border, an elaborate spiral of interwoven bands that looped

around each other in a frozen dance with the stem of the lily as their ending point. She selected a strand of colored thread and began her work, hoping that this time she would reach the mists and the forest, for in the last few days she had found it more and more difficult to do so.

The mists were thick, a dark gray that seemed to cling to her skirts and weigh them down. Try though she might, she could take no more than a few steps in any direction before exhaustion struck her and she was forced to rest. The silence oppressed her, and for the first time since she had discovered the mists, fear sent a chill down her spine. She longed to see Dirreth, and not knowing how to reach him, she spoke aloud.

"Dirreth, what am I to do? He's so kind, and Father insists that I must come to a decision, and soon. If I do not, I am afraid that he will make the decision for me . . ." She buried her face in her hands, standing alone in the misty no-place, and suddenly she knew he was there.

"Patience, my love," he murmured, and she turned on him in anger and frustration.

"How can I be patient? My father won't be patient, for I *must be wed.* I care not for the formalities, nor even for the fact that the heir must be wed before he or she is one-and-twenty. Let Lynore wed whom she chooses! Let her wed her King of the Silver Mountain, as it is prophesied to occur within a week." Not noticing the startled look Dirreth gave her, she went on. "It is she who craves the queenship, not I. It means nothing to me." She looked away, taking a long breath to calm herself. "I care only for you," she said, her voice thick with unshed tears.

Turning back to him, she saw that he seemed different somehow, paler, more of a dream or vision than he had ever appeared to her. She had always thought of him as being as real as she, there in the mists and the gardens, but the strange pallor of his skin made her wonder. He saw her fear and sighed, then took her hand and held it tight within his own.

"Though I seem far, know that I am closer to you than ever." He raised his other hand to forestall her protest. "You must trust that all will be well." The pressure of his hand on hers faded. When she looked at their linked fingers, she was able to see the outline of her own hand through his. Then he was gone and she was again alone, weeping in the mists.

King Beren drew himself up to his full height and frowned at his heir.

"Shalyssa, your stubborn behavior has caused me no end of trouble and embarrassment. A parade of suitors comes before you, and yet you reject each and every one. Only two days remain before the turning of the moon, and then you shall be one-and-twenty. The heir must be wed before reaching that age, or forfeit the throne to the next in line— and there is none to forfeit to, for Lynore will be one-and-twenty as well! The security of the throne will be shaken, and the fate of this kingdom cannot wait on your whims!" Beren paused, calming himself before he continued. "I will stand for this no longer, and surely Rolff deserves better than this from our hands. This marriage will go forth, whether you will it or not." His eyes softened at the distress in her face, and for the first time he regretted agreeing with his wife's ultimatum. "I would have you agree, daughter. Rolff is a good man, and Ixantria a fine kingdom," he continued in a pleading voice. "What say you?"

Shalyssa looked down at the stitchery in her hands for a long time, tears welling in her eyes, and gave a tiny nod.

All the folk of the city gathered in the great square to hear the king's announcement of Shalyssa's betrothal to Rolff of Ixantria. The king and court stood on the palace steps, watching the milling crowd while they waited for Shalyssa to arrive.

"Where is she?" Queen Lizaveta fretted, wringing her hands. "She agreed to this match. Why is she not here for the announcement?"

King Beren, having seen the tears in his eldest daughter's eyes, was more patient.

"Hush, love," he reassured her. "Shalyssa will be here. She knows the duty she owes her country and her people." He would have continued, but a great noise at the main gate drew the attention of all.

A magnificent procession approached, led by two riders clad all in black. The first was astride a great black stallion, whose trappings were black and silver. The second rode a white stallion with trappings also of black and silver, and carried a black banner with an emblem of a silver unicorn. Looking neither to the right nor to the left, the two rode straight to the castle, where the king and his court stood waiting in stunned silence.

When they pulled up in front of the king, the second man urged his horse a step forward and spoke in a voice for all to hear.

"The King of the Silver Mountain," he announced, "has come to claim his destined bride."

King Beren and Queen Lizaveta smiled at each other and stepped apart, leaving a space between them for Lynore to step forward. She looked up at the stranger, admiring his handsome form and giving him her most inviting smile.

The King of the Silver Mountain looked down at her from atop his black steed, frowned, and glanced over at his companion. The second man spoke again.

"You have another daughter, do you not, King Beren?"

"Why, yes, I do," he said, surprised that these strangers should know his name. "But she is this day to be betrothed to . . ." His voice trailed off as the King of the Silver Mountain swung off his horse and walked up to the castle, brushing past the royal family.

Lynore gave a strangled cry of denial and reached after him as though to hold him and keep him to her. When he continued to ignore her, she burst into tears, flinging herself on her mother's breast and weeping aloud. Queen Lizaveta patted her shoulder, but her attention was fastened on the young king, who disappeared into the castle. King Beren looked down at his younger daughter, but his curiosity defeated his concern for her.

"Hush, dear," he said, his tone sharper than he had ever used with her. Her only response was to wail louder. He glowered at the queen, who shrugged helplessly. He frowned once more at his daughter, then turned to follow the King of the Silver Mountain. Lizaveta gave Lynore a brisk shake and did the same, and the court went with her.

Rolff looked over at the weeping Lynore, who raised her head from her hands and turned piteous eyes on him. He shuddered and hurried after the court, following after this stranger who made his way unerringly through the palace.

*   *   *

Tears streaming down her face, Shalyssa set the last stitches in her embroidery. The last few times she had worked her sewing, she had not seen Dirreth even in the mists. Today, when she most needed the escape to the calm of the fog and forest, she had been unable to reach them, as hard as she concentrated.

She heeded not the opening of the door to her solar, sure that it was one of the ladies-in-waiting sent by her father to fetch her. She would not go, she had decided, until she had finished the pattern. Carefully, she placed the last stitch and set the knot. As she raised the work to her face so she could bite off the thread, she saw a glimpse of black clothing on the person who stood beside her. Her breath caught in her throat, for she knew of none who wore black, save for *him*. She closed her eyes to fight back the tears as she folded the fabric so the pattern was framed in the center and set the muslin on the low table beside her. Only then did she raise her gaze to the one who stood before her, one hand outstretched.

A smile lit her face as the tears spilled over her cheeks again. "Dirreth," she said, and all the court gasped, for her voice was as clear as silver.

Rolff stood by the door with the king and queen. A sad smile of understanding crossed his face when he saw the flower that the young king held out to Shalyssa, for he remembered the day she had fled from him in the garden. "Futile, to fight for a heart already another's," he murmured to no one, then turned and walked out the door.

Shalyssa stood, taking the ivory lily from Dirreth's hand and placing it atop the lily of her embroidery. Then she gasped, too, for the fresh flower melted into the fabric, uniting with the stitched flower.

"Did I not say you called me?" Dirreth said, smiling down at her amazed expression. "Come," he said.

Shalyssa took his hand and, leaving the embroidered dream behind them, they left the palace and joined his retinue for the journey to the Silver Mountain, where the mists and forests and gardens awaited.

THE FACE IN THE LEAVES

by Diane A.S. Stuckart

Having lived most of her life on the prairielands of North Central Texas, Diane A. S. Stuckart vows one day to move to the forest. She has a degree in Journalism from the University of Oklahoma and has published four critically acclaimed historical romances writing as Alexa Smart. This is her first foray into fantasy.

Miss Emma Pomeroy's Journal
Benbraver Abbey, Surrey, England

2 June 1881

Lord Hocksley attended the burial this morning. He was not difficult to spot among the mourners, his shock of golden hair and his pale gray morning suit a stark contrast to the somber black garb of the others. He was the last person I expected to see, given the enmity that had existed between him and my father. Death, however, has a way of putting an end to old grudges and putting a new face on the past. Thus, I politely greeted him after our other friends and neighbors had filed silently past the open grave.

"I realize we were not always the best of neighbors," his lordship said. The observation was something of an understatement, though I forbore to point that out. "However, I do hope you will let me express my condolences over the loss of your father. It was an accident, I understand?"

"We found him yesterday morning, in the small ravine

at the far edge of the woods," I replied. "Our stableboy reported a suspicious character lurking in that area, so Father and two of the men set out to investigate. They went separate directions, the better to cover more ground. He must have been walking along the ravine's edge. He lost his footing. It is a short drop, but in his fall he struck his head upon a rock. . . ."

At this point, I was forced to pause and dab at my eyes, which were welling again. Only a day before, Father had been hale and hearty, attending to the day's chores with his usual enthusiasm. Now he was dead, and I was, for all intents and purposes, an orphan . . . though perhaps this is a melodramatic term, given that I have reached the advanced age of four-and-twenty and am well able to take care of myself.

I snuffled a moment longer into my damp handkerchief, grateful that Lord Hocksley refrained from those well-meant if annoying reassurances regarding "better places," and simply waited for me to regain my composure. When I glanced back up again, however, a frown had replaced his previous expression of sympathy as he repeated my earlier words.

"A suspicious character. I presume that he—or she—was never apprehended?"

"Jeffers and Bart, the men who accompanied Father, said they saw no sign that anyone had been wandering about. Of course, the description they were given of the intruder was unusual, to say the least."

Indeed, I had strongly protested when Father set out so close to dusk on what was, to my mind, a wild goose chase. Late that afternoon, the stable boy had stumbled into the manor house to frantically report he'd seen . . . something . . . in the woods. A man, young Jem had finally concluded, but swathed in a strange brown robe and with his face covered all in greenery. The face in the leaves, he had called it, half-weeping.

Given that the lad had returned quite late from a village errand and was in danger of a caning from the stable master, I suspected he had concocted the outlandish tale to avoid punishment. Father, however, had been convinced the boy's apparent fright was genuine and insisted that they search for the stranger.

I said nothing of this to Lord Hocksley, however; neither did I mention what I had found clutched in my
father's stiff fingers as I helped prepare his body for
burial . . . a crimson-and-gold oak leaf, half the size of
my palm and made of silk, as if it had been plucked from
a clever arrangement pinned to a woman's hat. Perhaps
Father had been reaching for it when he lost his balance.
Whatever the case, some impulse had made me tuck it
away in my handkerchief case.

Hocksley did not press me for further explanation but,
briefly taking my gloved hand, wished me the best before
making his way back to his carriage. I returned home
with Biggers and the rest of the staff, then went about
Father's usual chores that had been left undone these
past two days. So preoccupied was I with those tasks that
I had almost forgotten my brief encounter with the
earl . . . that was, until late in the afternoon, when Biggers brought me a note, red-waxed and stamped with a
noble crest.

My Dear Miss Pomeroy, the missive read, *Let me again
offer my condolences on your loss. I have been reflecting
on our conversation earlier today and believe I have some
information you might find of interest. I would be hon-
ored if you would take tea with me tomorrow at 5 o'clock
so that we may discuss the matter. Respectfully, Hocksley.*

I considered the unexpected invitation for many moments, given the impropriety of an unmarried woman
calling upon a gentleman. Finally, I concluded it was a
business matter and that tea with him would, therefore,
be acceptable. For I must know any scrap of information
connected with my father's death; thus, I will be at Bisbee
Hall at the appointed time.

3 June, Morning

I lay awake much of last night thinking upon Lord
Hocksley's invitation . . . a welcome distraction, since
it kept my thoughts from more grievous musings. Our
conversation following the graveside service had been, to
my knowledge, only the second between his lordship and
a Pomeroy. The first had occurred almost ten years earlier and within days of our first settling at Benbraver
Abbey. True to its name, it once had housed an order

of monks . . . and, until our acquisition, it had been part of his lordship's family estate for generations.

Viscount Bisbee, as the earl had been known then (his father had not yet succumbed to the effects of strong drink and, thus, still held the title) had been outraged at the loss of the abbey and surrounding woods. But he'd not directed his anger at his own sire, whose gaming and overspending had brought them to such a pass. Rather, the young viscount had ridden to the abbey to confront my father, who had just set his men to clearing a section of the woods in preparation for next season's plowing.

Father had crisply pointed out that it was hardly his fault Lord Hocksley gambled beyond his means and was forced to sell off land to pay his debts; neither was he to blame that Hocksley's forebears had lacked the foresight to entail their lands to avoid such parceling. His observations had not endeared Father to the young viscount. The latter had countered with a few choice epithets before spurring his steed, vowing as he departed in a cloud of good Sussex dirt that Benbraver Abbey and its woods would one day be his.

Secretly, I had found his dramatic words quite thrilling . . . but then, I had been but a girl of four-and-ten and, thus, prone to mooning over handsome young gentlemen. Not that the viscount would have noticed me, for I was small and plump, with honey-colored hair pulled back into unfashionable plaits. I have grown taller and slimmer in the intervening years, and now wear my hair becomingly pinned atop my head; even so, I rather suspect his lordship would not have noticed me yesterday had we simply passed on the street.

I do not fault Hocksley for this, given our respective status; still, it is a blow to my feminine vanity to know that I might be accounted attractive within my own set and remain quite invisible to a man like the earl. But it is only here, in the pages of my journal, that I will admit to such conceit . . . or to the fact that I am not all that far removed from the girl who found that young man so dashing.

How fortunate that I am not one of those women whose complexion is ill-suited to mourning's ubiquitous black.

Evening

Had I harbored any secret hope that his lordship's intentions toward me were less than honorable, I would have been sorely disappointed this afternoon at tea. During the brief visit, both his butler and housekeeper hovered outside the drawing room's open door, lest propriety be compromised. The conversation, however, proved enlightening . . . and more than a bit puzzling.

"You have no other relatives, then?" the earl had asked after I had poured and we had dispensed with the ritual pleasantries. "No male cousin or uncle to take over the estate for you?"

I explained to him that both my mother and my younger brother, Will, had died of the influenza more than half a dozen years ago; moreover, she and my father had been estranged from their respective families, eliminating the likelihood of a stray male relative now stepping onto the scene. Not that it mattered, I told him, for my father had been a modern man and considered a female child equally capable of running the estate after him. Thus, Benbraver Abbey and the surrounding lands all fell to me.

The earl nodded. "I was not questioning your ability to run the estate. My concern is more for your well-being, given that you are a woman alone there." He paused, as if seeking the right words, then went on, "I feel you should know, Miss Pomeroy, that your stable boy's odd account is not the first rumor regarding something uncanny in Benbraver Woods."

"Something uncanny?" I masked the sudden shiver his words sent through me with a polite smile and a shrug. "Really, Lord Hocksley, I do not believe in such things; besides which, I am hardly alone at the abbey. I have quite a large staff and, among them, several burly men who would be the match of any ghost or goblin."

"It is not ghosts or goblins of which I speak, but an entity far older and more powerful. Have you heard tell, perhaps, of the green man of Benbraver Woods?"

When I shook my head, he set down his teacup and frowned. "Ah, well, your ignorance on this matter is hardly surprising, given the short time your family has lived in the Abbey. Let me assure you, however, that stories of our green man have been passed down in my family for generations. In fact, there exists a very fine stone representation of him in the abbey gardens."

I confessed that, although I'd spent countless hours in that place, played there daily as a child, I had never stumbled across any such stone carving. This time, the earl smiled. "Then perhaps I might pay you a call in return, tomorrow, and show it to you."

It was less any interest in this so-called green man and more a sudden, feminine desire to experience another of the earl's smiles that led me to accept his offer with alacrity. We settled on mid-afternoon for our rendezvous, then spent several minutes more in conversation. His lordship even indulged me as I related a few of my favorite anecdotes about my father. I left Bisbee Hall in a relatively cheerful frame of mind, considering my recent bereavement.

Would it be inappropriate, I wonder, to brighten my black gown with a touch of lace?

4 June

Lord Hocksley arrived promptly at three o'clock. We adjourned to the L-shaped, walled garden, a glorious tangle of vines and flowers that hugged the abbey's southeast corner. Before her untimely death, Mother had tried and failed to bring order to this botanical chaos. For my own part, I have always enjoyed the garden's unruly character. Other than keeping the paths clear and plucking the occasional bouquet, I am content to let it grow as it will.

Hocksley took in the riot of flowers and creepers with what appeared to be a satisfied smile, then led me to the garden's far corner, where the path forms a cul-de-sac. I glanced up at the leaded glass of my second-floor bedroom window, which overlooks the garden at that very spot, then dropped my gaze again. Save for a crumbling stone bench and the curtain of ivy obscuring the wall beneath my window, I saw nothing of note. Then the earl stepped forward and, with a flourish, swept aside that ivy cascade to reveal the pale stone beneath.

"This, my dear Miss Pomeroy, is the green man of Benbraver Woods."

Chiseled into the abbey's outer wall was a life-sized face of a man . . . and yet, not a man. His not-quite-human features were surrounded by elaborately carved leaves layered like a bird's feathers around his stone brow, cheeks, and chin. He stared out from behind the vines with a zealot's intensity, while his full lips—oddly sensuous, for all they were carved from rock—were parted as if he were about to speak. Indeed, it was the most magnificent face I had ever before seen, for all that it was undeniably disturbing.

"The face in the leaves," I murmured, abruptly recalling the stable boy's description of the trespasser he had seen. Surely, this had to be the inspiration for his extraordinary tale though, to my knowledge, young Jem had never set foot in this garden before.

The earl, meanwhile, was running his fingers along a knoblike carving beneath the bas-relief face. "The green man once was quite the popular motif," he explained in the well-rehearsed tones of a Tower guide showing off the Crown Jewels. "Some called him Jack-in-the-Green or John Barleycorn, but he is a far older figure than any of those fanciful folk creatures. He is an image of death and resurrection . . . the symbol of the changing seasons . . . the representation of the new crop and the harvest. In these times, however, he exists merely as a quaint conversation piece of the garden. I fear no one much worships or fears him any longer . . . which might be our very great misfortune, indeed."

I would have smiled at this last, save for the odd note in his voice that convinced me he was not making an attempt at humor. "But you cannot be serious, my lord. Surely you do not believe that some angry pagan deity has run amok in Benbraver Woods."

"These woods are filled with many strange things, Miss Pomeroy. I have long since learned to temper my own innate skepticism with a healthy dose of open-mindedness."

With those blunt words, he let the ivy curtain fall back into place, once more obscuring the green man's face. Then he gestured me to follow him a short distance away, almost if he feared the stone being might overhear him.

"I trust I have not alarmed you unduly; it's just that I would not have you come to any harm. You see, I rather regret my bad behavior toward your family all these years. Perhaps it is not yet too late for the two of us to be friends."

The admission, delivered as it was with almost boyish candor, made me forget my momentary uneasiness. We parted a few minutes later, the earl having secured my promise that I would send him word immediately should I see or hear anything untoward. I agreed, though I boldly added the condition that he must come again to visit, to which proviso he seemed to have no objection.

Perhaps the next time I see him, I will have shed my dull black gowns for a more becoming shade of gray.

5 June

I dreamed last night of the green man. He was no longer frozen into his prison of stone that was the abbey wall, but had taken on living form. His hand, when I touched it, held the warmth of human flesh. The sensation sent—dare I say it?—a shiver of womanly desire through me. I awoke far later than usual to find I had flung aside my coverlet as I slept and lay sprawled in a most unseemly manner across the bed.

Mortified, I hurried to dress, not softening my black gown with the usual lace collar as a penance for my nocturnal transgressions. I was not able, however, to resist stealing out into the garden. After a guilty glance around me, I lifted the ivy curtain and reached tentative fingers to touch his carved features, assuring myself the face was cool stone, just as it should be. Then, feeling rather foolish, I hurried back into the house, where I have spent the day in worthwhile endeavors. Tonight, I shall be too tired to indulge in wanton dreams.

8 June, Early morning

The last few days have passed uneventfully, but today brings a disturbing revelation. I awakened less than an hour ago to find that someone—or something—had made its way into my bedchamber last night! The discovery has left me quite shaken, so that my quivering fingers already have caused me to blot the page . . . yet, I hesi-

tate to question Biggers or any other of the staff. But
for my own peace of mind, I will record what has happened in these pages.

I retired last night at the regular hour, having sipped
my usual cup of chocolate before pinching out my candle.
I slept far more soundly than I have in recent days, not
stirring until well after dawn. As soon as I awoke, I realized something was amiss, for my bedcovers were folded
at my feet. Worse, the ribbons of my night rail had come
untied, leaving my bare breasts completely exposed. I
hurried to cover myself, blushing at the thought that I
might have lain that way for the entire night. But the
blood promptly drained from my cheeks when I glanced
at the floor and saw a series of muddy footprints surrounding my bed.

I stifled the reflexive gasp that rose in my throat and
hurriedly clambered back beneath my coverlet, swad-
dling myself in its familiar comfort as my thoughts frantically raced. Someone had been in my room, had
undressed me as I slept . . . yet he had moved so quietly
that I never awakened. I peered again at the muddy pattern of prints. Had I to guess, I would say they were not
made by a shod intruder, but by someone tiptoeing about
in his bare feet. And, most frightening of all, they did
not lead to or away from the bed. Rather, it seemed as
if my nocturnal visitor simply had appeared in the middle
of my room, circled my bed, and then vanished again.
But how could such a thing be possible?

With a cry, I scrambled from beneath the covers again
and, snatching a damp cloth from my washstand,
scrubbed away the incriminating trail. That accomplished, I settled myself more calmly and sought a logical
explanation. Perhaps the footprints were my own. I might
well have walked about in my sleep, having first stepped
in a bit of mud that one of the upstairs maids had inadvertently tracked into the room.

When I examined the soles of my feet, however, they
were scrubbed quite clean, so that I was forced to seek
another explanation. As the moments passed, and none
offered itself, the image of the green man lodged itself
in my mind. I recalled my previous dream, and Lord
Hocksley's warning. Could it be that the earl was right,

and that this ancient pagan deity has indeed returned to walk his woods . . . and, more frighteningly, my bedchamber?

Noon

I have had a few hours to contemplate the morning's discovery and have concluded that something *is* amiss, though I refuse to attribute it to supernatural causes. I should not forget that Lord Hocksley offered his assistance should I experience anything unusual. I shall set down my pen and call upon him to see what sort of explanation he might offer for this mystery.

Evening

I gave the earl an accounting of these most recent events, neglecting only to mention the fact that I'd been but half-dressed when I had awakened. His lordship—or rather, Quillan, as he has asked me to address him—was duly distressed by what had happened, so much so that he offered to post one of his own men outside my bedchamber to keep watch. I refused him, of course, but his concern warmed me. Instead, I agreed to have one of the maids sleep in the room, which seemed to satisfy him. Now, Nance is snuggled in the bed beside me, her wide-eyed gaze keeping watch while I finish this entry. She and the staff now know that an intruder made his way into the house last night, and they are determined to catch him should he try his nocturnal invasion again. Of course, I have mentioned nothing of the green man to them, lest they succumb to superstition and flee the abbey, instead!

Oh, but I wish Father were still with us. . . .

18 June

I've seen no further evidence of nighttime visitors. Unfortunately, whispers have begun among the staff that the green man of Benbraver Woods roams his forest once more. Cook even claims that, earlier in the week, she saw his leafy face peering in at her through the kitchen windows as she was preparing the day's breakfast. I was surprised to learn I was the only one unacquainted with this local legend, and that no one else is unduly frightened of the pagan deity. Had they seen those muddy footprints, however, the others might not be so sanguine in their dismissal of him.

As for Quillan, he has become a regular visitor over the past fortnight, so that I suspect his intentions might point in directions other than neighborly concern. The better acquainted I am with him, the more I regret our two families' estrangement all these years. I think Father would approve of him, after all.

Lady Hocksley's Journal
Bisbee Manor

7 July, Midnight
Quillan and I were married by special license today, so that I am now Lady Hocksley. I have left the care of Benbraver Abbey to our steward to take up residence at Bisbee Hall with my new husband.

Husband. The very word sends a delightful shiver through me, for I have been initiated this night into the mysteries of matrimony. I must confess, it was nothing at all like I had expected, armed as I was with little more than the knowledge of lesser creatures' mating habits. My only moment of disappointment came afterward, when Quillan kissed me and then departed for his own adjoining chambers. It is customary, I know, for the married nobility to sleep apart; still, I selfishly would prefer to bed down together at night, as did my parents and do the common folk. But I will not spoil our first night as a married couple with complaints. Perhaps when he is more accustomed to having a wife at his side, Quillan will be willing to forgo such tradition, at least upon occasion, and spend the entire night with me.

As it is, I will take advantage of this unwanted privacy to once more take up my journal . . . though perhaps such records will no longer be necessary. Save for the occasional eager report from one or another of our flighty young housemaids, our geen man seems to have ceased his nocturnal wanderings. And no longer am I gripped by the feeling of foreboding that had held me in sway for so long. Perhaps Quillan's presence—and now, our marriage—has broken the string of uncanny events.

The green man, if he indeed ever existed, is seemingly now appeased.

And as for myself, I am happier than I ever thought I could be.

17 July

Something is very wrong. This morning, I went in search of Quillan on a trivial domestic matter. His bedchamber door was open, so I stepped past the threshold only to discover he was not within. I had turned to continue my search elsewhere, when a sliver of color caught my gaze . . . a scrap of cloth protruding from beneath his wardrobe door. The color was oddly familiar, crimson fading into gold. I bit my lip, my heart pounding faster as I bent to retrieve it. The scrap proved to be a silk oak leaf, identical to the one I had found clutched in my dead father's hand, and which now is tucked in with my handkerchiefs.

Uncertain what I might find, yet sure I could not rest until I knew, I eased open the wardrobe. A few moments search uncovered a most extraordinary thing . . . a mask completely covered with layers of silken leaves in shades of red, gold and brown. Hands shaking, I went over to his washstand and gingerly pulled on the sacklike covering so that, save for slits cut for the eyes, nose, and mouth, it covered my entire face and head. Then, taking a deep breath, I gazed into the mirror.

The image that stared back at me bore a striking resemblance to the stone carving of the green man in the abbey garden. A terrible suspicion gripped me, and I swiftly tugged off the mask again. I shoved back into its hiding place and slammed the wardrobe doors upon it; then, snatching up my journal, I fled the house for the sanctuary of the abbey.

I have been here in the abbey gardens for almost two hours now, long enough for the summer sun to warm my chill flesh . . . long enough for my suspicions to solidify into certainty. But what will I do? I cannot confront Quillan with what I have learned, and I am uncertain who I can trust among the servants. Indeed, I dare not even commit what I most fear to paper. Yet I cannot return home as if nothing happened.

He is here! I can hear his stallion clomping around the crushed gravel drive that leads to the abbey's main entry. I do not know if he has deliberately come looking for me, or if he simply has business here with his steward. But I cannot let him find me, not yet. He would look into my eyes and read there the tragic knowledge that is carved upon my heart. What he would do then, I fear to guess. I must flee again. . . .

18 July

It is over. I will record the ending to my fantastic tale and then put aside this journal, never to open it again.

I managed to make my way, unseen, from the abbey garden to the edge of Benbraver Woods. I did not harbor any doubt that one or another of the servants had seen me arrive, or else had noted my unusual departure over the garden wall; still, I was certain that, unless Quillan asked for me, they would not volunteer the information. Even so, I hastened to put as much distance between me and the abbey as I could.

Afternoon shadows darkened the woods by the time I finally halted my swift pace through the trees and perched upon a broken stump to rest. Whether by accident or by unconscious design, my flight had taken me within yards of the very ravine where my father had met his end . . . though now, I was certain his death was no accident. Rather, it was cold-blooded murder. A thorn of anguish pierced my heart. If only I could have warned him . . . but how could I have known, how could anyone have suspected?

I had been sitting on my stump for many minutes, struggling not to give way to grief, when I heard behind me the sharp snap of a twig crushed beneath a foot. I leaped to my feet and swung about in the direction of the sound, then choked back a scream as I saw a menacing figure make its way from out of the shadows. It was swathed in a flowing, rough-woven brown robe that trailed the forest floor. A leafy mask obscured the being's features, though it bore a strong resemblance to the reflection I had earlier seen in Quillan's mirror.

"Really, Emma, you disappoint me," came a familiar voice from behind the layers of cleverly cut silk just before Quillan shrugged aside the crude robe and tugged off his mask. "I rather thought you would have enjoyed meeting our green man face-to-face, yet instead you appear quite distressed."

"How—how did you know I suspected you?" I demanded, ignoring his jibe even as I tried to control the quaver in my voice.

He smiled and held up the leafy mask like the Tower executioner displaying a severed head. "It's a clever little disguise, is it not? I found it in a London shop last year and intended to wear it to a costume ball one day, though I venture to say I have put it to a much more practical use, of late. But it does not suit you at all, my dear. You see, I was watching you from the hallway as you tried it on."

"And it was you who watched me that night in my bedchamber," I accused him. "How did you get in and out of the abbey with no one seeing you?"

"Surely you remember, my dear Emma, that Benbraver Abbey had belonged to my family for generations. The place is riddled with hidden passages, and your bedchamber is no exception. There's a secret panel along one wall that opens onto a stone staircase leading down to the garden. I even showed you how to access it, had you been clever enough to take my hint."

I recalled the knob-like carving beneath the green man's face and said as much. "But I cannot believe I did not awaken while you tromped about my room, unless—"

"Laudanum," he said, confirming my outraged guess. "I was already waiting behind the panel when the girl brought up your chocolate. It was a simple matter to slip into the room after she left, add a few drops to the cup, and then wait for you to drink it."

"And what of the footsteps that only encircled my bed, and led neither in nor out? How did you manage that?"

He flashed me a sly smile. "Now, that was a frightening little trick, was it not . . . but the explanation is quite simple. My feet were muddy, not my boots, which I did not remove until I was beside your bed. I strolled about in my bare feet for a long while, admiring your most charming . . . assets, then pulled on my boots again and left the way that I came."

His smug recitation banished the last of my fear, so that the only emotion gripping me as I faced him was anger. "Very well, Quillan, you have proved yourself the expert at schoolboy pranks. But why go to the trouble of this charade . . . and why murder my father?"

"How else was I to get back the lands that rightfully belong to me?" came his harsh reply. "Your father would not have sold the abbey and its woods, even if I'd had money enough to buy them. The only way I could get them back was through you . . . but first, your father had to die."

He tossed the mask aside and slowly advanced on me. "I had to make it look like an accident, but I could not risk his recognizing me should the attempt fail. That is why I wore the mask. I waited until he had split off from the others and then let him catch a glimpse of me, dressed like the green man. I led him a merry chase to this ravine, then circled back on him. He put up a fine struggle, you will be glad to know, but a single blow with the rock that I held ended it all. When I was certain he was dead, I dropped him into the ravine for the others to find. Then, all that was left was to make you my wife."

He favored me with another sly smile that twisted his features, so that I wildly wondered how I'd ever thought him handsome. "I must admit, I found that I rather enjoyed running amok in the woods, wearing a mask and frightening all and sundry. Winning you was rather less of a challenge, though I did enjoy our time together. We could have been very happy, my dear Em, had you not stuck your nose where you should not have. Now, I cannot risk your unmasking me as Benbraver Woods' green man."

So saying, he closed the distance between us and grasped my arm before I could protest. But even as his grip on me tightened, we were buffeted by a gust of wind, as if some unseen person suddenly passed between us.

The uncanny breeze was distraction enough even to pierce Quillan's murderous reverie. His fingers loosened their hold long enough so that I was able to jerk free. I began to run . . . only to catch my boot heel on an exposed root before I had managed more than a dozen paces. I tumbled in an ungainly heap upon the soft bed twigs and leaves at the ravine's edge, and I inwardly cursed myself for having bobbled my one chance at escape. Then I looked back at Quillan and nearly wept at the satisfaction that had frozen his finely sculpted features into an icy mask. His plan had succeeded, after all. My father and I would be dead, and a Bisbee would once again reign over Benbraver Abbey.

As I watched my husband advance upon me, murder in his eyes and heart, I opened my mouth for a frantic, final prayer. But, rather than the familiar words of supplication to my Christian God, I was appalled to hear a pagan curse drop from my lips.

"May your green man punish you, Quillan, for the sacrilege you commit here."

He halted, uncertainty flickering across his handsome face, and I knew a moment's satisfaction. Beneath his air of superiority lurked vestiges of the primitive forester who worshiped tree-dwelling deities. Kill me, Quillan might, but he would ever after step uneasily through these woods. It would be a small comfort to me, buried as I would be in the churchyard . . . but a comfort, nonetheless.

Barely had the echo of my words died amid the now-silent trees than the sighing of the wind began. It started softly, like a child's distant whimper, ruffling my tangled locks and caressing my flushed cheeks like a lover's touch. Reflexively, I drew myself up into a seated position, sensing that I had been served a reprieve of sorts. Yet even as I wondered whether to flee again now, or wait for some other sign, a mound of last season's long-dead leaves and vines skittered aimlessly at my feet. They danced about me for a moment, seeming to revel in their freedom, only to be caught in a gust that sent them swirling upward in a column of gold, red, and brown. The wind's low cry began to build as the bright leaves continued their concentric flight, rising ever higher between us.

And then, as I watched in amazement, the column began to take on human form.

It happened in the space of a few heartbeats, vines and

leaves weaving themselves into a multicolored pattern of
male limbs, torso, and head that towered half again as
high as a man. As the last leaf settled into place,
the wind abruptly ceased. Slowly, the figure turned
toward me, and I gasped, for I recognized this being.
Standing before me was the living embodiment of the
stone-carved green man that graced the abbey's gardens.

Distantly, I heard Quillan's strangled cry, but I paid
him no heed, for my attention was fixed upon the green
man. My first thought was that he was quite beautiful, a
living tapestry of the forest that was his domain. His face
was made up of small golden leaves, as were his upper
torso and the palms of his hands, while a subtle mottling
of darker gold and brown leaves covered the rest of his
body and his limbs. Tendrils of leafy, dark green vines
twisted from his head to form a tangled mane that
reached his shoulders and through which were scattered
crimson leaves the size of a woman's palm. The faint
scent of wood smoke and newly mown grass clung to
him . . . comforting, familiar scents that touched a place
deep inside me long buried under layers of civility.

Yet mixed with the soothing known was the terror of
the unknown . . . the same gut-wrenching fear that primitive man and woman must have felt upon first witnessing
an eclipse or some other awesome spectacle of nature.
He exuded raw power that belied the fragility of the
leaves and twigs through which he had taken shape. I
was acutely aware of my vulnerable pose, as I huddled
practically at his feet. Still, I sensed an air of calm
strength about him that allayed my reflexive fear. The
eyes which gazed back at me were disconcertingly
human, dark and warm as the rich brown earth beneath
me, wise and yet alight with sensuality. If this were the
same deity whose favor the ancient Britons had invoked,
then they had put their faith in a wondrous being, indeed.

The green man held my gaze a moment longer before
turning to Quillan who, after his first gasp of shock, had
dropped to his knees. Another wind gust shook us, and
I felt a shift in the air. A dangerous anger now emanated
from this forest god who my fearful words seemingly had
summoned. Whether Quillan sensed the same thing, I
could not guess, for he simply stared up at the apparition

like a peasant gazing upon a king. Then, after an interminable moment, the green man spoke.

"You have desecrated my forest and disturbed my slumber, human."

And, indeed, the accusation echoed with the rustiness of a voice that had been long silent. I shivered, even though the words were not meant for me. As for Quillan, he paled visibly, his lips moved soundlessly as he fruitlessly sought to reply.

"Your actions have unbalanced the scales of Nature," the green man continued in the same ponderous tones, "and forced me to wakefulness after centuries of rest. I cannot sleep again until matters are put to right."

"B-but you have it all wrong," Quillan finally managed, struggling to his feet. "It was she—" he stabbed a dramatic finger in my direction, "—she and her father who desecrated your forest. They cut down your trees and plowed your earth. I wanted only to preserve the lands."

"You wanted to preserve them, human . . . for yourself."

With those words, the green man turned in my direction again, and I could feel the heat of his anger momentarily cool. "Though I sleep now and no longer wander my forests, in my dreams I can see the hearts of those who would use them," he said in a low rumble, and I gasped as I remembered my own dream of him. "It is no desecration to work the earth if it is done with respect and for the benefit of others. But to spill the blood of an innocent man in my name, even to preserve a stand of my trees, that is a sacrilege I will not endure."

"Benbraver Woods are mine," Quillan countered, his handsome features drawn into lines of frightened anger. He snatched up a fallen branch and wielded it like a club. "I am no blue-painted pagan to fear forest spirits. Your time is long past, green man. You should have died along with Merlin and the Druids."

"No, human," the being thundered, his voice now loud enough to shake the very trees. "I shall live so long as the forests remain. You are the one who should have died for your arrogance and for your folly."

On the heels of those words came an ear-splitting

crack and the scream of tortured wood. My gaze flew upward to the branches of the great oak beneath which my husband stood. From its immense green crown was plummeting a limb nearly as thick as a man and four times as long. Quillan glanced up the same instant as I. He had time for but a single shriek of terror before the impact of the falling limb abruptly silenced him.

I gazed a long moment at the lifeless form of my husband, my would-be murderer, pinned to the dark earth beneath an oaken pillar. Thankfully, his face was turned away from me, so I did not have to witness his features twisted in final agony. But I was not spared the sight of the growing pool of blood beneath his head, nor the way the ground around him greedily sucked at that crimson puddle. Despite myself, tears welled in my eyes. Though he had killed my father and would have murdered me, he had shared my heart and my bed for a time, so that I could not witness his death with total indifference.

It wasn't until a broad shadow drifted over me that I belatedly recalled the true instrument of Quillan's demise. I tore my gaze from my dead husband and looked up at the green man, this pagan spirit into whose fantastic realm I had unwittingly strayed. Would he demand a blood sacrifice of me, as well?

As if reading my thoughts, he shook his head and then smiled. The gesture lit his face with an almost human warmth, so that a flicker of optimism rose in my breast. And then, in a courtly gesture, he reached down a viney hand toward me.

Hesitantly, I grasped it . . . him . . . half-expecting the leafy digits to crush at my touch. Yet the hand I clutched was as substantial as my own, the tapestry of leaves and vines smooth and warm as flesh. He pulled me to my feet, keeping hold of me as my unsteady knees sought to lock into place. Only when I had firmly regained my footing did I dare glance up at him again.

Up close, he was far more wonderful, so that I could have gazed at him in fascination for hours. And, terrifyingly regal as he was, he exuded a humanlike aura of maleness that sent an answering warmth through me. The question flashed through my mind if beings such as these ever sought and seduced human females . . . for surely there would be no shortage of women eager to couple with a deity. Then, just as swiftly, I recalled his claim that he could read the hearts of those who walked his forests, and I blushed.

His dark eyes, so human and yet so unearthly, burned with even warmer emotion as he released my hand. "You need never fear to walk these woods again," he softly rumbled. "The one who would harm you is no more, and you will remain under my protection for so long as you live here."

I nodded, the words to a dozen questions suddenly knotted upon my tongue. But when my tongue finally loosened, what I blurted with feminine illogic was, "Do you have a name?"

"My name," he replied, "is whatever you would call me in your dreams."

Then another breeze swept us, and I cried out in protest, knowing what would happen next. With the same swiftness that he had formed, the green man dissolved into a bright column of leaves and vines that momentarily swirled before me on that magical breeze. As the colorful whirlwind slowed and began to settle, I reached out to capture a single golden leaf. It fluttered an instant in my hand, then lay still upon my palm . . . just as the other leaves had subsided into a patchwork blanket of color upon the forest floor.

I sighed, and my breath sent the delicate leaf wafting once more. It drifted a moment upon the breeze, then finally settled with its fallen fellows at my feet. I gave my husband's crumpled form a final glance, then caught up the mask of silk leaves and started in the direction of Bisbee Hall to report his lordship's tragic death.

22 August

I had thought never to write within this journal again, but I feel the need for one final entry, and then I shall burn this book and be done with it. Life has returned somewhat to normal, for which I am grateful. I have been quite the object of sympathy these past few weeks, having lost both a father and a husband so tragically, and in so short a space of time. Everyone takes pains to assure me that Quillan was a fine, upstanding figure of a nobleman . . . a fiction I have not bothered to dispel.

For, by the time I made my way back to the manor house that tragic day, the mask of silken leaves was nothing more than a collection of bright-colored cloth fragments scattered through Benbraver Woods. The elements will do their work so that, when spring arrives next year, no evidence will remain of Quillan's evil scheme. Revealing it now will serve no purpose . . . nor will it bring back my father, or undo my pain. Besides, it is far more important that I shield my son from the cruel knowledge that his dead father was murderer.

Yes, one happy result has come of my ill-fated marriage. In a few months, I am to bear a child . . . a boy child, I am certain, who will be the next Earl of Hocksley. Of course, he is Quillan's son, for I have been with no other man save in my dreams.

In my dreams. The man in my dreams is no ordinary mortal but the face in the leaves, the same green man who protects our woods. He comes to me here, in my old room at Benbraver Abbey, where I have recently returned. With him, I know a far greater bliss than ever I found in Quillan's arms, so that I rush to my bed each night in hopes that this will be the night he will appear again. And, glorious as those nights are, the following dawn always brings with it a keen disappointment when I awaken to an empty bed once more.

Odd, though, that every time I dream of the green man, the next morning finds my coverlet strewn with a scattering of forest leaves . . . gold, red, and brown.

SUNRISE

by Michelle West

Michelle West is the author of The Sacred Hunter *du-ology,* The Broken Crown, *and* The Uncrowned King, *published by DAW Books. She reviews books for the on-line column* First Contacts, *and less frequently for* The Magazine of Fantasy & Science Fiction. *Other short fiction by her appears in* Black Cats and Broken Mirrors, Elf Magic, *and* Olympus.

THIS time at night, she always heard the screaming.

It wasn't like a real scream, or like real screams; those were always short, always sudden—a burst of something as damaging as gunfire, but more visceral, less obviously deadly. No, these were the screams of ghosts, and they lingered, always, after the fall of sunlight.

She lingered with them, one of five survivors of the slaughter of her graduating class, and the sole survivor of the subsequent slaughter of the family that she had returned to in such a state of shock. Four of her five year mates had moved on; this was a big city, but there were a lot of big cities, and none had the shadows and the memories of death that this one did.

But she stayed.

The old house wasn't empty; the corpses had been removed on stretchers bathed in the turning red and white of ambulance light. She could still see them if she closed her eyes: Her father's headless body, arranged in a shaky moment so that his head and his neck seemed connected; her brother's, torn from sternum to jaw; her mother's, fin-

gerless and toeless, throat a small explosion of artery, vein
and flesh, her eyes missing, her body otherwise whole.

It made the news, of course. There were pictures of the
house, and of her, standing in front of it, covered in blood
and clutching—of all things—a rosewood stake, sharpened,
blooded, the disturbing legacy of the graduation dance
nightmare. Her way of not feeling helpless.

She had come home to screaming: her mother's, a voice
so distorted she both knew it for what it was and didn't
recognize it.

At nineteen years of age, Jessica Mitchell—Jess to her
friends, not that any of them had survived—had killed her
first two vampires. The first was an act of self-defense and
denial, the second a sudden red rage. There was no third;
the police came. Special unit. Called in numbers that the
vampires didn't feel like facing.

They would, later; they would play cat and mouse with
the law—set traps, using live bait; play games that made
what she'd studied of Vietnam seem pleasant and tame by
comparison. But not that night. That night, they came just
as if they were cavalry. Rescued Jessica, but couldn't quite
make it in time for her mother. Her father and brother
were long gone by the time they arrived.

People threw up. She remembered that really well. She
was one of them. But she'd seen it once before.

Why me?

Not a thought she was proud of, but it still came up,
especially now, three years later, as she stood in her old
neighborhood.

Two months after the deaths, someone else had bought
the old place. She didn't know whether or not the history
meant anything to him. People could be damned ghoulish
when the death and destruction was something they could
study—or observe—rather than experience personally.

Didn't much matter, though; she couldn't have stayed in
that house.

Nineteen years old. Summer of her last year of high
school. Accepted into the Arts & Science program at the
University of Toronto. She hadn't meant to live on campus;
she'd mentioned it to her father and mother, and her father
had responded with absolute silence, her mother with heat
and concern. But she couldn't live at the House. She kept

the car, kept one or two of the things she best liked about her mother and her father's lives, kept things of her brother's because he'd turned into such a stranger during high school that she wanted to try to figure out who he was and who he might have become. The rest, she sold, or had sold.

Her mother had two sisters in the city, her father a sister and a brother. They were too shocked to be helpful, too grief-stricken to start, and by the time they recovered, she had already begun to pursue her studies with a focus and a concentration that she had never shown before the deaths. They worried; she knew it.

But she was driven.

Not, at first, by the need for vengeance. Not then. No more than she would have had her family died horribly in an earthquake, a tidal wave, a flood.

But by a need to understand what had happened. Why. As if understanding would somehow protect her. As if knowledge were power.

"It's like a murder," one of the two friends she made at U of T would say.

"According to the police, it *is* murder," she'd reply. But she could not—not quite—bring herself to think of the Vampires as human; they were like rabid, ravening, hungry things that walked upright. And without the humanity to underpin whatever it was they were, they were forces of nature.

Religion came less easily to her; her family was Anglican in the modern sense of the word: Easter and Christmas. For Jessica, that meant chocolate egg hunts on Easter Sunday and presents on the twenty-fifth of December. with a visit to the Church sandwiched twice in between. She had learned not to pay much attention, and as a child who had learned to sit quietly, had always gotten away with it. But at nineteen and twenty, she wanted the comfort of the cross without the belief in a just God.

After all, if there was a God, why in hell did He let vampires exist at all? How could He justify the hideous murder of the whole final grade?

Why, she was asked, did earthquakes exist? Famine? Floods? Unhappiness? The questions had baffled her at first, and then angered her. But she'd taken them, chewed on them, swallowed them.

"They died horribly," Father Thomsen told her, "but the

dead are dead. They way they died affects us far more than
it affects them."

She was twenty-one years old before she could take comfort from that. And she could take comfort at any time of
night but this one, in any other place but this: Galloway
Street. Home.

The moon was full. Clouds were few, scattered into a
thin stream that made them seem more like the afterburner
of a large jet than a natural phenomenon. She cast a long,
slender shadow against the flat sidewalk and the perfectly
kept grass. Not for Jessica the soldier-of-fortune look, but
she carried six stakes strapped from the small of her back
to the hollows of her shoulder blades, wore a thick cross
on a chain that couldn't be snapped without taking her
neck along for the ride, and carried a crossbow. It was the
bow that made her feel safe.

The police had experimented unsuccessfully with bullets
and gun delivery systems; she knew this because she worked
with the auxiliary as a volunteer. Night auxiliary. She wasn't
quite tall enough to be a patrolman, but she still wanted to
go into police work once she finished her degree—and she
wanted a degree because it had been so important to both of
her parents that she do well academically, and it was one of
the few things she could still do for them.

In the meantime, she kept her hand in. Her friends on
the force turned a blind eye to activities that were just this
side of legal, most of the time. They turned a blind eye to
the activities that were just the other side as well, but she
had to be careful there; they all did. They didn't speak
much about what they did, either as teams or as individuals.
They'd learned the hard way that it was really easy to get
at that information. Not by torture; they were pretty tor-
ture-proof as far as things went.

No, worse: by conversion. Vampires, it seems, retained
the memories of the living, but nothing else whatever about
the life. No heart, no soul, no humanity.

Safety existed in isolation.

And people weren't meant to be isolated.

Because isolation drove them to the edge, gave them the
leeway to do *really* stupid things. One of which was this:
To stand exposed on Galloway Street, a lone woman with

a crossbow, stakes, a cross, and a hand-written letter burning a hole in both pocket and memory.

I'm sure, it read—she knew it by heart, and she'd know it by heart even if she never opened it up and read it again—*you'd like to know exactly what happened on the night of the summer solstice. And why. You've proved such an interesting challenge, little Jess, I've a mind to discuss it with you after all these years. Meet me on Galloway Street, by the old house, on the anniversary of the event.*

It was signed, with a flourish, unreadably; the scrawl was male. But just in case she couldn't recognize the word for what it was, the author had taken the pains to print out, in even letters, a single name beneath the signature. *Lysander.*

And anyone who worked night auxiliary or night patrol knew who Lysander was. The head of the horde. The leader. She'd done her research; she knew that he didn't really play much in the way of games—not like these, not with a human that wasn't immediately under claw and fang. And in the end, what did that mean? Not much. They really didn't have a lot to go on. Vampires didn't take the time to talk or wheedle; they hissed, they raved, they threatened, they screamed, and they died. But conversation between hunter and hunter was generally kept to a minimum.

And Jessica Mitchell found that she very badly *did* want that conversation. So she kept the letter to herself. Noted the date. Hated it. And kept it.

It had seemed like a stupid idea at the time. It was far, far darker than the merely stupid now.

She waited; her shadow shortened. Moonrise. She wasn't about to look at her watch. Not and give the bastards a chance to catch her unaware.

"I'm here," she said, lifting her chin and raising her voice.

"So you are," a voice said.

She turned, slowly, toward the rooftop of the building two houses past the one she'd grown up in. There, perched like a living gargoyle, dressed like a bad television cat burglar, was death.

"But you see," another voice said, from another rooftop, "so are *we.*"

Female voice, that voice. It cut her, as it was no doubt meant to. "Amy," she said softly.

"Amy Amelia," the vampire replied, smiling an angelic, human smile that almost glittered across the night distance that separated them. "We used to be best friends, Jess. And I think we will be again, once we sort out your little problem."

"*My* little problem?"

"Well, all right, your two little problems." The blonde vampire—and she was still blonde, still beautiful, and still so damn slim and perfect—began to sidle her way off the edge of the roof. "First, you're alive. We can change that.

"Second, you're human. But you know what? Lysander can change that, too. You must have impressed him. He kept so very few of us after the slaughter."

Two vampires. Two. She'd faced that before.

But there was a third voice.

"I would have kept you, the night your family died. I *asked* for you, Jessica. I serve Lysander well. You weren't to be marked or scarred or harmed. But you couldn't leave well enough alone. You had to deprive us of eternity."

David's voice. Gods, she *hated* it. She had come here to face her past: she was facing it. She didn't like it and promised herself that in the future she'd face her past the way everyone else did: a therapist's nice, safe couch.

"I cried at your funeral," she whispered.

"I know. I heard about it. Touching."

"Probably wouldn't have lasted anyway."

"Probably not then. But now? We'll have forever."

"You are getting ahead of yourself, David, and that *never* pleases me."

The vampire who had David's voice—she couldn't quite make out his face in the darkness—suddenly hissed; he fell forward like an animal, scratching ground with his hands. Fourth vampire. She had no doubt at all, given David's sudden and dramatic loss of humanity and dignity—for which mercy she thanked a God she didn't quite worship—that Lysander had finally decided to show himself.

She had one crossbow, and no friends.

No brains, either. She was a prime candidate for the annual Darwin Award, although she wasn't certain it would count if the vampires brought her back.

"C'mon, Jess," Amy said quietly. "It's not bad, this life. No tanning, but you learn to get by."

"Yeah. And Lysander has more strings attached to you

than your parents did when they decided you were going
to get confirmed."

"He offers more."

"No, thanks."

"A pity," Lysander said, in a voice that dripped satisfaction.
"The problem with making a vampire, my dear, is that there
is *some* voluntary portion. The other problem, given our history together, is that you only get to die once." He stepped
out, stood beneath the perfect circle of a street lamp. He
wore a shirt, opened halfway down his chest; tight jeans, black
boots; his hair was cropped short on the sides, pulled back
along the top; she was certain—if he ever exposed his back
to her—he'd have it tied back in a long ponytail.

One bolt.

Four vampires that she knew of, but she was pretty sure
there would only be four: they liked to feel their power
before they fed, and that usually meant some sort of introduction. Of course, if she only had one bolt, she had other
ways of killing vampires. She'd have to be up close and
personal with at least two of them.

She fired the crossbow.

He *caught* the bolt.

She swore. He leaned back against the girth of the lamp
and smiled lazily. "All right, boys and girls. Bring her to
me."

They didn't know enough about how vampire compulsion
worked. There were stories, of course; always those. The
fevered imagination of the pens and keyboards of the civi-
lized world had responded poetically, savagely, and luridly
to the known existence of vampires. In the uncivilized
world, the responses were older, the stories deeper, wilder.

But what was accepted—by modernists such as Jessica—
as truth was this: Newly created vampires were under the
thrall of the creature that had created them. They had their
memories, but no more; they had volition only so long as
the attention of their creator wandered to his own concerns,
his own pleasures.

Except, of course, when those concerns and pleasures
dovetailed so neatly with a tight rein.

She reached over her shoulders with both hands; pulled
out two stakes, shaking loose a second cross to protect the

back of her neck. The first cross, heavy and unavoidable, started in the hollow of her neck and fell to just below where her heart beat; it wasn't heavy, but the chain it was on was tough enough to hang a man by. She'd learned the necessity of that the hard way. Taken her first scars that day, but she'd walked away with her throat intact.

"Jess, don't make us hurt you." David's voice, David's sweet voice. David's lips—familiar to her now, even though three years had passed. Not her first kiss, no—but her first serious boyfriend. Her dreams of marriage and children, her little, insular plans for The Future.

"Why not?" She replied. "Or does he get everything? That's not what you used to be like, David."

Vampires had mercurial tempers. You could sometimes shake them loose a bit—make them stupid.

But Lysander was *right here*. She tried out of habit, and not with any real hope for success.

"Jess, it's really not so bad. And Lysander will offer you eternity."

"Great. Eternity as a walking variant of a mosquito or a lamprey." She propped one sharpened spike against her hip. "Let's get this over with, shall we?"

They obliged. Three to one, with Lysander—lazy bastard—watching in the distance. She caught a flash of his eyes, no more, and she promised herself she wouldn't do that in again in a hurry; by the time she'd looked away, Amy's steel grip hands were a yard away from her arms. They looked soft enough, and she'd sheathed her claws, but her teeth were an elegant flash of pointed white beneath the glow of street lamps. A reminder.

But it *hurt*. She was surprised at how much it hurt. Amy Amelia, just this side of being too much of a diabetic-inducing nice girl, and David Johnson, the boy she'd planned to marry. Best friend. Boy friend.

Didn't make any damned sense that of all the people he could change over after the grad night slaughter, he'd choose these two. Hundreds just died in the carnage. Some disappeared.

She swung the sharp spike around and forward, forcing Amy to stop.

They'd thought—they'd thought that the ones who disappeared had escaped. Hope, there. She remembered that, because she *was* one of the ones who'd been listed as a disappearance. But it was worse than that. Still, it was terrible when hope died completely. She saw the past in the present, and knew that he'd hurt her, twice, just by ugly luck.

She was going to have to kill them. She desperately didn't want to have to kill them.

Don't go out on your own.

First rule for the Night Auxiliary. What the *hell* had she been thinking?

There was a third vampire. He looked vaguely familiar, but it took her a few minutes to place his ugly face. Ian Strocken. Smug sport jock bastard. God's gift to women and he knew it. He came in close; it didn't occur to him, even as a vampire, that he somehow didn't have the same tug on her, the same hooks in her, as the other two did. No claim to safety.

But then again, vampires probably didn't rule the world for just this reason: they were stupid. She brought the stake around in a sudden feint of motion, ducking under his underarm. He cried out in shock, and then the shock traveled up her arm, shuddering. She gave the stake a vicious shove and let it go, well aware that her right to call anyone else stupid had been severely compromised.

Amy's hands caught her hair; her nails ripped the topside of her skull. Just a little bit of pain, and not—quite—enough to draw blood. Drawing blood tended to change the appearance and the temperament of new vampires.

Drawing blood.

It made them savage, far more vicious, far less prone to use what brains they had. It brought out the animal; submerged the human.

Jessica Mitchell stared out of night eyes at Amy Amelia and David, and her heart bled. What difference did it make if the rest of her did? She reached over her back while they circled her; kept a stake forward and pulled out another one. She brought the second one up, and before she could change her mind, bit her lip and shoved its grisly, sharpened tip into the fleshy part of her hand.

Young vampires.

They lost control almost instantly; lost the solidity of their connection with her past.

Or they started to.

"Oh, very, very clever, Young Jessica. I am so impressed."

Lysander held their chains. Held them on such a short rein it was hard to believe he was as far away as the lamppost.

Amy Amelia screamed. It was a terrible, a horrible, sound. Jessica crouched slightly, held the stakes out. Waited. Some vampires could take to air; could shred their victims from the safety of height. But which ones did and which ones didn't weren't immediately obvious to her or her fellow vampire hunters, and the rhyme or reason for it was buried in the corpse of the undead.

David looked at her. "Jess," he said. And then, "you don't know what it's like. You can't know what it's like." But his voice had been stripped of all its latent sensuality, all of its promise of dark pleasure; it was a naked voice. David's voice. "I don't want to kill you," he said. "But I'm going to. I have to." He shuddered. "You're alive, and I'm not—and the closest I ever get to life is when—is when—"

"Is when," That lovely, rich, perfect voice interjected, "He takes it. It sometimes takes a while to addict a new young thing to an eternity of pleasure. A pity."

She learned something about herself all right. That night, she learned something big: she wasn't a killer. This David, artifice or no, she recognized, and she couldn't carve his heart out, cut his head off, bathe him in holy water. She backed up, backed up quickly; the stakes in her hands were a threat. She kept her expression locked down, kept the set of her lips rigid. But she didn't kill him.

Did she love David? Was she still in love with him?

No. But she knew him now, and that still meant something.

Lysander laughed. Laughed. She fled; David and Amy followed.

"Help us, Jess," Amy said, her voice as raw as—no, worse than—David's. Her eyes were dark eyes, vampire eyes; her teeth were fangs—but there was nothing at all cloying about that voice. Jessica's hand was bleeding. She fled, awkwardly now. She'd faced about as much of her past as she could take, and she was numb with it, raw as their voices.

Except that it wasn't done with her. Because she was

backing off the sidewalk and up the manicured walk of a house, and she was almost at the door when she realized whose house it was. Or rather, whose house it had been.

Her house.

Her past.

The death she'd avoided, maybe.

It was here that she'd first faced the vampires and won; walked out of the nightmare, changed its terms. The door hit her back squarely, she braced herself against it. What was, after all, the only thing she could do for David or Amy?

Swallow. Think.

Something dropped down on her from above.

The skin across her left shoulder broke cleanly in a solid stripe of red.

No time to think, then. She cried out; her arm spasmed. She lost one of the two pillars of her defense as the stake fell from her hand.

Lysander? No. She could see him silhouetted by lamplight, watching, his hands in his pockets. One of his servants, then. One of his.

A lot of lessons to be learned from tonight, if she survived. The biggest one: Vampires were a lot smarter if their master was pulling their strings. A lot smarter. And vampire hunters were a lot stupider if their master was pulling her strings. She didn't want to stoop to praying. Took too much time. Three against one—but the third one hadn't touched down yet.

And it wasn't going to.

She was ready for his attack—but Amy moved in when Jessica lifted her arm, exposing her throat. The cross saved her some contact; she could hear Amy hissing, but there was fresher blood across the length of her shoulder. They'd both lost a bit in the encounter.

David caught her arm.

His fingers pierced her skin, stopping just below the surface, causing little swells of blood to decorate the edges of his claws. His nostrils flared, his eyes widened; there was nothing at all about him that looked human.

Nothing at all about him that sounded human when he screamed.

*   *   *

It wasn't the sound she'd been expecting.

She didn't even wonder if this was one of Lysander's tricks; she knew it wasn't. There was a bolt that protruded its way out of the front of David's chest, smoking and blackening as the seconds passed. Night auxiliary experience told her one thing at a glance: the bolt had hit what had once been heart. The thing that had once been David was dead, and he'd realize it soon enough.

But Amy froze as well, and Jessica didn't have the time to run from her past. She did close her eyes as the stake struck home. Closed her eyes, put all of her weight behind driving the thin, straight column of wood where it had to go.

The third vampire, unnamed and unidentified, dropped again; she threw her arms up to cover her face, and he left his marks—deep, deep gashes now—where her eyes would have been. Games, it seemed, were over.

It fell again; she bled again; this time, the wound burned.

Not much time, then. Groping in the inside of her jacket pocket with hands that were shaking in reaction, she reached for something she could throw—

And the door at her back fell open. She fell over, across the threshold, into the house that had once been her home.

"Please," an unfamiliar voice said quietly, "come in."

Contained on the outside of a well-framed solid door, she got her first real glimpse of the vampire's face. Not a face she recognized; ears too long, jaw too elongated. It looked sort of like Man-bat from one of the really, really old comic books, but a little bit less intelligent and a lot less friendly.

"I—I hope you don't mind if I bleed on your carpet," she said lamely, not even turning to look at the man who the voice belonged to.

He laughed. That did catch her attention, and she turned a moment; she could spare that much time.

He was younger than she'd thought anyone who could just buy this house from her parent's estate could be, but he was probably about eight years older than she was, give or take a few. Tall, but not gangly. His hair was a blue-black that looked so perfect you usually only found it in boxes, his eyes were a shade of brown that made them look almost all pupil.

But what was remarkable about him was his stillness.

"Do not interfere," the vampire hissed, "in what does not concern you."

The man shrugged expansively. "I rarely do. You don't presume to threaten me when you can't even walk across the threshold, do you?"

"You have already been warned; the master will—"

His face twisted and then expanded, filling out to the sides. He threw up his hands, his face continuing its slow decline into humanity; Jessica could tell that he was clawing at his back. She'd once seen an older vampire literally cut a section of its spine out in order to preserve it from the effect of a blessed weapon that hadn't—quite—struck home. This was a lot like that.

And bleeding as she was from multiple cuts, she wasn't above taking a bit longer than normal to pull out her weapon and finish it off. But only a bit longer: there was something about the changing tenor of a scream uttered by a throat that was becoming more and more human that would cling to her nightmares and haunt her sleep if it went on for too long.

He couldn't enter where he wasn't invited.

She didn't have that problem. One of few human advantages.

She planted the stake in his chest as if he were a garden, taking care to stay near the open doorway. Just in case.

But when she looked up from the corpse, the spotlight had ceased to shine on Lysander; it was empty. He'd fled.

"Good work," another voice said.

Jessica turned to look up the barrel of a modern crossbow. "You've got good reflexes," the woman holding it added. "No brains, which is a pity, but good reflexes." The crossbow fell. "You piss off a master vampire?"

"Guess so," Jessica replied, a bit off her stride. She hated to be treated like an empty-headed idiot—and lord knows, at her age it happened a lot—but she knew when to be fair. She had been an empty-headed idiot. She'd take the rap. "Thanks," she added, straightening up. "I owe you my life. And possibly more than that."

"No problem. I'll be in town for a while." The woman yawned, stretched. "You'll probably have the chance to repay me in kind—and if you do, I'll appreciate it just as much." As the crossbow fell completely, she held out a gloved hand. "I'm Theo," she said quietly. "Theo Plokamakis."

"Jessica. Jessica Mitchell."

"Well, ladies, if the excitement is over for the evening, I'd be pleased if you'd join me. I don't get out often." The stranger smiled. "For obvious reasons. This neighborhood has proved most . . . interesting."

Theo shouldered the crossbow. Smiled, the curve of her lips just this side of wicked. "Thought you'd never ask," she said, laughing. "You got antiseptics and bandages?"

"Some, someplace." He gave Jessica a dubious look; she was bleeding profusely from at least three wounds. "I'm not much of a tailor, though—and some of those injuries are going to need a needle."

He was right. Jessica felt vaguely queasy. From blood loss, undoubtedly.

"Did you get the master?" She said, turning to the woman who called herself Theo.

Theo laughed. "Not hardly. But I will."

He lied.

He was, as it turned out, a pretty good tailor. And Jessica—who had once fainted at the sight of her own blood—had become a damn good patient over the last three years. "You need," she said, through gritted teeth, while Theo looked on with something approaching approval, "better anesthetics."

He laughed. His laugh was the strangest thing about him, and it took her the better part of the evening to realize why. It was completely free from that euphoric post-gallows edge that usually informed the laughter of the survivors of the Night Auxiliary after a particularly gruesome mission.

And why shouldn't it be? Short of opening a door, he hadn't actually stepped out into the darkness himself. And yet, he had opened the door on this night—and given his door setup, the infrareds would probably have given him a clear idea what he—or rather she—had been up against.

Sure, you didn't invite just anyone into your house anymore, and door-to-door canvassing or pleading for money just didn't happen after sunset, but that didn't mean you were safe. People had to eat; they had to work; they had

to travel to and from each other, and sometimes they had
to do those things at night. No one pissed off the vampires
if they weren't already in line to do so.

Like, say, Jessica Mitchell and the Night Auxiliary.

"You've done this before," Theo said quietly.

"Yeah."

"At your age," the older woman said, "I was daydreaming about boys and babies."

"When you were my age, there weren't any vampires."

Theo laughed, and the laugh was the bitterest thing about
her so far. "Yes," she said quietly. "There were. They just
weren't out in the open so much."

Jessica turned, the last of the clean up forgotten. "What
do you mean?"

"You think vampires are new? They're older than the
wheel. Older than sex for money; probably younger than
parenthood. But not by much." She rose, shoved her hands
into loose pockets, turned to the wide, wide windows that
fronted what looked to be, in the darkness, perfect lawn.
"They're sort of like the wheel, as far as I've been able to
tell: they get reinvented, but they basically spin in circles
until you stop them."

Jessica shrugged. "We've all read the stories," she said
softly. "We've done the research we can do. But it's so
hard to separate fact from fiction—"

"Isn't any easier on the vampires, not to defend them,"
Theo replied, picking up one of Jessica's stakes and examining it under the large chandelier in the dining room. It
cast the brightest light in the house, and since it was cleared
off, the dining room table made the best surface for emergency surgery; Jessica's arm, and Jessica's weaponry, were
laid out against its matte dark surface. "Vampires make
themselves as well." She stopped speaking for a moment,
turning the stake over and over in her hands. "These are
what, oak?"

"Something like that."

"Get a better tree." She put the stake down. "I don't
mean they literally make themselves; they need help for
that. But over time. Flight, for instance. Mutability of
shape."

"Allergy to religious symbol?"

"No, that comes for free." Theo laughed. "I'm not sure

they're allergic to garlic; holy water is the effective equivalent of very strong acid. What else? Can't cross a threshold. Can't stand sunlight. Don't deal well with fire."

"People don't deal well with fire."

"They've got a lot in common with people, especially as they get older." Theo shrugged. "They can cross running water; that one's a crock."

"Do they really need to sleep in their dirt?"

"Some do, to start; some don't. This coven master—I'd bet you even odds—actually, more like three to one—that he doesn't even remember where he was originally buried."

"You've been doing this for a long time." There wasn't much of a question in Jessica's words.

"Yeah. Long time. A damned long time." She shrugged. "If you survive it, you learn a helluva lot by trial and error. Mostly error, though. Blessed bolts," she added, pointing to the crossbow, "seem to go through most of the young ones like hot knives through butter." She turned in her seat. "Uh, sorry if this is boring you—we'll try to keep girl-talk down to a minimum."

"We?" His amusement was obvious, although the smile it came through was subtle.

"Obsessive and Compulsive Vampire Hunters."

"And you're all so-called girls?"

Theo shrugged. "It's the way the world works. If there's a dirty job, and someone's got to do it, it's usually the women."

He did laugh at that. His voice was low, smooth, almost pleasant; Jessica could forget, hearing him laugh, that he was also jabbing at the top of her skin with a sterilized needle and thread. Until he started again. "How very modest of you. You realize that if I said something remotely similar, I'd be lynched for sexism."

"Smart man. In this room, you would be." Theo's grin was wicked, and it was easy. Jessica suddenly envied her that; the ease of being wicked.

"I didn't catch your name, by the way," Theo added quietly.

The man's smile deepened. "I didn't give it."

"Oh?"

"Names have power, after all." Light, that. Teasing. He turned to look at Jessica. "I think you're done," he said, his tone of voice changing. "Bathroom's upstairs, if you want to wash off—I'd be careful, though."

She nodded. She almost told him that she knew where the bathroom was, but she stopped herself—because he'd had this house for years now, and she wasn't completely certain that she did know where the bathroom was anymore. It surprised her, because the uncertainty caused a stab of visceral pain. She'd never thought to stand in this house again.

Wasn't this what you wanted, you idiot? she asked herself. *To confront your past? To get some answers? To have some sort of peace? As if.* She walked, hesitant now, up to the staircase that hadn't been changed at all. Oh, the carpets were a different color, neutral gray as opposed to the soft cream that her mother and father had argued about, but the pickets and rails were the same solid wood, and they wound up the stairs in an open-step circle. She took those steps one at a time, testing the feel of the carpet. Or so she told herself; what she was actually doing was avoiding that first shock of sight as the stairs opened up onto the second story of the house she'd grown up in. There, at the end of the hall, the double doors into her parents—no, no call it what it was: the master bedroom. To the left of that, her brother's old room—no easy real estate definition for that—door closed. To the right, the bathroom, and to the right of that, her old room. The door to that was closed as well.

She fumbled a moment for the light switch, because she realized that the lights weren't actually on; she could see the doors from the hall light below, and memory filled in the details. Ah. There.

It hit her, suddenly; hit her much harder than she'd thought it would. She stumbled, half at a run, for the bathroom, and threw open the door. Toilet was there. Sink. Big, gorgeous bath unlike anything her parents had ever owned. Marble. Brass. Things that weren't part of her life as a member of the Night Auxiliary—or as a teenager at Sir John A. MacDonald.

She made it to the toilet, and there, as unglamorous as she'd ever been, she threw up.

Because she remembered, clearly, the last time she'd walked through this house. Remembered what she'd seen;

what they'd carried out, what they'd left behind. The blood
had been everywhere, and that was the easy part of it—it
didn't look like it had ever really belonged to anything
alive. But the pictures her mother scattered with such fond-
ness from one end of the house to the other had been
smashed and fragmented, glass from the frames used as
weapons or—*face it, face it Jessica*—cutlery. Her life had
been torn apart with a casual brutality, and she had spent
three goddamned years trying to put it all together again.

She rose from her half-crouch in a bathroom that was
familiar to her only in the placement of windows and shape
of the room. Stopped at the sink, to splash her face with
water, forgetting the new stitches, the new pain. Grabbed
a towel that was softer than anything she owned, wiped
herself clean. She even made it out of the bathroom as if
nothing at all had happened.

But she couldn't walk past her room. Couldn't do it.

It's not your house, Jessica. For God's sake, let it go. But
even as she thought it, her hand snaked out as if it belonged
to some other Jessica Mitchell, one over whom she had no
control—like, say, the idiot who had secretly accepted the
invitation of Lysander, coven master—and grabbed the
door knob. It was the same knob—boring brass, unremark-
able in every possible way.

She pushed the door open into a room she didn't recognize. There was a bed here, a single, much like the bed
she'd owned, but it was missing the frilly canopy that she'd
insisted on for her eighth birthday, and regretted every year
after her twelfth, and the shelf with her very few books
was, of course, in her new, small residence room. There
was no television, no roll-top desk, no armchair, no carpet.
The wood floors and closet door looked the same, and the
window hadn't changed much—if you could get beyond the
fact that the drapery was ugly and plain.

She hadn't meant to come here.

She told herself that she hadn't meant to come here.

There just wasn't anything to see.

And she couldn't see, that was the damnable thing; her
eyes were screwed up too tightly, or something. Something
in them, maybe. Yeah, something in her eyes. She raised
the back of her hand, scored lightly by years of vampire

claw wounds and splinters, and rubbed the back of her
eyes. Didn't help much.

It was gone; all of her past was gone. She'd sold it because she couldn't face it then, but she'd never really let
herself know how much she missed it. Until tonight.

David. Amy Amelia. And a house owned by an absolute
stranger. Death, she'd seen. She'd faced it a dozen times,
up close and personal. But it was her own death, and she'd
always managed to avoid that. This, this was loss, and it
was worse.

She began—and she hated herself for it—to weep, standing in the doorframe of a room that would never belong
to her again.

But Jessica Mitchell's grief wasn't a spectator sport; it
wasn't something she willingly shared with anyone. The
Night Auxiliary worried about that sometime, but they let
her be; most of the force had been driven to it by the same
demons that drove her, after all, and they knew how to
bide their time.

The stranger appeared at her elbow like a shadow.

He said nothing at all; he'd moved so quietly—or she'd
been sobbing so loudly—she hadn't heard him. Between
one breath and the next, she was choking, trying to pull
herself back to herself, away from loss and loss.

"I'm sorry," he said quietly, withdrawing even the hand,
although he didn't leave her. "But I thought you might like
to see it."

"You—"

"I know who you are, Jessica Mitchell. I knew the history
of the house when I bought it. I confess I didn't expect to
see you back here quite like this, but I thought a time
might come when you'd want to look at what was left of
your past."

She found his voice soothing, which was good, because
she couldn't bring herself to look at his face.

"I would have left the room the same—but it was the
only room in the house that came with no furniture."

Her throat tightened. She couldn't speak, not even to tell
him to leave. To ask him to leave. She stood, facing the
shadows in her room, the light of the hall at her back, the
stranger somewhere between the two. At last she squeezed
a single word out of a throat too swollen for it. "Why?"

His laugh was bitter. "I've seen such a loss in my time. Worse, in some ways. I know what it's like, to long for a past that others have destroyed."

His words were so soft, and so felt, she found a wary comfort in them. Enough to find her voice, at least, although she still couldn't meet his eyes. "Vampires?"

"Vampires, yes," he said. "And men. I come from a land that has seen a lot of war."

"Is that why you opened the door?"

He was silent a long time; so silent, in fact, that she did turn to face him because she wasn't certain that he was still there.

His face was like granite; chiseled, empty. But something in his eyes flickered to life when her eyes brushed them. "I don't know why I opened the door," he said quietly. "It's been a long time since I've actively interfered in anything. The cost is . . . high." He touched her elbow gently, and this time she allowed it. The shadows of the room pulled at her and pushed at her, and he brought her away from them into the light, gently, gently closing the door at her back.

As if he knew the answer, he didn't ask her whether or not she wanted to look at the rest of the house. "Theo's waiting for you," he said quietly. "And if you don't join her soon, she'll start to worry."

"Worry? About me?"

"She's been suspicious of anything that doesn't actively kill vampires since—as she said—a damned long time. You've got the weaponry. I don't." His smile was wry. "Attractive woman, if you're interested in big risks." He shrugged. "She said she has a car."

"I said," Theo broke in sharply, "I had what was left of a car."

It was true. Theo had, definitely, what was left of a car. "Don't you ever get pulled over in this thing?"

"Yeah."

"And they haven't impounded it as a road hazard?"

"Once or twice."

"You've got to have more money than it looks like you have." Jessica shook her head. "I've never heard an engine make a noise like that before and still start."

"Look, at least it's a car. What were you going to do? Take a cab back?"

"I can't afford a car. I'm theoretically a struggling student." She'd had a car; she'd lost it during her second encounter with vampires. Jessica shrugged, but she couldn't quite shake the shock of evening off. "I don't know," she said quietly. "I don't know what I was going to do." She was suddenly glad of the company. "Theo, why were you here tonight?"

Theo shrugged. Was silent for about five minutes; Jessica almost repeated the question.

"I've been in town for a while," the older woman said at last, tossing her hair over her shoulders. "About three weeks. I've been doing my research."

"Research?"

"What do you think I do for a living, Jessica?"

"I don't know. Judging by the car, though, it doesn't pay well."

Theo laughed. "All right, all right. If you can find a mechanic who keeps up with my hours, I'll get it fixed." The laughter passed into the night air that whistled in through rolled down windows. The window on Jessica's side was rolled down because it was jammed, she noted, when she tried to roll it up. "Seriously, though. I hunt vampires. In particular, this . . . type of vampire. I find out what they do, and when. I spend a few day days researching old newspaper clippings, old articles, video footage, things like that." She shrugged. "I've got an old powerbook in the back seat; it's great for dipping into twenty-four-hour resources. Because after a few days of day hopping, I get back to basics.

"You want to hunt these creatures, you really want to smoke them out—you live by their schedule. Not their whim, Jessica—never that. But their schedule."

"But if you find them during the day—"

"I know. That's the newcomer's dream. The daylight ambush. Even happens often enough that you start to believe in it. But I've seen more men lost to daylight ambush than were ever lost to night. First: The vampires don't all need to sleep. They just need to come in out of the light." She took a deep breath. "Do you smoke?"

Jessica frowned. "Does anyone these days?"

"Yeah. Women much older than you are who don't have time for anything more self-indulgent. Like, say, a life. I'll roll the window down. You can roll your eyes."

Jessica shook her head instead.

"The second problem with daytime raids, and the bigger one," Theo said, after she'd pulled out a cigarette and lit it with one of the few parts of the car that actually seemed to be working, "is the psychology of it. People are a lot more careless in the daylight. Don't know why. But I've seen it. I've done it. In this line of work, you don't live long if you're careless. How many of your Night force are as old as I am, Jessie?"

Jessie was not a name that she was used to being called by anyone but a great-aunt who had pinched her cheeks, patted her head, and had passed away unmourned—by her—when she'd been a bit too young to understand death. But it fit Theo well enough; she couldn't even find the energy to object.

"As old as you? I don't know. You don't look all that old."

Theo laughed. "Yeah, well. Not many. There're probably a lot more of 'em who are your age, and who won't break a quarter century. But I like you. You've got an edge buried under all that suburban weight, and if you'd like, you can tag along with me; we'll sharpen it."

"Tag along?"

"I told you. I hunt vampires. It's what I do." For just a minute, in the darkness of a night alleviated by streetlights above and the whole glow of a city that never quite slept, Theo's face went utterly still. She seemed to be looking down the road, but her eyes didn't waver when the car followed the off ramp; they continued, as glassy as the window.

"Theo?"

Her lips turned up briefly, and the expression might have been a smile if it weren't so bitter. "Yeah. I hunt vampires. But I've been looking for this particular vampire off and on for about seven years now. I'm sorry, Jessie," she added, turning to look at her companion.

While the car was moving.

"Theo, the car!"

"I've got it. I've got it. God, you kids these days—you don't smoke, you don't drink, and you drive like instructors. I bet you spend all day working out at the gym too. You eat meat?"

Jessica rolled her eyes. "What were you sorry about?"

"What? Oh, nothing. Come on, let's go get a coffee."

"You girls seen trouble?"

"Nah," Theo said smartly, "Why?"

"You're decked out like a no-gunpowder soldier of fortune."

"Ha ha ha."

The night manager of the donut store didn't crack a smile. "We've got our own early warning system," he said. "You can leave the bow and the sharp spikes in the car."

"You haven't seen her car."

"Everyone's a critic." Theo shrugged. "You want my business, you get the whole package."

"You're not legal even in Canada," the man replied. But it was North enough of the central core that he shrugged; this was the area of the city where the vampire murders were the worst. Sexism at work, Jessica thought; if they'd been men, his hand would've been on the red button to security central, and the police would have paid a nice, quiet visit. Or not so quiet, depending. But there was something about Theo that seemed sane—hard to imagine given the gear she was carrying, and short of being told to butt out, literally, she was given a cup of coffee, two donuts, and a tea.

"When I was your age, I could smoke anywhere," she grumbled.

"Well, people like to breathe. It's a failing." Jessica grimaced.

"Pain?"

"Some. It's not the worst I've been through."

"And you're still alive. I'm impressed. What the hell were you doing out there alone like that anyway? You don't seem stupid."

"I'm stupid. Lysander, as far as we can tell, is the head of what we call the coven—and sent me a letter."

"A . . . letter."

"Signed. Sealed."

"And it said?"

Jessica shrugged. She did not want to feel self-conscious

in front of this woman—but she did. She started to fiddle with the tea bag in the slowly cooling water. At last she said, quietly, "The past. He said—I thought—" She looked up at Jessica. "I want to be able to understand it all. I sometimes think, if I could only understand it—"

She half expected Theo laugh. But she didn't. "The past," the older woman said softly, cupping both hands around the pressed paper of coffee cup and staring down at her reflection in the—what else?—black coffee, "is a place for the damned. It keeps you coming back to places you barely escaped the first time. Sometimes it even has answers. Sometimes.

"I won't lecture you about hunting your past. I couldn't. I'm here hunting mine." She took a sip of the coffee. Looked up, past Jessica's shoulder. "Shit."

"What?" Jessica knew that tone of voice.

"Looks like the past is hunting me."

"What do you—"

The windows blew out.

The lights went down.

Governing rules of vampires: they couldn't come in where they weren't invited. Easy, that. But vampires were modern creatures. And creative thinkers. They didn't have to enter a place to destroy it.

Jessica thought they preferred it—it happened often enough. This despite the fact that vampires could almost always make their kill without resorting to it—there were always dark corners in any man or woman that responded to what was, in the end, exotic, attractive, forbidden. Like, say, death on two legs.

But expedience counted. Some of the vampires could drive. They obviously watched bad television, and they could figure out how to set off big, big guns. Jessica looked out the window, swore, and grabbed Theo in a pincer-tight grip. "Let's go!"

"But we—"

"Now!" She pulled out the flashlight she carried strapped to her thigh for lights-out situations. Lights out had special meanings for Jessica—and she didn't like any of them.

She ran for the bathroom. Men's room. Easy to reach. Window to the outside. "That thing—arm it."

"Done," Theo said, that fast. Jessica was impressed. She swung herself up on the sink, shoved the window out. It was wide enough to crawl through. "You've got the weapon," she said to Theo. "You want to go first?"

"Sure." Theo's smile was all teeth. "Don't let the noise disturb you."

Three. Two. One.

The building shook. Glass shattered. The ceiling tiles—old asbestos from the look of them, shuddered and buckled. She looked at Theo's long legs. *Lady, hurry.*

Over the roar of a sudden inferno, she couldn't hear anything. Three. Two. One. Ground shook. Destroy an entire building, and you know what? You didn't have to wait to be asked in. Of course, there wasn't usually anything left to eat, either, so the vampires had to want you pretty damn badly to take out a building to get you.

Looking at Theo's black boots—flat and practical, at that, but certainly not cheap, and certainly not new—Jessica was impressed in spite of herself. Impressed and, as black smoke started seeping in through the inch-wide gap between door and floor, a bit nervous. "Theo?"

"Just a minute!"

"We don't have a minute!"

"All right, all right for Christos' sake!" Her black boots disappeared out the window. "Get your ass out while I cover the window." As Jessica approached the window, she heard a feral shriek. Theo swore.

"Hurry up—I could use some help!"

Catching the ledge by the hands, Jessica pulled herself up. Caught a stake between her teeth; it was rough enough that there was a fifty-fifty chance she'd get a splinter in her lip. Hated those. She made her way out.

Theo was fighting two to one. Before Jessica could drop down and join her, she was fighting one to one. No telling what the odds had been when she started. Jessica didn't gape.

"Smart idea," the older woman said, over her shoulder. "Using the men's room. They'd staked out the window on the far side."

"I never said they were smart."

"Smarter than I thought. Shit—what was that? A rocket launcher?"

"It was a BFG."

"A what?"

"A Big effing Gun."

"Ha ha—Jessie, I think it's time to find some cover."

"Some—"

Good news: The vampires suddenly melted away. Bad news: Fire made a pit of the asphalt ten yards away from where they were standing. Cover, on the other hand, wasn't too hard to come by. If they could outrun the gunner. "You know what?" Theo shouted.

"What?"

"I think they know I'm here!"

We are going to have a long talk, Jessica thought. *If we survive this.*

Jessica'd been hunted by vampires before. She'd been cut half to ribbons, bleeding a trail of blood that must have been luminescent to their senses; she'd been caught in graveyards, in warehouses, in churches—although the circumstances for that were unusual to say the least—but she had to admit that this was unusual, too.

Theo took the lead, scanning the horizon every few seconds. "There," she said, at one point. You see that one?"

"Barely."

"Flyer."

"How can you tell? It's on the ground."

"Flyers have their own special look. We knock him out, we're probably safe for the night. They won't press it."

Jessica nodded. "You've got the only crossbow."

"I told you not to leave yours in the car."

"Later. Uh, Theo?"

"What?"

"What's that?"

Theo frowned. The frown deepened. "That," she said, "is trouble."

From above where they both stood, beneath the awning of a very solid house, a voice as soft as shadow settled around them. "Hello, Jessica," it said, and she recognized the speaker immediately. "I see you've met . . . Theo. A pity. She's not what I consider to be a good influence."

"Lysander," Theo said, her voice louder and stronger than it had been all evening, "I'm surprised. You don't usually have the courage to show yourself."

"Oh? Well, Theo, I think you'll find a welcome change in me, given how much you hate cowardice. I've grown, Theo. I've grown so strong, you'd hardly recognize me. Have you come to play, or are you still bound up in the rules of your little game, whatever it is?"

"Move," Theo said.

Jessica didn't wait to be told twice. She didn't, in fact, wait to be told once; there was something electric in Lysander's voice—something like lightning before the strike, the danger of the storm on high.

But she said a brief prayer for the people whose house was destroyed in the blast that followed.

Lysander was a flyer. Not much of a surprise, not really. Jessica had expected that. But she hadn't expected this: this cross-country hunt that lit up the sky, broke the earth, deafened the ears; it was almost— almost—as if they were being chased by a mythical dragon across a modern landscape.

The Night Auxiliary would soon be out—and so would police of every stripe and description. She couldn't understand what Lysander was doing; even for a vampire—even for this vampire, the most open of the coven rulers on this side of either the Pacific or the Atlantic—this was extreme. At this rate, Jessica wasn't going to make it to morning, and neither was half of North York.

"Can you see him?" Theo asked, over the sound of crackling timber. Jessica wondered what the hell there was left to burn.

Jessica shook her head: No.

Theo grimaced. "We'll get out of here."

Jessica nodded grimly. But she didn't ask how, and Theo didn't volunteer any information. They caught their breath. They had ducked for the moment between two houses that weren't packed together tightly enough. Vampires had perfect night vision, of course. The shrubs hiding them exploded in black and black; in the morning, their colors would be more distinct; pureed edge of green, black, and a lot of new dirt. Some blood, too. Jessica was tired. She stumbled. Felt the flames lap up her leg. Theo pulled her up and out. She looked up; shaded her eyes.

They ran. The lovely shrubbery that separated the next two houses went up in a blaze of fire; the dragon, such as

it was, was close. Never trust a vampire with a flame-
thrower. Jessica stumbled again. Loss of blood. Late night.
Maybe Theo was right: you want to be a hunter, you had
to live like the hunted did.

"Leave me," she said, sides heaving.

Theo squinted into night air. Started to speak.

Lysander spoke instead, and his voice was a roar, a
scream, a thing of beauty. A thing of pain.

Theo pulled Jessica to her feet; they stood there, on a
small stretch of grass, surrounded by an awkward, burning
circle. Waiting.

Through the fire, carrying two bows—modern crossbow
and something older—stepped the man who now lived in
Jessica's past. Surrounded by flame, he looked like an archangel; an angel against a dragon. Seemed fitting, somehow.
She thought his name might be Michael. She must have
spoken; he smiled.

"No, although you can call me Michael if you want; it's
better than the name my parents gave me."

"And that one?" Theo said, over the crackle of flame.

"You'll laugh."

"Too tired."

"Ambrose."

Theo laughed.

But Jessica didn't. She stared at his soot-blackened face
as if there were no distance at all between herself and the
flames that lit up his back like an orange halo. "Is he
dead?"

"No," Ambrose replied. "Not Lysander. Not yet. But
we've bought time." The sirens that she'd heard in the
background leaped to the foreground with a jarring blast
of sound. "And questions, if we want to answer them. I
don't. Theo?"

"Vampire vigilantes aren't as frowned on as normal
ones."

He smiled. "You're in Canada, lady. Come with me. I've
got a car that . . . runs."

Jessica was exhausted. Ambrose carried her to her room;
Theo followed. They stayed just long enough to make sure
the security system had kicked in—but no longer. "I'll be
back," Theo said softly. "Tonight. But I'm exhausted, and

I've still got some footwork to do if we're going to be ready. You need a better crossbow, for one."

"But—"

"Jessie, I've been doing this for a long time. Trust me." She ran a hand across her blackened brow. "And given the Lysander welcome party, I don't think we're going to have time for great subtlety. I think I can figure out where the bastard is—but we're going to need a helluva lot of fire power to actually finish him off."

"But—"

"No buts, Jessica," Ambrose said softly. "I'm exhausted, and I still have to rid myself of Theo before I have to be decent for work. Sleep."

"Ambrose—"

"Yes?"

"Thank you."

Theo laughed. "See? Pretty face gets you a thank you." But Jessica missed the good-humored jibe; she had already surrendered to darkness.

She slept through the entire day. The alarm clock failed to wake her—she could've sworn she'd turned it on the day before, so much for memory—and no one so much as phoned. She was certain she'd hear from the Night Auxiliary; the action in the North was just too big. But so far, nothing. Jessica Mitchell hadn't slept through an entire day since the day after her family—

She rolled up, into darkness. Early evening darkness, sky faded into pinks and purples, deep blue falling, but not quickly enough to quash the riot of color. No clouds tonight. Just clarity. The edge of a dream slipped out from beneath her consciousness like a hard-pulled rug. Nightmares were bad, but the dreams she had when she slept during the day were worse, somehow. She'd never understood why.

The knock at her door came again. Until she heard it the second time, she didn't realize that she'd heard the first one. She rose, still dressed in torn clothing that now had the added advantage of being stiff with dried blood, all of it hers. "Hang on a sec!" Rolling out of bed, she stopped, flipped on the television, checked the monitor picture. It wasn't much of a precaution as precautions went; most of

the heavy-duty equipment was up front with the night porter's office.

It was Ambrose. "Jessica?"

He looked straight into the camera.

"I'll be right there!" She stripped out of her old clothing,
frantically trying to find something half-decent to wear.
Something that didn't make her look like a girl who carried
crossbows and stakes the way some people carried powder
compacts. She settled for jeans and a T-shirt; on short notice, it was the best she could do.

Then she opened the door, knowing that she looked like
a mess. He didn't look much better, if she were honest.
And she'd seen him, outlined by fire and shadow; she knew
which gashes were new.

"You were—where were you?"

"That's a bit personal, isn't it?"

She started to apologize, stopped; his lips were turned
up in a quirky, subtle smile; the shadows hid it. "Sorry.
Someone I've never met saves my life not once but twice
in an evening—I almost feel like I know him."

"Dangerous, that." He was carrying his crossbow. It
looked a lot like Theo's. In fact, she wasn't certain it
wasn't Theo's.

"Where's Theo?"

"Out hunting."

"Doesn't she ever sleep?"

"Not today. Maybe tomorrow. She's . . . not happy."

Jessica ran out of words. Just like that. They were there
one minute, gone the next. She stood in the door to her
room, feeling like an awkward schoolgirl. Surprised that she
remembered what it was like, to feel awkward in that way.

"I thought you might like dinner company," he said at
last, when it became clear she wasn't going to keep talking.

"What, now?"

"Pretty close to now. They'll be out in full force in about
an hour."

They. The vampires. "I'll—I'll go get my stuff."

Jessica's big struggle for the evening was choosing the
restaurant. It was a ritual of University students to stand
in the front door of the porter's lodge and spend fifteen
minutes trying to decide *en masse* what to eat, and old

habits were hard to break. In the end, she let Ambrose
decide; he chose a small Japanese restaurant just off Queen
Street West whose heights of trendiness had long since become ossified. The restaurant itself was wonderful; quiet,
peaceful, dark in a restful and not a menacing way.

They sat together at a table meant for four, hot green
tea cooling between the hands they laid flat, palm out,
against the tabletop.

She hadn't expected to say much; there was something
about him that seemed to invite silence. But his eyes, dark
and unblinking, seemed to wait on a question, any question,
and she didn't want to embarrass herself by babbling like
a moron. Babbling, however, was probably better than
blurting. Years of killing and hiding didn't really hone con-
versational skills.

"Why did you buy my old house?" The minute the words
left her mouth, she wanted to take them back; she picked
up the tea and stared at it until his absolute stillness drew
the eye again. He was staring, unblinking, at her; his hands
hadn't moved.

"I'm—I'm sorry. That's really—it's none of my business.
I don't even know why—I mean, I, just forget it."

But he waited until she'd finished stammering what was
supposed to be an apology. Then he lifted his own cup,
infinitely more graciously than she'd lifted hers; the steam
rising from the water was like a ghost mask against the
lines of his face. "I bought your house," he said quietly,
"because I saw you standing in front of it."

He waited for her reaction; she didn't have one to offer
him. The words almost made no sense to her.

"I don't want to be despised as a curiosity seeker, Jessica.
But perhaps I am one. I . . . lived off the continent for a
number of years."

"You don't speak with—"

"An accent? No; I don't suppose I do. I can, if you'd
like. Some women desire the exotic."

That made her uncomfortable; he didn't seem to notice.

"I was living off the continent when I first saw your face.
Vampire problems are not . . . recent. They exist across
Europe, across the Middle East, across what used to be
called the Orient. In North and South America, though,
the young seem to gather, and they gather with impunity.

No one is completely certain why." He smiled; the smile wasn't particularly friendly. "The news of the events in Toronto filtered out across every form of media known to man. I will not lie to you, Jessica; if you pore over your history, or ours, you will discover slaughters of a similar nature buried in the annals of war, and they are the slaughters of vampires. But that is the nature of the creature; to kill under the cover of man, of man's darkness, man's night."

"But—but my house—"

He smiled. "You aren't patient, are you?" But he didn't wait for an answer. Just as well; she had no idea how to answer the question. "After the large slaughter, the smaller one took place: Your family. But because you were one of a handful of survivors—of both attacks—you were newsworthy. Maybe you don't remember."

Don't remember? The glare of the spotlights had caught her like a rabbit on the highway. How could she ever forget it? She shrugged, her lips twisting a moment. "Not my finest hour," she said at last.

"No?" He shrugged. "You survived. They failed. Some would count that highly." He lifted the menu; laid it flat between his palms. But he didn't look away from her face. "I came to Toronto a week after the death of your family. I come from a monied background. I'm not sure what I thought to do at the time, Jessica; I spent a month or two familiarizing myself with the city. But when I decided to stay here, and I started to look for a home, yours was for sale.

"I bought it. I bought it because it was the backdrop to the drama that had called me across the water." He flipped the menu open. "Do you despise that?"

And she could see, in the dim light of candle and flickering lamp, his face shadowed by the roar of flame, the bow in his hands. "Pardon?"

"You're special, Jessica. You're more than a victim, and God knows a victim is what you were marked to be."

"Is that why you're—"

"Hunting?" His smile was crooked. "Yes. It's been a long time since I've taken up a cause. I didn't expect to have yours fall across my threshold so neatly—but perhaps I should have."

He reached out, then. Touched her hand. She wasn't certain whose was shaking: hers or his.

Theo met them just outside of her residence building. Her face was darkened by something Jessica would have sworn was tar by its consistency, and she wore black and gray; she also wore more stakes than Jessica thought could actually fit around a body.

"Yeah," Theo said, before Jessica could ask, "I can move. I picked up a crossbow for you. It's not an autoloader."

"Is there any such thing?"

"You can custom make 'em. I don't have the time, not tonight. But here. It's sort of double barreled. Don't mess with the bowstrings, okay?"

Jessica nodded. "Are we going out hunting tonight?"

"You and I are. Ambrose here is going out as well, but he's on his own. This is girl work."

Ambrose raised a dark brow. "I see," he said wryly.

"You know what you're hunting."

"Yes."

"Go find it. She and I are going to clear out a pocket of difficulty first."

"Pocket of difficulty?"

"Munitions depot."

"Theo—can't we do what normal people do and just call the police?"

"I can't. You can call in the Night Auxiliary. Here," she added, handing Jessica a phone. "But don't call 'em until we're well in place and we've already started rolling. Let's go."

"Where are we going?"

"My car."

"Oh, great."

Warehouse. She'd done warehouses before. Warehouses, boarded up against the cracks of lights that tended to come through boards pried loose by homeless inner city kids. She'd found what was left of the kids, too, after the vampires were done and gone—or done and killed.

This wasn't an abandoned, creaky building; it looked solid, half-new.

"You're sure this is the right place?"

"I've been doing this for—"

"I know, I know. A long, long time. But the vampires—"

"I can almost smell them. This is the right place."

It was dark, it was quiet, it was creepy—and there was a blackened husk of car that might once have been roadworthy parked across the doors a tractor-trailer would have docked at. Theo had become more and more silent as they approached the building; the bantering good humor and the self-inflected smile left her face, bleaching it of animation and color. The cigarette stayed; it made Jessica think, for a moment, of old black-and-white movies. As if Theo had been caught out of time and place.

"I did a bit of hunting around in the day," Theo said quietly, as she drove a good way past the building her nod had pointed out. "And it's some setup. Here, Jessie. These are blessed; use 'em. The stakes are better wood than yours, but they're shorter—you might like to try one or two if you get into a pinch, but reach counts until you've got experience.

"You get to know the fliers by the look. Longer faces, longer ears; they don't seem halfway human, and they probably aren't. Primal vampires, that's what we used to call 'em back home. They're actually harder for a master to control. You've got to tell me, by the way, why you call them covens."

"I don't know."

"Figures."

"When the signal comes, attack. Kill everything that comes out of the building."

"There are about twenty exits."

Theo's smile was smooth as glass, cold as ice. "Not nearly," she said. "Not anymore. I told you, I've done my work for the day." She shrugged herself into her weapons. And then she slid something out of her front breast pocket. It was small, compact; in the growing darkness, Jessica thought it looked like a tiny radio.

She pulled up an antenna. "You ready, Jessie?"

"I think so."

"Good. Before the fireworks start, I want to have a little talk with you."

"About what?"

"Ambrose."

"Theo—"

"You want to be a hunter, you've got to hunt. Ambrose is dangerous. He knows what he's doing, and he knows it too well. There's a lot of stuff he hasn't told me; probably a lot more that he hasn't told you."

"That wouldn't be hard."

Theo shrugged. "Point," she said softly. "Maybe I'm being unfair. But . . . He's pretty. I hate pretty men." She was quiet a long time. "After this is over, you and I should talk a bit. If we survive tonight, I'll owe you that much." She reached out with the glowing remnant of her cigarette and butted it out against the dash. "Okay. Get the phone ready to call your friends." She opened the car door, stepped out in to the crisp, clear night.

Jessica followed her lead, although the passenger side door worked about as well as the passenger side window. She had to struggle to extricate herself. "But you said—"

Theo looked at the little radio. Pressed a delicate button.

The warehouse exploded.

Nothing Theo did was obvious. But Jessica put up the crossbow and waited, watching the night sky. Vampires, as Theo had said, didn't deal well with fire. Fire wasn't sunlight, but burning destroyed them, and it was probably the most painful of the deaths that did.

On the other hand, fire wasn't the only thing that gave them trouble. There were other doors out of the building still undamaged by the explosion, but for some reason, the vampires couldn't cross them. She'd have to ask Theo about that, later. Right now, she had her sights—literally—full. She knelt almost in direct line of sight of the door that Theo had chosen as an exit, turned the phone on, dialed a very familiar number.

The reception was pretty shaky. She'd expected that.

"Hayley?"

"Jess, is that you?"

"Yeah—I've found a cross between a coven and a munitions factory up on Laird Drive, and I could use a helluva lot of help. As in now."

The phone crackled in reply; Jessica hoped to hell her meaning had managed to fight its way through. Because she didn't have time to call again. She set her sights; the fire made a lovely background against which to pinpoint dark things on two legs.

"Jessie?" Theo shouted.

"What?"

"I'll take care of the fliers!"

Jessica nodded. No time for much else. She fired a bolt; fired a second one. Thought that Theo was right; this was definitely a better weapon than the one she'd had. She took the time to load it; figured she'd have just enough time to load and fire it again before she'd have to set it aside entirely.

But she stopped before she could look down the barrel, because she caught sight of Theo's face in the night sky. What had looked like black grease now just looked black; the lines of her face were set, like obsidian, into something hard and cold. She fired her weapon; loaded it; fired. These motions were almost balletic movements of hand, graceful in their own way, and utterly deadly.

Theo's lips didn't move; her face seemed to lose all of the expression that made her what she was.

Do I look like that? Jessica wondered, shaking herself out of the night chill that a vampire's death had caused. *Do I look like that when I'm hunting?*

She didn't know, and it didn't matter. In the end, it was only at times like this that the screaming of the past was muted and dull; she denied it by denying the vampires the curious life they called undeath.

The sirens started up in the background; more; the night sky became a symphony of chopper wings, of dust and dirt swept up in so much wind they stung the cheeks and the careless eye. Jessica expected them. Theo obviously did as well. She stood, her hands on the belt around her neck.

"C'mon, Jessica," she said quietly.

"Where?"

"Out of here. Your friends are more than equipped to take over."

"But—"

"You can stay and finish up if you want; I've got a lot to do before tomorrow night. Night after, maybe."

She almost stayed. Leaving would worry the Night Auxiliary members she'd called; they'd assume she'd been killed, or worse. But there was something moody and dark about Theo's face, something that she couldn't—quite—leave alone. "Yeah," Jessica said quietly. "They can mop up from here."

They found a quiet park. Most nights, that was all of them. No one went out for a pleasant stroll once the sun had started its descent toward horizon. Well, not no one. But teenagers were convinced of their own immortality; Jessica knew. She'd been one. She'd paid.

But she didn't feel particularly stupid now, now sitting under a tree by the side of a woman who had managed to track down a den of vampires during a single day's search. That den was homeless—and probably headless—by now; the fires that weren't quite distant enough lit the sky like a celebratory bonfire. Jessica lifted her mineral water in a quiet toast.

Theo lit a cigarette.

They were silent a long time. "Jessie," the older woman said at last, "that first night we met, those two vampires, the boy and the girl—what were they to you?"

Jessica grimaced. "That obvious?"

Theo shrugged.

"Amy Amelia was my best friend. David Johnson was my boyfriend." She tried to mimic Theo's shrug, but her shoulders froze.

"You didn't even try to kill them."

"I killed Amy Amelia."

"Are we being honest here, or just factual?"

Jessica understood the question. "Why are you asking me this, Theo? You probably already know the answer."

"Because what I'm doing here won't make any damned sense to you if you don't answer the question."

"You're hunting vampires. You say it's what you do. You've said it a hundred times."

"Yeah, well." Theo took a drag on the cigarette that seemed to burn through about half of it all at once. "It's truth of a sort. What I do is hunt Lysander. That means hunting vampires."

"Pardon?"

"I'm hunting Lysander, and he knows it."

"Theo—"

"No, listen to me. Because when we do meet up with Lysander—and we will, there's only one thing I want."

"What's that?"

She caught Jessica's wrist in a sudden flash of movement; her grip was strong, unshakable. "I kill him. Not you. Not Ambrose, if we can't get rid of him. Me."

Jessica didn't even try to free her wrist. "Does it matter, as long as he's dead?"

"Yes."

Silence. Then, "You hate him a lot. Did he—did he do to you what he did to me?"

Theo was perfectly still for a long time; so still, in fact, she seemed to have forgotten how to breathe. When she spoke, she released Jessica's hand. "No," she said softly. "Not at all. I knew Lysander when we were both young. You know what I told about what I was doing at your age—dreaming about boys and babies? He was the boy, and it was his babies I was hoping for." She returned all attention to the cigarette she was carrying between her lips. "When he was . . . changed . . . I couldn't believe it. I couldn't believe he'd become a monster. I thought—I thought that immortality didn't have to destroy him. He had all his memories, he had the whole history of his life." She laughed. It wasn't a pretty sound. "I guess you're smarter than I was. I don't think you've ever thought that."

"Not until I heard David and Amy," Jessica said. "Not until then."

"I searched the world over for a way to somehow redeem him. And Jessica, I know how to travel.

"But while I searched, he just kept getting more monstrous, more demonic, more insane. He has—I don't know if you noticed—the face of an angel. When he flies, when he's at the peak of his . . . I don't know what you want to call it—I call it glory—he's the most beautiful creature I've ever seen.

"Took me a long time to realize that it was hopeless. That the only thing I could do for him, for us, was to free him. Is to free him." The cigarette's glow was reflected in her unblinking gaze. "I owe it to him," she said quietly. "I used to tell him that I'd love him forever. I thought I knew what forever meant. What other act of love can I offer him? Can I offer what's left of him?" She rose, then. "All

I have are memories, really, and they cut and cut and cut. A lot to be laid to rest, Jessica."

"And it has to be you, that does it?"

"Yes. Because I did love him, and because this is the last act of love I can offer. I can't turn away from it; I turned away from it once. And what did that get you? Get any of the young women like you?" She started forward, restless animal now. "Sorry, Jessie—I hate talking about things like this—but you might hear things or see things when we finally catch up with Lysander, and you've got a right to know most of what they mean." She started to walk away, and Jessica let her, because there just wasn't anything she could offer.

It was only when she couldn't see Theo anymore that she rose herself, and realized she was standing alone in the middle of an empty park at evening's height.

"Jessica, you aren't very careful with your life, are you?"

She turned. Ambrose stood, hands shoved into deep pockets, at the base of the closest large tree.

"Don't you ever make any noise?"

"Some. What are you doing out here alone?"

"I was talking with Theo."

"And she left you here."

"I can take care of myself."

He said nothing, and she knew, with acute embarrassment, that he had every right to say worse. She might have even said something, but she noticed then that he looked to be in worse shape than Theo was. "Ambrose?"

He held out a hand palm out, in denial. "I'm . . . fine," he said quietly. "Theo and I have agreed to work together, but she's obviously better at this game than I am."

"You've been fighting."

"For my life." He shrugged. "I'd forgotten how much killing a vampire is just like killing. I've got my car. I'll take you home." His smile was slightly pained. "But you'll have to forgive me; I'm not up to the effort of being acceptable company tonight."

"You came here to take me home?"

He gazed off into the distance that had swallowed Theo entirely. "She . . . said she wanted to talk to you about personal things. That never comes easily to someone like Theo. And Jessica—I know you can take care of yourself,

but while Theo's in town, the game is far, far deadlier."
He laughed. "You're the first stranger I've let into my
home since I can't remember when. I don't want to—" He
shook his head. "I'll take you home."

And he did. But true to his word, he let her out of his
car; he didn't try to pass the porter or join her in a dorm
room that was, after all, barely large enough for one. She
thought—for just a second—he might try to kiss her. But
he didn't, and she stared at the back of his car for a long
time after he drove away, wondering why it mattered.

Three days passed; Jessica sleepwalked through all of
them. She had no way of reaching Theo; no way of reaching
Ambrose. It hadn't occurred to her to ask for phone numbers, and she would have felt self- conscious using them
anyway. But on the fourth night, on the fourth night she
woke to a scratching, of all things, at her window. Which
only struck her as odd when she was halfway to it; she
lived on the fourth floor.

She paused, armed herself, straightened out her cross,
and then nudged the window open with her foot. "Who's
there?"

"Santa Claus," Theo said, "but these rooms are too
damned cheap to have real chimneys."

"I told her," an equally familiar voice added, drifting
down from above, "that we could use the doors."

"Why're you two on the roof?"

"Well . . ." Theo began.

"You're really not going to like this," Ambrose said, at
the same time.

Jessica said, "While you both get your story straight, I'm
getting dressed. Am I getting dressed for a heavy duty evening, or are we just going out for drinks?"

"If we're going out for drinks," Theo replied, "We're the
keg or the bottle."

When Theo told her where they were going, Jessica
blanched. It was the first time that she had hesitated in any
way since Theo had given her permission—if grabbing an
arm and dragging a person along can be called permission—to accompany her.

"Here?"

Ambrose and Theo crossed glances. "I told you," he said softly.

Theo shrugged. "We need her."

"Yes," Ambrose said. "Here."

"I'll get expelled. I'll get worse than expelled! Do you have any idea how much that building is worth?"

"Not a lot; it's ugly as sin. Cheap poured concrete, steel girder construction. At least that'd be my guess."

"Thanks for the quick architecture lesson. That's the Robarts Library. And that," she added, "is the Thomas Fisher rare book library. The building might be worthless, but the contents are priceless!"

"Did I forget to mention that Lysander used to fancy himself a scholar?" The bitterness in Theo's voice was laced with a fatalistic humor.

"You haven't—you haven't done the explosive thing again, have you?"

"No," she said quietly.

"Good." Then, "Why not?"

"Because I can't linger too long before he knows I'm here. We're—we're still connected, he and I. It took me a while to make sure the warehouse was ready for our visit. We won't have that here. Plus, Ambrose tells me that changes have been made to the interior of the rare book library; most notably beneath the ground."

"I don't even know how to get in there without tripping off every alarm in the building."

"No problem," Theo said grimly. "That's what Ambrose has been doing for the last four days."

"But they—they caught him. Must have—he was in a fight."

"Not exactly." It was as curt as Theo ever got. "You two ready?"

No. Jessica thought. But her gaze went, in the darkness of streetlight and building light that bounced off—yes, ugly poured concrete—to Ambrose. His smile was one of the strangest smiles she'd ever seen.

"We're ready, Theo."

"Good. I'm tired. Let's get it done."

They moved in. In and down. There were elevators; neither Ambrose nor Theo paused to give them a glance before taking the stairs. They passed through a door that looked like part of the wood-paneled wall, and from there, descended into shadow, shadow, shadow.

Ambrose and Theo moved in concert. There was about them, the moment they entered the soft-edged darkness of the dramatically—and poorly—lit library, a grace and an almost utter silence that made Jessica feel awkward, clumsy, out of place. It didn't help that she carried two crossbows and one of Theo's heavy belts across her shoulder; she wasn't used to two weapons, found them cumbersome. Theo moved as if they were each a part of her arm. So did Ambrose. Old soldiers, Jessica thought.

And felt a twinge of something that might have been jealousy had she been three years younger. She followed them, looking over her shoulder, pretending that she'd been left at the rearguard for that reason, rather than because she didn't begin to attain their levels of competence.

The scream, cut short, slid that bare conceit out from under her feet. She knew it by tenor; not a human scream. Animal. Primal. Theo had loosed a bolt, let it fly. *When the screaming starts, you move, girl, and you don't stop moving until you're where we need you.*

Nice, sometimes, to have someone else think for you. She moved. She had moved, the night of the graduation dance. She had run. But not like this, not armed, not toward the danger. It felt better, but it opened wounds. Always did.

Another scream. She saw—or thought she saw—a head fly off the shoulders of a waiting sentry, but she didn't see the weapon that caused the damage; she thought it was Ambrose's work. Blood flew; the vampires weren't going hungry—although they didn't snack much at the university. Smart, if they were living here.

A set of double doors flew wide.

"Lights!" Theo shouted.

Lights flooded the room as if it were a movie set.

The vampires, momentarily blinded, cringed behind their forearms as Jessica Mitchell opened fire. This was her past. Because these were his permanent coven. The creatures that had come with him the night of the dance. The creatures that had come with him the night of her family's slaughter. She hadn't thought—hadn't thought to be so savage, facing them. Maybe she'd avoided thinking about it at all. The bow flew; the screaming started in earnest, the hissing, the growling.

And some of it, to her surprise, was her own.

They were three to thirteen—maybe that's why it was called a coven—but two of them had already died before the doors opened wide. Three to eleven; Theo brought down two before they'd had a chance to move. Ambrose brought down three—and Jessica herself matched that number; her first shot had gone wild at the last moment because it was aimed at Lysander, and she remembered what Theo had asked for.

That left close work; stake work—and that work had become Jessica's specialty over the past three years. It was more dangerous, but it was more personal, and her feelings for vampires were nothing if not personal. She closed.

"Jessica, no!" She froze, two stakes out, cross a symbol across back and chest.

Ambrose bore her weight down as a bullet ricocheted off the floor. Off something on the floor. She felt his weight as if he were earth, and she, buried in its safety. Another bullet; he rolled with her weight.

"There's a reason," he said, through gritted teeth, "that Theo and I didn't take on this coven by ourselves, for God's sake. It's old, powerful, deadly. Think."

How old can it be? But she didn't say it. Didn't ask. "Are you—did it hit you?"

"No—it—"

The lights went out.

Lights out was a situation that Jessica thought she'd come prepared for, even if it was one she didn't like—but not lights out like this. She had fought at night; fought in darkened houses and buildings—but here, nestled underground like a catacomb skeleton from the sight of open sky, the blackness was utter. Absolute. Above her, she heard the steady breath of the man who had probably saved her life for a third time.

And then it was gone. She bit her lip to stop from crying out. Heard, to her left, a sharp hiss, a cry of pain. She didn't think it was Ambrose.

The stakes! She pulled up; she scrambled at her thigh

for a moment, and then pulled out a flashlight. Not a heavy one. Not one that'd do her much damned good in a real fight, not in a place like this. She lit it; kept the glow cupped in the palm of her hand.

"Jessica." Ambrose' voice. She remembered to breathe; he caught her hand; his was slick and wet. "Here. There's a wall here. Find it with your back, and don't leave it. It's the only place you're not visible from the catwalk."

She nodded; the light caught his face, and she thought of flame and fire, not so much behind him, but within him; he looked, a moment, like a demon himself in the darkness.

She wasn't prepared for the mist.

She'd never seen it before, although she'd read about it often enough. Had always dismissed it as the fancy of hyperimaginative writers. But it rose, like smoke or steam, an inch—two inches—away from her feet. She shone light into it; it caught the light, devoured it; there was almost no reflection to see by.

The worst part about it was the eyes; it had eyes. And a voice, with no throat to utter it. "Jessica," it said, softly. "Jessica Mitchell." She hadn't meant to meet those eyes; she knew better.

But they swallowed her, the way the mist did; wrapping itself slowly and utterly painlessly around her body, little beads of something much lighter than the night, the darkness.

She tried to speak.

"Don't," the voice said, softly, softly, softly.

Her lips closed over the words. Her eyes, his eyes, were all that mattered, all that she could see. Even when the flashlight rolled out of her hands, she could still seem them, light in darkness, something other than night.

She was suddenly tired, so very, very tired. She had come here, she thought, to have peace, and she would have it; that's what the darkness was for, after all. Peace. Sleep.

Death.

But death without pain. She had never thought—

And then, there was pain. Her wrist blossomed with it, a fire that spread from the vein down her hand and up her arm, carrying something with it, something foreign, something that tasted like a name might taste if names had that texture.

She cried out, pulled back, but there was nothing to pull back from. The mist itself writhed and twisted, becoming a thing of storm and not a thing of peace. And it said, "I'll kill you for that!" But it wasn't speaking to her.

She didn't have time to think; she brought her hand to her wrist and clamped tight, pressing the vein down with bruising force. She had strips of cloth for exactly this purpose, but no light, and it took her a minute or two, while the wind whipped around in a room that wasn't open to it, to find them, to bind her wounds.

"Jessica—are you all right?"

Ambrose's voice. "No." She said, faintly. "Yes." She started to say something else, and then she heard it: Lysander's voice.

In the darkness, his voice.

"Well, Theo, it looks like you've come to spoil my little game again. I can't seem to be rid of you."

"Not for want of trying, Lysander." Theo's voice. Older, somehow. "It's been a long time. I hadn't realized you were off the continent, you'd become so . . . quiet.

"Isn't that what you wanted? Isn't that what you've always wanted? That I hide, that I grovel and cringe beneath the street or the night habitat of the rest of the cattle? Is that why I was given this gift? To be one step above a mosquito?"

"I don't know," Theo said. Her voice was like the mist had been; soft, now, soft in the shadow. Jessica was suddenly very glad that she couldn't see the older woman's face.

As if he were thinking the same thing, Ambrose appeared in the glow of her flashlight. He handed it to her; she took it—and where their hands touched, she felt a little spark of something. Shock, maybe. Electricity. She was very, very tired. He put an arm around her shoulder; drew her in. She'd realize later how odd it was—but not then. Then he was lost in the darkness.

"I don't know why you were given the gift, Lysander. Has it brought you much happiness?"

"What is happiness?" Lysander replied, his voice losing some of the velvet, some of the edge.

"Be careful, Theo," Ambrose said, but his words were not meant to carry.

"I don't know," Theo answered. "I'm not sure any of us does, anymore. But it can't be this—living in a hole in a basement and thinking of new ways to kill cows."

"Maybe we think of other things."

"Maybe. But I don't hear your music anymore. I don't hear the words that almost made you famous before your untimely death: the poetry, Lysander. The plays. I don't see the horses—do you remember the horses? You rode when I couldn't because it made you feel alive—"

He cried out, then, wordless, angry.

Theo's voice responded; a grunt of pain. Jessica started forward and the gentle arm around her shoulders became a vice.

"It's been a long time, Lysander," Theo continued. "It's been too long."

"And what can you offer me? I have eternity," he said, but his voice was shorn, more and more, of whatever it was that spoke of power. Jessica didn't understand.

As if he could hear the confusion, Ambrose said, "People are complicated, Jessica, even when they're dead. Especially when they're dead. We should probably leave them."

But they didn't; they were meant to be witnesses, even if they couldn't do a damned thing.

"I can offer you peace," Theo answered wearily, wearily.

"And will you take that peace as well?" Sarcasm, anger.

"Yes."

"You always were such a fool."

"Especially for a pretty voice, pretty words. But Lysander—when you wrote about life, when you spoke about love, you gave it to me, whole. I swallowed it, I believed in it. I should have known, then. Do you even remember the sunrise, the sunset, the birthings?"

"Theo—" Something in his voice, a change, a turn of tide; some momentary edge.

"I loved you. I love you. I hope—I hope there's forgiveness on the other side of the divide."

"Theo—"

A grunt, then. Pain. Anger, maybe—hard to say. She couldn't tell whose voice was whose, until she heard the weeping. Weeping.

Her own eyes closed over with something unshed, unsheddable; she felt like a vulture, like a voyeur; was fiercely, suddenly glad of the darkness.

Ambrose picked her up; she didn't resist him; she put her arms around his neck, winced, and pulled them back, cradling her throbbing wrist in her hand. He led her out of the darkness, never stumbling, never jarring her, and she let him.

He left her at the residence, and in the moonlight that seemed brighter than most days, she could see the gouges across his throat, his cheek, his forehead. She wondered how much cosmetic damage had been done, and how much real. He carried no weapons; she still had her crosses, her stakes, for all the good they'd done. "Ambrose—"

He lifted a finger. Placed it, gently, against her lips. "Not tonight," he said softly. "Not tonight, but tomorrow, or tomorrow, or tomorrow. I've—" she shook his head. "I won't be good company tonight, Jessica."

She swallowed. Nodded. Let him leave, and wondered why it bothered her; in total, she hadn't spent more than a day in his company if you added up the hours.

"I thought I'd find you here."

The woman was weeping. Still weeping. In her arms, she cradled the headless body of a man that she had crossed continents to kill. Or to save. The dead were so complicated.

"Theophanu."

She turned, and in the scant light of star and the bright light of moon, her teeth glimmered; no strength now, for subterfuge, and no need for it. Her arms tightened around the corpse, around the blood that was, after all, part hers.

"Leave me," she said. A command.

But he stood, quietly, as she rocked. "Dawn," he told her. "Dawn is coming."

She said nothing.

"You didn't tell her the truth."

At that, a glimmer of the Theo that Jessica Mitchell would know shone through. "Neither did you, Ambrosios. Neither did you."

He did not answer the accusation, not directly. Instead,

he looked at Lysander's headless corpse. "Is that why you called me? Is that why you asked for my help?"

She rocked the body as if it still had a beating heart. As if, with the rising sun, some life would return to it. Vampires never wept. And Theo, Theophanu in the times of the ancient Greeks, was weeping.

"Maybe," she said, as the tears ceased to fall. "He was the first . . . mortal . . . that I loved. I did not lie to him. He reminded me of life—not of taking it, but of living it. He was, in all things, what I was not, what I'd never been. I wanted his daylight, Ambrosios. I wanted to keep it with me.

"And I was caught by just a look, by a vulnerability, by something that spoke across distance. I had to seek him out. Does this sound familiar? I had to seek him.

"I loved him. He loved me." She cradled what was left. "And I wanted what every fool in love wants: eternity." She waited for a response; there was none. "You understand," she said. "He was dying. That's what mortality is, although the living don't understand it. Every day, a march toward change and death. Every hour. Every minute.

"I offered it. I offered him the gift. He accepted it." She shook her head. "But he was not like my . . . other children. Not to me. I could not bear to hold him. I couldn't bear to contain him, to mold him, to make him what I desired. I wanted—I thought—"

She laughed. "I was too old, Ambrosios. I had forgotten my own youth, and my youth as one of the newly dead. I was . . . almost your age."

He was silent. Rigid now, with the effort of silence.

Theophanu, ancient as dead gods, rose, carrying the body of her lover as if it were a child. "Even the dead change," she said softly. "You've seen Jessica. You were called across the waters because of what you saw. But what you desire—it is life; it cannot be held, it cannot be contained. Death will take it—but not the death you offer, unless you want to hasten the end. You've already marked her, and I understand why; it saved her life. But it binds you, it weakens you. Remember what I have learned. There is no eternity, not for love, not for—

"Love is a human thing, I think."

He was silent. Silent a long time. And then he said, "A

bitter lesson, Theophanu. Bitter. But I thank you for it. I will . . . think on what you've said.

"And while I think, where will you be?"

She turned, night eyes meeting night eyes, all pretense gone; her face was the face of a goddess, cold, eternal, ageless. "I think," she said quietly, "that I have a desire to see the sun rise. I do not recommend that you join me; there are things that we all must do in private."

He bowed. The dawn was very, very close.

Theophanu walked away, to find privacy, to find light; Ambrose stayed, a sentry and a witness, until she had passed, like a mortal, from his vision.

And when he turned, when he turned, Jessica Mitchell was staring up at his face from the end of a crossbow.

He didn't blanch. Didn't blink. Didn't speak.

She waited, watching him, angry at him, angry at Theo. "Well? Aren't you going to say something? To say anything?"

He met her eyes. "What would you have me say?"

"Why did she call you Ambrosios?"

"It is my given name. As Theophanu was hers. She was young long, long before I was born; young long before I died."

"Don't move."

He hadn't. She knew he wouldn't. "You're one of them. You both are."

"Yes."

"Why? Why?"

"We are both very old," he replied. It wasn't much of an answer.

"What did she mean—you've marked me, you're bound to me?"

He said nothing, but his gaze fell to her bandaged wrist. "I'm sorry," he said quietly. "But there was no other way to save your life. I told you, the coven was an old coven. Lysander and his chosen were very powerful, very skilled."

"That was you? You bit me?"

"Jessica—"

The bow came up, and up; her hands were shaking. "How many people have you killed while you've been living here?"

"How many people do you think I've killed?"

"Don't play games with me, Ambrose. Answer my question while I still feel like asking questions."

He smiled. The smile was almost gentle. She hated it. And wanted to see it. That was the truth, and she had come to face truth, one way or the other.

"Six," he said quietly.

And she knew he was lying. Didn't know how. "You're not telling me the truth."

He raised a brow; the surprise was genuine. At least she would have bet it was genuine. But she would have bet Theo was, too.

Theo, at least, she understood.

"We give ourselves away," he said at last, to himself. "I am not . . . telling you the truth. I have not killed six men—six mortals—in my time here. It appears that you are more sensitive than I would have thought possible given the . . . events that occurred. I have not killed a single mortal in this city, that I am aware of."

She knew it shouldn't have made a difference, but it did.

He must have seen it on her face; the lines of his own shifted beneath the night sky; for a moment she thought there was something like contempt—but not quite—in his expression. "Make no mistake. I have killed, Jessica, many, many people in my time. Innocents, murderers—the living." He looked beyond her; his eyes seeing past her shoulders, past her. "I've killed for sport; I've killed in rage; I've killed out of boredom. I've made my followers, just as Lysander made his, and I've used them just as poorly in my time." When he smiled, his teeth were long and slender, and his face was the face of—

Of an angel.

"Is that not what you wanted to hear, Jessica? It is the truth."

An archangel.

She knew better than to turn her back on a vampire. But she didn't want to look at his face, because she could see in it, framed by fire, hallowed by it, a type of salvation that she had both looked for and never thought to find under the night sky of this city, during this war.

"She—she made Lysander."

"Yes."

"Did you—did you bring your—your coven with you?"

"My coven, as you call it, is long since scattered to wind and geography. I neither know where it is, nor care. I have played all of my games, Jessica, and I have come to be here, as you see me now, because there are no games left to play."

"And what's this, then?" she asked, bitterly.

He did not reply.

"Am I supposed to just let you walk? So you've decided in the last year or two—or decade, whatever— that killing cattle isn't fun anymore, and that's it? What about the people you killed? What about the crimes you committed?"

"Justice," he said quietly, "has many faces."

"How convenient."

"Not really, Jessica." He put his hands behind his back. Turned away. "The dawn is very near, and I've no desire to face it; not today. Maybe soon. Sooner or later, we all do.

"When I was younger—closer to your age, in our terms— I didn't even understand the desire." He spoke at a distance. "I didn't kill anyone here, Jessica, because this is your city. Because I didn't know how to approach you; I didn't know how to begin. I knew what you were. I saw it, then, when I first saw your face. I knew how you'd feel about, and I knew—because I am somewhat self-aware at times—that you'd find out, eventually.

"And if you do not choose to kill me, here and now, I will not take the lives of your kind, because to me this is still your city, your home.

"I would like to learn about it, with you, now that we have met." He met her eyes then, and she let him. Even though she knew that he was older than Lysander. Knew that he was more dangerous.

She lifted the bow.

He lifted his arms, a lazy gesture, a sweep of motion in cool night air. And he began to rise. There was nothing long about his face, nothing feral, nothing batlike; the air took him, the wind bore him aloft.

Like, she thought, an angel. A dark angel.

She caught him in the sight of the bow. Held him there an instant.

Fired.

Two days later, she sat by the window of her small residence room. Waiting. Tears, what tears there were, had dried; she was nervous. She hadn't been nervous like this in so long, she almost didn't know what it was, what it meant.

But she knew it meant something. As soon as the sun had finally disappeared from the swell of the building-laden horizon, she'd felt it in the air; purpose. A hunt of its own.

The tapping at her window was soft.

It reminded her of Theo.

She rose at once, knowing that Theo was gone. Rose and pushed the window open. He was there. Just there; the three stories of building below him had vanished beneath his feet.

"Ambrose," she said. And then, "Ambrosios."

"Jessica." He held out a hand; she pulled back.

"I'm—I'm—"

"I know. I don't ask you to invite me in; not yet. Maybe not ever. But if I invite you out, will you come, little Jessica? The world is a night world."

He didn't ask her why she'd missed when she shot at him. They both knew she could have killed him then, so easily. She had some sort of answer, some sort of complicated personal denial, all set to go—but the words faded; fell from her lips. She met his eyes, saw in them the fire, saw in him a darkness to escape to, not to escape from.

For just a minute, Jessica Mitchell held her breath. And then she climbed up, as carefully as she could, and stood on the old stone windowsill. Balanced there. When he offered her a hand, she took it.

And closed her eyes. And stepped off the window's ledge. For just a second, she floated in the air beside him, and then gravity rushed up to meet her.

He caught her. Held her.

"Jessica," he said, quietly.

She said nothing at all, afraid, willing to be afraid for just a minute, just an hour, just an evening.

Perhaps, just perhaps, she'd found the way to put her past behind her.

Perhaps, just for tonight, she could begin again.